**Praise for #1 *New York Times* bestselling author
Debbie Macomber**

"Debbie Macomber's name on a book is a guarantee of delightful, warmhearted romance."
—Jayne Ann Krentz, *New York Times* bestselling author

"No one writes better women's contemporary fiction."
—*RT Book Reviews*

"Debbie Macomber is…a bona fide superstar."
—*Publishers Weekly*

**Praise for *New York Times* bestselling author
Lee Tobin McClain**

"Lee Tobin McClain dazzles with unforgettable characters, fabulous small-town settings and a big dose of heart. Her complex and satisfying stories never disappoint."
—Susan Mallery, #1 *New York Times* bestselling author

"Fans of Debbie Macomber will appreciate this start to a new series by McClain that blends sweet, small-town romance with such serious issues as domestic abuse…. Readers craving a feel-good romance with a bit of suspense will be satisfied."
—*Booklist* on *Low Country Hero*

Debbie Macomber is a #1 *New York Times* bestselling author and a leading voice in women's fiction worldwide. Her work has appeared on every major bestseller list, with more than 170 million copies in print, and she is a multiple award winner. Hallmark Channel based a television series on Debbie's popular Cedar Cove books. For more information, visit her website, www.debbiemacomber.com.

New York Times and *USA TODAY* bestselling author **Lee Tobin McClain** read *Gone with the Wind* in the third grade and has been an incurable romantic ever since. When she's not writing angst-filled love stories with happy endings, she's probably on Snapchat with her college-student daughter, mediating battles between her goofy goldendoodle and her rescue cat, or teaching aspiring writers in Seton Hill University's MFA program. She is probably not cleaning her house. For more about Lee, visit her website at www.leetobinmcclain.com.

#1 *New York Times* Bestselling Author

DEBBIE MACOMBER

THE COURTSHIP OF CAROL SOMMARS

**HARLEQUIN
BESTSELLING
AUTHOR
COLLECTION**

**HARLEQUIN®
BESTSELLING
AUTHOR
COLLECTION**

Recycling programs
for this product may
not exist in your area.

ISBN-13: 978-1-335-40620-0

The Courtship of Carol Sommars
First published in 1990. This edition published in 2021.
Copyright © 1990 by Debbie Macomber

The Nanny's Secret Baby
First published in 2019. This edition published in 2021.
Copyright © 2019 by Lee Tobin McClain

This edition published by arrangement with Harlequin Books S.A.

For questions and comments about the quality of this book, please contact
us at CustomerService@Harlequin.com.

Harlequin Enterprises ULC
22 Adelaide St. West, 40th Floor
Toronto, Ontario M5H 4E3, Canada
www.Harlequin.com

Printed in Lithuania

MIX
Paper from
responsible sources
FSC® C021394

CONTENTS

Also available from Debbie Macomber and MIRA

Blossom Street

Cedar Cove

Visit her Author Profile page at Harlequin.com,
or debbiemacomber.com, for more titles!

THE COURTSHIP
OF CAROL SOMMARS

Debbie Macomber

In loving memory of
David Adler, Doug Adler and Bill Stirwalt
Beloved Cousins
Beloved Friends

Special thanks to
Pat Kennedy and her endearing Italian mother,
and Ted Macomber and Bill Hall
for the contribution of their rap music
and all the lessons about living with teenage boys

Chapter 1

Carol Sommars swore the entire house shook from her fifteen-year-old son's sound system, which was blasting out his favorite rap song.

> I'm the Wizard MC and I'm on the mike
> I'm gonna tell you a story that I know you'll like
> 'Cause my rhymes are kickin', and my beats do flash
> When I go to the studio, they pay me cash

"Peter!" Carol screamed from the kitchen, covering her ears. She figured a squad of dive-bombers would've made less of a racket.

Realizing that Peter would never be able to hear her above the din, she marched down the narrow hallway and pounded on his door.

Peter and his best friend, Jim Preston, were sitting on Peter's bed, their heads bobbing in tempo with the music. They both looked shocked to see her.

Peter turned down the volume. "Did you want something, Mom?"

"Boys, please, that music is too loud."

Her son and his friend exchanged a knowing glance, no doubt commenting silently on her advancing age.

"Mom, it wasn't *that* bad, was it?"

Carol met her son's cynical look. "The walls and floors were vibrating."

"Sorry, Mrs. Sommars."

"It's okay, Jim. I just thought I'd save the stemware while I had a chance." Not to mention warding off further hearing loss...

"Mom, can Jim stay for dinner? His dad's got a hot date."

"Not tonight, I'm afraid," Carol said, casting her son's friend an apologetic smile. "I'm teaching my birthing class, but Jim can stay some other evening."

Peter nodded. Then, in an apparent effort not to be outdone by his friend, he added, "My mom goes out on hot dates almost every weekend herself."

Carol did an admirable job of disguising her laugh behind a cough. Oh, sure! The last time she'd gone out had been...she had to think about it...two months ago. And that had been as a favor to a friend. She wasn't interested in remarrying. Bruce had died nearly thirteen years earlier, and if she hadn't found another man in that time, she wasn't going to now. Besides, there was a lot to be said for the benefits of living independently.

She closed Peter's bedroom door and braced her shoulder against the wall as she sighed. A jolt of deafening music brought her upright once more. It was immediately lowered to a respectable level, and she continued back to the kitchen.

At fifteen, Peter was moving into the most awkward teenage years. Jim, too. Both boys had recently obtained their learner's permits from the Department of Motor Vehicles and were in the same fifth-period driver training class at school.

Checking the time, Carol hurried into the kitchen and turned on the oven before popping two frozen meat pies inside.

"Hey, Mom, can we drive Jim home now?"

The operative word was *we,* which of course, meant Peter would be doing the driving. He was constantly reminding her how much practice he needed if he was going to pass the driving part of the test when he turned sixteen. The fact was, Peter used any excuse he could to get behind the wheel.

"Sure," she said, forcing a smile. These "practice" runs with Peter demanded nerves of steel.

Actually, his driving skill had improved considerably in the last few weeks, but the armrest on the passenger side of the car had permanent indentations. Their first times on the road together had been more hair-raising than a horror movie—another favorite pastime of her son's.

Thanks to Peter, Carol had been spiritually renewed when he'd run the stop sign at Jackson and Bethel. As if to make up for his mistake, he'd slammed on the brakes as soon as they'd cleared the intersection, catapulting them both forward. They'd been saved from injury by their seat belts.

They all clambered into her ten-year-old Ford.

"My dad's going to buy me a truck as soon as I get my license," Jim said, fastening his seat belt. "A red four-by-four with flames painted along the sidewalls."

Peter tossed Carol an accusing glare. With their budget, they'd have to share her cantankerous old sedan for a while. The increase in the car insurance premiums with an additional driver—a male teenage driver—meant frozen meat pies every third night as it was. As far as Carol was concerned, nurses were overworked, underpaid and underappreciated.

"Mom—hide!"

Her heart vaulted into her throat at the panic in her son's voice. "What is it?"

"Melody Wohlford."

"Who?"

"Mom, please, just scoot down a little, would you?"

Still not understanding, she slid down until her eyes were level with the dashboard.

"More," Peter instructed from between clenched teeth. He placed his hand on her shoulder, pushing her down even farther. "I can't let Melody see me driving with my *mother!*"

Carol muttered under her breath and did her best to keep her cool. She exhaled slowly, reminding herself *this, too, shall pass.*

Peter's speed decreased to a mere crawl. He inadvertently poked her in the ribs as he clumsily lowered the window, then draped his left elbow outside. Carol bit her lower lip to prevent a yelp, which probably would've ruined everything for her son.

"Hey, Melody," he said casually, raising his hand.

The soft feminine greeting drifted back to them. "Hello, Peter."

"Melody," Jim said, leaning across the backseat. He spoke in a suave voice Carol hardly recognized.

"Hi, Jimmy," Melody called. "Where you guys off to?"

"I'm driving Jim home."

"Yeah," Jim added, half leaning over Carol, shoving

her forward so that her head practically touched her knees. "My dad's ordered me a truck, but it hasn't come in yet."

"Boys," Carol said in a strangled voice. "I can't breathe."

"Just a minute, Mom," Peter muttered under his breath, pressing down on the accelerator and hurrying ahead.

Carol struggled into an upright position, dragging in several deep gulps of oxygen. She was about to deliver a much-needed lecture when Peter pulled into his friend's driveway. Seconds later, the front door banged open.

"James, where have you been? I told you to come directly home after school."

Carol blinked. Since this was the boys' first year of high school and they'd come from different middle schools, Carol had never met Jim's father. Now, however, didn't seem the appropriate moment to leap out and introduce herself.

Alex Preston was so angry with Jim that he barely glanced in their direction. When he did, he dismissed her and Peter without a word. His dark brows lifted derisively over gray eyes as he scowled at his son.

Carol suspected that if Jim hadn't gotten out of the car on his own, Alex would have pulled him through the window.

Carol couldn't help noting that Alex Preston was an imposing man; he had to be easily six-two. His forehead was high and his jaw well-defined. But his eyes were what immediately captured her attention. They held his son's with uncompromising authority.

There was an arrogant set to his mouth that Carol found herself disliking. Normally she didn't make snap judgments, but one look told her she wasn't going to get along with Jim's father, which was unfortunate since the boys had become such fast friends.

Not that it really mattered. Other than an occasional

phone conversation, there'd be no reason for them to have any contact with each other.

She didn't know much about the man, other than his marital status (single—divorced, she assumed) and the fact that he ran some sort of construction company.

"I told you I was going out tonight," Alex was saying. "The least you could've done was have the consideration to let me know where you were. You're lucky I don't ground you for the next ten years."

Jim dropped his head, looking guilty. "Sorry, Dad."

"I'm sorry, Mr. Preston," Peter said.

"It's not your fault."

To his credit, Alex Preston glanced apologetically at Peter and Carol as if to say he regretted this scene.

"It might be a good idea if you hurried home yourself," Alex told her son.

Carol stiffened in the front seat. She felt like jumping out of the car and informing him that they had no intention of staying anyway. "We should leave now," she said to Peter with as much dignity as she could muster.

"Later," Peter called to his friend.

"Later," Jim called back, still looking chagrined.

Peter had reversed the car out of the driveway and was headed toward the house before either of them spoke.

"Did you know Jim was supposed to go home right after school?" Carol asked.

"How could I know something like that?" Peter flared. "I asked him over to listen to my new CD. I didn't know his dad was going to come unglued over it."

"He's just being a parent."

"Maybe, but at least you don't scream at me in front of my friends."

"I try not to."

"I've never seen Mr. Preston blow his cool before. He sure was mad."

"I don't think we should be so hard on him," she said, feeling generous despite her earlier annoyance. Adults needed to stick together. "He was obviously worried."

"But, Mom, Jim's fifteen! You shouldn't have to know where a kid is every minute of the day."

"Wanna bet?"

Peter was diplomatic enough not to respond to that.

By the time they'd arrived at the house and Carol had changed clothes for her class, their dinner was ready.

"Mom," Peter said thoughtfully as she brought a fresh green salad to the table. "You should think about going out more yourself."

"I'm going out tonight."

"I mean on dates and stuff."

"Stuff?" Carol repeated, swallowing a smile.

"You know what I mean." He sighed loudly. "You haven't lost it yet, you know."

Carol wasn't sure she did. But she was fairly certain he meant to compliment her, so she nodded solemnly. "Thanks."

"You don't even need to use Oil of Olay."

She nodded, although she didn't appreciate such close scrutiny of her skin.

"I was looking at your hair and I don't see any gray, and you don't have fat folds or anything."

Carol couldn't help it—she laughed.

"Mom, I'm serious. You could probably pass for thirty."

"Thanks... I think."

"I'm not kidding. Jim's dad is going out with someone who's twenty-one, and Jim told me she's tall and blond and pretty with great big...you know." He cupped his hands over his chest.

Carol sat down at the table. Leaning her elbows on it, she dangled her fork over her plate. "Are you suggesting I find myself a twenty-one-year-old guy with bulging muscles and compete with Jim's dad?"

"Of course not," Peter said scornfully. "Well, not exactly. I'm just saying you're not over the hill. You could be dating a whole lot more than you do. And you should before...well, before it's too late."

Carol pierced a fork full of lettuce and offered a convenient excuse. "I don't have time to get involved with anyone."

Peter took a bite of his own salad. "If the right guy came along, you'd make time."

"Perhaps."

"Mr. Preston does. Jim says his dad's always busy with work, but he finds time to date lots of women."

"Right, but most of the women he sees are too young to vote." Instantly feeling guilty for the catty remark, Carol shook her head. "That wasn't nice. I apologize."

"I understand," Peter said, sounding mature beyond his years. "The way I see it, though, you need a man."

That was news to her. "Why? I've got you."

"True, but I won't be around much longer, and I hate the thought of you getting old and gray all alone."

"I won't be alone. Grandma will move in with me and the two of us will sit side by side in our rocking chairs and crochet afghans. For entertainment we'll play bingo every Saturday afternoon." Even as she spoke, Carol realized how ridiculous that was.

"Grandma would drive you crazy in three days," Peter

said with a know-it-all smile, waving his fork in her direction. "Besides, you'd get fat eating all her homemade pasta."

"Maybe so," Carol agreed, unwilling to argue the point. "But I have plenty of time before I have to worry about it. Anything can happen in the next few years."

"I'm worried *now*," Peter said. "You're letting your life slip through your fingers like…like the sand in an hourglass."

Carol's eyes connected with her son's. "Have you been watching soap operas again?"

"Mom," Peter cried, "you're not taking me seriously."

"I'm sorry," she said, trying to hide the smile that raised the corners of her mouth. "It's just that my life is full. I'm simply too busy to spend time developing a relationship." One look from her son told her he didn't accept her explanation. "Sweetheart," she told him, setting her fork aside, "you don't need to worry about me. I'm a big girl. When and if I decide to see another man, I promise it'll be someone muscular so you can brag to your friends. Would a wrestler be all right?"

"The least you could've done was get married again," he muttered, his patience clearly strained. "Dad would've wanted that, don't you think?"

Any mention of Peter's father brought with it a feeling of terror and guilt. They'd both been far too young and foolish to get married. They were high school seniors when Carol learned she was pregnant. Given her very traditional Catholic family, marriage had seemed the only option. She'd also believed her love and their baby would change Bruce. For those reasons, Carol had agreed to marry him. But from that point to the moment Bruce had died in a terrible car accident three years later, Carol's life had been a living hell. She'd have to be crazy to even consider remarriage.

"Peter," she said, pointedly glancing at her watch and pushing her plate away. "I'm sorry to end this conversation so abruptly, but I've got to get to class."

"You're just being stubborn, but fine. It's your decision."

Carol didn't have time to argue. She dumped the remainder of her meal in the garbage, rinsed off her plate and stuck it in the dishwasher. She left Peter after giving him instructions to take care of his own dishes, then she hurried into the bathroom.

She refreshed her makeup and ran a brush though her shoulder-length dark hair, then examined her reflection in the mirror.

"Not bad," she muttered, eyeing herself critically. Thirty-four wasn't exactly retirement age.

Releasing her breath, Carol let her shoulders fall. "Who are you kidding?" she said with a depressed sigh. She faced the mirror and glared at her image again. Peter might not think she needed Oil of Olay, but the dew was definitely off the rose.

Tugging at the skin on her cheekbones until it was stretched taut, she squinted at her reflection, trying to remember what she'd looked like at eighteen. Young. Pretty. Stupid.

She wasn't any one of those now. And even if she'd had the opportunity, she wouldn't go back. She'd made plenty of mistakes, but there wasn't a single, solitary thing she'd change about her current life. Although after Peter got his driver's license, she might modify that thought.

No, the only option open to her was the future, and she'd face that, sagging skin and all.

"Hey, Mom." Peter's voice cut into her musings. "Can I invite a friend over tonight?"

Carol opened the bathroom door and frowned at her son.

"I can't believe you'd even ask that. You know the rules. No one's allowed here when I'm not home."

"But, Mom," he whined.

"No exceptions."

"You don't trust me, do you?"

"We're not discussing this now. I have a class to teach, and I'm already five minutes behind schedule." She blamed Peter for that. If he hadn't tried to convince her how attractive she was, she wouldn't be late in the first place.

Class went well. They were into the third week of the eight-week course sponsored by Ford Hospital in a suburb of Portland, Oregon. The couples were generally first-time parents, and their eagerness and excitement for the adventure that lay before them filled each session with infectious enthusiasm.

If Carol had known when she was carrying Peter that he was to be her one and only pregnancy, she would've taken time to appreciate it more.

Since she was the last to leave the building, Carol turned off the lights and hauled her material out to her car. The parking lot was well lit, and she hurried through the rain, sliding inside the car. She drew in a deep breath and turned the ignition key. The Ford coughed and objected before roaring to life. Her car had been acting a little funny lately, but it was nothing she could pinpoint. Satisfied that there wasn't anything too terribly wrong, she eased into traffic on the busy street.

It wasn't until she'd stopped for the red light at the first intersection that her car released a series of short pathetic coughs, only this time it really sounded…sick.

"What's wrong?" she cried as the light turned green. Pushing down on the accelerator, she leaped ahead, but it was apparent that the problem, whatever it might be, was serious.

"All right, all right," she said, "I get the message. You need a mechanic and fast." A quick glance down the business-lined thoroughfare revealed there wasn't a single service station in sight.

"Great," she moaned. "How about if I promise not to let Peter behind the wheel for a while. Will that help?"

The ailing car belched loudly and a plume of black smoke engulfed the rear end.

"Okay, so you're not interested in a deal." Turning into the first driveway she happened upon, Carol found herself in a restaurant parking lot. The minute she entered an empty space, the car uttered one last groan and promptly died. And of course she'd left her cell phone charging—at home.

For a full minute Carol just sat here. "You can't do this to me!" Her car disagreed. Climbing out, she walked around it, as if she'd magically discover a cure lying on the ground. The rain was coming down in sheets, and within seconds, she was drenched.

In an act of angry frustration, she kicked a tire, then yelped when the heel of her pump broke off. She wanted to weep.

With no other alternative, she limped into the restaurant, intent on heading for the ladies' room. Once she composed herself, she'd deal with the car and call Peter to tell him she was going to be late.

Alex thought that if his date giggled one more time, he'd have to walk away from the table. Thanks to this woman, he was going slowly insane. He should know by now never to accept a blind date.

The first thing Bambi did when they were seated at the restaurant was to pick up the saltshaker and start discussing the "amazing" qualities of crystal.

It took Alex five minutes to make the connection. The saltshaker was made of crystal.

"I'm crazy about hot tubs," Bambi said, leaning forward to offer him a generous view of her ample breasts.

"They're...hot, all right," Alex murmured, examining the menu without much enthusiasm. His friend—at least someone he *used* to consider a friend—claimed Bambi was every man's dream. Her name should have been his first clue. Once they'd met, he'd learned her given name was Michelle, but she'd started calling herself Bambi because she loved forest animals so much. Animals like deer and chipmunks and hamsters.

Alex didn't have the heart to tell her that in all the years he'd been camping, he had yet to stumble upon a single family of hamsters grazing in a meadow.

When the waitress came to take their order, it took Bambi five minutes to explain how she wanted her salad served. Okay, he was exaggerating. Four minutes. He ordered a steak and asked for it rare.

"I'm on a diet," Bambi said, once the waitress had left.

He smiled benignly.

"Do you think I'm fat, Alex?" she asked.

Her big brown eyes appealed to him to lie if he must. Once more she bunched her full breasts together and leaned toward him. It was more than obvious that she wasn't wearing a bra. He suspected that he was supposed to swoon at the sight.

"You do think I'm fat, don't you?" Bambi asked, pouting prettily.

"No," Alex told her.

"You're just saying that to be nice," she purred, and demurely lowered her lashes against the high arch of her cheek.

Alex smoothed out the linen napkin on his lap, thinking he was getting old. Far too old for someone like Bambi/Michelle. His teenage son might appreciate her finer qualities, but he suspected even James had better sense than that.

"Do you have a hot tub?"

Alex was so caught up in his thoughts, mentally calculating how long it would take to get through dinner so he could drive her home, that he didn't immediately realize she'd directed the question at him.

"I love hot tubs," she reminded him. "I even carry a swimsuit with me just in case my date has a tub. See?" She reached inside her purse and held up the skimpiest piece of material Alex had seen in his entire life. It was all he could do not to grab it out of her hand and shove it back in her purse.

"I don't have a hot tub," he said, making a strenuous effort to remain civil.

"Oh, that poor, pathetic thing," Bambi said, looking past him to the front of the restaurant.

"I beg your pardon?"

Bambi used this opportunity to lean as far forward as possible, drape her breasts over his arm and whisper, "A bag lady just came into the restaurant. She's drenched, and I think she might be hurt because she's limping pretty bad."

Although he really wasn't interested, Alex glanced over his shoulder. The instant his gaze connected with the woman Bambi was referring to, he twisted his chair around for a better view. "That's no bag lady," he said. "I know that girl."

"You do?"

"Yes, she was with my son and his best friend this afternoon. I think she's another friend of theirs." He paused. "She might be in some kind of trouble." He wasn't in the business of rescuing maidens in distress, but someone had to do something. "Will you excuse me a moment?"

"Alex," Bambi cried, reaching out for his arm, stopping him. Half the restaurant turned to stare at them—including the woman at the front. Even from halfway across the room, Alex could feel her eyes on him.

"You can't involve yourself in other people's problems," Bambi insisted.

"She's just a kid." He pulled his arm free.

"Honey, one look at her and I can tell you she's no kid."

Disregarding Bambi's unsought advice, Alex dropped his napkin on the table, stood and walked away.

"Hello, again," he said when he reached his son's friend. Bambi was right about one thing. She looked terrible— nothing like the way she'd looked earlier. Her hair fell in wet tendrils that dripped on her jacket. Her mascara had left black streaks down her face, and she held the heel of her shoe in one hand. "I'm James's dad—we met briefly this afternoon." He held out his hand to her. "Do you remember me?"

"Of course I do," she said stiffly, clearly resenting this intrusion. She glanced longingly at the ladies' room.

"Is something wrong?"

"Wrong?" she echoed. "What could possibly be wrong?"

She thrust out her chin proudly, but he resisted the urge to shake some sense into her. Sarcasm always set his teeth on edge. "I'd like to help if I could."

"I appreciate the offer, but no thanks. Listen, I think you'd better get back to your date." She nodded toward

Bambi, and a smile quivered at the corners of her mouth. She had difficulty meeting his eyes.

Briefly Alex wondered what she found so amusing. But then again…he knew.

"I thought she was supposed to be tall," she said next, and it sounded like she was trying not to laugh outright. Alex didn't appreciate her sense of humor, but he wasn't going to respond in kind. She was the one standing there looking like a drowned rat. Not him.

Her brows rose as she studied Bambi. "Actually two out of three isn't bad."

Alex had no idea what she was talking about. His expression must have said as much because she added, "Jim was telling Peter how your date for this evening was tall and blond and had big—"

She stopped abruptly, and Alex could swear she was blushing. A bright pink color started creeping up her neck and into her cheeks. "I'm sorry, that was uncalled for."

Bambi apparently wasn't about to be the center of their conversation while sitting down. She pushed back her chair, joined them near the hostess desk and slipped her arm through Alex's. "Perhaps you'd care to introduce us, Alex darling."

Alex wanted to roll his eyes at the way she referred to him as "darling." They'd barely met. He doubted Bambi knew his last name. He certainly didn't remember hers.

Since he wasn't sure of anyone's name, Alex gestured toward Carol and said, "This is a friend of my son's…."

"Carol Sommars," she supplied.

Alex was surprised. "I didn't know Peter had a sister."

Carol shot him a look. "I'm not his sister. I'm his mother."

Chapter 2

"His mother," Alex echoed, clearly distressed. "But I thought... I assumed when you were with the boys that..."

"She's got to be *way* over thirty!" the blonde with her arm wrapped around Alex's exclaimed, eyeing Carol as possible competition.

Unwilling to be subjected to any debate over her age, Carol politely excused herself and headed blindly toward the ladies' room. The way her luck had been going this evening, it shouldn't be any shock that she'd run into Alex Preston of all people—and his infamous "hot date."

As soon as Carol examined herself in the mirror, she groaned and reached for her purse, hoping to repair the worst of the damage. No wonder Alex had mistaken her for a teenager. She looked like Little Orphan Annie on a bad day.

To add to her consternation, he was waiting for her when she left the restroom.

"Listen," he said apologetically. "We got off to a bad start. Can I do something to help?"

Carol thanked him with a smile. "I appreciate that, but I don't want to ruin your evening. My car broke down and I don't have my cell. I'm just going to call the auto club from here and have them deal with it." She already had the phone number and a quarter in her hand. The pay phone was just outside the restrooms.

"All right." Carol was grateful when he left. She was horrified by the way she'd spoken to him earlier and wanted to apologize—later. Alex had caught her at a bad moment, but he'd made up for it by believing she was Peter's sister. That was almost laughable, but exceptionally flattering.

She finished her call and tried three frustrating times to get through to Peter, but the line was busy. Sitting in the restaurant foyer, she decided to give her son a few more minutes before calling again.

Alex strolled toward her. "Is the auto club coming?"

"They're on their way," she answered cheerfully, flashing him a smile.

"Did you get hold of Peter?"

Her facade melted away. "I tried three times and can't get through. He's probably talking to Melody Wohlford, the love of his life."

"I'll contact James on my cell and have him get in touch with Peter for you. That way, you won't have to worry about it."

"Thank you." She was more gracious this time. "Knowing Peter, he could be on the phone for hours."

Alex stepped away and returned a minute later. "Jim was talking to Peter. Fortunately we have call waiting so I got through to him." He shook his head slightly. "They're doing their algebra homework together, which is probably good because Jim needs all the help he can get."

"In this case it's the blind leading the blind."

Alex grinned, and the mouth she'd found so arrogant and haughty earlier now seemed unusually appealing. His smile was sensual and affable at the same time and Carol liked it a whole lot. It had been a good many years since she'd caught herself staring at a man's mouth. Self-conscious, she dragged her gaze away and looked past him into the restaurant.

Alex glanced uncomfortably at his table, where the other woman was waiting impatiently. "Would you like to join us and have something to eat?" he asked eagerly.

"Oh, no," Carol said, "I couldn't do that."

Alex's gray eyes reached out to hers in blatant appeal. "*Please* join us."

Carol wasn't sure what was going on between Alex and his date, and she was even less sure about putting herself in the middle of it, but... Oh, well, why not?

"All right," she agreed in a tentative voice.

Alex immediately looked grateful. He glanced back at the woman who was glaring at him, clearly displeased that he was paying so much attention to Carol.

However, if her disapproval bothered him, he didn't show it. He led Carol back to the table and motioned for the waitress to bring a menu.

"I'll just have coffee."

As soon as the waitress was gone, Alex introduced the two women. "Bambi, Carol. Carol, Bambi."

"I'm pleased to make your acquaintance," Bambi said formally, holding out her hand. Carol thought she'd never seen longer nails. They were painted a fire engine red and were a good inch in length.

"Alex and I have sons the same age," Carol explained. Her coffee arrived, and she quickly took a sip to disguise her uneasiness.

"Eat your dinner, Alex," Bambi instructed. "There's no need to let our evening be ruined by Carol's problems."

"Yes, please," Carol said hurriedly. "By all means, don't let me keep you from your meal."

Alex reached for the steak knife. "Is Peter trying out for track this year?"

"He wouldn't miss it. I'm positive that's the only reason he's managed to keep his grades up. He knows the minute he gets a D, he's off the team. Who knows what'll happen next year when he takes chemistry."

"Jim's decided to take chemistry his junior year, too."

"I took chemistry," Bambi told them. "They made us look inside a worm."

"That's biology," Carol said kindly.

"Oh, maybe it was."

"I need to apologize for the way I blew up this afternoon," Alex continued. "I felt bad about it afterward. Yelling at Jim in front of his friends was not the thing to do. It's just that there are times my son frustrates me no end."

"Don't worry about it. I feel the same way about Peter when he does something I've specifically asked him not to do." Feeling guilty for excluding Bambi from the conversation, Carol turned toward her and asked, "Do you have children?"

"Heavens, no. I'm not even married."

"Children can be extremely wonderful and extremely frustrating," Carol advised Bambi, who seemed far more interested in gazing lovingly at Alex.

"Jim only has one chore around the house during the week," Alex went on to say. "He's supposed to take out the garbage. Every week it's the same thing. Garbage starts stacking up against the side of the refrigerator until it's as high as the cabinets, and Jim doesn't even notice. I end up having to plead with him to take it out."

"And two days later he does it, right? Peter's the same."

Alex leaned forward and braced his forearms against the table, pushing his untouched steak aside. "Last week, I didn't say a word, wanting to see how long it would take him to notice. Only when something began to stink did he so much as—"

"Pass the salt," Bambi said, stretching her arm between Carol and Alex and reaching for it herself. She shook it over her salad with a vengeance, then slammed it down on the table.

Apparently Alex felt contrite for having ignored his date. He motioned toward her salad. "Bambi's on a diet."

"I am not fat!" Bambi cried. "You said so yourself."

"I…no, I didn't mean to imply that you *needed* to be on a diet, I was just…making small talk."

"Well, if you don't mind, I'd prefer it if you didn't discuss my eating habits."

"Where's the protein?" Carol asked, examining Bambi's plate of greens. "You should be having some protein—eggs, lean meat, that sort of thing."

"Who are you?" Bambi flared. "Jenny Craig?"

"You're right, I'm sorry. It's just that I'm a nurse, and I work with pregnant women, and nutrition is such an important part of pregnancy that—"

"Are you suggesting I'm pregnant?"

"Oh, no, not in the least." Every time Carol opened her mouth, it seemed she made an even worse mess of the situation. "Look, I think the auto club might need some help finding me. If you'll both excuse me, I'll wait outside."

"You should," Bambi said pointedly. "You're over thirty, so you can take care of yourself."

Carol couldn't get away fast enough. The rain was coming down so hard it was jitterbugging across the asphalt parking lot. Standing just inside the restaurant doorway, Carol buried her hands in her pockets and shivered. She hadn't been there more than a few minutes when Alex joined her.

Before she could say anything, he thrust his hands in his own pockets, sighed and said, "I gave her money for a taxi home."

Carol wasn't sure how to respond. "I hope it wasn't on account of me."

"No." He gave her another of his warm, sensual smiles. "It was a blind date. I should've known better than to let myself get talked into it."

"I went out on one a while ago, and it was a disaster, too." It got worse the longer she was single. Her friends seemed to believe that since she'd been alone for so many years, she should be willing to lower her standards. "How long have you been single?" she asked Alex.

"Two years. What about you?"

"Thirteen."

He turned to face her. "That's a long time."

"So Peter keeps telling me. According to him, I'm about to lose it and need to act fast. I haven't figured out precisely what *it* is, but I have a good idea."

"Jim keeps telling me the same thing. Between him and Barney—that's the guy who arranged this date—they're driving me crazy."

"I know what you mean. My brother's wife calls me at least once a week and reads me ads from the personal columns. She's now progressed to the Internet, as well. The one she picked out last week really got me. It was some-thing like—Male, thirty-five, dull and insecure, seeks ex-citing, wealthy female any age who's willing to love too much. Likes string cheese and popcorn. If you can do *Su-doku for Dummies,* I'm the man for you."

"Maybe we should introduce him to Bambi."

They laughed together, and it felt natural.

"Give me your car keys," Alex said suddenly. "I'll check it out and if it's something minor, I might be able to fix it."

"I don't think it is. When the engine died, it sounded pretty final." Nevertheless, she handed him her key ring and stood under the shelter while Alex ran across the park-ing lot to test her car. She stood on her tiptoes and watched him raise the hood, disappear under it for a few minutes and then close it and come running back to her.

"I think you're right," he said, rubbing the black grease from his hands with a white handkerchief.

"Excuse us, please," a soft feminine voice purred from behind Carol. Bambi slithered past them, her arm looped through that of a much older gentleman. She cast Carol a dirty look and smiled softly in Alex's direction before turn-ing her attention to her most recent admirer. "Now, what were you saying about your hot tub?"

The two were barely out of earshot when Alex started to chuckle. "It didn't take her long, did it?"

"I really am sorry," Carol felt obliged to say. "I feel ter-rible...as though I personally ruined your evening."

"No," he countered. "On the contrary, you saved me. By the time you arrived, I was trying to figure out how long my patience was going to hold out. I had the distinct im-pression that before the evening was over I was going to be fighting her off."

Carol laughed. It didn't require much imagination to

see Bambi in the role of aggressor. Come to think of it, Carol had dealt with a handful of Bambi's male counterparts over the years.

The rain had diminished and it was drizzling when the auto club van arrived. Alex walked the driver to Carol's car, and together the two men tried to determine what was wrong with her faithful Ford. They decided that whatever the problem was, it couldn't be fixed then and there and that the best thing to do was call a tow truck.

Carol agreed and signed on the dotted line.

"I'll give you a lift home," Alex volunteered.

"Thanks." She was already in his debt; one more thing wouldn't matter.

Within minutes, they were sitting inside Alex's car with the heater running full blast. Carol ran her hands up and down her arms to warm them.

"You're cold."

"I'll be fine in a minute. If I wasn't such a slave to fashion," she said with self-deprecating humor, "I would've worn something heavier than this cotton jacket. But it's the same pale green as my slacks and they go so well together."

"You sound just like Jim. It was forty degrees yesterday morning, and he insisted on wearing a shirt from last summer."

They smiled at each other, and Carol was conscious of how close they were in the snug confines of Alex's sports car. Her dark eyes met his warm gray ones. Without warning, the laughter faded from Alex's lips, and he studied her face. After viewing the damage earlier, Carol knew her hair hung in springy ringlets that resembled a pad used to scrub pots and pans. She'd done the best she could, brushing it away from her face and securing it at the base of her neck with a wide barrette she'd found in the bottom of her purse. Now she was certain the tail that erupted from her nape must be sticking straight out.

A small lump lodged in her throat, as though she'd tried to swallow a pill without water. "You never did get your dinner, did you?" she asked hastily.

"Don't worry about it."

"Listen, I owe you. Please...stop somewhere and let me treat you. It's after nine—you must be starved." She glanced at her watch and felt a blush heat her cheeks. It'd been longer than she could recall since a man had unsettled her quite this much.

"Don't worry about it," he said again. "I'm a big boy. I'll make myself a sandwich once I get home."

"But—"

"If you insist, you can have me over to eat sometime. All right? When it comes to dinner, Jim and I share the duties. A good home-cooked meal would be welcome."

Carol didn't have any choice but to agree, and she did so by nodding her damp head briskly until she realized she was watering the inside of his car. "Oh, sure, I'd like that." She considered saying that she came from a large Italian family and was an excellent cook, but that would sound too much like the personal ads her sister-in-law, Paula, insisted on reading to her.

"You *do* cook?"

"Oh, yes." Once more she held her tongue. Whereas a few moments earlier she'd been cold, now she felt uncomfortably warm. Her hands were clammy and her stomach was filled with what seemed like a swarm of bees.

They chatted amicably on the rest of the drive to her house. When Alex pulled into her driveway, she turned and smiled at him, her hand on her door handle. "I'm really grateful for all your help."

"No problem."

"And... I'm sorry about what happened with Bambi."

"I'm not," he said, then chuckled. "I'll give you a call later, all right? To check on your car...."

The question seemed to hang between them, heavy with implication. It was the "all right" that told her he was referring to something beyond the state of her car.

"Okay," she said almost flippantly, feeling more than a little light-headed.

"So, tell me about this man who brings color back to my little girl's cheeks," Angelina Pasquale said to Carol as she carried a steaming plate of spaghetti to the table.

Carol's mother didn't know how to cook for three or four; it was twelve or fifteen servings for each and every Sunday dinner. Her two older sisters lived in California now, and only Tony and Carol and their families came religiously for Sunday dinner. Her mother, however, continued to cook as if two or three additional families might walk in unannounced for the evening meal.

"Mama, Alex Preston and I just met last week."

"That's not what Peter said." The older woman wiped her hands on the large apron tied around her thick waist. Her dark hair, streaked with gray, was tucked into a neat bun. She wore a small gold crucifix that had been given to her by Carol's father forty-two years earlier.

Carol brought the long loaves of hot bread from the oven. "Alex is Jim's father. You remember Peter's friend, don't you?"

"He's not Italian."

"I don't know what he is. Preston might be an English name."

"English," Angelina said as if she was spitting out dirty dishwater. "You gonna marry a non-Italian again?"

"Mama," Carol said, silently laughing, "Alex helped me when my car broke down. I owe him dinner, and I insisted on taking him out to repay him. We're not stopping off at the church to get married on the way."

"I bet he's not even Catholic."

"Mama," Carol cried. "I haven't the faintest clue where he attends church."

"You taking a man to dinner instead of cooking for him is bad enough. But not even knowing if he's Catholic is asking for trouble." She raised her eyes as if pleading for patience in dealing with her youngest daughter; when she lowered her gaze, they fell to Carol's feet. She folded her hands in prayerlike fashion. "You wear pointed-toe shoes for this man?"

"I didn't wear these for Alex. I happen to like them—they're in style."

"They're gonna deform your feet. One day, you'll trip and end up facedown in the gutter like your cousin Celeste."

"Mama, I'm not going to end up in a gutter."

"Your cousin Celeste told her mother the same thing, and we both know what happened to her. She had to marry a foot doctor."

"Mama, please don't worry about my shoes."

"Okay, but don't let anyone say your mama didn't warn you."

Carol had to leave the room to keep from laughing. Her mother was the delight of her life. She drove Carol crazy with her loony advice, but Carol knew it was deeply rooted in love.

"Carol," Angelina said, surveying the table, "tell everyone dinner's ready."

Peter was in the living room with his younger cousins, who were watching the Dodgers play Kansas City in a hotly contested baseball game.

"Dinner's on the table, guys."

"Just a minute, Mom. It's the bottom of the eighth, with two out." Peter's intense gaze didn't waver from the screen. "Besides, Uncle Tony and Aunt Paula aren't back from shopping yet."

"They'll eat later." Carol's brother Tony and his wife had escaped for the afternoon to Clackamas Town Center, a large shopping mall south of Portland, and they weren't expected back until much later.

"Just a few more minutes," Peter pleaded.

"Mama made zabaglione," Carol said.

The television went off in a flash, and four children rushed into the dining room, taking their places at the table like a rampaging herd of buffalo. Peter was the oldest by six years, which gave him an air of superiority over his cousins.

Sunday dinner at her mother's was tradition. They were a close-knit family and helped one another without question. Her brother had lent her his second car while hers was being repaired. Carol didn't know what she'd do without him. She'd have her own car back in a few days, but Tony's generosity had certainly made her life easier.

Mama treasured these times with her children and grandchildren, generously offering her love, her support and her pasta. Being close to her family was what had gotten Carol through the difficult years following Bruce's death. Her parents had been wonderful, helping her while she worked her way through college and the nursing program, caring for Peter when she couldn't and introducing her to a long list of nice Italian men. But after three years of dealing with Bruce's mental and physical abuse, she wasn't interested. The scars from her marriage ran deep.

"I'll say grace now," Angelina said. They all bowed their heads and closed their eyes.

No one needed any encouragement to dig into the spaghetti drenched in a sauce that was like no other. Carol's mother was a fabulous cook. She insisted on making everything from scratch, and she'd personally trained each one of her three daughters.

"So, Peter," his grandmother said, tearing off a thick piece from the loaf of hot bread. "What do you think of your mother marrying this Englishman?"

"Aw, Grandma, it's not like that. Mr. Preston called and Mom's treating him to dinner 'cause he gave her a ride home. I don't think it's any big deal."

"That was what she said when she met your father. 'Ma,' she told me, 'it's just dinner.' The next thing I know, she's standing at the altar with this non-Italian and six months later the priest was baptizing you."

"Ma! Please," Carol cried, embarrassed at the way her mother spoke so freely—although by now she should be used to it.

"Preston." Her mother muttered the name again, chewing it along with her bread. "I could accept the man if he had a name like Prestoni. Carol Prestoni has a good Italian ring to it…but Preston. Bah."

Peter and Carol exchanged smiles.

"He's real nice, Grandma."

Angelina expertly wove the long strands of spaghetti around the tines of her fork. "Your mama deserves to meet a nice man. If you say he's okay, then I have to take your word for it."

"Mama, it's only one dinner." Carol wished she'd never

said anything to her mother. Alex had called the night before, and although he sounded a little disappointed that she wouldn't be making the meal herself, he'd agreed to let her repay the favor with dinner at a local restaurant Monday night. Her big mistake was mentioning it to her mother. Carol usually didn't say anything to her family when she was going out on a date. But for some reason, unknown even to herself, she'd mentioned Alex as soon as she'd walked in the door after church Sunday morning.

"What color eyes does this man have?"

"Gray," Carol answered and poured herself a glass of ice water.

Peter turned to his mother. "How'd you remember that?"

"I… I just recall they were…that color." Carol felt her cheeks flush. She concentrated on her meal, but when she looked up, she saw her mother watching her closely. "His eyes are sort of striking," she said, mildly irritated by the attention her mother and her son were lavishing on her.

"I never noticed," Peter said.

"A boy wouldn't," Angelina told him, "but your mother, well, she looks at such things."

That wasn't entirely true, but Carol wasn't about to claim otherwise.

As soon as they were finished with the meal, Carol's mother brought out the zabaglione, a rich sherry-flavored Italian custard thick with eggs. Angelina promptly dished up six bowls.

"Mama, zabaglione's high in fat and filled with cholesterol." Since her father's death from a heart attack five years earlier, Carol worried about her mother's health, although she wasn't sure her concern was appreciated.

"So zabaglione's got cholesterol."

"But, Mama, cholesterol clogs the veins. It could kill you."

"If I can't eat zabaglione, then I might as well be dead."

Smiling wasn't what Carol should have done, but she couldn't help it.

When the dishes were washed and the kitchen counters cleaned, Carol and her mother sat in the living room. Angelina rocked in the chair her mother's mother had brought from Italy seventy years earlier. Never one for idle hands, she picked up her crocheting.

It was a rare treat to have these moments alone with her mother, and Carol sat on the sofa, feet tucked under her, head back and eyes closed.

"When am I gonna meet this Englishman of yours?"

"Mama," Carol said with a sigh, opening her eyes, "you're making me sorry I ever mentioned Alex."

"You didn't need to tell me about him. I would have asked because the minute you walked in the house I could see a look in your eyes. It's time, my *bambina*. Peter is growing and soon you'll be alone."

"I… I'm looking forward to that."

Her mother discredited that comment with a shake of her head. "You need a husband, one who will give you more children and bring a sparkle to your eyes."

Carol's heart started thundering inside her chest. "I… I don't think I'll ever remarry, Mama."

"Bah!" the older woman said. A few minutes later, she murmured something in Italian that Carol could only partially understand, but it was enough to make her blush hotly. Her mother was telling her there were things about a man that she shouldn't be so quick to forget.

The soft Italian words brought a vivid image to Carol's mind—an image of Alex holding her in his arms, gazing down at her, making love to her. It shocked her so much that she quickly made her excuses, collected Peter and drove home.

Her pulse rate hadn't decreased by the time she arrived back at her own small house. Her mother was putting too much emphasis on her dinner date with Alex…far more than necessary or appropriate.

As soon as Peter went over to a neighbor's to play video games, Carol reached for the phone. When voice mail kicked in on the fourth ring, she immediately hung up.

On second thought, this was better, she decided, and dialed again, planning to leave a message. "You're a coward," she muttered as she pushed down the buttons.

Once more the recorded message acknowledged her call. She waited for the greeting, followed by a long beep.

"Hello… Alex, this is Carol… Carol Sommars. About our dinner date Monday night… I'm sorry, but I'm going to have to cancel. Something…has come up. I apologize that thisissuchshortnotice. Bye." The last words tumbled together in her haste to finish.

Her face was flushed, and sweat had beaded on her upper lip as she hung up the phone. With her hand on the receiver, she slowly expelled her breath.

Her mother was right. Alex Preston was the one man who could bring the light back into her eyes, and she'd never been more frightened in her life.

Chapter 3

Carol's hand remained closed around the telephone receiver as she heaved in a giant breath. She'd just completed the most cowardly act of her life.

Regretting her actions, she punched out Alex's phone number again, and listened to the recorded message a third time while tapping her foot. At the beep, she paused, then blurted out, "I hope you understand... I mean...oh...never mind." With that, she replaced the receiver, pressed her hand over her brow, more certain than ever that she'd just made a world-class idiot of herself.

Half an hour later, Carol was sorting through the dirty clothes in the laundry room when Peter came barreling into the house.

He paused in the doorway, watching her neatly organize several loads. "Hey, Mom, where's the TV guide?"

"By the television?" she suggested, more concerned about making sure his jeans' pockets were empty before putting them in the washer.

"Funny, Mom, real funny. Why would anyone put it there?"

Carol paused, holding a pair of dirty jeans to her chest. "Because that's where it belongs?" she said hopefully.

"Yeah, but when's the last time anyone found it there?"

Not bothering to answer, she dumped his jeans in the washing machine. "Did you look on the coffee table?"

"It's not there. It isn't by the chair, either."

"What are you so keen to watch, anyway? Shouldn't you be doing your homework?"

"I don't have any…well, I do, but it's a snap."

Carol threw another pair of jeans into the churning water. "If it's so easy, do it now."

"I can't until Jim gets home."

At the mention of Alex's son, Carol hesitated. "I…see."

"Besides, it's time for wrestling, but I don't know what channel it's on."

"Wrestling?" Carol cried. "When did you become interested in *that?*"

"Jim introduced me to it. I know it looks phony and stuff, but I get a kick out of those guys pounding on each other and the crazy things they say."

Carol turned and leaned against the washer, crossing her arms. "Personally I'd rather you did your homework first, and if there's any time left over you can watch television."

"Of course you'd prefer that," Peter said. "You're a mom—you're supposed to think that way. But I'm a kid, and I'd much rather watch Mr. Muscles take on Jack Beanstalk."

Carol considered her son's argument for less than two seconds. "Do your homework."

Peter sighed, his shoulders sagging. "I was afraid you'd say that." Reluctantly he headed toward his bedroom.

It was still light out, and with the wash taken care of,

Carol ventured into the backyard, surveying her neatly edged flower beds. Besides perennials, she grew Italian parsley, basil and thyme and a few other herbs in the ceramic pots that bordered her patio. One of these days she was going to dig up a section of her lawn and plant an honest-to-goodness garden.

"Mom…" Peter was shouting her name from inside the house.

She turned, prepared to answer her son, when she saw Alex walk out the back door toward her. Her heart did a somersault, then vaulted into her throat and stayed there for an uncomfortable moment.

"Hello, Alex," she managed to say, suspecting that her face had the look of a cornered mouse. She would gladly have given six months' mortgage payments to remove her messages from his voice mail. It wasn't easy to stand there calmly and not run for the fence.

"Hello, Carol." He walked toward her, his gaze holding hers.

He sounded so…relaxed, but his eyes were a different story. They were like the eyes of an eagle, sharp and intent. They'd zeroed in on her as though he was about to swoop down for the kill.

For her part, Carol was a wreck. Her hands were clenched so tightly at her sides that her fingers ached. "What can I do for you?" she asked, embarrassed by the way her voice pitched and heaved with the simple question.

A brief smile flickered at the edges of Alex's mouth. "You mean you don't know?"

"No…well, I can guess, but I think it would be best if you just came out and said it." She took a couple of steps toward him, feeling extraordinarily brave for having done so.

"Will you offer me a cup of coffee?" Alex asked instead.

The man was full of surprises. Just when she was convinced he was about to berate her for behaving like an utter fool, he casually suggested she make coffee. Perhaps he often confronted emotionally insecure women who left him nonsensical messages.

"Coffee? Of course...come in." Pleased to have something to occupy her hands, Carol hurried into the kitchen. Once she'd added the grounds to the filter and filled the coffeemaker with water, she turned and leaned against the counter, hoping to look poised. She did an admirable job, if she did say so herself—at least for the first few minutes. After all, she'd spent the last thirteen years on her own. She wasn't a dimwit, although she'd gone out of her way to give him that impression, and she hadn't even been trying. That disconcerted her more than anything.

"No, I don't understand," Alex said. He opened her cupboard and took down two ceramic mugs.

"Understand what?" Carol decided playing dumb might help. It had worked with Bambi, and who was to say it wouldn't with her? However, she had the distinct notion that if she suggested they try out a hot tub, Alex would be more than willing.

"I want to know why you won't have dinner with me."

Carol was completely out of her element. She dealt with pregnancy and birth, soon-to-be mothers and terrified fathers, and she did so without a pause. But faced with one handsome single father, she was a worthless mass of frazzled nerves. Fearing her knees might give out on her, she walked over to the table, pulled out a chair and slumped into it. "I didn't exactly say I wouldn't go out with you."

"Then what did you say?"

She lowered her gaze, unable to meet his. "That...something came up."

"I see." He twisted the chair around and straddled it. The coffeemaker gurgled behind her. Normally she didn't even notice it, but now it seemed as loud as the roar of a jet plane.

"Then we'll reschedule. Tuesday evening at six?"

"I… I have a class… I teach a birthing class to expectant parents on Tuesday evenings." Now that was brilliant! Who else would attend those classes? But it was an honest excuse. "That's where I'd been when my car broke down in the parking lot of the restaurant where I met you…last Tuesday…remember?"

"The night I helped you," Alex reminded her. "As I recall, you claimed you wanted to repay me. Fact is, you insisted on it. You said I'd missed my dinner because of you and that you'd like to make it up to me. At first it was going to be a home-cooked meal, but that was quickly reduced to meeting at a restaurant in separate cars, and now you're canceling altogether."

"I…did appreciate your help."

"Is there something about me that bothers you? Do I have bad breath?"

"Of course not."

"Dandruff?"

"No."

"Then what is it?"

"Nothing," she cried. She couldn't very well explain that their one meeting had jolted to life a part of her that had lain dormant for years. To say Alex Preston unsettled her was an understatement. She hadn't stopped thinking about him from the moment he'd dropped her off at the house. Every thought that entered her mind was linked to those few minutes they'd spent alone in his car. She was an adult, a professional, but he made her forget everything—except him. In thinking about it, Carol supposed it was because she'd married so young and been widowed shortly afterward. It was as though she didn't know how to behave with a man, but that wasn't entirely true, either. For the past several years, she'd dated numerous times. Nothing serious of course, but friendly outings with "safe" men. One second with Alex, and she'd known instantly that an evening with him could send her secure, tranquil world into a tailspin.

"Wednesday then?"

Carol looked warily across the kitchen, wanting to weep with frustration. She might as well be a good sport about it and give in. Alex wasn't going to let her off the hook without a fuss.

"All right," she said, and for emphasis, nodded. "I'll see you Wednesday evening."

"Fine." Alex stood and twisted the chair back around. "I'll pick you up at seven." He sent her one of his smiles and was gone before the coffee finished brewing.

Once she was alone, Carol placed her hands over her face, feeling the sudden urge to cry. Closing her eyes, however, was a mistake, because the minute she did, her mother's whispered words, reminding her of how good lovemaking could be, saturated her thoughts. That subject was the last thing Carol wanted to think about, especially when the man she wanted to be making love with was the one who had so recently left her kitchen.

Abruptly she stood and poured herself a cup of coffee. It didn't help to realize that her fingers were shaking. What was so terrific about men and sex, anyway? Nothing that *she* could remember. She'd been initiated in the backseat of a car at eighteen with the boy she was crazy in love with. Or the boy she *thought* she was in love with. More likely it had been hormones on the rampage for both of them.

After she'd learned she was pregnant, Carol was never

convinced Bruce had truly wanted to marry her. Faced with her hotheaded father and older brother, he'd clearly regarded marriage as the more favorable option.

In the last of her three years with Bruce, he'd been drunk more than he was sober—abusive more than he was considerate. Lovemaking had become a nightmare for her. Feeling violated and vaguely sick to her stomach, she would curl up afterward and lie awake the rest of the night. Then Bruce had died, and mingled with the grief and horror had been an almost giddy sense of relief.

"I don't want a man in my life," she said forcefully.

Peter was strolling down the hallway to his room and stuck his head around the doorway. "Did you say something?"

"Ah…" Carol wanted to swallow her tongue. "Nothing important."

"You look nice," Peter told Carol on Wednesday when she finished with her makeup.

"Thanks," she said, smiling at him. Her attitude toward this evening out with Alex had improved now that she'd had time to sort through her confused emotions. Jim's father was a nice guy, and to be honest, Carol didn't know what had made her react the way she did on Sunday. She was a mature adult, and there was nothing to fear. It wasn't as though she was going to fall into bed with the man simply because she was attracted to him. They'd have the dinner she owed him and that would be the end of it.

But, as much as she would've liked to deny it, Alex was special. For the first time since she could remember, she was physically attracted to a man. And what was wrong with that? It only went to prove that she was a normal, healthy woman. In fact, she should be grateful to Alex for helping her realize just how healthy she was.

"Where's Mr. Preston taking you?" Peter asked, plopping himself down on the edge of the tub.

"Actually I'm taking him, and I thought we'd go to Jake's." Jake's was a well-known and well-loved Portland restaurant renowned for its Cajun dishes.

"You're taking Mr. Preston to Jake's?" Peter cried, his voice shrill with envy. "Are you bringing me back anything?"

"No." As it was, she was stretching her budget for the meal.

"But, Mom—Jake's? You know that's my favorite restaurant in the whole world." He made it sound as though he were a global traveler and connoisseur of fine dining.

"I'll take you there on your birthday." The way she had every year since he was ten.

"But that's another five months," Peter grumbled.

She gave him what she referred to as her "Mother Look," which generally silenced him.

"All right, all right," he muttered. "I'll eat frozen pot pie for the third time in a week. Don't worry about me."

"I won't."

Peter sighed with feeling. "You go ahead and enjoy your *étouffée*."

"I'm sure I will." She generally ordered the shrimp dish, which was a popular item on the menu.

Peter continued to study her, his expression revealing mild surprise. "Gee, Mom, don't you have a heart anymore? I used to be able to get you with guilt, but you hardly bat an eyelash anymore."

"Of course I've got a heart. Unfortunately I don't have the wallet to support it."

Peter seemed about to speak again, but the doorbell chimed and he rushed out of the tiny bathroom to answer it as though something dire would happen if Alex was kept waiting more than a few seconds.

Expelling a sigh, Carol surveyed her appearance in the mirror one last time, confident that she looked her best. With a prepared smile on her face, she headed for the living room.

The instant she appeared, Alex's gaze rushed to hers. The impact of seeing him again was immediate. It was difficult to take her eyes off him. Instead, she found herself thinking that his build suggested finely honed muscles. He was tall, his shoulders were wide and his chest solid. Carol thought he was incredibly good-looking in his pin-striped suit. His face was weathered from working out of doors, his features bronzed by the sun.

So much for the best-laid plans, Carol mused, shaking from the inside out. She'd planned this evening down to the smallest detail. They would have dinner, during which Carol would subtly inform him that she wasn't interested in anything more than a casual friendship, then he'd take her home, and that would be the end of it. Five seconds after she'd walked into the living room, she was thinking about silk sheets and long, slow, heart-melting kisses.

Her mother was responsible for this. Her outrageous, wonderful mother and the softly murmured Italian words that reminded Carol she was still young and it was time to live and love again. She was alive, all right. From the top of her head to the bottom of her feet, she was *alive*.

"Hello, Carol."

"Alex."

"Mom's taking you to Jake's," Peter muttered, not both-

ering to hide his envy. "She can't afford to bring me anything, but that's okay."

"Peter," she chastised, doubting Alex had heard him.

"Are you ready?"

She nodded, taking an additional moment to gather her
composure while she reached for her jacket and purse.
Glancing at her son, she felt obliged to say, "You know the
rules. I'll call you later."

"You don't need to phone," he said, making a show of
rolling his eyes as if to suggest she was going overboard
on this parental thing.

"We'll be back early."

Alex cupped her elbow as he directed her to the door.
"Not too early," he amended.

By the time they were outside, Carol had bridled her
fears. Her years of medical training contributed to her skill
at presenting a calm, composed front. And really, there
wasn't a reason in the world she should panic....

They talked amicably on the drive into downtown Portland, commenting on such ordinary subjects as the weather,
when her car would be fixed and the approach of summer,
which they both dreaded because the boys would be constantly underfoot.

Alex managed to find parking on the street, which was
a feat in its own right. He opened her car door and took her
hand, which he didn't release.

Since Carol had made a reservation, they were immediately seated in a high-backed polished wood booth and
greeted by their waiter, who brought them a wine list and
recited the specials of the day.

"Jim tells me you're buying him a truck," Carol said
conversationally when they'd placed their order.

"So he'd like to believe."

Carol hesitated. "You mean you aren't?"

"Not to the best of my knowledge," Alex admitted, grinning.

Once more, Carol found herself fascinated by his smile. She found herself wondering how his mouth would feel on hers. As quickly as the thought entered her mind, she discarded it.

"According to Jim it's going to be the latest model, red with flames decorating the sidewalls."

"The boy likes to dream," Alex said, leaning back. "If he drives any vehicle during the next two years, it'll be because he's impressed me with his grades and his maturity."

"Oh, Alex," Carol said with a sigh, "you don't know how relieved I am to hear that. For weeks, Peter's been making me feel as though I'm an abusive mother because I'm not buying him a car—or, better yet, a truck. Time and time again he's told me that *you're* buying one for Jim and how sharing the Ford with me could damage his self-esteem, which might result in long-term counseling."

Alex laughed outright. "By the way," he added, "Jim isn't Jim anymore, he's James."

"James?"

"Right. He noticed that his learner's permit listed his name as James Preston, and he's insisting everyone call him that. Actually, I think he came up with the idea after I spoke to him about driving and his level of maturity. Apparently, James is more mature-sounding than Jim."

"Apparently," Carol returned, smiling. "Well, at least if Peter does end up having to go to a counselor, he'll have company."

Their wine arrived and they both commented on its delicious flavor and talked about the quality of Walla Walla area wineries.

Their meal came soon after. The steaming *étouffée* was placed before her, and she didn't experience the slightest bit of guilt when she tasted the first bite. It was as delicious as she remembered.

"Have you been a nurse long?" Alex asked, when their conversation lagged.

"Eight years. I returned to school after my husband was killed, and nursing was a natural for me. I was forever putting Band-Aids on my dolls and treating everyone from my dog to my tolerant mother."

"Next time I have a cold, I'll know who to call," Alex teased.

"Oh, good. And when I'm ready to put the addition on the house, I'll contact you," Carol told him.

They both laughed.

The evening wasn't nearly as difficult as Carol had feared. Alex was easy to talk to, and with the boys as common ground, there was never a lack of subject matter. Before Carol was aware of it, it was nearly ten.

"Oh, dear," she said, sliding from the booth. "I told Peter I'd check in with him. Excuse me a minute."

"Sure," Alex said, standing himself.

Carol was in the foyer on her cell, waiting for Peter to answer when she looked over and saw that Alex was using his own cell phone.

"Hello."

"Peter, it's Mom."

"Mom, you said you were going to phone," he said, sounding offended. "Do you know what time it is? When you say you're going to phone you usually do. James is worried, too. Where have you guys been?"

"Jake's—you knew that."

"All this time?"

"Yes. I'm sorry, sweetheart, the evening got away from us."

"Uh-huh," Peter said and paused. "So you like Mr. Preston?"

Carol hedged. "He's very nice," she murmured.

"Do you think you'll go out with him again? What did you guys talk about? Just how long does it take to eat dinner, anyway?"

"Peter, this isn't the time or place to be having this discussion."

"Were there any leftovers?"

"None."

Her son sighed as if he'd actually been counting on her to bring home her untouched dinner—a reward for the supreme sacrifice of having to eat chicken pot pie, which just happened to be one of his favorites.

"When will you be home? I mean, you don't have to rush on my account or anything, but you'd never let *me* stay out this late on a weeknight."

"I'll be back before eleven," she promised, ignoring his comment about the lateness of the hour. Sometimes Peter forgot who was the adult and who was the child.

"You *do* like Mr. Preston, don't you?" His tone was too smug for comfort.

"Peter," she moaned. "I'll talk to you later." She was about to replace the receiver when she heard him call her name. "What is it now?" she said sharply, impatiently.

He hesitated, apparently taken aback by her brusqueness. "Nothing, I just wanted to tell you to wake me up when you get home, all right?"

"All right," she said, feeling guilty.

She met Alex back at their table. "Everything okay at home?" he asked.

"Couldn't be better." There was no need to inform Alex

of the inquisition Peter had attempted. "What about Jim—James?"

"He's surviving."

"I suppose we should think about getting home," Carol suggested, eager now to leave. The evening had flown by. At some point during dinner, her guard had slipped and she'd begun to enjoy his company. There'd been none of the terrible tension that had plagued her earlier.

"I suppose you're right," Alex said with enough reluctance to alarm her. He'd obviously enjoyed their time as much as she had.

They had a small disagreement over the check, which Alex refused to let her take. He silenced her protests by reminding her that she owed him a home-cooked meal and he wasn't accepting any substitutes. After a couple of glasses of wine and a good dinner, Carol was too mellow to put up much of an argument.

"Just don't let Peter know," she said as they walked toward the car. Alex held her hand, and it seemed far too natural, but she didn't object.

"Why?"

"If Peter discovers you paid, he'll want to know why I didn't bring anything home for him."

Alex grinned as he unlocked his car door and held it open. He rested his hand on the curve of her shoulder. "You *will* make me that dinner sometime, won't you?"

Before she realized what she was doing, Carol found herself nodding. She hadn't had a chance to compose herself by the time he'd walked around the front of the car and joined her.

Neither of them spoke on the drive back to her house. Carol's mind was filled with the things she'd planned to tell him. The things she'd carefully thought out beforehand—

about what a nice time she'd had, and how she hoped they'd stay in touch and what a good boy Jim—James—was and how Alex was doing a wonderful job raising him. But the trite, rehearsed words refused to come.

Alex pulled into her driveway and turned off the engine. The living room was dark and the curtains drawn. The only illumination was the dim light on her front porch. When Alex turned to face her, Carol's heart exploded with dread and wonder. His look was warm, eager enough to make her blood run hot…and then immediately cold.

"I had a good time tonight." He spoke first.

"I did, too." How weak she sounded, how tentative…

"I'd like to see you again."

They were the words she'd feared—and longed for. The deep restlessness she'd experienced since the night her car had broken down reverberated within her, echoing through the empty years she'd spent alone.

"Carol?"

"I…don't know." She tried to remind herself of what her life had been like with Bruce. The tireless lies, the crazy brushes with danger as though he were courting death. The anger and impatience, the pain that gnawed at her soul. She thought of the wall she'd so meticulously constructed around her heart. A wall years thick and so high no man had ever been able to breach it. "I…don't think so."

"Why not? I don't understand."

Words could never explain her fear.

"Let me revise my statement," Alex said. "I *need* to see you again."

"Why?" she cried. "This was only supposed to be one night…to thank you for your help. I can't give you any more… I just can't and…" Her breath scattered, and her lungs burned within her chest. She couldn't deny the things he made her feel.

"Carol," he said softly. "There's no reason to be afraid."

But there was. Except he wouldn't understand.

He reached up and placed his calloused palm against her cheek.

Carol flinched and quickly shut her eyes. "No...please, I have to go inside... Peter's waiting for me." She grabbed the door handle, and it was all she could do not to escape from the car and rush into the house.

"Wait," he said huskily, removing his hand from her face. "I didn't mean to frighten you."

She nodded, opening her eyes, and her startled gaze collided with his. She watched as he slowly appraised her, taking in her flushed face and the rapid rise and fall of her breasts. He frowned.

"You're trembling."

"I'm fine...really. Thank you for tonight. I had a marvelous time."

His hand settled over hers. "You'll see me again."

It wasn't until she was safely inside her living room and her heart was back to normal that Carol realized his parting words had been a statement of fact.

Chapter 4

"So, Dad, how did dinner go with Mrs. Sommars?" James asked as he poured himself a huge bowl of cornflakes. He added enough sugar to make eating it worth his while, then for extra measure added a couple of teaspoons more.

Alex cupped his steaming mug of coffee as he considered his son's question. "Dinner went fine." It was afterward that stayed in his mind. Someone had hurt Carol and hurt her badly. He'd hardly touched her and she'd trembled. Her dark brown eyes had clouded, and she couldn't seem to get out of his car fast enough. The crazy part was, Alex felt convinced she was attracted to him. He knew something else—she didn't want to be.

They'd spent hours talking over dinner, and it had seemed as though only a few moments had passed. There was no need for pretense between them. She didn't pretend to be anything she wasn't, and he was free to be himself as well. They were simply two single parents who had a lot in common. After two years of dealing with the singles scene,

Alex found Carol a refreshing change. He found her alluringly beautiful and at the same time shockingly innocent. During the course of their evening, she'd argued with him over politics, surprised him with her wit and challenged his opinions. In those few hours, Alex learned that this intriguing widow was a charming study in contrasts, and he couldn't wait to see her again.

"Mrs. Sommars is a neat lady," James said, claiming the kitchen chair across from his father. "She's a little weird, though."

Alex looked up from his coffee. "How's that?"

"She listens to opera," James explained between bites. "Sings it, too—" he planted his elbows on the tabletop, leaned forward and whispered "—in Italian."

"Whoa." Alex was impressed.

"At the top of her voice. Peter told me she won't let him play his rap CDs nearly as loud as she does her operas."

"The injustice of it all."

James ignored his sarcasm. "Peter was telling me his grandmother's a real kick, too. She says things like 'Eat your vegetables or I'm calling my uncle Vito in Jersey City.'"

Alex laughed, glanced at his watch and reluctantly got to his feet. He finished the last of his coffee, then set the mug in the sink. "Do you have your lunch money?"

"Dad, I'm not a kid anymore. You don't have to ask me stuff like that."

"Do you?" Alex pressed.

James stood and reached inside his hip pocket. His eyes widened. "I…guess I left it in my room."

"Don't forget your driver's permit, either."

"Dad!"

Alex held up both hands. "Sorry."

He was all the way to the front door when James's shout stopped him.

"Don't forget to pick me up from track practice, all right?"

Alex pointed his finger at his son and calmly said, "I'll be there."

"Hey, Dad."

"What now?" Alex complained.

James shrugged and leaned his shoulder against the door leading into the kitchen. "In case you're interested, Mrs. Sommars will be there, too."

Alex was interested. Very interested.

He left the house and climbed inside his work van, sitting in the driver's seat with his hands on the steering wheel. He mulled over the events of the night before. He'd dated several women recently. Beautiful women, intelligent women, wealthy women. A couple of them had come on hot and heavy. But not one had appealed to him as strongly as this widow with the dark, frightened eyes and the soft, delectable mouth.

A deep part of him yearned to stroke away the pain she held on to so tightly, whatever its source. He longed to watch the anxiety fade from her eyes when she settled into his arms. He wanted her to feel secure enough with him to relax. The urge to hold her and kiss her was strong, but he doubted Carol would let him.

"Okay, Peggy, bear down...push...as hard as you can," Carol urged the young mother-to-be, clutching her hand. Peggy did as Carol asked, gritting her teeth, arching forward and lifting her head off the hospital pillow. She gave it everything she had, whimpering softly with the intensity of the labor pain. When the contraction had passed, Peggy's head fell back and she took in several deep breaths.

"You're doing a good job," Carol said, patting her shoulder.

"How much longer before my baby's born?"

"Soon," Carol assured her. "The doctor's on his way now."

The woman's eyes drifted closed. "Where's Danny? I need Danny."

"He'll be back in a minute." Carol had sent her patient's husband out for a much-needed coffee.

"I'm so glad you're here."

Carol smiled. "I'm glad I'm here, too."

"Danny wants a son so much."

"I'm sure he'll be just as happy with a little girl."

Peggy smiled, but that quickly faded as another contraction started. She reached for Carol's hand, her face marked by the long hours she'd struggled to give birth. Carol had spent the past hour with her. She preferred it when they weren't so busy and she could dedicate herself to one patient. But for more days than she cared to remember, the hospital's five labor rooms had been full, and she spent her time racing from one to the other.

Peggy groaned, staring at a focal point on the wall. The technique was one Carol taught in her classes. Concentrating on a set object helped the mother remember and practice the breathing techniques.

"You're doing just fine," Carol said softly. "Take a deep breath now and let it out slowly."

"I can't do it anymore… I can't," Peggy cried. "Where's Danny? Why's he taking so long?"

"He'll be back any second." Now that her patient was

in the final stages of labor, the pains were stronger and closer together.

Danny walked into the room, looking pale and anxious…and so very young. He moved to the side of the bed and reached for his wife's hand, holding it to his cheek. He seemed as relieved as Peggy when the contraction eased.

Dr. Adams, old and wise and a hospital institution, sauntered into the room, hands in his pockets, smiling. "So, Peggy, it looks like we're going to finally have that baby."

Peggy grinned sheepishly. "I told Dr. Adams yesterday I was sure I was going to be pregnant until Christmas. I didn't think this baby ever wanted to be born!"

Phil Adams gave his instructions to Carol, and within a few minutes the medical team had assembled. From that point on, everything happened exactly as it should. Before another hour had passed, a squalling Danny, Jr., was placed in his father's arms.

"Peggy…oh, Peggy, a son." Tears of joy rained down the young man's face as he sobbed unabashedly, holding his son close.

Although Carol witnessed scenes such as this day in and day out, the thrill of helping to bring a tiny being into the world never left her.

When her shift was over, she showered and changed clothes, conscious of the time. She had to pick Peter up from track practice on her way home, and she didn't want to keep him waiting, although she was the one likely to be twiddling her thumbs.

The first thing Carol noticed when she pulled into the school parking lot was a van with Preston Construction printed in large black letters on the side. Alex. She drew in a shaky breath, determined to be friendly but reserved.

After the way she'd escaped from his car the night before, it was doubtful he'd want anything to do with her, anyway.

The fact was, she couldn't blame him. She wasn't sure what had come over her. Then again, she did know…and she didn't want to dwell on it.

She parked a safe distance away, praying that either Peter would be finished soon and they could leave or that Alex wouldn't notice her arrival. She lowered the window to let in the warm breeze, then turned off the ignition and reached for a magazine, burying her face in its pages. For five minutes nothing happened.

When the driver's side of the van opened, Carol realized her luck wasn't going to hold. She did her best to concentrate on a recipe for stuffed pork chops and pretend she hadn't seen Alex approach her. When she glanced up, he was standing beside her car. Their eyes met for what seemed the longest moment of her life.

"Hello again." He leaned forward and rested his hands on her window.

"Hello, Alex."

"Nice day, isn't it?"

"Lovely." It wasn't only his smile that intrigued her, but his eyes. Their color was like a cool mist rising off a pond. Would this attraction she felt never diminish, never stop? Three brief encounters, and she was already so tied up in knots she couldn't think clearly.

"How was your day?" His eyes were relentless, searching for answers she couldn't give him to questions she didn't want him to ask.

She glanced away. "Good. How about yours?"

"Fine." He rubbed a hand along the back of his neck. "I was going to call you later."

"Oh?"

"To see if you'd like to attend the Home Show with me next Friday night. I thought we could have dinner afterward."

Carol opened her mouth to refuse, but he stopped her, laying his finger across her lips, silencing her. The instant his hand touched her, the warm, dizzy feeling began. As implausible, as preposterous as it seemed, a deep physical sensation flooded her body. And all he'd done was lightly press his finger to her lips!

"Don't say no," Alex said, his voice husky.

She couldn't, at least not then. "I... I'll have to check my schedule."

"You can tell me tomorrow."

She nodded, although it was an effort.

"Good... I'll talk to you then."

It wasn't until he'd removed his finger, sliding it across her moist lips, that Carol breathed again.

"What do you mean you can't pick me up from track?" Peter complained the next morning. "How else am I supposed to get home? Walk?"

"From track practice, of all things." She added an extra oatmeal cookie to his lunch because, despite everything, she felt guilty about asking him to find another way home. She was such a coward.

"Mom, coach works us hard—you know that. I was so stiff last night I could barely move. Remember?"

Regretfully, Carol did. A third cookie went into the brown-paper sack.

"What's more important than picking me up?"

Escaping a man. If only Alex hadn't been so gentle. Carol had lain awake half the night, not knowing what was wrong with her or how to deal with it. This thing with

Alex, whatever it was, perplexed and bewildered her. For most of her life, Carol had given and received countless hugs and kisses—from relatives, from friends. Touching and being touched were a natural part of her personality. But all Alex had done was press his finger to her lips, and her response...her response still left her stunned.

As she lay in bed, recalling each detail of their brief exchange, her body had reacted again. He didn't even need to be in the same room with her! Alone, in the wee hours of the morning, she was consumed by the need to be loved by him.

She woke with the alarm, in a cold sweat, trembling and frightened, convinced that she'd be a fool to let a man have that kind of power a second time.

"Mom," Peter said impatiently. "I asked you a question."

"Sorry," she said. "What was it you wanted to know?"

"I asked why you aren't going to be at track this afternoon. It's a simple question."

Intuitively Carol knew she wouldn't be able to escape Alex, and she'd be a bigger fool than she already was even to try.

She sighed. "I'll be there," she said, and handed him his lunch.

Peter stood frozen, studying her. "Are you sure you're not coming down with a fever?"

If only he knew...

When Carol pulled into the school parking lot later that same day, she saw Alex's van in the same space as the day before. Only this time he was standing outside, one foot braced against it, fingers tucked in his pockets. His jeans hugged his hips and fit tight across his thighs. He wore a checked work shirt with the sleeves rolled up past his elbows.

When she appeared, he lowered his foot and straightened, his movement leisurely and confident.

It was all Carol could do to slow down and park her car next to his. To avoid being placed at a disadvantage, she opened her door and climbed out.

"Good afternoon," she said, smiling so brightly her mouth felt as though it would crack.

"Hello again."

A lock of his dark hair fell over his forehead, and he threaded his fingers through its thickness, pushing it away from his face.

His gaze tugged at hers until their eyes met briefly, intently.

"It's warmer today than it was yesterday," she said conversationally.

"Yes, it is."

Carol lowered her eyes to his chest, thinking she'd be safe if she practiced what she preached. Find a focal point and concentrate. Only it didn't work as well in situations like this. Instead of saying what had been on her mind most of the day, she became aware of the pattern of his breathing, and how the rhythm of her own had changed, grown faster and more erratic.

"Have you decided?"

Her eyes rushed to his. "About..."

"Going to the home show with me."

She wished it could be the way it had been in the restaurant. There was something about being with a crowd that relaxed her. She hadn't felt intimidated.

"I...don't think seeing each other is such a good idea. It'd be best if we...stayed friends. I can foresee all kinds of problems if we started dating, can't you?"

"The Home Show's going to cause problems?"

"No...our seeing each other will."

"Why?"

"The boys—"

"Couldn't care less. If anything, they approve. I don't understand why there'd be any problems. I like you and you like me—we've got a lot in common. We have fun together. Where's the problem in that?"

Carol couldn't very well explain that when he touched her, even lightly, tiny atoms exploded inside her. Whenever they were within ten feet of each other, the air crackled with sensuality that grew more intense with each encounter. Surely he could feel it, too. Surely he was aware of it.

Carol held a hand to her brow, not knowing how to answer him. If she pointed out the obvious, she'd sound like a fool, but she couldn't deny it, either.

"I...just don't think our seeing each other is a good idea," she repeated stubbornly.

"I do," he countered. "In fact, it appeals to me more every minute."

"Oh, Alex, please don't do this."

Other cars were filling the parking lot, and the two of them had quickly become the center of attention. Carol glanced around self-consciously, praying he'd accept her refusal and leave it at that. She should've known better.

"Come in here," Alex said, opening the side panel to his van. He stepped inside and offered her his hand. She joined him before she had time to determine the wisdom of doing so.

Alex closed the door. "Now, where were we...ah, yes. You'd decided you don't want to go out with me again."

That wasn't quite accurate, but she wasn't going to argue.

She'd rarely wanted anything more than to continue seeing him, but she wasn't ready. Yet... Bruce had been dead for thirteen years. If she wasn't ready by now, she never would be. The knowledge hit her hard, like an unexpected blow, and her eyes flew to his.

"Carol?" He moved toward her. The walls of the van seemed to close in around her. She could smell the scent of his after-shave and the not unpleasant effects of the day's labor. She could feel the heat coming off his body.

Emotion thickened the air, and the need that washed through her was primitive.

She backed as far as she could against the orderly rows of tools and supplies stacked on the shelves. Alex towered above her, studying her with such tenderness and concern that she had to repress the urge to weep.

"Are you claustrophobic?"

She shook her head.

His eyes settled on her mouth, and Carol felt her body's reaction. She unconsciously held her breath so long that when she released it, it burned her chest. If she hadn't been so frightened, she would have marveled at what was happening between them, enjoyed the sensations.

Gently Alex whisked back a strand of hair from her face. At his touch, Carol took a deep breath, but he seemed to gain confidence when she didn't flinch away from him. He cupped her cheek.

Her eyes momentarily drifted shut, and she laid her own hand over his.

"I'm going to kiss you."

She knew it and was unwilling to dredge up the determination to stop him.

His hands slipped to her shoulders as he slowly drew

her forward. She considered ending this now. At the least amount of resistance, he would have released her; she didn't doubt that for a second. But it was as if this moment had been preordained.

At first all he did was press his lips to hers. That was enough, more than enough. Her fingers curled into his shirt as he swept his mouth over hers.

She whimpered when he paused.

He sighed.

Her breathing was shallow.

His was harsh.

He hesitated and lifted his head, eyes wide and shocked, his brow creased with a frown. Whatever he'd decided, he didn't share, letting her draw her own conclusions.

Her hands were braced against his chest when he sought her mouth again. This time, the force of his kiss tilted back her head as he fused their lips together, giving her no choice but to respond. The heat, hot enough to scorch them both, intensified.

He kissed and held her, and her lungs forgot it was necessary to breathe. Her heart forgot to beat. Her soul refused to remember the lonely, barren years.

From somewhere far, far away, Carol heard voices. Her ears shut out the sound, not wanting anything or anyone to destroy this precious time.

Alex groaned, not to communicate pleasure but frustration. Carol didn't understand. Nor did she comprehend what was happening when he released her gradually, pushing himself away. He turned and called, "The door's locked."

"The door?" she echoed. It wasn't until then that she realized Alex was talking to the boys. Peter and Jim were standing outside the van, wanting in. She'd been so involved with Alex that she hadn't even heard her own son calling her name.

"Please open that door," she said, astonished by how composed she sounded. The trembling hadn't started yet, but it would soon, and the faster she made her escape, the better.

"I will in just a minute." He turned back to her and placed his hands on her shoulders. "You're going with me next Friday night. Okay?"

"No…"

He cradled her face with his hands and kissed her once more, forcefully.

She gasped with shock and pleasure.

"I'm not going to argue with you, Carol. We've got something good between us, and I'm not about to let you run away from it."

Standing stock-still, all she could do was nod.

He kissed the tip of her nose, then turned again and slid open the van door.

"What are you doing with Mrs. Sommars?" Jim demanded. "I've been standing out here for the past five minutes."

"Hi, Mom," Peter said, studying her through narrowed eyes. "Everyone else has gone home. Did you know you left your keys in the ignition?"

"I… Mr. Preston was showing me his…van." She was sure her face was as red as a fire truck, and she dared not meet her son's eyes for fear he'd know she'd just been kissed. Good heavens, he probably already did.

"Are you all right?" Peter asked her.

"Sure. Why?" Stepping down onto the pavement she felt as graceful as a hippo. James climbed in when she'd climbed out; she and Peter walked over to her car.

"I think you might be coming down with something," Peter said as he automatically sat in the driver's seat, assuming he'd be doing the honors. He snapped the seat belt into place. "There were three cookies in my lunch, and no sandwich."

"There were?" Carol distinctly remembered spreading peanut butter on the bologna slices—Peter's favorite sandwich. She must have left it on the kitchen countertop.

"Not to worry, I traded off two of the cookies." He adjusted the rearview mirror and turned the key. He was about to pull out of the parking space when a huge smile erupted on his face. "I'm glad you and Mr. Preston are getting along so well," he said.

Alex sat at his cluttered desk with his hands clasped behind his head, staring aimlessly into space. He'd finally kissed her. He felt like a kid again. A slow, easy smile spread across his face, a smile so full, his cheeks ached. What a kiss it had been. Seductive enough to satisfy him until he could see her again. He was going to kiss her then, too. He could hardly wait.

The intercom buzzed. "Mr. Powers is here."

Alex's smile brightened. "Send him in." He stood and held out his hand to Barney, his best friend. They'd been in college together, roommates their senior year, and had been close ever since. Barney was a rare kind of friend, one who'd seen him through the bad times and the good times and been there for both in equal measure.

"Alex, great to see you." He helped himself to a butterscotch candy from the bowl on the edge of the desk and sat down. "How you doing?"

"Fine." It was on the tip of his tongue to tell Barney

about Carol, but everything was so new, he didn't know if he could find the words to explain what he was feeling.

"I've decided to forgive you."

Alex arched his eyebrows. "For what?"

"Bambi. She said you dumped her at the restaurant."

"Oh, that. It wouldn't have worked, anyway."

"Why not?" Barney said, unwrapping the candy and popping it in his mouth.

"I don't have a hot tub."

"She claimed you left with another woman. A bag lady?"

Alex chuckled. "Not exactly."

"Well, you needn't worry, because ol' Barn has met Ms. Right and is willing to share the spoils."

"Barn, listen…"

Barney raised his hand, stopping him. "She's perfect. I swear to you she's bright, beautiful and buxom. The three *b*'s—who could ask for anything more?"

"As I recall, that's what you told me about Bambi," Alex countered, amused by his friend's attempts to find him a wife. It wouldn't be quite as humorous if Barney could stay married himself. In the past fifteen years, his friend had gone through three wives. Each of them bright, beautiful and buxom.

They might've been the best of friends, but when it came to women, their tastes were as dissimilar as could be. Barney went for breasts, whereas Alex was far more interested in brains.

"You're going to let me introduce her, aren't you? I mean, the least you can do is meet Babette."

"No, thanks." The guy had an obsession with *B*-words, Alex thought. The next woman would probably be named Brandy. Or Barbie.

"You won't even have a drink with her?"

"Sorry, not interested."

Barney leaned back and crossed his legs, sucking on the butterscotch candy for a few seconds before he spoke. "She was first runner-up for Miss Oregon several years back. Does that tell you anything?"

"Sure," Alex said, reaching for a candy himself. "She looks terrific in a swimsuit and is interested in world peace."

Barney slowly shook his head. "I don't understand it. I thought you were ready to get back into dating."

"I am."

"Listen, buddy, take a tip from me. Play the field, sample the riches available, then settle down. I'm happier when I'm married, and you will be, too. Frankly, with your looks and money, I don't think you'll have much of a problem. There are plenty of willing prospects out there. Only I notice you aren't doing anything to meet one."

"I don't have to, with you around. You're worse than a matchmaker."

Barney ignored that. "It's time, Alex. You said so yourself. Just how long are you going to wait? Gloria's been gone two years now. She wouldn't have wanted this."

"I know." At the mention of his late wife, Alex felt a twinge of pain. Time had healed the worst of it, but he'd always remember the agony of watching the woman he loved die.

"You want me to give you Babette's phone number?" his friend asked gently.

Alex shook his head. "Don't bother to introduce me to any more of your women friends."

Barney's mouth sagged open. "But you just admitted I was right, that it's time to get out there and—"

"Remember the bag lady Bambi was telling you about?"

Alex asked, interrupting his friend before he could deliver the entire five-minute lecture.

"Yeah, what about her?"

"I'm going to marry her."

Chapter 5

"You know, Mom, I like Mr. Preston," Peter announced over dinner as though this was a secret he'd been waiting to share.

"He seems very nice," Carol agreed, reaching for a slice of tomato. She didn't want to say anything more to encourage this topic, so she changed it. "How was school?"

"Fine. James was telling me about all the neat things him and his dad do together, like camping and fishing and stuff like that."

"Your uncle Tony takes you with him."

"Not camping or fishing and besides, it's not the same," Peter murmured. "Uncle Tony's my *uncle*."

Carol paused, her fork over the plump red tomato. "Now, that was profound."

"You don't know what I mean, do you?"

"I guess not," Carol said.

"Going camping with Mr. Preston would be like having a dad."

"How's that?" She took a bite of her roast, then braced her elbows on the tabletop.

"You know."

"No, I don't."

Peter lapsed into silence as he mulled over his thoughts. "I guess what I'm trying to say is that James and I talked it over and we decided we'd like it if the two of you got married."

Carol was so shocked by her son's statement that she stopped eating. Peter was staring at her intently, waiting for some sign or reaction.

"Well?" he pressed. "Is it going to happen? I can tell you like each other."

Chewing furiously, Carol waved her fork at her son, letting it speak for her. The meat, which had been so tender a moment before, took on the quality of leather. The faster she chewed, the more there seemed to be.

"You may think I'm still a kid and I don't know much," Peter continued, "but it didn't take James and me long to figure out what was going on inside his dad's van."

The piece of meat finally slid down Carol's throat. She blinked, uncertain if she could speak normally.

Peter was grinning from ear to ear. "I wish you could've seen your face when Mr. Preston opened the door of the van." Peter didn't bother to disguise his amusement. "If I hadn't been arguing with James, I would've started laughing right then."

"Arguing with James?" Those three words were all she could force past her lips. From the moment the two boys had met on the first day of high school, they'd been the best of friends. In all the months since September, Carol couldn't remember them disagreeing even once.

"We had an argument when we couldn't get his dad to

open the van," Peter admitted, his mouth twitching. "Your face was so red, and you had this stunned look, like an alien had hauled you inside his spaceship." Peter's deepening voice vibrated with humor.

"Peter," she demanded, furiously spearing another piece of meat. "What did you argue about?"

"We argued over what his father was doing with you in that van. What kind of son would I be if I didn't defend your...honor?"

"What did James say?"

Peter shrugged. "That his dad wouldn't do anything you didn't want him to."

"*Those* were fighting words?"

Peter shrugged again. "It was the way he said them."

"I see."

Peter scooped himself a second helping of the scalloped potatoes. "Getting back to the marriage part. What do you think?"

"That you need to finish your peas and carrots."

Peter's eyes rushed to hers, but only for a moment. Then he grinned. "Oh, I get it—you want me to mind my own business. Right?"

"Exactly."

"But think about it, Mom. Promise me you'll at least do that much. Meeting Mr. Preston could be the greatest thing that's ever happened to us."

"And when you're finished with your dinner, I want you to stack the dirty dishes in the dishwasher," Carol said without a pause. She ate the last bite of her roast, although it tasted more like rubber.

"Every time I mention Mr. Preston, are you going to give me another job to do?"

Her son was a quick study, Carol would grant him that.

"But you *are* going to see him again, aren't you?" he asked hopefully.

"The garbage should be taken out, and I noticed that the front flower beds should be weeded. I know you worked out there last Saturday, but—"

"All right, all right," Peter cried, throwing his hands in the air. "Enough—I get the message."

"I certainly hope so," she said and got up to carry her plate to the sink.

Carol waited until Peter was busy with his homework and the dishes were done before she snuck into the kitchen and turned off the light. Then she called Alex. She wasn't sure what she'd do if James answered.

"Hello."

"Alex?" She cupped her hand over the receiver and kept her eye on the doorway in case Peter strolled past.

"I can't talk long. Listen, did James happen to have a heart-to-heart discussion with you about…us?"

"Not exactly. He said something about the two of them having a talk about you and me. Why?"

"That's what I'm talking about," she whispered, ignoring his question. "Over dinner Peter threw a grenade at my feet."

"He did *what?*"

"It's a figure of speech—don't interrupt me. He said the two of them argued when you didn't open the van door and afterward decided it would be just great if the two of us… that's you and me…got *married.*" She could barely get the words past the growing lump in her throat.

"Now that you mention it, James did say something along those lines."

Carol pressed her back to the kitchen wall, suddenly

needing its support. "How can you be so casual about this?" she burst out.

"Casual?"

"My son announced that he knew what was going on inside the van and that I should've seen my face and that fishing and camping with you would be like having a father." She paused long enough to draw in a breath.

"Carol?"

"And then when I try to calmly warn you what these two are plotting, you make it sound like… I don't know…like we're discussing basketball or something."

"Carol, slow down, I can barely understand you."

"Of course you can't understand me—I'm upset!"

"Listen, this is clearly disturbing you. We need to talk about it. Can you meet me for lunch tomorrow?"

"I'm working tomorrow. And can't go out for lunch, for heaven's sake—I'm a nurse."

"Okay, I'll meet you in the hospital cafeteria at noon."

Just then Peter strolled nonchalantly into the kitchen. He stood in the doorway, turned on the light and stared curiously at his mother.

"Sure, Mama, whatever you say," Carol said brightly—too brightly.

"Mama?" Alex echoed chuckling. "Okay, I get the picture. I'll see you tomorrow at noon."

Agreeing to meet Alex at the hospital was a mistake. Carol should have realized it immediately, but she'd been so concerned with the shocking news Peter had delivered over dinner that she didn't stop to consider what could happen once she was spotted with Alex in the gossip-rich cafeteria at Ford Memorial.

"Sorry I'm late," Carol murmured as she joined him

at a table for two, sliding her orange tray across from his. A couple of nurses from surgery walked past, glanced at Alex, then at Carol, and then back at Alex. Carol offered her peers a weak smile. Once she returned to the obstetrics ward, she was in for an inquisition that could teach the Spaniards a lesson.

"I haven't been here long." Alex grinned and reached for his ham sandwich. "How much time do you have?"

Carol checked her watch. "Forty-five minutes."

He opened a carton of milk. "All right. Do you want to tell me what upset you so much about last night?"

"I already did."

"Refresh my memory."

Carol released a slow sigh. Several more of her friends had seen her and Alex, including Janice Mandle, her partner in the birthing classes. By this time, the probing stares being sent their way were rattling Carol's shaky composure. "Apparently James and Peter have come to some sort of agreement...about you and me."

"I see." Humor flashed through his eyes like a distant light.

"Alex," she cried. "This is serious. We've gone out to dinner *once,* and our sons are talking about where the four of us are going to spend our honeymoon."

"And that bothers you?"

"Of course it does! And it should bother you, too. They already have expectations about how our relationship's going to develop. I don't think it's a healthy situation, and furthermore, they know about next Friday." She took a bite of her turkey sandwich and picked up her coffee.

"You mean that we're going to the Home Show?"

Carol nodded. "Yes, but I think we should forget the whole thing. We're looking at potential trouble here, and

I for one have enough problems in my life without dealing with the guilt of not giving my son a father to take him fishing." She breathed deeply, then added, "My brother doesn't camp or fish. Actually no one in our family does."

Alex held his sandwich in front of his mouth. He frowned, his eyes studying hers, before he lowered his hands to the plate. "I beg your pardon?"

Carol shook her head, losing patience. "Never mind."

"No," he said after a thoughtful pause. "Explain to me what taking Peter fishing has to do with us seeing each other Friday night and your brother Tony who doesn't camp and hunt."

"Fish," Carol corrected, "although he doesn't hunt, either."

"That part makes sense."

Curious stares seemed to come at Carol from every corner of the room. Alex had finished his sandwich, and Carol wasn't interested in eating any more of hers.

"Do you want to go outside?" she suggested.

"Sure."

Once they'd disposed of their trays, Carol led him onto the hospital grounds. The weather had been beautiful for April. It wouldn't last much longer. The rains would return soon, and the "Rose City" would blossom into the floral bouquet of the Pacific Northwest.

With her hands in the front pockets of her uniform, Carol strolled in the sunshine, leading them away from the building and toward the parking lot. She saw his van in the second row and turned abruptly in the opposite direction. That construction van would be nothing but a source of embarrassment to her now.

"There's a pond over this way." With its surrounding green lawns, it offered relative privacy.

An arched bridge stretched between its banks, and gold-fish swam in the cold water. Sunlight rippled across the pond, illuminating half, while the other half remained in enigmatic shadow. In some ways, Carol felt her budding relationship with Alex was like sun and shadow. When she was with him, she felt as though she was stepping into the light, that he drew her away from the shade. But the light was brilliant and discomfiting, and it illuminated the dark-est corners of her loneliness, revealing all the imperfections she hadn't noticed while standing numbly in the shadows.

Although gentle, Alex had taught her painful lessons. Until she met him, she hadn't realized how hungry she was to discover love in a man's arms. The emptiness inside her seemed to echo when she was with him. The years hadn't lessened the pain her marriage had brought into her life, but seemed to have intensified her self-doubts. She was more hesitant and uncertain now than she'd been the year following Bruce's death.

With his hand on her elbow, Alex guided her to a park bench. Once they were seated, he reached for her hand, lacing their fingers together.

"I don't want you to worry about the boys," he said.

She nodded and lowered her eyes. She couldn't help being worried, but Alex didn't understand her fears and revealed no distress of his own. That being the case, she couldn't dwell on the issue.

He raised her fingers to his mouth. "I suppose what I'm about to say is going to frighten you even more."

"Alex...no."

"Shh, it needs to be said." He placed his finger across her lips to silence her, and who could blame him, she mused. It had worked so well the first time. "The boys are going to come to their own conclusions," he continued, "and that's fine, they would anyway. For Peter to talk so openly with you about our relationship is a compliment. Apparently he felt comfortable enough to do so, and that reflects well on the kind of mother you are."

Carol hadn't considered it in those terms, but he was right. She and Peter were close.

"Now, about you and me," Alex went on, "we're both adults."

But Carol felt less mature than an adolescent when it came to Alex. She trembled every time she thought of him, and that was far more often than she would've liked. When he touched and kissed her, her hormones went berserk, and her heart seemed to go into spasms. No wonder she was frightened by the things Alex made her experience.

"I like you, and I'm fairly confident you like me."

She agreed with a sharp nod, knowing it wouldn't do any good to deny it.

"The fact is, I like everything about you, and that feeling increases whenever we're together. Now, if it happens that this attraction between us continues, then so be it. Wonderful. Great. It would be a big mistake for us to allow two teenage boys to dictate our relationship. Agreed?"

Once more, Carol nodded.

"Good." He stood, bringing her with him. "Now we both have to get back to work." Tucking her hand in the crook of his arm, he strode back toward the parking lot, pausing when he came to his van. He opened the door, then turned to face her.

"It seems to me we should seal our agreement."

"Seal it? I don't understand." But she did.... His wonderful, mist-gray eyes were spelling out exactly what he meant.

He caressed her cheek, then traced the outline of her lips. Whatever it was about his touch that sent her heart into such chaos, Carol couldn't understand. She reacted by instinct, drawing his finger between her lips, touching it with the tip of her tongue. The impact of her action showed in his eyes with devastating clarity.

He leaned forward and slipped his finger aside, replacing it with his mouth. His kiss was exquisitely slow and wildly erotic.

When he broke away they were both shaking. Carol stared up at him, her breath ragged, her lips parted and eager.

"I've got to get back to work…." she whispered.

"I know," Alex said. But he didn't make any effort to leave.

Instead he angled his head and dropped tiny kisses on her neck, then her ear, taking the lobe in his mouth before trailing his lips in heart-stopping increments back to hers. She was ready for him this time, more than ready.

The sound of a car door slamming somewhere in the distance abruptly returned them to the real world. Carol leaped back, her eyes startled, her breathing harsh and uneven. She smoothed her hands down the front of her uniform, as though whisking away wrinkles. She'd been kissing him like a lover and in broad daylight! To her chagrin, Alex didn't look at all dismayed by what had happened between them, just pleased.

"I wish you hadn't done that," she said, knowing he wasn't the only one to blame—but at the moment, the most convenient.

"Oh, baby, I don't regret a thing."

She folded her arms over her chest. "I've got to get back inside." But she had to wait until the flush of desire had left her face and her body had stopped trembling.

"It seems to me," Alex said with a smile of supreme

confidence, "that if kissing you is this good, then when we finally make love it'll be downright dangerous." With that, he climbed into the driver's seat, closed the door and started the engine.

"You didn't call me," Carol's mother complained the following Friday evening. "All week I waited for you to phone and tell me about your date with the non-Italian."

"I'm sorry, Mama," Carol said, glancing at the kitchen clock. Alex was due to pick her up for the Home Show in ten minutes. Peter was staying overnight at a friend's, and she was running behind schedule as it was. The last thing she wanted to do was argue with her mother.

"You *should* be sorry. I could have died this week and you wouldn't have known. Your uncle in Jersey City would've had to call you and tell you your mother was dead."

"Mama, Peter started track this week, and we've gotten home late every single night."

"So don't keep me in suspense. Tell me."

Carol paused. "About what?"

"Your date with that Englishman. Did he take you to bed?"

"Mama!" Sometimes the things her mother said actually shocked Carol. "Of course not."

"It's a shame. Are you seeing him again? But don't wear those shoes with the pointed toes or he'll think you're a loose woman. And to be on the safe side, don't mention your cousin Celeste."

"Mama, I can't talk now. Alex will be here any minute—we're going to the Home Show. His company has a booth there, and it'd be impolite to keep him waiting."

"Do you think he'll convert?"

"Mama, I'm not marrying Alex."

"Maybe not," her mother said with a breathless sigh, "but then again, who knows?"

The doorbell chimed, and Carol, who'd been dreading this evening from the moment she'd agreed to it, was flooded with a sense of relief.

"Bye, Mama."

Angelina said her farewells and added something about bringing Alex over to try her pasta. Carol was putting down the receiver by the time her mother had finished issuing her advice.

The doorbell rang again as Carol hurried into the living room. She rushed to open the door. "I'm sorry it took me so long to answer. My mother was on the phone."

"Did she give you any advice?" Alex teased.

"Just a little. She said it might not be a good idea if I mentioned my cousin Celeste."

"Who?"

"Never mind." Carol laughed a little nervously. Alex looked too good to be true, and the warm, open appreciation in his eyes did wonders for her self-esteem.

"You were worth the wait."

Carol could feel the blush in her cheeks. She wasn't used to having men compliment her, although her family was free with praise and always had been. This was different, however. Alex wasn't family.

His eyes compelled her forward, and she stepped toward him without question, then halted abruptly, realizing she'd very nearly walked into his arms.

"I'll…get my purse." She turned away, but his hand at her shoulder turned her back.

"Not yet."

"Alex… I don't think we should—"

But that was all the protest she was allowed. She closed her eyes as he ran his hand through her hair, then directed her mouth to his with tender restraint. He kissed her lightly at first, until she was pliant and willing in his arms....

When he pulled away from her, she slowly, languorously, opened her eyes to meet his.

"Don't look at me like that," he groaned. "Come on, let's get out of here before we end up doing something we're not ready to deal with yet."

"What?" Carol asked, blinking, still too dazed to think coherently.

"I think you know the answer to that."

They were in Alex's car before either of them spoke again. "If it's okay with you, I've got to stop at the office and pick up some more brochures," Alex said. "We're running low already."

"Of course it's okay," Carol told him. It was a good thing she was sitting down because her legs seemed too weak to support her. She was sure her face was flushed, and she'd rarely felt this shaky.

Her mind became her enemy as Alex headed toward the freeway. Try as she might, she couldn't stop thinking about how he'd felt against her. So strong and warm. A thin sheen of perspiration moistened her upper lip, and she swiped at it, eager to dispel the image that refused to leave her mind.

"How far is your office?" Carol asked after several strained minutes had passed. Alex seemed unusually quiet himself.

"Another quarter of an hour."

Not knowing how else to resume the conversation, she dropped it after that.

"Peter's staying with Dale tonight?" he finally asked.

"Yes. James, too?"

"Yes."

That was followed by ten more minutes of silence. Then Alex exited the freeway.

Carol curled her fingers around the armrest when he stopped at the first red light. The district was an industrial area and well lit.

As soon as he pulled into a side street, she saw his company sign. She'd never asked about his business and was impressed when she saw a small fleet of trucks and vans neatly parked in rows outside. He was apparently far more successful than she'd assumed.

Unlocking the door, Alex let her precede him inside. He flicked a switch, and light immediately flooded the office. One entire wall was lined with filing cabinets. Three desks, holding computers, divided the room. Carol didn't have time to give the room more than a fleeting glance as Alex directed her past the first desk and into another large office. She saw his name on the door.

The room was cluttered. The top of his desk looked as if a cyclone had hit it.

"The brochures are around here someplace," he muttered, picking up a file on a corner of the credenza. "Help yourself to a butterscotch candy."

"Thanks." As Carol reached for one, her gaze fell on the two framed photographs hidden behind a stack of computer printouts. The top of a woman's head showed on one of the photos, but that was all she could see. The second one was of James.

"I've got to get organized one of these days," Alex was saying.

Curious, Carol moved toward the credenza and the two photographs. "Who's this?" She asked, lifting the picture of the woman. She was beautiful. Blond. Blue-eyed. Wholesome. Judging by the hairstyle and clothes, the picture had been taken several years earlier.

Alex paused. "That's Gloria."

"She was your wife?"

Alex nodded, pulled out the high-backed cushioned chair and sank into it. "She died two years ago. Cancer."

It was all Carol could do to hold on to the picture. The pain in his voice stabbed through her.

"I… I thought you were divorced."

"No," Alex said quietly.

Carol continued to study the beautiful woman in the photo. "You loved her, didn't you?"

"So much that when the time came, I wanted to die with her. Yes, I loved her."

With shaking hands, Carol replaced the photograph. Her back was to Alex, and she briefly closed her eyes. She made a rigorous effort to smile when she turned to face him again.

He frowned. "What's wrong?"

"Nothing," she said breezily.

"You look pale all of a sudden. I thought you knew…. I assumed James or Peter had told you."

"No—neither of them mentioned it."

"I'm sorry if this comes as a shock."

"There's no reason to apologize."

Alex nodded, sighed and reached for her hand, pulling her down into his lap. "I figured you'd understand better than most what it is to lose someone you desperately love."

Chapter 6

"Gloria had problems when James was born," Alex began. His hold on Carol's waist tightened almost painfully, but she was sure he wasn't aware of it. "The doctors said there wouldn't be any more children."

"Alex, please, there's no need to tell me this."

"There is," he said. "I want you to know. It's important to me...."

Carol closed her eyes and pressed her forehead against the side of his head. She knew intuitively that he didn't often speak of his late wife, and that he found it difficult to do so now.

Alex wove his fingers into her hair. "In the years after Jim's birth, Gloria's health was never good, but the doctors couldn't put their finger on what was wrong. She was weak and tired a lot of the time. It wasn't until Jim was in junior high that we learned she had leukemia—myelocytic leukemia, one of the most difficult forms to treat." He paused and drew in an unsteady breath.

"Alex," she pleaded, her hands framing his face. "Don't, please—this is obviously so painful for you." But the moment her eyes met his, she knew nothing she said or did would stop him. She sensed that only sharing it now, with her, would lessen the trauma of his memories.

"We did all the usual things—the chemotherapy, the other drugs—but none of it helped, and she grew steadily worse. Later, when it was clear that nothing else could be done, we opted for a bone-marrow transplant. Her sister and mother flew in from New York, and her sister was the better match. But…that didn't work, either."

Carol stroked his cheek, yearning to do anything she could to lessen the pain.

He hesitated and drew in a quavering breath. "She suffered so much. That was the worst for me to deal with. I was her husband, and I'd sworn to love and protect her, and there wasn't a thing I could do…not a single, solitary thing."

Tears moistened Carol's eyes, and she struggled to keep them at bay.

Alex's voice remained firm and controlled, but Carol recognized the pain he was experiencing. "I didn't know what courage was until I watched Gloria die," he whispered. He closed his eyes. "The last three weeks of her life, it was obvious she wasn't going to make it. Finally she fell into a coma and was put on a respirator. The doctors knew she'd never come out of it and so did the nurses. I could see them emotionally removing themselves, and I couldn't bear it. I became a crazy man, refusing to leave her side, letting no one care for her but me. I held on to her hand and silently willed her to live with every breath I took. I honestly believe I kept her alive by the sheer force of my will. I was afraid to leave her, afraid that when I did, she'd slip silently into death. Eventually that was exactly what happened. I left her because Jim needed me and because I knew that at some point I'd have to leave. I sat in the hospital waiting room with my son, telling him about his mother, and suddenly a pain, an intense stabbing pain, shot through me—" he hesitated and gave a ragged sigh "—and in that instant, I knew she was gone. I've never felt anything like it. A few minutes later, a nurse came for me. I can remember that scene so vividly—my mind's played it back so many times.

"I stood up and Jim stood with me, and I brought my son as close to my side as I could, looked the nurse in the eye and said, 'She's gone, isn't she?' The nurse nodded and Jim started to cry and I just stood there, dazed and numb. I don't remember walking back to Gloria's room, but somehow I found myself there. I lifted her into my arms and held her and told her how sorry I was that I'd been so stubborn and selfish, keeping her with me those three weeks, refusing to let her die. I told her how I would much rather have been with her, how I'd wanted to hold her hand as she stepped from one life into the next."

By now Carol was weeping softly, unabashedly.

Alex's fingers stroked her hair. "I didn't mean for you to cry," he whispered, and his regret seemed genuine. "You would have liked her."

Carol had felt the same way from the first moment she'd seen Gloria's photograph. Nodding, she hid her face in the strong curve of his neck.

"Carol," he whispered, caressing her back, "look at me."

She sniffled and shook her head, unwilling to let him witness the strength of her emotion. It was one thing to sit on his lap, and entirely another to look him in the eye after he'd shared such a deep and personal part of himself.

His lips grazed the line of her jaw.

"No," she cried softly, her protest faint and nearly inaudible, "don't touch me…not now." He'd come through hell, suffered the torment of losing his wife, and he needed Carol. He was asking for her. But her comfort could only be second-best.

"Yes," he countered, lifting her head so he could look at her. Against her will, against her better judgment, her gaze met his. His eyes were filled with such hunger that she all but gasped. Again and again, they roamed her face, no doubt taking in the moisture that glistened on her cheeks, the way her lips trembled and the staggering need she felt to comfort him. Even if that comfort was brief, temporary, a momentary solace.

"I'm sorry I upset you." He wove his fingers into her hair and directed her lips to his. His mouth was warm and moist and gentle. No one had ever touched her with such tenderness and care. No kiss had ever affected her so deeply. No kiss had ever shown her such matchless beauty.

Tears rained down Carol's face. Sliding her fingers through his hair, she held him close. He was solid and muscular and full of strength. His touch had filled the hollowness of her life and, she prayed, had helped to ease his own terrible loneliness.

"Carol," he breathed, sounding both stunned and dismayed, "what is it? What's wrong?"

"Nothing," she whispered. "Everything."

"I'm sorry…so sorry," he said in a low voice.

Confused and uncertain, Carol turned to face him. "You are? Why?"

"For rushing you. For thinking of my own needs instead of yours."

"No…" She shook her head, incapable of expressing what she felt.

"Are you going to be all right?"

She nodded, still too shaken to speak.

He placed his hands on the curve of her shoulder and kissed the crown of her head. "Thank you."

"For what?" Reluctantly her eyes slid to his.

"For listening, for being here when I needed you."

All she could manage in response was a tremulous smile.

For the rest of the evening, Alex was a perfect gentleman. He escorted her to the Home Show, where they spent several hours wandering from one display to another, discussing the ideas and products represented. They strolled hand in hand, laughing, talking, debating ideas. Carol was more talkative than usual; it helped disguise her uneasiness. She told him about her plan to dig up a portion of her back lawn and turn it into an herb garden. At least when she was talking, her nerve endings weren't left uncovered and she didn't have to deal with what had happened a few hours before...

After they'd toured the Home Show, Alex took her out to eat at a local Greek restaurant. By that time of the evening, Carol should have been famished, since they were having dinner so late. But whatever appetite she'd had was long gone.

When Alex dropped her off at the house, he kissed her good-night, but if he was expecting an invitation to come inside, he didn't receive one.

Hours later, she lay staring at the ceiling, while shadows of the trees outside her window frolicked around the light fixture like dancing harem girls. Glaring at the clock radio, Carol punched her pillow several times and twisted around so she lay on her stomach, her arms cradling her head. She *should* be sleepy. Exhausted. Drained after a long, trying week. Her job took its toll in energy, and normally by Friday night, Carol collapsed the moment she got into bed, waking refreshed Saturday morning.

She would've liked to convince herself that Alex had nothing to do with this restless, trapped feeling. She tried to analyze what was bothering her so much. It wasn't as though Alex had never kissed her before this evening. The impact he had on her senses shouldn't come as any surprise. She'd known from the first night they'd met that Alex had the power to expose a kaleidoscope of emotions within her. With him, she felt exhilarated, excited, frightened, reborn.

Perhaps it was the shock of passion he'd brought to life when he'd kissed her. No, she mused, frowning, she'd yearned for him to do exactly that even before they'd arrived at his office.

Squeezing her eyes closed, she tried to force her body to relax. She longed to snap her fingers and drift magically into the warm escape of slumber. It was what she wanted, what she needed. Maybe in the morning, she'd be able to put everything into perspective.

Closing her eyes, however, proved to be a mistake. Instead of being engulfed by peace, she was confronted with the image of Alex's tormented features as he told her about Gloria. *I figured you'd understand better than most what it is to lose someone you desperately love.*

Carol's eyes flew open. Fresh tears pooled at the edges as her sobs took control. She'd loved Bruce. She'd hated Bruce.

Her life ended with his death and her life had begun again.

It was the end; it was the beginning.

There hadn't been tears when he'd died—not at first but later. Plenty of tears, some of profound sadness, and others that spoke of regrets. But there was something more. A release. Bruce had died, and at the same moment, she and Peter had been set free from the prison of his sickness and his abuse.

The tears burned her face as she sobbed quietly, caught in the horror of those few short years of marriage.

Bruce shouldn't have died. He was too young to have wasted his life. Knowing he'd been drunk and with another woman hadn't helped her deal with the emotions surrounding his untimely death.

I figured you'd understand better than most what it is to lose someone you desperately love. Only Carol didn't know. Bruce had destroyed the love she'd felt for him long before his death. He'd ravaged all trust and violated any vestiges of respect. She'd never known love the way Alex had, never shared such a deep and personal commitment with anyone—not the kind Alex had shared with Gloria, not the kind her mother had with her father.

And Carol felt guilty. Guilty. Perhaps if she'd been a better wife, a better mother, Bruce would have stopped drinking. If she'd been more desirable, more inventive in the kitchen, a perfect housekeeper. Instead she felt guilty. It might not be rational or reasonable but it was how she felt.

"Well?" Peter asked as he let himself in the front door the next morning. He dumped his sleeping bag on the kitchen floor, walked over to Carol and dutifully kissed her cheek.

"Well, what?" Carol said, helping herself to a second cup of coffee. She didn't dare look in the mirror, suspecting there were dark smudges under her eyes. At most, she'd slept two hours all night.

"How did things go with Mr. Preston?"

Carol let the steam rising from her coffee mug revive her. "You never told me James's mother had died."

"I didn't? She had leukemia."

"So I heard," Carol muttered. She wasn't angry with her son, and Alex's being a widower shouldn't make a whole lot of difference, but for reasons she was only beginning to understand, it did.

"James said it took his dad a long time to get over his mother's death."

Carol felt her throat muscles tighten. He wasn't over her, not really.

"James keeps a picture of her in his room. She was real pretty."

Carol nodded, remembering the bright blue eyes smiling back at her from the framed photograph in Alex's office. Gloria's warmth and beauty were obvious.

"I thought we'd work in the backyard this morning," Carol said, as a means of changing the subject.

"Aw, Mom," Peter groaned. "You know I hate yard work."

"But if we tackle everything now, it won't overwhelm us next month."

"Are you going to plant a bunch of silly flowers again? I don't get it. Every year you spend a fortune on that stuff. If you added it all up, I bet you could buy a sports car with the money."

"Buy who a sports car?" she challenged, arms akimbo.

"All right, all right." Peter clearly didn't want to argue. "Just tell me what I have to do."

Peter's attitude could use an overhaul, but Carol wasn't in the best of moods herself. Working with the earth, thrusting her fingers deep into the rich soil, was basic to her nature and never more than now.

The sun was out when Carol, dressed in her oldest pair of jeans and a University of Oregon sweatshirt, knelt in front of her precious flower beds. She'd tied a red bandanna around her head, knotting it at the back.

Peter brought his portable CD player outside and plugged it into the electrical outlet on the patio. Next, he arranged an assortment of CDs in neat piles.

Carol glanced over her shoulder and groaned inwardly. She was about to be serenaded with music that came with words she found practically impossible to understand. Although maybe that was a blessing…

"Just a minute," Peter yelled and started running toward the kitchen.

That was funny. Carol hadn't even heard the phone ring. Ignoring her son, she knelt down, wiping her wrist under her nose. The heat was already making her perspire. Bending forward, she dug with the trowel, cultivating the soil and clearing away a winter's accumulation of weeds.

"Morning."

At the sound of Alex's voice, Carol twisted around to confront him. "Alex," she whispered. "What are you doing here?"

"I came to see you."

"Why?"

He joined her, kneeling beside her on the lush, green grass. His eyes were as eager as if it had been weeks since he'd seen her instead of a few hours.

"What are you doing here?" she demanded again, digging more vigorously than necessary. She didn't want to have this conversation. It was too soon. She hadn't fully recovered from their last encounter and was already facing another one.

"I couldn't stay away," he said, his voice harsh and husky at once, and tinged with a hint of anger as if the lack of control bothered him. "You were upset last night, and we both ignored it instead of talking about it the way we should have."

"You were imagining things," she said, offering him a false smile.

"No, I wasn't. I felt guilty, too."

"Guilty?" she cried. "Whatever for?"

"Because I told you about Gloria and didn't ask about your husband. It would've been the perfect time for you to tell me."

Carol's stomach lurched. "That was a long time ago... and best forgotten."

"But you loved him and were saddened by his death, and I should've realized that talking about Gloria would be especially painful for you. I should have been more sensitive."

She shut her eyes. "There's no reason to feel guilty. You talked openly and honestly, and I appreciated knowing about your wife."

"Maybe so," Alex conceded, "but I frightened you, and now you're feeling confused."

"Nothing could be further from the truth." She continued to work, dragging the trowel through the damp soil.

Alex chuckled softly. He gripped her shoulders and turned her toward him as he scanned her features. "You shouldn't lie, Carol Sommars. Because you blush every time you do."

"That's ridiculous." As if on cue, she felt her cheeks grow pink. Carol groaned inwardly, furious with Alex and even more so with herself.

"No, it isn't ridiculous." He paused, and his mouth quivered as he studied her. "You're doing it now."

"Where are the boys?"

Alex's chuckle deepened. "Don't try changing the subject—it isn't going to work."

"Alex, please."

"Hey, Mom, you'll never guess what!"

Grateful for the distraction, Carol dragged her eyes away from Alex and turned to her son, who stood on the patio, looking exceptionally pleased.

"What is it, Peter?"

"James and Mr. Preston brought over one of those fancy, heavy-duty tillers. They're going to dig up that garden space you've been talking about for the past two summers."

Carol's gaze flew back to Alex's, full of unspoken questions.

"You said something last night about wanting to grow an herb garden, didn't you?"

"Yes, but why… I mean, you don't have to do this." She felt flustered and surprised and overwhelmed that he'd take a casual comment seriously and go out of his way to see that her wish was fulfilled.

"Of course I don't have to, but I want to. Peter and James and I are your willing servants, isn't that right, boys?" Neither bothered to answer, being far more interested in sorting through the CDs Peter had set out.

Two hours later, Carol had been delegated to the kitchen by all three men, who claimed she was a world-class nuisance.

"Mom," Peter said, "do something constructive like make lunch. You're in the way here."

Slightly taken aback by her son's assessment of her role, Carol muttered under her breath and did as he asked. Her ego suffered further when James sent his friend a grateful glance. Even Alex seemed pleased to have her out from under their capable feet.

Twenty minutes later, Alex entered the kitchen. He paused when he saw her stacking sandwiches on a platter.

He walked over to her, slipped his arms around her waist and nuzzled her neck.

"Alex," she protested in a fierce whisper, "the boys will see you."

"So?"

"So, what they're thinking is bad enough without you adding fuel to the fire."

"They're too busy to care."

"I care!"

His growl was low as he slid his hand from her navel up her midriff. "I know."

"If you don't stop I'll… I'll… I'm not sure what I'll do— but it won't be pleasant." Her threat was an empty one, and Alex knew it as well as she did. She was trembling the way she always did when he touched her. The more intimate the caress, the more she shivered.

"I told the boys I was coming inside to pester you, and I'm nothing if not a man of my word," Alex informed her, clearly relishing her shyness.

"Alex…"

"Don't say it," he murmured. "I already know—this isn't the time or the place. I agree, but I don't have to like it." Slowly and with great reluctance, he released her.

Carol was aware of every nuance of this man. He made the most innocent caress sweet with sensations. His touch only created a need for more. Much more.

Once he'd released her, Carol sighed with relief—or was it regret? She no longer had any idea. She carried the platter of sandwiches to the table and brought out a pitcher of fresh lemonade.

Alex pulled out a chair and sat down. "I like watching you move," he whispered. "I like touching you even more."

"Alex…please don't. You're making me blush."

He laughed lightly. "I like that, too. Being with you makes me feel alive again. I hadn't realized how…desensitized I'd become to life. The first time we kissed I discovered what I'd been missing. All those arranged dates, all those wasted evenings—and all that time you were right under my nose and I didn't even know it."

"I… I think I'll put out two kinds of chips," Carol said, completely unsettled by the way he spoke so openly, so frankly.

"You're beautiful." His eyes were dark, filled with the promise of things to come. "So beautiful…"

"Alex, please." She leaned against the counter, overwhelmed by his words.

"I can't help it. I feel as though I've been granted a second chance at life. Tell me I'm not behaving like an idiot. Tell me you feel it, too."

She did feel everything he did, more profoundly than she dared let him know. "We've both been alone too long," she said. "People in situations like ours must think these kinds of thoughts all the time."

Her comment didn't please him. He frowned and slowly stood. "You may find this difficult to believe, Carol, but there hasn't been anyone since Gloria who made me feel the things you do. And trust me, there've been plenty who tried."

Gulping, Carol whirled around and made busy work opening a bag of potato chips.

Alex joined her, leaning against the counter and facing her so she couldn't ignore him. "You, on the other hand, don't even need to touch me to make me respond. You might not want to admit it, but it's the same for you."

"When you decide to pester someone, you don't do it by half measures, do you?" she muttered.

"Admit it, Carol."

"I…"

He slid his lips across hers. "Are you ready to admit it yet?"

"No, I—"

He bent forward and kissed her again.

Carol's knees buckled and she swayed toward him.

Alex instantly reached for her. Without question, without protest, Carol fell into his arms, so hungry for his touch, she felt as if she were on fire.

The sound of someone clearing his throat was followed by, "Hey, we're not interrupting anything, are we?" Peter was standing just inside the kitchen. "In case you two haven't noticed, it's lunchtime."

Chapter 7

Alex pressed one knee down on the green and stretched out his putter, judging the distance to the hole with a sharp eye. He'd been playing golf with Barney every Sunday afternoon for years.

"So when do I get to meet this female dynamo?" Barney asked after Alex had successfully completed the shot.

"I don't know yet," Alex said as he retrieved his golf ball. He inserted the putter back inside his bag before striding toward the cart.

"What do you mean, you don't know?" Barney echoed. "What's with you and this woman? I swear you've been a different man since you met her. You stare off into space with this goofy look on your face. I talk to you and you don't hear me, and when I ask you about her, you get defensive."

"I'm not defensive, I'm in love."

"Alex, buddy, listen to the voice of experience. You're not in love, you're in lust. I recognize that gleam in your eye. Ten to one you haven't slept with her yet. So I recommend that you get her in the sack and be done with it before you end up doing something foolish."

Alex's gaze fired briefly as he looked at his friend. How did Barney know the progress of his relationship with Carol?

"I have every intention of sleeping with her. Only I plan to be doing that every night for the rest of my life. Carol's not the type of woman to have a fling, and I refuse to insult her by suggesting one."

Barney stared at Alex as if seeing him for the first time. "I don't think I ever realized what an old-fashioned guy you are. Apparently you haven't noticed, but the world's become a lot more casual. Our clothes are casual, our conversations are casual and, yes, even our sex is casual. In case you hadn't heard, you don't have to marry a woman to take her to bed."

"Continue in this vein," Alex said, "and you're going to become a casual friend."

Barney rolled his eyes dramatically. "See what I mean?"

If three wives hadn't been able to change Barney's attitude, Alex doubted he could, either. "As I recall, the last time we had this conversation," Alex reminded him, "you said settling down was the thing to do. I'm only following your advice."

"But not yet," Barney said. "You haven't played the field enough. There are riches out there—" he gestured with his hands "—female gold nuggets just waiting to be picked up, then set gently back in place for the next treasure-hunter."

"You mean like Bambi and what was the name of the other one? Barbie?"

"Stop being clever," Barney snickered. "I have your best interests at heart, and frankly I'm concerned. Two years after Gloria's gone, you suddenly announce it's time to start dating again. Man, I was jumping up and down for joy. Then you go out with a grand total of ten different women—most of them only once—and calmly inform me you've met *the one*. You plan to marry her, just like that, and you haven't even slept with her yet. How are you going to find out if you're sexually compatible?"

"We're compatible, trust me."

"You may think so now, but *bingo*, once she's got a wedding band, it's a totally different story."

"Stop worrying, would you?" Alex eased his golf cart into his assigned space. From the day he'd decided to look for another wife, Barney had been a constant source of amusement. The problem was, his most hilarious moments had come in the form of women his friend had insisted he meet.

"But, Alex, I *am* worried about you," Barney muttered as he lifted his clubs from the back of the cart. "You don't know women the way I do. They're scheming, conniving, money-hungry, and how they get their clutches into you is by marriage. Don't be so eager to march up the aisle with Carol. I don't want you to go through what I have."

After three wives, three divorces and child support payments for two separate families, Barney was speaking from experience—of a particularly negative sort.

"Gloria was special," his longtime friend said. "You're not going to find another one like her. So if it's those qualities that attract you to Carol, look again. You may only be seeing what you want to see."

"You wanna yell?" Angelina Pasquale shouted from the doorway of the kitchen into the living room where her grandchildren were squabbling. "Then let's have a contest.

But remember—I've been doing it longer. They can hear me all the way in Jersey City."

Peter and his younger cousins ceased their shouting match, and with a nod of her head, Angelina returned to the kitchen, satisfied that a single threat from her was enough to bring about peace that would last through the afternoon.

Carol was busy slicing tomatoes for the salad, and her sister-in-law, Paula, was spreading garlic butter on thick slices of French bread.

The sauce was warming on the stove, and the water for the long strands of fresh pasta was just starting to boil. The pungent scent of basil and thyme circled the kitchen like smoke from a campfire. From Carol's earliest memory, her mother had cooked a pot of spaghetti sauce every Saturday evening. The unused portion from Sunday's dinner was served in a variety of ways during the week. Leftover pot roast became something delectable with her mother's sauce over top. And chicken with Mama's sauce rivaled even the Cajun chicken at Jake's restaurant.

"So, Carol," her mother began, wiping her hands on the ever-present apron. She took a large wooden spoon and stirred the kettle of simmering sauce. "I suppose your English friend thinks good spaghetti sauce comes from a jar," she said disparagingly. This was her way of letting Carol know the time had come to invite Alex and his son to Sunday dinner.

"Mama, Alex plays golf on Sundays."

"Every Sunday?"

Carol nodded.

"That's because he's never tasted my sauce." Angelina shook her head as though to suggest Alex had wasted much of his life walking from green to green when he could've been having dinner at her house.

Adding serving utensils to the salad, Carol set the wooden bowl on the dining room table.

Tony, Carol's brother, sauntered into the kitchen and slipped his arms around Paula's waist. "How much longer until dinner? The natives are getting restless."

"Eleven minutes," Angelina answered promptly. She tasted the end of the wooden spoon and nodded in approval.

Carol returned to the kitchen and noticed that her mother was watching her under the guise of waiting for the water to boil. The question Carol had expected all day finally came.

"You gonna marry this non-Italian?" her mother asked, then added the noodles, stirring with enough energy to create a whirlpool in the large stainless-steel pot.

"Mama," Carol cried. "I barely know Alex. We've only gone out a handful of times."

"Ah, but your eyes are telling me something different."

"The only thing my eyes are interested in is some of that garlic bread Paula's making," Carol said, hoping to divert her mother's attention from the subject of Alex.

"Here." Her sister-in-law handed her a slice. "But it's no substitute for a man." Paula turned her head to press a quick kiss on her husband's cheek.

Tony's hands slipped further around Paula's waist as he whispered in his wife's ear. From the way her sister-in-law's face flooded with warm color, Carol didn't need much of an imagination to guess what Tony had said.

Carol looked away. She wasn't embarrassed by the earthy exchange between her brother and his wife; instead, she felt a peculiar twinge of envy. The realization shocked her. In all the years she'd been alone, Carol had never once longed for a pair of arms to hold her or for a man to whisper suggestive comments in her ear. Those intimacies were reserved for the happily married members of her family.

Yet, here she was, standing in the middle of her mother's kitchen, yearning for Alex to stroll up behind her, circle her waist and whisper promises in her ear. The image was so vivid that she hurried into the living room to escape it.

It wasn't until later, when the dishes were washed, that Carol had a chance to sort through her thoughts. Tony and Peter were puttering around in the garage. Paula was playing a game of Yahtzee with the younger children. And Angelina was rocking in her chair, nimble fingers working delicate yarn into a sweater for her smallest grandchild.

"So are you gonna tell your mama what's troubling you?" she asked Carol out of the blue.

"Nothing's wrong," Carol fibbed. She couldn't discuss what she didn't understand. For the first time, she felt distanced from the love and laughter that was so much a part of Sunday dinner with her family. For years she'd clung to the life she'd built for herself and her son. These few, short weeks with Alex had changed everything.

Alex had discovered all her weaknesses and used them to his own advantage. Digging up the earth for her herb garden was a good example. She could've asked her brother to do it for her. Eventually she probably would have. But Tony did so much to help her already that she didn't want to burden him with another request. It wasn't as if tilling part of the backyard was essential. But one casual mention to Alex, and next thing she knew, there was freshly tilled earth waiting for basil and Italian parsley where before there'd been lawn.

"You like this man, don't you?"

Carol responded with a tiny nod of her head.

A slow, easy smile rose from her mother's mouth to her eyes. "I thought so. You got the look."

"The look?"

"Of a woman falling in love. Don't fight it so hard, my *bambina*. It's time you met a man who brings color to your cheeks and a smile to your lips."

But Carol wasn't smiling. She felt confused and ambivalent. She was crazy about Alex; she prayed she'd never see him again. She couldn't picture her life with him; she couldn't picture her life without him.

"I lit a candle in church for you," her mother whispered. "And said a special prayer to St. Rita."

"Mama…"

"God and I had a good talk, and He told me it's predestined."

"What's predestined?"

"You and this non-Italian," her mother replied calmly.

"Mama, that doesn't make the least bit of sense. For years you've been telling me to marry a rich old man with one foot in the grave and the other on a banana peel. You said everyone loves a rich widow."

"Keep looking for the rich old man, but when you find him, introduce him to me. With any luck his first wife made spaghetti sauce with tomato soup and he'll worship at my feet."

Carol couldn't keep from smiling. She wasn't so sure about her mother lighting candles on her behalf or deciding that marrying Alex was predestined, but from experience she'd learned there wasn't any point in arguing.

Tony, Paula and their two children left around five. Usually Carol headed for home around the same time, but this afternoon she lingered. The 1940s war movie on television held Peter's attention, and her eyes drifted to it now and again.

It wasn't until she felt the moisture on her cheeks that she realized she was crying.

Doing what she could to wipe away the tears so as not to attract attention to herself, she focused on the television screen. Her mother was right; she was falling in love, head over heels in love, and it was frightening her to death.

Silently Angelina set her knitting aside and joined Carol on the sofa. Without a word, she thrust a tissue into Carol's hand. Then she wrapped her arm around her daughter's shoulders and pressed her head tenderly to her generous bosom. Gently patting Carol's back, Angelina whispered soothing words of love and encouragement in a language Carol could only partially understand.

Alex didn't see Carol again until Monday afternoon when he pulled into the high school parking lot. He angled his van in front of the track, four spaces down from her car. He waited a couple of minutes, hoping she'd come and see him of her own free will. He should've known better. The woman wasn't willing to give an inch.

Deciding to act just as nonchalant, Alex opened his door, walked over to the six-foot-high chain-link fence and pretended to be watching the various groups participate in field events. Neither James nor Peter was trying out for any of those positions on the team.

Then he walked casually toward Carol, who was determined, it seemed, to ignore him, hiding behind the pages of a women's magazine.

"Hello, Carol," he said after a decent interval.

"Oh—Alex." She held the magazine rigidly in place.

"Mind if I join you?"

"Not at all." The hesitation was long enough to imply that she would indeed mind. Regardless, he opened the passenger door and slid inside her car. Only then did Carol bother to close the magazine and set it down.

By now, Alex told himself, he should be accustomed to her aloof attitude toward him. It was like this nearly every time they were together. She'd never shown any real pleasure at seeing him. He had to break through those chilly barriers each and every encounter. The strangest part was that he knew she was as strongly attracted to him as he was to her. And not just in the physical sense. Their lives were like matching bookends, he thought.

"Did you have a good day?" he asked politely.

She nodded and glanced away, as though she thought that sharing even a small part of her life with him was akin to admitting she enjoyed his company.

"I suppose it would be too much to hope that you missed me the last couple of days?" he asked.

"Yes."

Alex was almost embarrassed by the way his heart raced. "You missed me," he repeated, feeling like a kid who'd been granted free rein in a candy store.

"No," Carol said, clearly disconcerted. "I meant it would be too much to hope I did."

"Oh." The woman sure knew how to deflate his pride.

"It really was thoughtful of you to dig up that area in my backyard on Saturday. I'm grateful, Alex."

Crossing his arms, Alex leaned against the back of the seat and tried to conceal his injured pride with a lazy shrug. "It was no trouble." Especially since the two boys had done most of the work, leaving him free to "pester" Carol in the kitchen. With everything in him, he wished they were back in that kitchen now. He wanted her in his arms the way she'd been on Saturday afternoon, her lips moist and swollen with his kisses, her eyes dark with passion.

"The boys will be out any minute," Carol said, studying the empty field.

Alex guessed this was his cue to leave her car, but he wasn't taking the hint. When it came to Carol Sommars, he was learning that his two greatest allies were James and Peter.

It was time to play his ace.

Alex waited until the last possible minute. Both boys had walked onto the parking lot, their hair damp from a recent shower. They were chatting and joking and in a good mood. Climbing out of Carol's car, Alex leaned against the fender in a relaxed pose.

"Peter, did you say something about wanting to go camping?" he said, casting Carol a defiant look. "James and I were thinking of heading for the Washington coastline this coming weekend and thought you and your mother might like to go with us."

"We are?" James asked, delighted and surprised.

Peter's eyes widened with excitement. "Camping? You're inviting Mom and me to go camping?"

At the mention of the word *camping,* Carol opened her car door and vaulted out. Her eyes narrowed on Alex as if to declare a foul and charge him a penalty.

"Are you two free this weekend?" Alex asked with a practiced look of innocence, formally extending the invitation. The ball was in her court, and he was interested in seeing how she volleyed this one.

"Yes," Peter shouted. "We're interested."

"No," Carol said at the same moment. "We already have plans."

"We do?" her son moaned. "Come on, Mom, Mr. Preston just offered to take us camping with him and James. What could possibly be more important than that?"

"I wanted to paint the living room."

"What? Paint the living room? I don't believe it." Peter

slapped his hands against his thighs and threw back his head. "You know how I feel about camping," he whined.

"Give your mother time to think it over," Alex urged, confident that Carol would change her mind or that Peter would do it for her. "We can talk about it tomorrow evening."

James gave Peter the okay signal, and feeling extraordinarily proud of himself, Alex led the way to his van, handing his son the keys.

"You're going to let me drive?" James asked, sounding more than a little stunned. "Voluntarily?"

"Count your blessings, boy, and drive."

"Yes, sir!"

Carol was furious with Alex. He'd played a faultless game, and she had to congratulate him on his fine closing move. All day she'd primed herself for the way she was going to act when she saw him again. She'd allowed their relationship to progress much further than she'd ever intended, and it was time to cool things down.

With her mother lighting candles in church and having heart-to-heart talks with God, things had gotten completely out of hand. Angelina barely complained anymore that Alex wasn't Catholic, and worse, not Italian. It was as if those two prerequisites no longer mattered.

What Carol hadn't figured on was the rush of adrenaline she'd experienced when Alex pulled into the school parking lot. She swore her heart raced faster than any of the runners on the track. She'd needed every ounce of determination she possessed not to toss aside the magazine she'd planted in the car and run to him, bury her face in his chest and ask him to explain what was happening to her.

Apparently Alex had read her perfectly. He didn't appear at all concerned about her lack of welcome. That hadn't even fazed him. All the arguments she'd amassed had been for naught. Then at the last possible minute he'd introduced the subject of this camping trip, in what she had to admire was a brilliant move. Her chain of resistance was only as strong as the weakest link. And her weakest link was Peter.

Grudgingly she had to admire Alex.

"Mom," Peter cried, restless as a first grader in the seat beside her. "We're going to talk about it, aren't we?"

"About the camping trip?"

"It's the chance of a lifetime. The Washington coast— I've heard it's fabulous—"

"We've got plans."

"To paint the living room? We could do that any old time!"

"Peter, please."

He was silent for a minute or so. The he asked, "Do you remember when I was eleven?"

Here it comes, Carol mused darkly. "I remember," she muttered, knowing it would've been too much to expect him not to drag up the lowest point of her life as a mother.

"We were going camping then, too, remember?"

He said *remember* as though it was a dirty word, one that would get him into trouble.

"You promised me an overnight camping trip and signed us up for an outing through the Y? But when we went to the meeting you got cold feet."

"Peter, they gave us a list of stuff we were supposed to bring, and not only did I not have half the things on the list, I didn't even know what they were."

"You could have asked," Peter cried.

"It was more than that."

"Just because we were going to hike at our own pace?

They said we'd get a map. We could've found the camp, Mom, I know we could have."

Carol had had visions of wandering through the woods for days on end with nothing more than a piece of paper that said she should head east—and she had the world's worst sense of direction. If she could get lost in a shopping mall, how would she ever find her way through dense forest?

"That wasn't the worst part," Peter murmured. "Right there in the middle of the meeting you leaned over and asked me what it would cost to buy your way out of the trip."

"You said you wouldn't leave for anything less than a laser tag set," Carol said, tormented by the unfairness of it all. The toy had been popular and expensive at the time and had cost her a pretty penny. But her son had conveniently forgotten that.

"I feel like I sold my soul that day," Peter said with a deep sigh.

"Peter, honestly!"

"It wasn't until then that I realized how much I was missing by not having a dad."

The kid was perfecting the art of guilt.

"Now, once again," he argued, "I have the rare opportunity to experience the great out-of-doors, and it's like a nightmare happening all over again. My own mother's going to pull the rug out from under my feet."

Carol stopped at a red light and pretended to play a violin. "This could warp your young mind for years to come."

"It just might," Peter said, completely serious.

"Twenty years from now, when they lock those prison doors behind you, you can cry out that it's all my fault. If only I'd taken you camping with Alex and James Preston, then the entire course of your life would have been different."

A short pause followed her statement.

"Sarcasm doesn't suit you, Mother."

Peter was right, of course, but Carol was getting desperate. At the rate this day was going, she'd end up spending Saturday night in front of a campfire, fighting off mosquitoes and the threat of wild beasts.

Because she felt guilty, despite every effort not to, Carol cooked Peter his favorite chicken-fried steak dinner, complete with gravy and mashed potatoes.

After the dishes had been cleared and Peter was supposed to be doing his homework, Carol found him talking on the phone, whispering frantically. It wasn't hard to guess that her son was discussing strategies with James. The three of them were clearly in cahoots against her.

Carol waited until Peter was in bed before she marched into the kitchen and righteously punched out Alex's phone number. She'd barely given him a chance to answer before she laid into him with both barrels.

"That was a rotten thing to do!"

"What?" he asked, feigning innocence.

"You know darn well what I'm talking about. Peter's pulled every trick in the book from the moment you mentioned this stupid camping trip."

"Are you going to come or is this war?"

"It's war right now, *Mister* Preston."

"Good. Does the victor get spoils? Because I'm telling you, Carol Sommars, I intend to win."

"Oh, Alex," she said with a sigh, leaning against the wall. She slid all the way down to the floor, wanting to weep with frustration. "How could you do this to me?"

"Easy. I got the idea when you told me it was too much to hope that you'd miss me."

"But I don't know anything about camping. To me, roughing it is going without valet service."

"It'll be fun, trust me."

Trusting Alex wasn't at the top of her priority list at the moment. He'd pulled a fast one on her, and she wasn't going to let him do it again.

"Is Peter sleeping?" Alex asked softly.

"If he isn't, he should be." She didn't understand where this conversation was heading.

"James is asleep, too," he said. "After the cold shoulder you gave me this afternoon, I need something to warm my blood."

"Try a hot water bottle."

"It won't work. Keep the door unlocked and I'll be right over."

"Absolutely not. Alex Preston, listen to me, I'm not dressed for company and—"

It was too late. He'd already disconnected.

Chapter 8

Standing in front of her locked screen door, Carol had no intention of letting Alex inside her home. It was nearly eleven, and they both had to work in the morning. When his car pulled into the driveway, she braced her feet apart and stiffened her back. She should be furious with him. Should be nothing; she *was* furious!

But when Alex climbed out of his car, he stood in her driveway for a moment, facing the house. Facing her. The porch light was dim, just bright enough to outline his handsome features.

With his hands in his pockets, he continued to stand there, staring at her. But that seemed such an inadequate way to describe the intensity of his gaze as his eyes locked with her own. Not a muscle moved in the hard, chiseled line of his jaw, and his eyes feasted on her with undisguised hunger. Even from the distance that separated them, Carol saw that his wonderful gray eyes had darkened with need.

He wanted her.

Heaven help her, despite all her arguments to the contrary, she wanted him, too.

Before he'd marched two steps toward her, Carol had unlocked the screen door and held it open for him.

"I'm not going camping," she announced, her voice scarcely audible. Her lips felt dry and her hands moist. Once she'd stated her position, her breath escaped with a ragged sigh. She thought of ranting at him, calling him a coward and a cheat to use her own son against her the way he had, but not a word made it from her mind to her lips.

Alex turned and shut the front door.

The only light was a single lamp on the other side of the room.

They didn't move, didn't breathe.

"I'm not going to force you to go camping," Alex whispered. "In fact, I..." He paused as he lowered his eyes to her lips, and whatever he intended to say trailed into nothingness.

Carol felt his eyes on her as keenly as she had his mouth.

In an effort to break this unnatural spell, she closed her eyes.

"Carol?"

She couldn't have answered him had her life depended on it. Her back was pressed to the door, and she flattened her hands against it.

Not once during her marriage had Carol felt as she did at that moment. So...needy. So empty.

He came to her in a single, unbroken movement, his mouth descending on hers. Carol wound her arms around him and leaned into his solid strength, craving it as never before. Again and again and again he kissed her.

"Alex." She tore her lips from his. "Alex," she breathed again, almost panting. "Something's wrong...."

She could feel his breath against her neck and his fingers in her hair, directing her mouth back to his, kissing her with such heat, Carol thought she'd disintegrate.

Her tears came in earnest then, a great profusion that had been building inside her for years. Long, lonely, barren years.

With the tears came pain, pain so intense she could hardly breathe. Agony spilled from her heart. The trauma that had been buried within her stormed out in a torrent of tears that she could no more stop than she could control.

Huge sobs shook her shoulders, giant hiccupping sobs that she felt all the way to her toes. Sobs that depleted her strength. Her breathing was ragged as she stumbled toward the edge of hysteria.

Alex was speaking to her in soft, reassuring whispers, but Carol couldn't hear him. It didn't matter what he said. Nothing mattered.

She clutched his shirt tighter and tighter. Soon there were no more tears to shed, no more emotion to be spent. Alex continued to hold her. He slid his arms all the way around her, and although she couldn't understand what he was saying, his voice was gentle.

Once the desperate crying had started to subside, Carol drew in giant gulps of air in a futile effort to gain control of herself.

Slowly Alex guided her to the sofa and sat her down, then gathered her in his arms and held her tenderly.

Time lost meaning to Carol until she heard the clock chime midnight. Until then she was satisfied with being held in Alex's arms. He asked no questions, demanded no explanations. He simply held her, offering comfort and consolation.

This newfound contentment in his arms was all too short-lived, however. Acute embarrassment stole through the stillness, and fresh tears stung Carol's eyes. Her mind, her thoughts, her memories were steeped in emotions too strong to bear.

"I... I'll make some coffee," she whispered, unwinding her arms from him, feeling she had to escape.

"Forget the coffee."

She broke away and got shakily to her feet. Before he could stop her, she hurried into the kitchen and supported herself against the counter, not sure if she could perform the uncomplicated task of making a pot of coffee.

Alex followed her into the darkened room. He placed one hand on her shoulder and gently turned her around, so she had no choice but to face him. "I want to talk about what happened."

"No...please." She leveled her eyes at the floor.

"We *need* to talk."

"No." She shook her head emphatically. "Not now. Please not now."

A long, desperate moment passed before he gently kissed the crown of her head. "Fine," he whispered. "Not now. But soon. Very soon."

Carol doubted she could ever discuss what had happened between them, but she didn't have the strength or the courage to say so. That would only have invited argument.

"I... I think you should go."

His nod was reluctant. "Will you be all right?"

"Yes." A bold-faced lie if ever there was one. She would never be the same again. She was mortified to the very marrow of her bones by her behavior. How could she ever see him again? And then the pain, the memories came rushing back...

No, she wouldn't be all right, but she'd pretend she was, the same way she'd been pretending from the moment she married Bruce.

The message waiting for Alex when he returned to his office the following afternoon didn't come as any surprise. His secretary handed him the yellow slip, and the instant he saw Carol's name, he knew. She was working late that evening and asked if he could pick up Peter from track and drop him off at the house.

The little coward! He sat at his desk, leaned back in his chair and frowned. He hadn't wanted to leave her the night before. Hadn't wanted to walk out of her kitchen without being assured she was all right. Carol, however, had made it clear that she wanted him to leave. Equally apparent was the fact that his being there had only added to her distress. Whatever Carol was facing, whatever ghost she'd encountered, was ugly and traumatic.

So he'd left. But he hadn't stopped thinking about her all day. The thought of her had filled every waking minute.

Even now, hours later, he could remember in vivid detail the way she'd started to unfold and blossom right before his eyes. Because of him. For him.

His frown deepened. She'd never talked about her marriage. Alex assumed it had to be the source of her anguish, but he didn't know why. He didn't even know her late husband's name. Questions bombarded him, and he cursed the lack of answers.

And now, his sweet coward had gone into hiding.

"Will you talk to her, Mr. Preston?" Peter begged as he climbed inside the van in the school parking lot. "Mom's never gone camping, and I think she'd probably like it if she gave it half a chance."

"I'll talk to her," Alex promised.

Peter sighed with relief. "Good."

Sounding both confident and proud, James said, "My dad can be persuasive when he wants to be."

Alex intended to be *very* persuasive.

"I tried to reason with Mom this morning, and you know what she said?" Peter's changing voice pitched between two octaves.

"What?"

"She said she didn't want to talk about it. Doesn't that sound just like a woman? And I thought Melody Wohlford was hard to understand."

Alex stifled a chuckle. "I'll tell you boys what I'm going to do. We'll pick up hamburgers on the way home, and I'll drop you both off at my house. Then I'll drive over to your place, Peter, and wait for your mother there."

"Great idea," James said, nodding his approval.

"But while I'm gone, I want you boys to do your homework."

"Sure."

"Yeah, sure," James echoed. "Just do whatever it takes to convince Mrs. Sommars to come on our camping trip."

"I'll do everything I can," Alex said.

Carol let herself in the front door, drained from a long, taxing day at the hospital and exhausted from the sleepless night that had preceded it. That morning, she'd been tempted to phone in sick, but with two nurses already out due to illness, there wasn't anyone to replace her. So she'd gone to work feeling emotionally and physically hungover.

"Peter, I'm home," she called. "Peter?"

Silence. Walking into the kitchen, she deposited her purse on the counter and hurried toward her son's bedroom. She'd contacted Alex and asked that he bring Peter home, with instructions to phone back if he couldn't. She hadn't heard from him, so she'd assumed he'd pick up her son and drop him off at the house.

Peter's room was empty, his bed unmade. An array of clean and dirty clothes littered his floor. Everything was normal there.

This was what she got for trying to avoid Alex, Carol mused, chastising herself. Peter was probably still waiting at the high school track, wondering where she could possibly be.

Sighing, she hurried back into the kitchen and reached for her purse. She had to get him his own cell phone, she decided—it would help in situations like this.

The doorbell rang as she walked through the living room. Impatiently she jerked open the door and her eyes collided with Alex's. She gasped.

"Hello again," he said in the warm, husky way that never failed to affect her. "I didn't mean to startle you."

"You didn't." He had, but she wasn't about to admit it. "Apparently you didn't get my message.... Peter must still be at the school."

"No. He's at my house with James."

"Oh." That hardly expressed the instant dread she felt. They were alone, and there was no escape, at least not by the most convenient means—Peter.

Alex stepped into the house and for the first time, she noticed he was carrying a white paper bag. Her gaze settled on it and she frowned.

"Two Big Macs, fries and shakes," he explained.

"For whom?"

Alex arched his eyebrows. "Us."

"Oh…" He honestly expected her to sit down and eat with him? It would be impossible. "I'm not hungry."

"I am—very hungry. If you don't want to eat, that's fine. I will, and while I'm downing my dinner, we can talk."

It wouldn't do any good to argue, and Carol knew it. Without another word, she turned and walked to the kitchen. Alex followed her, and his movements, as smooth and agile as always, sounded thunderous behind her. She was aware of everything about him. When he walked, when he breathed, when he moved.

His eyes seemed to bore holes in her back, but she ignored the impulse to turn and face him. She couldn't bear to look him in the eye. The memory of what had happened the night before made her cheeks flame.

"How are you?" he asked in that husky, caring way of his.

"Fine," she answered cheerfully. "And you?"

"Not so good."

"Oh." Her heart was pounding, clamoring in her ears. "I'm…sorry to hear that."

"You should be, since you're the cause."

"Me? I'm…sure you're mistaken." She got two plates from the cupboard and set them on the table.

As she stepped past him, Alex grabbed her hand. "I don't want to play word games with you. We've come too far for that…and we're going a lot further."

Unable to listen to his words, she closed her eyes.

"Look at me, Carol."

She couldn't do it. She lowered her head, eyes still shut.

"There's no need to be embarrassed."

Naturally he could afford to be generous. He wasn't the one who'd dissolved in a frenzy of violent tears and emotion. She was just grateful that Peter had slept through the whole episode.

"We need to talk."

"No…" she cried and broke away. "Couldn't you have ignored what happened? Why do you have to drag it up now?" she demanded. "Do you enjoy embarrassing me like this? Do you get a kick out of seeing me miserable?" She paused, breathless, her chest heaving. "Please, just go away and leave me alone."

Her fierce words gave birth to a brief, tense silence.

Grasping her chin between his thumb and forefinger, Alex lifted her head. Fresh emotion filled her chest, knotting in her throat as her eyes slid reluctantly to his.

"I don't know what happened last night," he said. "At least not entirely." His voice was gruff, angry, emotional. "All I know is that I've never felt closer to anyone than I did to you—and I've never felt more helpless. But we've got something special, Carol, and I refuse to let you throw it away. Understand?"

She bit her lower lip, sniffled, then slowly nodded.

The tension eased from Alex, and he reached for her, gently taking her in his arms. She went without question, hiding her face against his neck.

Long, lazy moments passed before he spoke. "I want you to tell me about your marriage."

"No!" she cried and frantically shook her head.

He was silent again, and she could feel him withdrawing from her—or maybe she was the one withdrawing. She wanted to ask him to be patient with her, to give her breathing room, time to analyze what was happening between them.

Just when she was ready to speak, she felt him relax. He chuckled softly, his warm breath mussing her hair. "All right, I'll strike a bargain with you. If you go camping with me this weekend, I'll drop the subject—not forever, mind you, but until you're comfortable enough to talk about it."

Carol raised her head, her eyes meeting his. "You've got a black heart, Alex Preston."

He chuckled and kissed the tip of her nose. "When it comes to courting you, I've learned I need one."

"I can't believe I'm doing this," Carol muttered as she headed up the steep trail into the trees. The surf pounded the Washington beach far below. But directly in front of her was a narrow path that led straight into the rain forest.

"We don't have to wait for you guys, do we?" James whined. He and Peter were obviously eager to do some exploring on their own.

Carol was about to launch into a long list of cautions when Alex spoke. "Feel free," he told the two boys. "Carol and I will be back at camp in time for dinner. We'll expect you to be there then."

"Great!"

"All *right*."

Within minutes both boys were out of sight, and Carol resumed the increasingly difficult climb. A mountain goat would've had trouble maneuvering this path, she told herself.

"You're doing fine," Alex said behind her. Breathless from the physical exertion required by the steep incline, Carol paused and took a couple of minutes to breathe deeply.

"I love it when you get all hot and sweaty for me."

"Will you stop," she cried, embarrassed and yet amused by his words.

"Never."

To complicate things, Alex moved with grace and skill, even while carrying a backpack. So far, he hadn't even worked up a sweat. Carol, on the other hand, was panting. She hadn't realized how out of shape she was until now.

"The view had better be worth all this effort," she said with a moan five minutes later. The muscles in her calves were beginning to protest, and her heart was pounding so hard it echoed in her ears.

To make matters worse, she'd worn the worst possible combination of clothes. Not knowing what to expect weatherwise, she'd donned heavy boots, jeans and a thick sweatshirt, plus a jacket. Her head was covered with a bright pink cap her mother had knitted for her last Christmas. Should they happen upon a snowstorm, Carol was prepared.

"It's worth the climb," Alex promised. "Do you want me to lead?"

"No way," she said, dismissing his offer. "I'd never be able to keep up with you."

A little while later, Carol staggered into a clearing. She stopped abruptly, astonished by the beauty that surrounded her. The forest she'd just left was dense with a variety of evergreens. Huge limbs were draped with mossy green blankets that hung down so far they touched the spongy ground. Moss-coated stumps dotted the area, some sprouting large white mushroom caps. Wildflowers carpeted the earth and a gentle breeze drifted through the meadow and, catching her breath, Carol removed her hat in a form of worship.

"You're right," she murmured. "This is wonderful… I feel like I'm standing in a cathedral…this makes me want to pray."

"This isn't what I wanted you to see," Alex said, resting his hand on the curve of her shoulder.

"It isn't?" she whispered in disbelief. "You mean there's something better than this?"

"Follow me."

Carol pulled off her jacket, stuffed her hat into one of the pockets and tied the sleeves around her waist. Eagerly she trailed Alex along the winding narrow pathway.

"There's a freshwater cove about a mile from here," he explained, turning back to look at her. "Are you up to the trek?"

"I think so." She felt invigorated. More than that, she felt elated. *Alive.*

"You're being a good sport about all this," Alex said, smiling at her.

"I knew I was going to be okay when I saw that you'd pitched the tents close to the public restrooms. I'm not comfortable unless I'm near something that goes flush in the night."

Alex laughed. They hiked for another twenty minutes and eventually came to the edge of a cliff that fell sharply into the water. The view of bright green waves, contrasted by brilliant blue skies, was beautiful enough to bring tears to Carol's eyes. The park department had set up a chain-link fence along the edge, as well as a rough-hewn bench that had been carved out of an old tree trunk.

Alex gestured for her to sit down. Spreading her coat on the bench, Carol sat down and gazed out at the vista before her.

"You hungry?"

"Starving."

"I thought you would be." He slipped off his pack and set it in front of them. Then he unfastened the zipper and removed a folded plastic bag that resembled the ones Carol used to line her garbage cans.

"What's that?" she asked.

"A garbage bag."

"Oh." Well, that was what it looked like.

Next, he took out a whistle, which he held up for her inspection. "A whistle," he announced unnecessarily. Finally he found what he was searching for and placed a thick chocolate bar and two apples on the bench.

"Without appearing completely stupid," Carol said, biting into her apple, "may I ask why you hauled a garbage bag all the way up here?"

"In case we get lost."

"What?" she cried in alarm. She'd assumed Alex knew his way back to their campsite. He'd certainly implied as much.

"Even the best of hikers have been known to get lost. This is just a precaution."

"When... I mean, I thought you were experienced."

He wiggled his eyebrows suggestively. "I am."

"Alex, this is no time to joke."

"I'm not joking. The garbage bag, the whistle and the chocolate are all part of the hug-a-tree program."

"Hug-a-tree?"

"It's a way of preparing children, or anyone else for that matter, in case they get lost in the woods. The idea is to stay in one place—to literally hug a tree. The garbage bag is for warmth. If you slip inside it, feet first, and crouch down, gathering the opening around your neck, you can keep warm in near-freezing temperatures. It weighs practically nothing. The whistle aids rescuers in locating whoever's lost, and the reason for the candy is obvious."

"Do you mean to tell me we're chowing down on our limited food rations?" Carol bit into her apple again before Alex could change his mind and take it away from her.

"Indeed we are, but then we're practically within sight of the campground, so I don't think we're in any danger of getting lost."

"Good." Too ravenous to care, Carol peeled the paper from the chocolate bar and took a generous bite.

"I was waiting for that," Alex murmured, setting aside his apple.

Carol paused, the candy bar in front of her mouth. "Why?"

"So I could kiss you and taste the chocolate on your lips." He reached for her, and his mouth found hers with such need, such hunger, that Carol groaned. Alex hadn't touched her in days, patiently giving her time to determine the boundaries of their relationship. Now she was starving for him, eager for his kiss, his touch.

His kiss was slow, so slow and deliberate. When he lifted his head Carol moaned and sagged against him.

"You taste sweet," he whispered, tugging at her lower lip with his teeth. "Even sweeter than I expected. Even sweeter than chocolate."

Chapter 9

Her sleeping bag and air mattress didn't look as comfortable as a bed at the Hilton, but they appeared adequate, Carol decided later that night. At least Alex had enough equipment for the four of them. All Carol and Peter owned was one GI Joe sleeping bag, decorated with little green army men, and Carol wasn't particularly excited about having to sleep in that.

They'd hiked and explored most of the afternoon. By the time everything was cleared away after dinner, dusk had settled over Salt Creek Park. Carol was out of energy, but Peter and James insisted they couldn't officially call it camping unless everyone sat around the campfire, toasted marshmallows and sang silly songs. And so a lengthy songfest had ensued.

Carol was yawning when she crawled inside the small tent she was sharing with Peter. Alex and James's larger tent was pitched next to theirs. By the dim light of the lantern hanging from the middle of the tent, Carol undressed, cleaned her face and then slipped into the sleeping bag.

"Is it safe yet?" Peter yelled impatiently from outside the tent.

"Safe and sound," Carol returned. She'd just finished zipping up the bag when Peter pulled back the flap and stuck his head in.

Smiling, he withdrew, and she heard him whisper something to James about how unreasonable women could be. Carol didn't know what she'd done that could be considered unreasonable, and she was too drained to ask.

"Good night, everyone," Carol called out when Peter dimmed the lantern.

There was a mixed chorus of "good nights." Content, she rolled onto her stomach and closed her eyes.

Within minutes Carol was fast asleep.

"Carol."

She woke sometime later as her name was whispered close to her ear. Jerking her head up, she saw Alex kneeling just inside the tent, fully dressed. A shaft of moonlight showed her that he'd pressed his finger to his lips, indicating she should be quiet.

"What is it?"

"I want to show you something."

"Now?"

He grinned at her lack of enthusiasm and nodded.

"It can't wait until morning?" she said, yawning.

"It'll be gone by morning," he whispered. "Get dressed and meet me in five minutes."

She couldn't understand what was so important that she couldn't see it by the light of day.

"If you're not out here in five minutes," he warned in

a husky voice from outside her tent, "I'm coming in after you."

Carol grumbled as she scurried around looking for her clothes. It was difficult to pull on her jeans in the cramped space, but with a few acrobatic moves, she managed. Before she crawled out, she tapped Peter's shoulder and told him she'd be back in a few minutes.

Peter didn't seem to care one way or the other.

Alex was waiting for her. His lazy smile wrapped its way around her heart and squeezed tight. For all her moaning and complaining about this camping trip, Carol was having a wonderful time.

"This had better be good," she warned and ingloriously yawned.

"It is," he promised. He held a flashlight and a blanket in one hand and reached for hers with the other. Then he led her toward the beach. Although she was wearing her jacket, the wind made her shiver. Alex must have noticed, because he slid his arm around her shoulder and drew her closer.

"Where are we going?" She found herself whispering, not sure why.

"To a rock."

"A rock," she repeated, incredulous. "You woke me from a sound sleep so I could see a *rock?*"

"Not see, sit on one."

"I couldn't do this at noon in the warm sun?" she muttered, laughing at him.

"Not if you're going to look at the stars."

Carol's step faltered. "Do you mean to tell me you rousted me from a warm, cozy sleeping bag in the middle of the night to show me a few stars? The very same stars I could see from my own bedroom window?"

Alex chuckled. "Are you always this testy when you just wake up?"

"Always," she told him. Yawning again, she covered her mouth with one hand.

Although the campsite was only a few feet away, it was completely hidden behind a clump of trees. Carol could hear the ocean—presumably at the bottom of some nearby cliff—but she couldn't see it.

"I suppose I should choose a tree now. Which one looks the friendliest to you?" Carol asked.

"A tree? Whatever for?"

"To hug. Didn't you tell me this afternoon that if I ever get lost in the woods a tree is my friend? If we get separated, there's no way I'd ever find my way back to camp."

Alex dropped a kiss on her head. "I won't let you out of my sight for a minute, I promise."

"The last time I trusted a guy, I was eighteen and I was pregnant three weeks later." She meant it as a joke, but once the words were out they seemed to hang in the air between them.

"You were only eighteen when you got married?"

Carol nodded, pulled her hand free from his and shoved it in the pocket of her jacket. She could feel herself withdrawing from him. She drew inside herself a little more.

They walked in silence for several minutes.

Suddenly Alex aimed the flashlight at the ground and paused. "This way."

"Over there?" Carol asked. She squinted but couldn't see any rock.

"Just follow me," Alex said. "And no more wisecracks about what happened the last time you listened to a guy. I'm not your first husband, and it would serve us both well if you remembered that." His words were light, teasing, but they sent Carol reeling.

He reached for her hand, lacing his fingers through hers. She could almost hear the litany of questions in Alex's mind. He wanted her to tell him about Bruce. But no one fully knew what a nightmare her marriage had been. Not even her mother. And Carol wasn't about to drag out all the pain for Alex to examine.

Within a couple of minutes, Alex had located "his" rock. At first Carol thought it looked like all the other rocks, silhouetted against the beach.

He climbed up the side, obviously familiar with its shape and size, then offered Carol his hand. Once they were perched on top, he spread out the blanket and motioned for her to sit down.

Carol did and pulled her knees under her chin.

Alex settled down beside her. "Now," he said, pointing toward the heavens, "can you see *that* outside your bedroom window?"

Having forgotten the purpose of this outing, Carol cast her gaze toward the dark sky, then straightened in wonder and surprise. The sky was so heavy with stars—hundreds, no, thousands of them—that it seemed to sag down and touch the earth. "Oh, Alex," she breathed.

"Worth waking up for?" he asked.

"Well worth it," she said, thanking him with a smile.

"I thought you'd think so." His returning smile flew straight into her heart.

She'd been struck by so much extraordinary beauty in such a short while that she felt almost overwhelmed. Turning her head slightly, she smiled again at this man who had opened her eyes to life, to beauty, to love and whispered fervently, "Thank you, Alex."

"For what?"

"For the hike in the rain forest, for the view of the cove, for ignoring my complaints and showing me the stars, for... everything." For coming into her life. For leading her by the hand. For being so patient with her.

"You're welcome."

Lost in the magic, Carol closed her eyes and inhaled the fragrant scent of the wind, the ocean and the night. Rarely had she experienced this kind of contentment and uncomplicated happiness.

When the breeze came, the trees whispered, and the sound combined with the crashing of the surf below. The scents of pine and sea drifted over her. Throwing back her head, Carol tried to take it all in.

"I don't think I appreciated how truly beautiful you are until now," Alex murmured. His face was carved in severe but sensual lines, and his eyes had darkened with emotion.

Carol turned, and when she did, he brushed back the curls from her cheek. His hand lingered on her face, and Carol covered it with her own, closing her eyes at all the sensations that accompanied his touch.

He brought his free hand to her hair, which he threaded through his fingers as though the texture was pure silk. He traced her lower lip with his finger. Unable to resist, Carol circled it with the tip of her tongue....

Time seemed to stand still as Alex's eyes sought and held hers.

He kissed her, and it was excruciatingly slow. Exquisitely slow.

He pressed warm kisses in the hollow of her neck and slipped his hands inside her jacket, circling her waist and bringing her closer. "The things you do to me," he said in a low voice.

"The things I do to *you?*" She rested her forehead against

his own. "They can't compare to what you do—have always done—to me."

His lips twitched with the beginnings of a smile, and Carol leaned forward just enough to kiss him again.

Under her jacket Alex slid his hands up her back. He stopped abruptly, went still and tore his mouth from hers.

"What's wrong?" Carol asked, lifting her head. Her hands were on his shoulders.

"You're not wearing a bra, are you?"

"No. You said I had only five minutes to dress, so I hurried."

His eyes burned into hers, then moved lower to the snap of her jeans. "Did you…take any other shortcuts?"

"Wanna find out?"

He shook his head wildly. "I… I promised myself when you agreed to go camping that I'd do everything I could to keep my hands off you." Although she was still in his arms, Carol had to strain to hear him.

"I think that was a wise decision," she murmured, looking up at him. Alex's expression was filled with surprise. An inner happiness she'd banished from her life so long ago she hadn't known it was missing pulsed through her now.

When he finally released her, Carol was so weak with longing that she clung to him, breathing deeply.

"Carol," he said, watching her closely as she shifted positions. She climbed onto his lap, wrapped her legs around his waist and threw her arms around his neck.

"Oh… Carol." Alex moaned and closed his eyes.

"Shhh," she whispered, kissing him deeply. He didn't speak again for a long, long time. Neither did she…

Thursday afternoon, with a stethoscope around her neck, Carol walked down the hospital corridor to the nurses' station. Her steps were brisk and her heart heavy. She hadn't talked to Alex since late Sunday, when he'd dropped Peter and her at the house after their camping trip. There could be any number of excellent reasons why he hadn't called or stopped by. Maybe he was simply too busy; that made sense. Maybe he didn't want to see her again; perhaps he'd decided to start dating other women. Younger women. Prettier women. He was certainly handsome enough. Perhaps aliens had captured him, and he was trapped in some spaceship circling uncharted universes.

Whatever the reason, it translated into one glaring, inescapable fact. She hadn't seen or heard from Alex in four days. However, she reminded herself, she didn't need a man to make her happy. She didn't need a relationship.

"There's a call for you on line one," Betty Mills told her. "Want me to take a message?"

"Did the person give a name?"

"Alex Preston. He sounds sexy, too," Betty added in a succulent voice. "I don't suppose he's that handsome guy you were having lunch with a little while ago."

Carol's heart slammed against her ribs—first with alarm and then with relief. She'd done everything she could to ignore the gaping hole in her life without Alex there. All it would've taken was a phone call—she could have contacted him. She could've asked Peter to talk to James. She could've driven over to his house. But she'd done none of those things.

"Carol? Do you want me to take a message or not?" Betty asked.

"No, I'll get it."

Betty laughed. "I would, too, if I were you." With that, she turned and marched away.

Carol moved to the nurses' station and was grateful no

one else was around to overhear her conversation. "This is Carol Sommars," she said as professionally as she could manage.

"Carol, it's Alex."

His words burned in her ears. "Hello, Alex," she said, hoping she didn't sound terribly stiff. Her pulse broke into a wild, absurd rhythm at his voice, and despite her best efforts, a warm sense of happiness settled over her.

"I'm sorry to call you at the hospital, but I haven't been able to reach you at home for the past few nights."

"I've been busy." Busy trying to escape the loneliness. Busy ignoring questions she didn't want to answer. Busy hiding.

"Yes, I know," Alex said impatiently. "Are you avoiding me?"

"I… I thought you…if you want the truth, I assumed you'd decided not to see me again."

"Not *see* you," he repeated loudly. "Are you crazy? I'm nuts about you."

"Oh." Her mouth trembled, but whether it was from irritation or sheer blessed relief, Carol didn't know. If he was nuts about her, why had he neglected her all week? Why hadn't he at least left her a message?

"You honestly haven't figured out how I feel about you yet?"

"You haven't been at the school in the past few days, and since I didn't hear from you it made sense—to me, anyway—that you wanted to cool things down, and I don't blame you. Things are getting much too hot and much too… well, fast, and personally I thought that…well, that it was for the best."

"You thought *what?*" he demanded, his voice exploding

over the wire. "When I get home the first thing I'm going to do is kiss some sense into you."

"When you get home?"

"I'm in Houston."

"Texas?"

"Is there any other?"

Carol didn't know. "What are you doing there?"

"Wishing I was in Portland, mostly. A friend of mine, another contractor, is involved in a huge project here and ran into problems. There must've been five messages from him when we returned from the camping trip. He needed some help right away."

"What about James? He isn't with you, is he?"

"He's staying with another friend of mine. I've probably mentioned him before. His name is Barney."

Vaguely Carol *did* remember either Alex or James mentioning the man, but she couldn't remember where or when she'd heard it. "How…long will you be gone?" She hated the way her voice fell, the way it made her need for him all too evident.

"Another week at least."

Her heart catapulted to her feet, then gradually righted itself. "A *week?*"

"I don't like it any better than you do. I can't believe how much I miss you. How much I needed to hear your voice."

Carol felt that, too, only she hadn't been willing to admit it, even to herself.

There was a slight commotion on Alex's end of the line and when it cleared, he said, "I'll try to call you again, but we're working day and night and this is the first real break I've had in three days. I'm glad I got through to you."

Her grip tightened on the receiver. "I'm glad, too."

"I have to go. Bye, Carol. I'll see you Thursday or so of next week."

"Goodbye, Alex…and thanks for phoning." She was about to hang up when she realized there was something else she had to say. She cried his name, desperate to catch him before he hung up.

"I'm here. What is it?"

"Alex," she said, sighing with relief. "I've… I want you to know I… I've missed you, too."

The sound of his chuckle was as warm and melodious as a hundred-voice choir. "It's not much, but it's something. Keep next Thursday open for me, okay?"

"You've got yourself a date."

Tuesday evening of the following week, Carol was teaching her birthing class. Ten couples were sprawled on big pillows in front of her as she led them through a series of exercises. She enjoyed this work almost as much as she did her daytime job at the hospital. She and Janice Mandle each taught part of the class, with Carol handling the first half.

"Everyone's doing exceptionally well tonight," Carol said, praising the teams. "Okay, partners, I have a question for you. I want you to tell me, in number of seconds, how long you think a typical labor pain lasts."

"Thirty seconds," one young man shouted out.

"Longer," Carol said.

"Sixty seconds," yelled another.

Carol shook her head.

"Ninety?"

"You don't sound too sure about that," Carol said, smiling. "Let's stick with ninety seconds. That's a nice round number, although in the final stages of labor it's not unusual for a contraction to last much longer."

The pregnant women eyed each other warily.

"All right, partners, I want you to show me your biceps. Tighten them as hard as you can. Good. Good," she said, surveying the room, watching as several of the men brought up their fists until the muscles of their upper arms bulged. "Make it as tight and as painful as you can," she continued. Most of the men were gritting their teeth.

"Very good," she went on to say. "Now, hold that until I tell you to relax." She walked to the other side of the room. "As far back as 1913, some doctors and midwives recognized that fear and tension could interfere with the birthing process. Even then they believed that deep breathing exercises and relaxation could aid labor." She paused to glance at her watch. "That's fifteen seconds."

The look of astonishment that crossed the men's faces was downright comical.

"Keep those muscles tightly clenched," Carol instructed. She strolled around the room, chatting amiably as the men held their arms as tight as possible. Some were already showing the strain.

"Thirty seconds," she announced.

Her words were followed by a low groan. Carol couldn't help smiling. She hated to admit how much she enjoyed their discomfort, but this exercise was an excellent illustration of the realities of labor, especially for the men. The smile remained on her lips as the door in the back of the room opened to admit a latecomer. Carol opened her mouth to welcome the person, but the words didn't reach her lips.

There, framed inside the door, stood Alex Preston.

Chapter 10

Carol stared at Alex. Alex stared at Carol.

The room went completely still; the air felt heavy, and the quiet seemed eerie, unnatural. It wasn't until Carol realized that several taut faces were gazing up at her anxiously that she pulled her attention away from Alex and back to her class.

"Now, where were we?" she asked, flustered and nervous.

"Ninety seconds," one of the men shouted.

"Oh. Right." She glanced at her watch and nodded. "Ninety seconds."

The relief could be felt all the way across the room.

A few minutes later Carol dismissed everyone for a fifteen-minute break. Janice strolled over to Carol and eyed the back of the room, where Alex was patiently waiting. He was leaning against the back wall, his ankles crossed and his thumbs hooked in the belt loop of his jeans.

"He's gorgeous."

Carol felt too distracted and tongue-tied to respond, although her thoughts had been traveling along those same lines. Alex was the sexiest man Carol had ever known. Unabashedly wonderful, too.

"He's…been out of town," she said, her eyes magnetically drawn to Alex's.

Janice draped her arm across Carol's shoulders. "Since your portion of tonight's class is finished, why don't you go ahead and leave?"

"I couldn't." Carol tore her eyes from Alex long enough to study her co-teacher. They were a team, and although they'd divided the class into two distinct sections, they stayed and lent each other emotional support.

"Yes, you can. I insist. Only…"

"Only what?" Carol pressed.

"Only promise me that if another gorgeous guy walks in off the street and looks at me like he's looking at you, you'll return the favor."

"Of course," Carol answered automatically.

Janice's voice fell to a whisper. "Good. Then we'll consider this our little secret."

Carol frowned. "I don't understand—what do you mean, our little secret?"

"Well, if my husband found out about this agreement, there could be problems."

Carol laughed. Janice was happily married and had been for fifteen years.

"If I were you I wouldn't be hanging around here talking," Janice murmured, giving Carol a small shove. "Don't keep him waiting any longer."

"Okay…thanks." Feeling unaccountably shy, Carol retrieved her purse and her briefcase and walked toward Alex. With each step that drew her nearer, her heart felt lighter.

By the time she made her way to the back of the room, she felt nearly airborne.

He straightened, his eyes warm and caressing. "Hello."

"Hi."

"Peter told me you were teaching tonight and where. I hope you don't mind that I dropped in unexpectedly."

"I don't mind." *Mind?* Her heart was soaring with gladness. She could've flown without an airplane. No, she didn't mind that he'd dropped in—not in the least.

For the longest moment all they did was gaze at each other like starry-eyed lovers.

A noise at the front of the room distracted Carol. She glanced over her shoulder and saw several couples watching them with undisguised curiosity.

"Janice said she'd finish up here, and I could…should leave now."

Alex grinned, and with that, Carol could feel whole sections of the sturdy wall around her heart start to crumble. This man's smile was nothing short of lethal.

"Remind me to thank her later," Alex said. He removed the briefcase from her unresisting fingers and opened the door, letting her precede him outside.

They hadn't taken two steps out the door when Alex paused. Carol felt his hesitation and stopped, turning to face him. That was when she knew Alex was going to kiss her. It didn't matter that they were standing in front of a public building. It didn't matter that it was still light enough for any number of passersby to see them. It didn't matter that they were both respected professionals.

Alex scooped her into his arms and with a lavish sigh lowered his head and covered her lips in the sweetest, wildest kiss of her life.

"I've missed you," he whispered. "The hours felt like years, the days like decades."

Carol felt tears in the corners of her eyes. She hadn't thought about how empty her life had felt without him, how bleak and alone she was with him away. Now it poured out of her in a litany of sighs and kisses. "I... I missed you, too—so much."

For years she'd been content in her own secure world, the one she'd created for herself and her son. The borders had been narrow, confining, but she'd made peace with herself and found serenity. Then she'd met Alex, and he'd forced her to notice how cramped and limited her existence was. Not only that, he'd pointed toward the horizon, to a new land of shared dreams.

When Alex spoke again, his voice was heavy with need. "Come on, let's get out of here."

She nodded and followed him to his car, ready to abandon her own with little more than a second thought.

He unlocked the passenger door, then turned to face her. His eyes were dancing with excitement. "Let's dispense with formalities and elope. Now. Tonight. This minute."

The words hit her hard. She blinked at the unexpectedness of his suggestion, prepared to laugh it off as a joke.

But Alex was serious. He looked as shocked as Carol felt, but she noted that the idea had begun to gain momentum. The mischievous spark in his eyes was gone, replaced by a solemn look.

"I love you, Carol. I love you so much that my buddy in Texas practically threw me on the plane and told me to get home before I died of it. He said he'd never seen anyone more lovesick and made me promise we'd name one of our children after him."

The mention of a child was like a right cross to the jaw

after his punch to her solar plexus, and she flinched involuntarily.

Alex set his hands on her shoulders, and a smile touched his eyes and then his mouth. He smiled so endearingly that all of Carol's arguments fled like dust in a whirlwind.

"Say something."

"Ah...my car's parked over there." She pointed in the general vicinity of her Ford. Her throat was so tight she could hardly speak.

He laughed and hugged her. "I know this is sudden for you. I'm a fool not to have done it properly. I swear I'll do it again over champagne and give you a diamond so large you'll sink in a swimming pool, but I can't keep the way I feel inside anymore."

"Alex..."

He silenced her with a swift kiss. "Believe me, blurting out a proposal like this is as much of a surprise to me as it is to you. I had no idea I was going to ask you tonight. The entire flight home I was trying to figure out how I could make it as romantic as possible. The last thing I expected to do was impulsively shout it out in a parking lot. But something happened tonight." He reached for her limp hands and brought them to his lips, then kissed her knuckles with reverence. "When I walked into your class and saw you with all those pregnant women, I was hit with the most powerful shock of my life." His voice grew quiet. "All of a sudden, my mind conjured up the image of you pregnant with our child, and I swear it was all I could do not to break down and weep." He paused long enough to run his fingers through his hair. "Children, Carol...our children." He closed his eyes and sighed deeply.

Carol felt frozen. The chill worked its way from her heart, the icy circles growing larger and more encompassing until the cold extended down her arms and legs and into her fingers and toes.

"I know this is abrupt, and I'm probably ruining the moment, but say something," Alex urged. "Anything."

Carol's mind refused to function properly. Panic was closing in, panic and a hundred misgivings. "I...don't know what to tell you."

Alex threw back his head and laughed. "I don't blame you. All right," he said, his eyes flashing, "repeat after me. I, Carol Sommars." He glanced expectantly at her.

"I... Carol Sommars..."

"Am crazy in love with Alex Preston." He waited for her to echo his words.

"Am crazy in love with Alex Preston."

"Good," he whispered and leaned forward just enough to brush his mouth over hers. His arms slipped around her, locking at the small of her back and dragging her unresistingly toward him. "You know, the best part about those babies is going to be making them."

A blush rose up her neck, coloring her cheeks with what she felt sure was a highly uncomplimentary shade of pink. Her eyes darted away from his.

"Now all you need to do is say *yes,*" Alex said.

"I can't. I...don't know." To her horror, she started to sob, not with the restrained tears of a confused woman, but the harsh mournful cries of one in anguish.

Alex had apparently expected anything but tears. "Carol? What's wrong? What did I say?" He wrapped his arms around her and brought her head to his shoulder.

Carol wanted to resist his touch, but she so desperately needed it that she buried her face in the curve of his neck and wept. Alex's arms were warm and safe, his hands gentle. She did love him. Somewhere between his rescue the night her car broke down and the camping trip, her well-guarded heart had succumbed to his appeal. But falling in love was one thing; marriage and children were something else entirely.

"Come on," Alex finally said. He opened the car door for her.

"Where are we going?" she asked, sniffling.

"My house. James won't be home yet, and we can talk without being disturbed."

Carol wasn't sure what more he could say, but she agreed with a nod of her head and climbed inside. He closed the door for her, then paused and ran a hand over his eyes, slumping wearily.

Neither of them said much during the ten-minute drive. He helped her out of his car, then unlocked the front door to his house. His suitcases had been haphazardly dumped on the living room carpet. When he saw Carol looking at them, he said simply, "I was in a hurry to find you." He led the way into the kitchen and started making a pot of coffee.

Carol pulled out a stool at the counter and seated herself. His kitchen—in fact, his home—wasn't at all what she expected. A woman's touch could be seen and felt in every room. The kitchen was yellow and cheery. What remained of the evening light shone through the window above the sink, sending warm shadows across the polished tile floor. Matching ceramic canisters lined the counter, along with a row of well-used cookbooks.

"Okay, Carol, tell me what's on your mind," Alex urged, facing her from behind the tile counter. Even then Carol wasn't safe from his magnetism.

"That's the problem," she said, swallowing hard. "I don't *know* what's on my mind. I'm so confused...."

"I realize my proposal came out of the blue, but once

you think about it, you'll understand how perfect we are for each other. Surely you've thought about it yourself."

"No," she said quickly, and for emphasis, shook her head. "I hadn't...not once. Marriage hadn't occurred to me."

"I see." He raised his right hand to rub his eyes again.

Carol knew he must be exhausted and was immediately overcome with remorse. She *did* love Alex, although admitting it—to herself as much as to him—had sapped her strength.

"What do you want to do?" he asked softly.

"I'm not sure," she whispered, staring down at her hands, which were tightly clenched in her lap.

"Would some time help?"

She nodded eagerly.

"How long?"

"A year. Several months. At the very least, three or four weeks."

"How about two weeks?" Alex suggested.

"Two weeks," she echoed feebly. That wasn't nearly enough. She couldn't possibly reach such an important decision in so little time, especially when there were other factors to consider. Before she could voice a single excuse, Alex pressed his finger to her lips.

"If you can't decide in that length of time, then I doubt you ever will."

A protest came and went in a single breath. There were so many concerns he hadn't mentioned—like their sons!

She was about to bring this up when Alex said, "I don't think we should draw the boys into this until we know our own minds. The last thing we need is pressure from them."

Carol agreed completely.

The coffee had finished perking, and Alex poured them each a cup. "How about dinner Friday night? Just the two of us." At her hesitation, he added, "I'll give you the rest of this week to sort through your thoughts, and if you still have any questions or doubts by Friday, we can discuss them then."

"But not a final decision?" Carol murmured, uneasy with the time limitation. He'd said two weeks, and she was going to need every minute to make up her mind.

Carol woke around three with her stomach in painful knots. She lay on her side and at a breath-stopping cramp, she tucked her knees under her chin. A wave of nausea hit her hard, and she couldn't stifle a groan. Despite her flu shot last fall, maybe she'd caught one of the new strains that emerged every year.

She lay perfectly still in the fervent hope that this would ward off her growing need to vomit. It didn't work, and a moment later she was racing for the bathroom.

Afterward, sitting on the floor, her elbows on the edge of the toilet, she breathed deeply.

"Are you all right?" Peter asked from behind her.

"I will be. I just need a couple more minutes."

"What's wrong?" Peter asked. He handed her a warm washcloth, following that with a cup of water.

"The flu, I guess."

He helped her to her feet and walked her back to her bedroom. "I appreciate the help, Peter, but it would be better if you went back to bed. I'll be fine by morning."

"I'll call work for you and tell them you're too sick to come in."

She shook her head. "No… I'll need to talk to them myself." Her son dutifully arranged the blankets around her, giving her a worried look before he slipped out of her bedroom.

Peter must have turned off her alarm because the next thing Carol knew it was eight-thirty. The house was eerily silent.

Sitting up, she waited for an attack of nausea. It didn't come. She'd slept without waking even once. She was astonished that she hadn't heard Peter roaming about. He was usually as noisy as a herd of rampaging buffalo. Perhaps he'd overslept as well.

In case he had, she threw the sheets back, sat on the edge of the bed and shoved her feet into slippers before wandering into the kitchen. The minute she stepped inside, it was obvious that her son had been up and about. A box of cold cereal stood in the middle of the kitchen table, along with a bowl half-filled with milk and crusts from several pieces of toast.

Posted on the refrigerator door was a note from Peter, informing her that he'd phoned the hospital and talked to her supervisor, who'd said Carol didn't need to worry about coming in. He proudly added that he'd made his own lunch and that he'd find a ride home from track practice, so she should stay in bed and drink lots of fluids. In a brief postscript he casually mentioned that he'd also called Grandma Pasquale.

Carol's groan had little to do with the way she was feeling. All she needed was her mother, bless her heart, hovering over her and driving her slowly but surely crazy. No sooner had the thought formed in her mind than the doorbell chimed, followed by a key turning in the lock and the front door flying open. Her mother burst into the house as though Carol lay on her deathbed.

"Carol," she cried, walking through the living room. "What are you doing out of bed?"

"I'm feeling much better, Mama."

"You look terrible. Get back in bed before the under-taker gets wind of how you look."

"Ma, please, I'm just a little under the weather."

"That's what my uncle Giuseppe said when he had the flu, God rest his soul. His wife never even got the chicken stewed, he went that fast." She pressed her hands together, raised her eyes to the ceiling and murmured a silent prayer.

"Peter shouldn't have phoned you," Carol grumbled. She certainly didn't need her mother fussing at her bedside, spooning chicken soup down her throat every time she opened her mouth.

"Peter did the right thing. He's a good boy."

At the moment Carol considered that point debatable.

"Now back to bed before you get a dizzy spell." Her mother made a shooing motion with her hands.

Mumbling under her breath, Carol did as Angelina insisted. Not because she felt especially ill, but because arguing required too much energy. Carol might as well try to talk her mother into using canned spaghetti sauce as convince her she wasn't on her deathbed.

Once Carol was lying down, Angelina dragged the rocking chair into her bedroom and sat down. Before another minute had passed, she was busy with her knitting. Several balls of yarn were lying at her feet in case she wanted to start a second or third project in the next few hours.

"According to Peter you were sick in the middle of the night," Angelina said. Eyes narrowed, she studied Carol, as if staring would reveal the exact nature of her daughter's illness. She shook her head, then paused to count the neat row of stitches before glancing back at Carol, clearly expecting an answer.

"It must've been something I ate for dinner," she suggested lamely.

"Peter said you were looking at parts of a toilet no one should see that close up."

Her teenage son certainly had a way with words. "I'm feeling better," she said weakly.

"Your face is paler than bleached sheets. Uncle Giuseppe has more color than you, and he's been in his grave for thirty years."

Carol leaned back against the pillows and closed her eyes. She might be able to fool just about anyone else, but her mother knew her too well.

Several tense minutes passed. Angelina said not a word, patient to a fault. Yes, her mother knew; Carol was sure of it. She kept her eyes closed, afraid that another searching look would reveal everything. Oh, what the heck, Angelina would find out sooner or later.

"Alex asked me to marry him last night." Carol tried to keep her voice even, but it shook noticeably.

"Ah," her mother said, nodding. "That explains everything. From the time you were a little girl, you got an upset stomach whenever something troubled you, although why you should be troubled when this man tells you he loves you is a whole other question."

Carol didn't need to hear stories from her childhood to recognize the truth.

"So what did you say to him?"

"Nothing," she whispered.

"This man brings color to your cheeks and a smile to your eyes and you said *nothing?*"

"I...need time to think," Carol cried. "This is an important decision.... I've got more than myself and my own life to consider. Alex has a son and I have a son.... It isn't as simple as it sounds."

Her mother shook her head. Her rocker was going ninety

miles an hour, and Carol was positive the older woman's thoughts were churning at equal speed.

"Don't be angry with me, Mama," she whispered. "I'm so frightened."

Angelina stopped abruptly and set her knitting aside. She reached for Carol's hands, holding them gently. A soft smile lit her eyes. "You'll make the right decision."

"How can you be so sure? I've been wrong about so many things—I've made so many mistakes in my life. I don't trust my own judgment anymore."

"Follow your heart," Angelina urged. "It won't lead you wrong."

But it would. She'd followed her heart when she married Bruce, convinced their love would see them through every difficulty. The marriage had been a disaster from the honeymoon on, growing more painful and more difficult with each passing day. The horror of those years with Bruce had shredded her heart and drained away all her self-confidence. She'd offered her husband everything she had to give, relinquished her pride and self-respect— and to what end? Bruce hadn't appreciated her sacrifices. He hadn't cherished her love, but turned it into something cheap and expendable.

"Whatever you decide will be right," her mother said once again. "I know it will be."

Carol closed her eyes to mull over her mother's confidence in her, which she was sure was completely unfounded. Angelina seemed to trust Carol's judgment more than Carol did herself.

A few minutes later, her mother started to sing softly, and her sweet, melodious voice harmonized with the clicking of the needles.

The next thing Carol knew, it was early afternoon and she could smell chicken soup simmering in the kitchen.

Angelina had left a brief note for her that was filled with warmth and encouragement. Feeling much better, Carol helped herself to a bowl of the broth and noodles and leisurely enjoyed her first nourishment of the day.

By the time Peter slammed into the house several hours later, she was almost back to normal.

"Mom," he said rushing into the room. His face was flushed and his eyes bright. It looked as though he'd run all the way home. His chest was heaving as he dropped his books on the table, then tried to catch his breath, arms waving excitedly.

"What is it?" Carol asked, amused by the sight her son made.

"Why didn't you *say* anything?" he demanded, kissing both her cheeks the way her mother did whenever she was exceptionally pleased. "This is great, Mom, really great! Now we can go fishing and camping and hiking all the time."

"Say anything about what?" she asked in bewilderment. "And what's this about fishing?"

"Marrying Mr. Preston."

Carol was half out of her seat before she even realized she'd moved. "Who told you…who so much as mentioned it was a possibility?"

"A possibility?" Peter repeated. "I thought it was a done deal. At least that's what James said."

"James told you?"

Peter gave her a perplexed look. "Who else? He told me about it first thing when I got to school this morning." He studied her, his expression cautious. "Hey, Mom, don't look so upset—I'm sorry if you were keeping it a secret.

Don't worry, James and I think it's a great idea. I've always wanted a brother, and having one who's my best friend is even better."

Carol was so outraged she could barely talk. "H-he had no business saying a word!" she stammered.

"Who? James?"

"Not James. Alex." If he thought he'd use the boys to influence her decision, he had another think coming.

Carol marched into her bedroom, throwing on a pair of jeans and an old sweatshirt. Then she hurried into the living room without bothering to run a brush through her tousled hair.

"Where are you going?" Peter demanded. He'd ladeled himself a bowl of soup and was following her around the house like a puppy while she searched for her purse and car keys.

"Out," Carol stormed.

"Looking like that?" He sounded aghast.

Carol whirled around, hands on her hips, and glared at him.

Peter raised one hand. "Sorry. Only please don't let Mr. Preston see you, all right?"

"Why not?"

Peter raised his shoulder in a shrug. "If he gets a look at you, he might withdraw his proposal. Honestly, Mom, this is the best thing that's happened to us in years. Don't go ruining it."

Chapter 11

James answered the door, and a smile automatically came to his lips when he saw it was Carol. Then his eyes narrowed as though he wasn't sure it was her, after all. Carol realized he was probably taken aback by her appearance. Normally she was well-dressed and well-groomed, but what Alex had done—had tried to do—demanded swift and decisive action. She didn't feel it was necessary to wear makeup for this confrontation.

"Where is he?" Carol asked through gritted teeth.

"Who? Dad?" James frowned. "He's watching the news." The teenager pointed toward the family room, which was adjacent to the kitchen.

Without waiting for James to escort her inside, Carol burst past him, intent on giving Alex a piece of her mind. She was furious. More than furious. If he'd honestly believed that involving the boys would affect her decision, then he knew absolutely nothing about her. In fact, he knew so little, they had no business even considering marriage.

She refused to be pressured, tricked, cajoled or anything else, and before this day was over Alex would recognize that very clearly indeed.

"Carol?" Alex met her halfway into the kitchen. His eyes softened perceptibly as he reached for her.

Carol stopped just short of his embrace. "How dare you," she snapped.

"How dare I?" Alex repeated. His eyes widened with surprise, but he remained infuriatingly calm. "Would you elaborate, please, because I'm afraid I have no idea what you're talking about."

"Oh, yes, you do."

"Dad?" James ventured into the kitchen, giving Carol a wide berth. "Something must really be wrong," the boy said, and then his voice dropped to a whisper as he pointed to Carol's feet. "Mrs. Sommars is wearing two different shoes."

Carol's gaze shot downward, and she mentally groaned. But if either of the Preston men thought they'd throw her off her guard by pointing out that she'd worn a blue tennis shoe on her right foot and a hot-pink slipper on her left, then she had news for them both.

"I have the feeling Mrs. Sommars was in a hurry to talk to me," Alex explained. The smile that quivered at the corners of his mouth did little to quell her brewing temper.

James nodded. "Do you want me to get lost for a few minutes?"

"That might be a good plan," Alex replied.

James exchanged a knowing look with his father before discreetly vacating the room. As soon as Carol heard

James's bedroom door close, she put her hands on her hips, determined to confront Alex.

"How dare you bring the boys into this," she flared.

"Into what?" Alex walked over to the coffeepot and got two mugs. He held one up to her, but she refused the offer with a shake of her head. "I'm sorry, Carol, but I don't know what you're talking about."

Jabbing her index finger at him, she took several steps toward him. "Don't give me that, Alex Preston. You know very well what I mean. We agreed to wait, and you saw an advantage and without any compunction, you took it! Did you really think dragging Peter and James into this would help? How could you be so foolish?" Her voice shook, but her eyes were as steady as she could make them.

"I didn't mention the possibility of our getting married to James, and I certainly didn't say anything to Peter." He leaned against the kitchen counter and returned her disbelieving glare with maddening composure.

Angrily Carol threw back her head. "I don't believe you."

His eyes hardened but he didn't argue with her. "Ask James then. If he heard that I'd proposed to you, the information didn't come from me."

"You don't expect me to believe that, do you?" she cried, not nearly as confident as she'd been earlier. The aggression had gone out of her voice, and she lowered her hands to her sides, less certain with each minute. The ground that supported her outrage started to shift and crumble.

"I told you I wouldn't bring the boys into this," he reminded her smoothly. "And I didn't." He looked over his shoulder and shouted for James, who opened his bedroom door immediately. Carol didn't doubt for an instant that he'd had his ear pressed to it the entire time they'd been talking.

With his hands in his jean pockets, James strolled casually into the room. "Yes, Dad?"

"Do you want to tell me about it?"

"About what?" James wore a look of complete innocence.

"Apparently you said something to Peter about the relationship between Mrs. Sommars and me. I want to know what it was and where you found out about it." Alex hadn't so much as raised his voice, but Carol recognized that he expected the truth and wouldn't let up until he got it.

"Oh…that," James muttered. "I sort of overheard you saying something to Uncle Barn."

"Uncle Barn?" Carol asked.

"A good friend of mine. He's the one I was telling you about who kept Jim while I was out of town."

"Call me *James*," his son reminded him.

Alex lifted both hands. "Sorry."

"Anyway," James went on to say, "you were on the phone last night talking to him about the basketball game tonight, and I heard you say that you'd *asked* Carol—Mrs. Sommars. I'm not stupid, Dad. I knew you were talking about the two of you getting married, and I thought that Peter and I had a right to know. You should've said something to us first, don't you think?"

"For starters, this whole marriage business is up in the air—when and if anything's decided, you two boys will be the first to find out."

"What do you mean, the wedding's up in the air?" This piece of information obviously took James by surprise. "Why? What's the holdup? Peter and I think it's a great idea. We'd like it if you two got married. It'd be nice to have a woman around the house. For one thing, your cooking could use some help. But if you married Mrs. Sommars—"

"James," Alex broke in, "I think it's time for you to go back to your room before Carol decides she wants nothing more to do with the likes of us."

James looked affronted, but without further questions, he pivoted and marched back into his bedroom.

Alex waited until his son was out of sight. He sighed loudly and rammed his fingers through his hair. "I'm sorry, Carol. I had no idea James overheard my conversation with Barney. I thought he was asleep, but I should've been more careful."

"I…understand," Carol whispered, mollified.

"Contrary to what James just said," Alex continued, the line of his mouth tight and unyielding, "I don't want to marry you for your cooking skills. I couldn't care less if you never cooked again. I love you, and I'm hoping we can make a good life together."

James tossed open his bedroom door and stuck out his head. "Peter says she's as good a cook as his grandmother. She's—"

Alex sent his son a look hot enough to melt tar.

James quickly withdrew his head and just as quickly closed his door.

"I'll talk to Peter and explain the mix-up, if you'd like," Alex offered.

"No… I'll say something to him." Suddenly self-conscious, Carol swung her arms at her sides and retreated a couple of steps. "I suppose I should get home…."

"You were sick last night?" Alex asked, his expression concerned. "James told me when I picked him up after school. I would gladly have given Peter a ride, but he'd apparently found another way because he was gone before James could find him."

"Peter decided to run home."

"But you *had* been ill?"

She nodded. "I…must've caught a twenty-four-hour bug." Her eyes darted around the room. She felt so foolish, standing there with her hair a tangled mess, wearing the oldest clothes she owned, not to mention mismatched shoes.

"You're feeling better today?"

"A lot better. Thank you." She was slowly but surely edging toward the front door. The sooner she escaped, the better it would be for everyone involved. If Alex was merciful, he'd never mention this visit again.

She was all the way across the living room and had just reached the front door, when Alex appeared behind her. As she whirled around, he flattened his hands on either side of her head.

"Have you come to a decision?" he asked softly. His gaze dropped to her mouth. "Do you need any help?"

"The only thing I've managed to come up with is the flu," she murmured in a feeble attempt at humor. Alex wasn't amused, however, and she rushed to add, "Obviously you want to know which way I'm leaning, but I haven't had time to give your proposal much thought. I will, I promise I will…soon." She realized she was chattering, but couldn't seem to stop. "We're still on for Friday night, aren't we? We can discuss it then and—"

The doorbell chimed, frightening Carol out of her wits. She gasped and automatically catapulted herself into Alex's arms. He apparently didn't need an excuse to hold her close. When he released her several awkward seconds later, he smiled at her, then kissed the tip of her upturned nose.

"That'll be Barney now. It's time the two of you met."

"*That* was Carol Sommars?" Barney asked for the third time. He scratched his jaw and continued to frown. "No wonder Bambi mistook her for a bag lady. I'm sorry, man, you're my best friend and we've been buddies for a lot of years, but I've got to tell you, you can do better than that."

Chuckling, Alex dismissed his friend's statement and walked into the family room. If he lived to be a hundred, he'd never forget Carol's mortified look as she bolted from the house.

Barney certainly hadn't helped the situation any. Doing his best to keep a straight face, Alex had introduced the two. Barney's eyes had widened and his mouth had slowly dropped open in disbelief. It took a moment before he had the presence of mind to step forward and accept Carol's outstretched hand. Barney had mumbled that it was a pleasure to finally meet her, but his eyes had said something else entirely.

"Trust me," Alex felt obliged to explain, "she doesn't always look like that."

Barney stalked over to the refrigerator and opened it. He stared inside for a long time before he reached for a cold beer. "What time do the Trail Blazers play?"

Alex checked his watch. Both he and Barney were keen fans of Portland's professional basketball team. The team had been doing well this year and were in the first round of the play-offs. "Seven."

"So," Barney said, making himself comfortable in the overstuffed chair. He crossed his legs and took a long swig of beer. "What happened to her foot?" he asked casually. "Did she sprain it?"

"Whose foot?"

"Carol's," Barney said, casting Alex a questioning glance. "She was wearing a slipper—you mean you didn't notice? Did she twist her ankle?"

"Nah," James answered for Alex, wandering into the

family room holding a bag of pretzels. He plopped himself down on the sofa, resting his legs on the coffee table. "Peter says she does weird stuff like that all the time. Once she wore his swimming goggles in the shower."

Barney raised his eyebrows. "Should I ask why?"

"It made sense—sort of—when Peter explained it. His mother had gone to one of those cosmetics stores and they put some fancy makeup on her eyes, and she didn't want to ruin it when she took a shower, so she wore Peter's rubber goggles."

"Why didn't she just take a bath?" Barney asked. He threw Alex a look that suggested his friend have his head examined.

"She couldn't take a bath because the faucet was broken," James said, "and her brother hadn't gotten around to fixing it yet."

"That makes sense," Alex said in Carol's defense.

Barney rolled his eyes and tipped the beer bottle to his lips.

To his credit, Barney didn't say anything else about Carol until James was out of the room. "You're really serious about *this* woman?" His question implied that Alex had introduced Barney to the wrong one, and that the whole meeting was a setup to some kind of joke that was to follow.

"I'm totally serious. I told you I asked her to marry me—I can't get any more serious than that."

"And she's *thinking* about it?" Barney asked mockingly. Being the true friend he was, Barn clearly couldn't understand why Carol hadn't instantly leaped at Alex's offer.

To be honest, Alex wondered the same thing himself. True, he'd blurted out his proposal in a parking lot. He still had trouble believing he'd done anything so crazy. As a contractor, he'd sold himself and his company hundreds of times. He'd prepared bids and presented them with polish and professionalism. He always had solid arguments that made his proposals sound attractive and intelligent. Carol deserved nothing less.

But something had happened to him when he'd visited her birthing class. Something enigmatic and profound. Even now he had to struggle not to get choked up when he thought about it.

After nearly two weeks in Texas, Alex had been starved for the sight of her, and he'd barely noticed the others in the class. In retrospect, he was sure his reaction could be attributed to seeing all those soon-to-be mothers.

In fifteen years Alex hadn't given babies more than a passing thought. He had a son and was grateful for that. He might have suffered a twinge of regret when he learned there'd be no more children, but he'd been more concerned about his wife's well-being than the fact that they wouldn't be adding to their family.

Then he'd watched Carol with those pregnant couples, and the desire for another child, a daughter, had suddenly overwhelmed him. He'd decided while he was in Texas that he loved Carol and wanted to marry her, but the idea of starting a family of their own hadn't so much as crossed his mind. But why not? They were both young enough and healthy enough to raise a houseful of children.

He'd been standing at the back of her class, waiting for her, when it happened. Out of nowhere, yet as clear as anything he'd ever seen or felt, Alex saw Carol pregnant with a child. *His* child. He'd realized at the time that this—he used the word *vision* for lack of a better one—was probably due to physical and emotional exhaustion. Wanting to hold on to the image as long as he could, he'd closed his eyes. He'd pictured her…. Her breasts were full, and when she smiled at him, her eyes had a radiance that couldn't be described. She'd taken his hand and settled it on her protruding stomach. In his fantasy he'd felt their child move.

This fantasy was what had prompted the abrupt marriage proposal. He wanted to kick himself now. If he'd taken her in his arms, kissed her and said all the things she deserved to hear, things might have gone differently. He hadn't meant to rush her, hadn't meant to be so pushy, but once he'd realized how resistant she was to the idea, he'd panicked. The two-week ultimatum was unfair. He'd tell her that on Friday night when they went out for dinner.

Then again, maybe he wouldn't. He'd wait to hear what she was thinking, which way she was leaning, before he put his foot any farther down his throat.

Then he began to smile. Perhaps it wasn't too late for a proper proposal, after all.

"Alex?"

His name seemed to be coming from some distance away.

"What?" he asked, pulling himself out of his thoughts.

"The game's started," Barney said. "Don't you want to see it?" He peered closely at Alex. "Is something wrong with you?"

Yes, something *was* wrong, and there was only one cure. Carol Sommars.

Carol dressed carefully for her dinner date with Alex Friday evening. After going through her closet and laying half of everything she owned across the bed, she chose a demure, high-necked dress of soft pink that buttoned down the front. That seemed safe enough, especially with a shawl.

She'd hardly ever felt this awkward. Trying to make her decision, she'd swayed back and forth all week. One day she'd decide she would be a fool *not* to marry him, and the next, she'd been equally convinced she'd be crazy to trust a man a second time.

Marrying Alex meant relinquishing her independence. It meant placing herself and her son at the mercy of another human being. Memories of her marriage to Bruce swiped at her viciously, and whenever she contemplated sharing her well-ordered life with another man, she broke into a cold sweat.

Years ago, someone had told her it took a hell of a man to replace no man. It wasn't until Carol graduated from college with her nursing degree and was completely on her own that she fully understood that statement. Her life was good, too good to tamper with, and yet...

Her thoughts were more confused than ever when the doorbell chimed. She paused, took a calming breath and headed across the room.

"Hello, Alex," she said, smiling stiffly.

"Carol."

He looked gorgeous in a three-piece suit. Her eyes took him in, and she felt some of the tension leave her muscles. It was when she met his eyes that she realized he was chuckling.

"We're going to dinner," he said, nodding at her dress, "not a baptism."

She blinked, not sure she understood.

"If that collar went any higher up your neck, it'd reach your nose."

"I... I was removing temptation," she said, embarrassed by the blush that heated her face.

"Honey, at this rate, the only thing we'll be removing is that dress."

Carol decided the best thing to do was ignore his remark. "Did you say where we're going for dinner?"

"No," he answered cryptically, and his warm eyes caressed her with maddening purposefulness. "I didn't. It's a surprise."

"Oh." After all the time they'd been together, after all the moments she'd spent in his arms, after all the dreams she'd had about Alex, she shouldn't feel this uncomfortable. But her heart was galloping, her hands felt damp, her breath was coming in soft gasps—and they hadn't even left her house yet.

"Are you ready?"

It was a question he shouldn't have asked. *No*, her mind screamed. *Yes*, her heart insisted. "I guess so," her lips answered.

Alex led her outside and held open his car door.

"It was thoughtful of you to drop the boys at the theater. Personally I don't think they were that keen on seeing a Disney movie," she said, slipping inside his car.

"Too bad. I gave them a choice of things to do this evening."

"Attending a kids' movie on the other side of town or being set adrift in the Columbia River without paddles probably isn't their idea of a choice."

Alex chuckled. "I don't want anyone disturbing us tonight."

Their eyes met. Alex's were hot and hazy and so suggestive, Carol's heart skipped a beat. For sanity's sake, she looked away.

"I hope you like steak."

"I love it."

"The champagne's cooling."

"You must've ordered in advance," she murmured, having difficulty finding something to do with her hands. Her fingers itched to touch him...*needed* to touch him. A need that only confused her more.

"I...hope you explained to Barney—your friend—that I...that I don't normally look the way I did the evening we met. When I got home and saw myself in the mirror...well, I could just imagine what he must've thought." Carol cursed the madness that had sent her rushing out of her house that evening to confront Alex.

"Barney understood."

"Oh, good."

A couple of minutes later, Alex turned into his own driveway. Carol looked at him, somewhat surprised. "Did you forget something?"

"No," he said.

A moment later, he let her into the house. She paused in the doorway, and her heart gave a sudden, sharp lurch. They weren't going to any restaurant. Alex had always planned to bring her back to his house.

The drapes were drawn, and the lights had been lowered. Carol saw that the dining room table was set with crystal and china. Two tapered candles stood in the middle of the table, waiting to be lit.

Alex went over to the stereo and pushed a single button. Immediately the room was drenched with the plaintive sound of violins.

Carol was still trying to assimilate what was happening when he walked over to the table and lit the candles. Tiny flames sent a golden glow shimmering across the pristine white cloth.

"Shall we?" Alex said, holding out his hands.

Carol was too numb to reply. He took the lacy shawl from her shoulders and draped it over the back of the sofa.

Then he pulled her purse from her unresisting fingers and set it next to the shawl. When he'd finished, he turned and eased her into his arms.

Their bodies came gently together, and a shudder went through her. She wasn't a complete fool—she knew what Alex was planning. She lowered her eyelids. Despite her doubts and fears, she wanted this, too.

For a moment, she battled the feeling, then with a deep sigh, she surrendered.

Alex wrapped his arms around her. "Oh, baby," he whispered in her ear. "You feel so good."

She emptied her lungs of air as his hands slid down her back, to her waist.

There was music, such beautiful music, and then Carol realized they were supposed to be dancing. She rested her fingertips on his shoulders as his mouth moved toward hers. Carol sighed. Alex's breath was moist and warm, his hands gentle as they pressed her closer and closer.

When he kissed her, the moment of anticipation ended, and Carol felt a tremendous surge of relief. He groaned. She groaned. He leaned back and began to unfasten the buttons at her throat.

That all too brief pause helped Carol collect her scattered senses. "Alex," she whispered, "what are you doing?"

"Undressing you."

"Why?" she asked breathlessly, knowing what a stupid question it was.

"Why?" he repeated with amusement. "Because we're going to make love."

Her pulse went wild.

"I love you," he said. "You love me. Right?"

"Oh...yes."

"Good." He kissed her again, so passionately she could

hardly resist—and yet she had to. She broke away from him with what little strength she still possessed.

"Alex…please don't."

"Tonight's a new beginning for us. I'm crazy in love with you. I need you so much I can't think straight anymore."

"You brought me here to make love to me, didn't you?"

"You mean it wasn't obvious?" he asked as he nibbled kisses along the side of her neck.

"Why now? Why not that night on the Washington coast…? Why tonight?"

"Carol, do we need to go through this evaluation?"

"I have to know," she cried, pushing herself away from him. Her hands trembled, and it was with some difficulty that she rebuttoned her dress. "The truth, Alex. I want the truth."

"All right," he murmured. "I thought… I believed that if we made love, it would help you decide you wanted to marry me."

Carol felt as though he'd tossed a bucket of ice water in her face. She raised her hand to her pounding heart. "Oh, no…" she whispered. "Not again."

"Carol? What's wrong?"

"Bruce did this to me, too…pressured me into giving in to him…then he hated me…punished me…." Blindly she reached for her purse and shawl, then headed for the front door.

Alex caught up with her before she made it outside. His hand clasped her shoulder as he turned her to face him. By then she was sobbing, her whole body trembling with terror. Stark terror—stark memories.

Alex took one look at her and hauled her into his arms. "Carol." He threaded his fingers through her hair. "It's all right, it's all right. I would *never* have forced you."

Chapter 12

All Carol could do was cry, and the pile of used tissues was mounting. Alex tried to comfort her, to help her, but everything he did seemed to make matters worse. One thing he'd immediately recognized—she didn't want him to touch her.

She'd curled herself up on his sofa and covered her face as she wept. She wouldn't talk to him. She wouldn't look at him. The only comprehensible statement she'd made in the last fifteen minutes had been a demand that he take her home.

Fear knotted his stomach. He had the inexplicable feeling that if he did as she asked, he'd never see her again. He had tonight and only tonight to repair the trust he'd unwittingly destroyed.

"Carol, I'm sorry." He must have told her that twenty times. It was true enough. Everything he tried to do with this woman was wrong. Tonight was the perfect example.

For days he'd been searching for a way to prove to Carol how much he loved her and how right they were for each other.

This evening had seemed the perfect place and time. He'd planned it all—the music, champagne, the carefully worded proposal, the diamond ring.

He'd thought that if everything went well, they'd make love, and afterward, they could discuss the details of their wedding and their lives. He wanted her in his bed, and although it was more than a little arrogant of him, he didn't think he'd have any problem getting her there.

He'd also come to the conclusion that once they made love, she'd be convinced that they belonged together, and their marriage would naturally follow.

At first, his plan had worked flawlessly. Carol had walked into the house, seen that the table was set and the candles ready to light. She'd looked at him with those huge eyes of hers and given him a seductive smile. Then, with barely a pause, she'd waltzed into his arms.

From there everything had gone downhill.

One minute he was kissing her, marveling at the power she had over his body, and the next, she was cold and trembling, demanding answers that should've been obvious.

"Would you like some coffee?" he asked her gently for the second—or was it the third?—time. Although his arms ached with the need to hold her, he resisted.

"No," she whispered. "I want to go home."

"We need to talk first."

"Not now. I *need* to go home." She rubbed her face and plucked a clean tissue from the nearby box. Apparently she'd regained her resolve because she stood, wrapped her shawl around her, and stumbled to the door. "If you won't drive me, then I'll walk."

Alex heard the desperation in her voice and was helpless to do anything other than what she asked. As he stood, the regret swept through him. If there was anything he could do to ease her pain, he would've done it. If there were any words he could have uttered to comfort her, he would've said them gladly. But all she wanted him to do was take her back to her own home. Back to her own bed. Her own life.

Who did he think he was? Some Don Juan who could sweep this beautiful, sensitive woman into his bed and make love to her? He felt sick to his stomach at the way he'd plotted, the way he'd planned to use her body against her, to exploit the attraction between them to serve his own ends.

Now he was losing her, and there wasn't anyone he could blame but himself. He'd known his chances weren't good the night he'd asked her to marry him. He'd hoped to see joy in her eyes when he suggested it. He'd longed to see happiness on her face. He'd wanted Carol to hurl herself into his arms, excited and overcome with emotion.

He should've known he'd been watching too many old movies.

He'd asked Carol to marry him, and none of the things he'd hoped for had happened. Instead, her eyes had reflected fear. And tonight…tonight he'd witnessed stark terror.

Alex was astute enough to realize the problem lay in Carol's brief marriage. Whatever had gone on had left deep emotional scars. Even when he'd felt the closest to her, Alex had learned very little about her relationship with her late husband. She'd let tidbits of information drop now and then, but every time she did, Alex had the feeling she'd regretted it.

On her way out the door, Carol grabbed a handful of

fresh tissues, and with nothing more to say, Alex led the way to his car.

He opened the passenger door, noticing how she avoided any possibility of their accidentally touching as she climbed inside.

The tension inside the car made the air almost too thick to breathe. He could hardly stand it and he wondered how she could.

When he braked at a stop sign, he decided to make one last effort.

"Carol, please, how many times do I have to tell you how sorry I am? I made a mistake. I behaved like a jerk. Tell me what you want me to do, because I'll do it. Anything you say. I love you! You've got to believe I'd never intentionally do anything to hurt you."

His pleas were met with more of the same strained, intolerable silence.

In frustration he pressed his foot to the gas, and they shot ahead. The seat belts were all that kept them from slamming forward with the car.

The fiercest argument of their courtship now ensued, and the crazy part was, neither of them uttered a word. Every once in a while, Alex could hear Carol drag a breath through her lungs, and he knew she was doing everything in her power not to cry. Each tear she shed, each sob she inhaled, felt like a knife wound.

He was losing her, and there wasn't a thing he could do about it. It wouldn't be so tragic if he didn't care for her so much. After Gloria's death, Alex had never truly believed he'd fall in love again. Even when he'd made the decision to remarry, he hadn't expected to find the depth of emotion he'd experienced with Carol.

And now it might be too late.

* * *

"Hey, Mom, did you and Mr. Preston have a fight or something?" Peter asked the following morning.

"W-why do you ask?"

Peter popped two frozen waffles in the toaster, then stood guard over them as though he expected Carol to snatch them out of his hands.

"I don't know. Mr. Preston was acting strange last night when he picked us up from the movie."

"Strange?"

"Sad. Mr. Preston's usually loads of fun. I like him, I mean, he's about the neatest adult I know. He doesn't treat me like I'm a kid, and he likes the same things I like and—I don't know—I just think he's an all-around great guy. Fact is, Mom, men don't come much better than James's dad."

"He is...nice, isn't he?" she agreed. She tightened her fingers around the handle of her coffee mug and looked anywhere but at her son.

Peter leaned toward her and squinted. "Have you been crying?"

"Don't be silly," she said lightly, trying to make a joke out of it.

"Your eyes are all puffy and red like you have an allergy or something."

"Pollen sometimes affects me that way." Which was the truth. It just didn't happen to be affecting her eyes at that particular moment.

The waffles popped up, and Peter grabbed them, muttering under his breath when he burned his fingers. He spread a thin layer of butter on them and followed that with a puddle of syrup. Once that task was complete, he added two more waffles to the toaster, then sat across the table from Carol.

"I kind of thought you and Mr. Preston might've had a fight," Peter said, obviously feeling it was safe to probe some more. "That would've been too bad because on the way to the movie he was telling us that he wanted to make this dinner the most romantic night of your life. Was it?"

"He...tried."

"How did the Baked Alaska taste?"

"The Baked Alaska?" Carol made a nondescript gesture. "Oh...it was great."

"Mr. Preston made everything himself. Right down to the salad dressing. James told me he'd been shopping for days. It would've been terrible if you'd had a fight and ruined it.... You love Mr. Preston, don't you?" Peter asked earnestly.

Carol closed her eyes to the emotion assaulting her from all sides. She would be lying if she didn't admit it. And her heart refused to let her lie. But no one seemed to understand that love wasn't a cure-all. She'd loved Bruce, too—or thought she did—and look where that had gotten her.

"Yes," she whispered. She'd averted her gaze, but she could hear Peter's sigh of relief.

"I knew you did," he said cheerfully, slicing into his waffle. "I told James you were wild about his dad and that whatever happened at dinner would be okay in the morning."

"I'm sure you're right," Carol murmured.

An hour later, Carol was working in the garden space Alex had tilled for her several weeks earlier. She was cultivating the soil, preparing it to plant several different herbs that afternoon. She'd done her homework and discovered a wide variety that grew well in the moist climate of the Pacific Northwest.

Her back was to the kitchen, and she hadn't heard the doorbell. Nor was there the usual commotion that occurred whenever Peter let someone in.

Yet without a doubt, she knew Alex was standing in the doorway watching her. She felt his presence in the same way she experienced his absence.

Running her forearm across her damp brow, she leaned back and removed her gloves. "I know what you want to say," she said, "and I think it would be best if we just dropped the whole issue."

"Unfortunately that's a luxury neither of us can afford."

"I knew you were going to say that," she sighed, awkwardly struggling to an upright position. The knees of her jeans were caked with mud and the sweat was pouring down her flushed face.

There'd probably been only two other times in her life when she'd looked worse, and Alex had seen her on both occasions.

With the cultivator gripped tightly in her fist, she walked over to the patio and sank down on a deck chair. "All right, say what you have to say."

Alex grinned. "Such resignation!"

"I'd rather be working in my garden."

"I know." He flexed his hands a couple of times. "I suppose I should start at the beginning."

"Oh, Alex, this isn't necessary, it really isn't. I overreacted last night. So, you made a mistake—you're only human and I forgive you. Your intentions weren't exactly honorable, but given the circumstances they were understandable. You wanted to take me into your bed and afterward make an honest woman of me." She made quotation marks with her fingers around the words *honest woman.* "Right?"

"Something like that," he mumbled. Although of course the issue was much more complicated than that....

"The thing is, I've been made an honest woman once and it was the biggest mistake of my life. I'm not planning to repeat it."

"What was your husband's name?" Alex asked without preamble.

"Bruce...why?"

"Do you realize you've never told me?"

She shrugged; she never talked about Bruce if possible.

"Tell me about him, Carol," Alex pleaded, "tell me everything. Start with the minute you noticed each other and then lead me through your relationship to the day you buried him."

"I can't see how that would solve anything."

"Tell me, Carol."

"No." She jumped to her feet, her heart in a panic. "There's nothing to say."

"Then why do you close up tight anytime someone mentions him?"

"Because!" She paced the patio. Stopping abruptly, she whirled around and glared at him, angry all over again. "All right, you want to know? I'll tell you. We were teenagers—young, stupid, naive. We made out in the back seat of a car...and when I got pregnant with Peter we got married. Bruce died three years later in a car accident."

An eternity passed before Alex spoke again. "That's just a summary. Tell me what *really* happened in those three years you were married." His voice was soft and insistent.

Her chest constricted painfully. Would nothing satisfy him short of blood? How could she ever hope to describe three years of living in hell? She couldn't, and she didn't even want to try.

Alex wouldn't understand, and nothing she could ever say would help him. What purpose would it serve to dredge up all that misery? None that she could see.

Slowly she lowered herself onto the deck chair again, trying to still her churning thoughts, to nullify the agonizing memories. The pain was so distinct, so acute, that she opted for the only sane solution. She backed away.

Alex reached for her hand, holding it loosely. "I know this is difficult."

He didn't know *how* difficult.

"Bruce and I were married a long time ago. Suffice it to say that the marriage wasn't a good one. We were much too young…and Bruce had…problems." She bit her lip, not willing to continue. "I don't want to drag up the past. I don't see how it would do any good."

"Carol, please."

"No," she said sharply. "I'm not about to dissect a marriage that ended thirteen years ago simply because *you're* curious."

"We *need* to talk about it," he insisted.

"Why? Because I get a little panicky when you start pressuring me into bed? Trust me, any woman who's gone through what I did would react the same way. You know the old saying—once burned, twice shy." She tried to make light of it and failed. Miserably.

For the longest time Alex said nothing. He did nothing. He stared into the distance, and Carol couldn't tell where his thoughts were taking him.

"I never expected to fall in love again," he said.

Carol frowned at the self-derision in his words.

"Gloria knew I would, but then she always did know me better than I knew myself." He paused for a moment, and he gave a sad, bitter smile. "I'll never forget the last time we were able to talk. The next day she slipped into a coma, and soon afterward, she died. She knew she was dying and had accepted it. The hospital staff knew it was only a matter of time. But I couldn't let go of her. I had such faith that God would save her from this illness. Such unquestionable trust. He did, of course, but not the way I wanted."

"Alex…" Tears were beginning to blur her vision. She didn't want to hear about Gloria and the wonderful marriage he'd had with her. The contrast was too painful. Too bleak.

"Gloria took my hand and raised her eyes to mine and thanked me for staying at her side to the very end. She apologized because she'd been ill. Can you imagine anyone doing that?"

"No." Carol's voice was the faintest of whispers.

"Then she told me God would send another woman into my life, someone healthy and whole who'd love me the way I deserved to be loved. Someone who'd share my success and who'd love our son as much as she did." He paused and smiled again, but it was the same sad smile. "Trust me, this was the last thing I wanted to hear from my wife. First of all, I was in denial, and I refused to believe she was dying, and second, nothing could have convinced me I'd ever love another woman as much as I loved Gloria."

Carol shut her eyes tightly and took deep breaths to keep from weeping openly.

"She told me that when I met this other woman and decided to marry her, I shouldn't feel guilty for having fallen in love again. She must've known that would be something powerful I'd be dealing with later. She squeezed my fingers—she was so weak, and yet, so strong. And wise, so very wise. Within a few hours she was gone from me forever." He rubbed his eyes and hesitated before continuing.

"I didn't believe her. I didn't think it would be possible to love anyone as much as I loved her.

"Then I met you, and before I knew it, I was falling in love all over again." Once more he brought a weary hand to his face. His expression was blank, his eyes unrevealing. "And again I'm relinquishing the woman I love." He paused. "I'll give you the two weeks to make your decision, Carol. In fact, I'll make it easy for you. I won't call or contact you until the seventh—that's exactly two weeks from the day we talked about it. You can tell me your decision then. All right?"

"All right," she agreed, feeling numb.

Slowly he nodded, then stood and walked out of her house.

"The way I see it," Peter said, holding a red Delicious apple in one hand and staring at his mother, "James's dad can adopt me."

Carol felt the fleeting pain that tore through her every time Peter not-so-casually mentioned Alex's name. He seemed to plan these times with precision. Just when she least expected it. Just when she was sure she knew her own mind. Just when she was feeling overly confident. Then *pow*, right between the eyes, Peter would toss some remark carefully chosen for its effect. It was generally preceded by some bit of information about Alex or a comment about how wonderful life would be when they were one big, happy family.

"I'd have to marry Alex first, and I'm not sure that's going to happen," she said reproachfully. One challenging look defied him to contradict her.

"Well, it makes sense, doesn't it? *If* you marry him, naturally." Peter took a huge bite of the apple. Juice dribbled down his chin, and he wiped it away with the back of his hand. "I haven't heard from Dad's family in years, and they wouldn't even care if someone adopted me. That way we could all have the same last name. Peter Preston has a cool sound to it, don't you think?"

"Peter," she groaned, frustrated and angered by the way he turned a deaf ear to everything she said. "If this is another tactic to manipulate me into marrying Alex so you can go fishing, then I want you to know right now that I don't appreciate it."

She was under enough pressure—mainly from herself—and she didn't need her son applying any more.

"But, Mom, think about how good our lives would be if you married Mr. Preston. He's rich—"

"I've heard all of this conversation that I want to. Now sit down and eat your dinner." She dished up the crispy fried pork chop and a serving of rice and broccoli, and set the plate on the table.

"You're not eating?" Peter asked, looking mildly disappointed. "This is the third night you've skipped dinner this week."

Carol's appetite had been nil for the entire two weeks. "No time. I've got to get ready for class."

"When will these sessions be over?"

"Two more weeks," she said, walking into her bedroom. *Two weeks* seemed to be the magical time period of late. Alex had given her two weeks to decide if she'd accept his proposal. Two weeks that were up today. He'd granted her the breathing space she needed to come to a sensible decision. Only "sensible" was the last thing Carol felt. It shouldn't be this difficult. She wondered why she had so many doubts if she loved Alex—which she did. But Carol knew the answer to that.

Alex's marriage had been wonderful.

Hers had been a disaster.

He was hoping to repeat what he'd shared with Gloria.

She wanted to avoid the pain Bruce had brought into her life.

"Mom...phone."

Carol froze. She'd been on tenterhooks waiting for Alex to contact her. All day she'd felt a growing sense of dread. She'd expected Alex to come strolling out from behind every closed door, to suddenly appear when she least expected him.

The last thing she'd figured he'd do was phone.

With one shoe on, she hobbled over to her nightstand and picked up the phone, wondering what she was going to say.

"Hello."

"Carol, it's your mother."

"Hello, Ma, what can I do for you?" Relief must have been evident in her voice.

Angelina Pasquale said, "I was in church this morning, lighting a candle to St. Rita, when something happened to my heart."

"Did you see your doctor?" Carol's own heart abruptly switched gears. Her greatest fear was losing her mother to heart disease the way she'd lost her father.

"Why should I see a doctor?" her mother protested. "I was talking to God—in my heart—and God was telling me I should have a talk with my daughter Carol, who's deciding if she's going to marry this rich non-Italian or walk away from the best thing since the invention of padded insoles."

"Mama, I've got a class—I don't have time to talk."

"You've seen Alex?"

"Not...yet."

"What are you going to tell him?"

Her mother was being as difficult as Peter. Everyone wanted to make up her mind for her. Everyone knew what she should do. Everyone except Carol.

"You know he's not Catholic, don't you?" she told her mother, who had once considered that an all-important factor in choosing a husband. Religion and an equally vital question—whether her potential husband was allergic to tomatoes.

Her mother snickered. "I know he's not Catholic! But don't worry, I've got that all worked out with God."

"Mama, I'm sorry, but I have to leave now or I'll be late for my class."

"So be late for once in your life. Who's it gonna hurt? All day I waited, all day I said to myself, my *bambina's* going to call and tell me she's going to marry again. I want to do the cooking myself, you tell him that."

"Mama, what are you talking about?"

"At the wedding. No caterers, understand? I got the menu all planned. We'll serve—"

"Ma, please."

It took Carol another five minutes to extricate herself from the conversation. Glancing at her watch, she groaned. Rushing from room to room, she grabbed her purse, her other shoe and her briefcase. She paused on her way out the door to kiss Peter on the cheek and remind him to do his homework. Then she jumped in the car, still wearing only one shoe.

Her breathing was labored by the time she raced through traffic and pulled into the parking lot at the community center where the birthing classes were held.

She'd piled everything she needed in her arms, including her umbrella, when she realized she'd left her lecture notes at the house.

"Damn," she muttered. She took two steps before she remembered she was carrying her shoe.

"It might help if you put that on instead of holding it in your arms."

Carol froze. She whirled around, angry and upset, directing all her emotion at Alex. "This is *your* fault," she said, dropping her shoe to the ground and positioning it with her toe until she could slip her foot inside. "First, Peter's on my case, and now my mother's claiming she received a message directly from God and that He's worked out a deal with her, since you're not Catholic, and frankly, Alex—don't you dare laugh." She finished with a huge breath. "I swear, if you laugh I wouldn't marry you if you were the last living male in the state of Oregon."

"I'm sorry," he said, holding up both hands.

"I should hope so. You don't know what I've been through this past week."

"Your two weeks are up, Carol."

"You don't need to tell me that. I know."

"You've decided?"

Her eyes shut, and she nodded slowly. "I have," she whispered.

Chapter 13

"Before you tell me what you've decided," Alex said, moving toward Carol, his eyes a smoky gray, "let me hold you."

"Hold me?" she echoed meekly. Alex looked one-hundred-percent male, and the lazy smile he wore was potent enough to tear through her defenses.

"I'm going to do much more than simply hold you, my love," he whispered, inching his way toward her.

"Here? In a parking lot?"

Alex chuckled and slipped his arms around her waist, tugging her closer. Carol had no resistance left in her. She'd been so lonely, so lost, without him. So confused.

His mouth brushed hers. Much too briefly. Much too lightly.

Carol didn't want him to be gentle. Not when she was this hungry for his touch. Her lips parted in a firm and wanting kiss. Alex sighed his pleasure and she clung to him, needing him.

When they drew apart, she rested her forehead against his. "Okay," Alex said, his breath warm and heavy. "Tell me. I'm ready now."

"Oh, Alex," she murmured, and her throat constricted with ready tears. "I can't decide. I've tried and tried and tried, and the only thing I really know is I need more time."

"Time," he repeated. Briefly he closed his eyes. His shoulders sagged with defeat. "You need more time. How much? A week? A month? Six months? Would a year fit into your schedule?" He broke away from her and rubbed his hand along the back of his neck. "If you haven't made up your mind by now, my guess is you never will. I love you, Carol, but you're driving me insane with this waiting."

"Can't you see things from my point of view?" she protested.

"No, I can't," he said. "I'm grateful for this time we've had, because it's taught me something I hadn't been willing to recognize before. I'm lonely. I want someone in my life—someone permanent. I want you as my wife. I *need* you as my wife. But if you don't want what I'm offering, then I should cut my losses and look elsewhere."

A strangled cry erupted from her lips. He was being so unfair, pressuring her like this. Everything had to be decided in *his* time frame, without any allowance for doubts or questions. Something broke in Carol. Control. It was all about control. She couldn't—wouldn't—allow another man to control her the way Bruce had.

"I think you're right, Alex," she finally said. "Find yourself someone else."

The shock of her words hit him like a blow to the head. He actually flinched, but all the while his piercing eyes continued to hold hers. Carol saw the regret and the pain flash through his burning gaze. Then he buried his hands in his pockets, turned and marched away.

It was all Carol could do not to run after him, but she knew that if she did she'd be giving up her self-respect.

Janice Mandle stuck her head out the door and scanned the parking lot. She looked relieved when she saw Carol, and waved.

Carol waved back. Although she wanted nothing more than to be alone, she didn't have any choice but to teach her class.

Janice called, mentioning the time.

Still Carol couldn't seem to tear her gaze from Alex, holding on to him for as long as she could. He made her feel things she'd never known she was capable of experiencing. When he kissed her, she felt hot and quivery, as though she'd just awakened from a long, deep sleep. Spending time with him was fun and exciting. There'd been adventures waiting to happen with this man. Whole new worlds in the making. Yet something was holding her back. Something powerful. She wanted everything Alex was offering, and at the same time her freedom was too precious, too important.

Carol didn't see Alex again until the end of the week, when the boys were participating in the district track meet. James was running in the four-hundred-and eight-hundred-meter races, and Peter was scheduled for the 1500-meter. On their own, the two friends had decided to choose events in which they weren't competing together. Carol had been impressed with their insight into each other's competitive personalities.

Carol's mother had decided to attend the meet with her. Angelina was as excited as a kid at the circus. They'd just settled themselves in the bleachers when out of the corner of her eye, Carol saw Alex. Since they both had sons involved in track, she knew avoiding him would be nearly impossible, but she hadn't expected to see him quite so soon. Although, in retrospect, she should've realized he'd be attending this important meet.

Preparing herself, she sat stiffly on the bleachers as Alex strolled past. Instantly her heart started to thunder. His friend was with him, the one she'd met briefly—Barney or Bernie... Barney, she decided. Her hands were tightly clenched in her lap, and she was prepared to exchange polite greetings.

To her consternation, Alex didn't so much as look in her direction. Carol knew it would've been nearly impossible for him to have missed seeing her. If he'd wanted to hurt her, he'd done so—easily.

"So when does the man running with the torch come out?" Angelina asked.

"That's in the Olympics, Mama," Carol answered, her voice weak.

Her mother turned to look in Carol's direction, and her frown deepened. "What's the matter with you?" she demanded. "You look as white as bleached flour."

"It's nothing."

"What is it?" Angelina asked stubbornly.

"Alex...just walked past us."

"Not *the* Alex?"

Carol nodded. Before she could stop her mother, Angelina rose to her feet and reached for Carol's binoculars. "Where is he? I want to get a good look at this man who broke my daughter's heart."

"Ma, please, let's not get into that again." The way her mother had defended her had touched Carol's heart, although Angelina hadn't wasted any time berating her daughter's foolishness, either. She'd spent most of Sunday muttering at Carol in Italian. Carol wasn't fluent enough to understand everything, but she got the gist of it. Angelina thought Carol was a first-class fool to let a man like Alex slip through her fingers.

"I want one look at this Alex," Angelina insisted. She raised the binoculars to her face and twisted the dials until she had them focused correctly. "I'm gonna give this man the eye. Now tell me where he's sitting."

Carol knew it would be easier to bend a tire iron than persuade her mother to remove the binoculars and sit down before she made a scene.

"He's on your left, about halfway up the bleachers. He's wearing a pale blue sweater," she muttered. If he glanced in her direction, she'd be mortified. Heaven only knew what interpretation he'd put on her mother glaring at him through a set of field glasses, giving him what she so quaintly called "the eye."

Her mother had apparently found him, because she started speaking in Italian. Only this time her comments were perfectly understandable. She was using succulent, suggestive phrases about Alex's sexual talents and how he'd bring Carol pleasure in bed.

"Ma, *please*," Carol wailed. "You're embarrassing me."

Angelina sat down and put the glasses on her lap. She began muttering in Italian again, leaning her head close to Carol.

"Ma!" she cried, distressed by the vivid language her mother was using. "You should have your mouth washed out with soap."

Angelina folded her hands and stared at the sky. "Such beautiful *bambinos* you'd have with this man."

Carol closed her eyes at the image of more children—hers and Alex's. Emotion rocked through her.

Her mother took the opportunity to make a few more succinct remarks, but Carol did her best to ignore them. It seemed as if the track meet wasn't ever going to begin. Carol was convinced she'd have to spend the afternoon listening to her mother whispering in her ear. Just when she couldn't endure it any longer, the kids involved in the hurdle events walked over to the starting line. They shook their arms at their sides and did a couple of stretching exercises. Carol was so grateful to have her mother's attention on the field that it was all she could do not to rush out and kiss the coach.

The four-hundred-meter race followed several hurdle events. Carol watched James through the binoculars as he approached the starting line. He looked confident and eager. As they were taking their positions, he glanced into the stands and cocked his head just slightly, acknowledging his father's presence. When his gaze slid to Carol, his eyes sobered before he smiled.

At the gun, the eight boys leapt forward. Carol immediately vaulted to her feet and began shouting at the top of her lungs.

James crossed the finish line and placed second. Carol's heart felt as though it would burst with pride. Without conscious thought her gaze flew to Alex, and she saw that he looked equally pleased by his son's performance. He must have sensed her watching him because he turned his head slightly and their eyes met. He held on to hers for just a moment, and then with obvious reluctance looked away.

Carol sagged onto her seat.

"So who is this boy you scream for like a son?" her mother demanded.

"James Preston—the boy who finished second."

"So that was Alex's son?" Angelina asked slowly, as she took the binoculars and lifted them to her eyes once more. She was apparently satisfied with what she saw, because she grinned. "He's a fine-looking boy, but he's a little on the thin side. He needs my spaghetti to put some meat on those bones."

Carol didn't comment. She *did* love James like a son. That realization forced a lump into her throat. And her heart—her poor, unsuspecting heart—was fluttering hard enough to take flight and leave her body behind.

Feeling someone's eyes on her, she glanced over her shoulder. Instantly Alex turned away. Carol's hands began to tremble, and all he'd done was look in her direction....

James raced again shortly afterward, placing third in the eight-hundred-meter. For a high school sophomore, he was showing a lot of potential, Carol mused, feeling very proud of him.

When her own son approached the starting line for his race, Carol felt as nervous as she ever had in her life....

Since the 1500-meter meant almost four long turns around the track, it didn't have the immediacy of the previous races. By the time Peter was entering the final lap, Carol and her mother were on their feet, shouting their encouragement. Carol in English. Angelina in Italian. From a distance, Carol heard a loud male voice joining theirs. Alex.

When Peter crossed the finish line in a solid third position, Carol heaved a sigh of pride and relief. Tears dampened her lashes, and she raised her hands to her mouth. Both the first-and second-place winners were seniors. As a sophomore, Peter had done exceptionally well.

Again, without any conscious decision on her part, Carol found herself turning to look at Alex. This time he was waiting for her, and they exchanged the faintest of smiles. Sad smiles. Lonely smiles. Proud smiles.

Carol's shoulders drooped with defeat. It was as if the worlds of two fools were about to collide.

He was pushy. She was stubborn.

He wanted a wife. She wanted time.

He refused to wait. She refused to give in.

Still their eyes held, each unwilling to pull away. So many concerns weighed on Carol's heart. But memories, too—good memories. She remembered how they'd strolled through the lush green foliage of the Washington rain forest. Alex had linked his fingers with hers, and nothing had ever felt more right. That same night they'd sat by the campfire and sung with the boys, and fed each other roasted marshmallows.

The memories glided straight to Carol's heart.

"Carol?"

Dragging her gaze away from Alex, Carol turned to her mother.

"It's time to leave," Angelina said, glancing into the stands toward Alex and his friend. "Didn't you notice? The stadium's almost empty, and weren't we supposed to meet Peter?"

"Yes…" Carol murmured, "we were…we are."

Peter and James strolled out of the locker room and onto the field together, each carrying a sports bag and a stack of school books. Judging by their damp hair, they'd just gotten out of the shower.

Carol and her mother were waiting where Peter had suggested. It seemed important to keep them as far away from the school building as possible for fear any of his friends would realize he had a family.

Alex didn't seem to be anywhere nearby, and for that

Carol was grateful. And even if it made no sense, she was also regretful. She wanted to be as close to him as she could. And yet she'd happily move to the Arctic Circle to escape him. Her thoughts and desires were in direct contrast and growing more muddled every second.

Peter and James parted company about halfway across the field. Before they went their separate ways, they exchanged a brief nod, apparently having agreed or decided upon something. Whatever it was, Peter didn't mention it.

He seemed unusually quiet on the ride home. Carol didn't question her son until they'd dropped her mother off. "What's bothering you?"

"Nothing." But he kept his gaze focused straight ahead.

"You sure?"

His left shoulder rose and fell in an indecisive shrug.

"I see."

"Mr. Preston was at the meet today. Did you see him?"

"Ah…" Carol hedged. There was no reason to lie. "Yeah. He was sitting with his friend."

"Mr. Powers and Mr. Preston are good friends. They met in college."

Carol wasn't sure what significance, if any, that bit of information held.

"According to James, Mr. Powers's been single for the past couple years, and he dates beautiful women all the time. He's the one who arranged all those hot dates for James's dad…and he's doing it again."

"That's none of our business." Her heart reacted to that, but what else could she expect? She was in love with the man. However, it wasn't as if Alex hadn't warned her; he'd said that if she wasn't willing to accept what he was offering, it was time to cut his losses and look elsewhere. She just hadn't expected him to start so soon.

"James was telling me his dad's been going out every night this week."

"Peter," she said softly, "I think it would be best if we made it a rule not to discuss Alex or his dating practices. You know, and, I hope, have accepted, the fact that the relationship between James's dad and me is over...by mutual agreement."

"But, Mom, you really love this guy!"

She arched her eyebrows at that.

"You try to fool me, but I can see how miserable you've been all week. And Mr. Preston's been just as unhappy, James says, and we both think he's going to do something stupid on the rebound, like marry this Babette girl."

"Peter, I thought I just said I don't want to talk about this."

"Fine," he muttered, crossing his arms and beginning to sulk. Five minutes passed before he sighed heavily. "Babette's a singer. In a band. She's not like the run-of-the-mill bimbos Barney usually meets. Mom, you've got to *do* something. Fast. This woman is real competition."

"Peter!" she cried.

"All right. All right." He raised both hands in surrender. "I won't say another word."

That proved to be a slight exaggeration. Peter had ways of letting Carol know what was going on between Alex and his newfound friend without ever having to mention either name.

Saturday, after playing basketball with James in the local park, Peter returned home, hot and sweaty. He walked straight to the refrigerator and took out a cold can of soda, taking the first swallows while standing in front of the open refrigerator.

Carol had her sewing machine set up on the kitchen

table. Pins pressed between her lips, she waved her hand, instructing her son to close the door.

"Oh, sorry," Peter muttered. He did as she asked, then wiped his face. "Ever hear of a thirty-six-year-old man falling head over heels in love with a twenty-three-year-old woman?" Peter asked disdainfully.

Stepping on a nail couldn't have been more painful—or more direct—than her son's question. "No. Can't say that I have," she said, so flustered she sewed a seam that was so crooked she'd have to immediately take it out. With disgust, she tossed the blouse aside, and when her son had left the room, she trembled and buried her face in her hands.

On Sunday morning, Peter had stayed in church a few extra minutes after Mass, walking up to the altar. When he joined Carol in the vestibule, she placed her hand on his shoulder and studied him carefully. She'd never seen her son quite so serious.

"What's on your mind, honey?"

He gave her another of his one-shoulder rolls. "I thought if Grandma could talk to God, then I'd try it, too. While I was up there, I lit a candle to St. Rita."

Carol didn't respond.

After that, she and her son drove over to her mother's house. The tears started when she was in the kitchen helping Angelina with dinner. It surprised Carol, because she had nothing to cry about—not really. But that didn't seem to matter. Soon the tears were flowing from her eyes so hard and fast that they were dripping from her chin and running down her neck.

Standing at the sink washing vegetables helped hide the fact that she was weeping, but that wouldn't last long. Soon someone would see she was crying and want to know why.

She tried desperately to stop, but to no avail. If anything, her efforts only made her cry more.

She must've made more noise than she realized, because when she turned to reach for a hand towel to wipe her face, she found her mother and her sister-in-law both staring at her.

Her mother was murmuring something to Paula in Italian, which was interesting since the other woman didn't understand a word of the language. But Carol understood each and every one. Her mother was telling Paula that Carol looked like a woman who was in danger of losing the man she loved.

With her arm around Carol's shoulders, Angelina led her into her bedroom. Whenever Carol was ill as a little girl, her mother had always brought her to her own bed and taken care of her there.

Without resistance, Carol let her mother lead her through the house. By now the tears had become soft sobs. Everyone in the living room stopped whatever they were doing and stared at her. Angelina fended off questions and directed Carol to her bed, pulling back the blankets. Sniffling, Carol lay down. The sheets felt cool against her cheeks, and she closed her eyes. Soon she was asleep.

She woke an hour later and sat bolt upright. Suddenly she knew what she had to do. Sitting on the edge of the bed, she held her hands to her face and breathed in deep, steadying breaths. This wasn't going to be easy.

Her family was still busy in the living room. The conversation came to an abrupt halt when Carol moved into the room. She picked up her purse, avoiding their curious eyes. "I...have to go out for a while. I don't know when I'll be back."

Angelina and Peter walked to the front door with her, both looking anxious.

"Where are you going?" her son asked.

She smiled softly, kissed his cheek and said, "St. Rita must have heard your prayers."

Her mother folded her hands and raised her eyes to heaven, her expression ecstatic. Peter, on the other hand, blinked, his gaze uncertain. Then understanding apparently dawned, and with a shout, he threw his arms around Carol's neck.

Chapter 14

Alex was in the kitchen fixing himself a sandwich when the doorbell chimed. From experience, he knew better than to answer it before James did. Leaning against the counter, Alex waited until his son had vaulted from the family room couch, passed him and raced toward the front door.

Alex supposed he should show some interest in his unannounced guest, but frankly he didn't care—unless it was one stubborn Italian woman, and the chances of that were more remote than his likelihood of winning the lottery.

"Dad," James yelled. "Come quick!"

Muttering under his breath, Alex dropped his turkey sandwich on the plate and headed toward the living room. He was halfway through the door when he jerked his head up in surprise. It was Carol. Through a fog of disbelief, he saw her, dressed in a navy skirt and white silk blouse under a rose-colored sweater.

At least the woman resembled Carol. His eyes must be

playing tricks on him, because he was sure this woman standing inside his home was the very one who'd been occupying his thoughts every minute of every hour for days on end.

"Hello, Alex," she said softly.

It sounded like her. Or could it be that he needed her so badly that his troubled mind had conjured up her image?

"Aren't you going to say anything?" James demanded. "This is Carol, Dad, Carol! Are you just going to stand there?"

"Hello," he finally said, having some trouble getting his mouth and tongue to work simultaneously.

"*Hello?* That's it? You aren't saying anything more than that?" James asked, clearly distressed.

"How are you?" Carol asked him, and he noticed that her voice was husky and filled with emotion.

Someday he'd tell her how the best foreman he ever hoped to find had threatened to walk off the job if Alex's foul mood didn't improve. Someday he'd let her know he hadn't eaten a decent meal or slept through an entire night since they'd parted. Someday he'd tell her he would gladly have given a king's ransom to make her his wife. In time, he *would* tell her all that, but for now, all he wanted to do was enjoy the luxury of looking at her.

"Carol just asked you a question. You should answer her," James pointed out.

"I'm fine."

"I'm glad," she whispered.

"How are you?" He managed to dredge up the polite inquiry.

"Not so good."

"Not so good?" he echoed.

She straightened her shoulders, and her eyes held his as

she seemed to be preparing herself to speak. "Do you…are you in love with her, because if you are, I'll… I'll understand and get out of your life right now, but I have to know that much before I say anything else."

"In love with her?" Alex felt like an echo. "With whom?"

"Babette…the singer you've been dating."

James cleared his throat, and, looking anxious, glanced at his father. "I…you two obviously need time alone. I'll leave now."

"James, *what* is Carol talking about?"

His son wore an injured look, as if to suggest Alex was doing him a terrible injustice by suspecting he had anything to do with Carol's belief that he was seeing Babette.

"James?" He made his son's name sound like a threat.

"Well," the boy admitted with some reluctance, "Mrs. Sommars might've gotten the impression that you were dating someone else, from…from something I said to Peter. But I'm sure whatever I said was very nebulous." When Alex glared at him, James continued. "All right, all right, Peter and I got to talking things over, and the two of us agreed you guys were wasting a whole lot of time arguing over nothing.

"Mrs. Sommars is way, way better than any of the other women you've dated. Sometimes she dresses a little funny, but I don't mind. I know Peter would really like a dad, and he says you're better than anyone his mom's ever dated. So when Uncle Barn started pressuring you to date that Babette, we… Peter and I, came up with the idea of…you know…"

"I don't know," Alex said sternly, lacing his words with steel. "Exactly what did you say to Carol?"

"I didn't," James was quick to inform him. "Peter did all

the talking, and he just casually let it drop that you were dating again and…"

"And had fallen head over heels in love with someone else," Carol supplied.

"In the space of less than a week?" Alex demanded. Did she really think his love was so fickle he could forget her in a few short days? He'd only retreated to fortify himself with ideas before he approached her again.

"You said it was time to cut your losses and look else-where," she reminded him.

"You didn't believe that, did you?"

"Yes… I thought you must've done it, especially when Peter started telling me about you and…the singer. What else was I supposed to believe?"

"I'll just go to my room now," James inserted smoothly. "You two go ahead and talk without having to worry about a kid hanging around." He quickly disappeared, leaving only the two of them.

"I'm not in love with anyone else, Carol," Alex said, his eyes holding hers. "If you came because you were afraid I was seeing another woman, then rest assured it isn't true. I'll talk to James later and make sure this sort of thing doesn't ever happen again."

"It won't be necessary."

"It won't?" he asked, frowning. They stood across the room from each other, neither of them making any effort to bridge the distance. The way Alex felt, they might as well have been standing on opposite ends of a football field… playing for opposing teams.

Her eyes drifted shut, and she seemed to be gathering her courage. When she spoke, her voice was low and trem-bling. "Don't be angry with James…"

"He had no right to involve himself in our business."

"It worked, Alex. It...worked. When I believed I was losing you, when I thought of you with another woman in your arms, I... I wanted to die. I think maybe I did, just a little, because I realized how much I love you and what a fool I've been to think I could go on without you. I needed time, I *demanded* time, and you wouldn't give it to me..."

"I was wrong—I understood that later."

"No," she countered, "you were right. I would never have made up my mind because...because of what happened in my marriage. With Bruce."

The whole world seemed to go still as comprehension flooded Alex's soul. "Are you saying...does this mean you're willing to marry me?" he asked, barely able to believe what she was saying. Barely able to trust himself to stay where he was a second longer.

Alex didn't know who moved first, not that it mattered. All that did matter was Carol in his arms, kissing him with a hunger that seemed to consume them both.

"Yes...yes, I'll marry you," she cried between kisses. "When? Oh, Alex, I'm so anxious to be your wife."

Alex stifled the sudden urge to laugh, and the equally powerful urge to weep. He buried his face in the soft curve of her neck and swallowed hard before dragging several deep breaths through his lungs. He slid his hands into her hair as he brought his mouth to hers, exploring her lips in all the ways he'd dreamed of doing for so many sleepless nights.

Her purse fell to the floor, and she wound her arms around him, moved against him, whispering over and over how much she loved him.

"I missed you so much," he told her as he lifted her from the carpet and carried her across the room. He was so famished for her love that he doubted he'd ever be satisfied.

"I thought I'd never kiss you again," she moaned. "I couldn't bear the thought of not having you in my life."

Alex made his way to the sofa, throwing himself on the cushions, keeping her in his lap. He stroked her hair as he gazed into her beautiful dark eyes. Unable to resist, he kissed her again.

When they drew apart, Alex rested his forehead against hers and closed his eyes, luxuriating in the warm sensations inside him. He didn't want to talk, didn't want to do anything but hold her and love her.

"Alex," she whispered. "You asked me about Bruce, and I didn't tell you. I was wrong to hold back, wrong not to explain before."

"It's all right, my..."

She gently stroked his face. "For both our sakes, I need to tell you."

"You're sure?"

She didn't *look* sure, but she nodded, and when she started speaking, her voice trembled with pain. "I was incredibly young and naive when I met Bruce. He was the most fun-loving, daring boy I'd ever dated. The crazy things he did excited me, but deep in my heart I know I'd never have married him if I hadn't gotten pregnant with Peter."

Alex kissed her brow and continued to stroke her hair.

"Although Bruce seemed willing enough to marry me," she began, "I don't know how much pressure my father applied." Her voice was gaining strength as she spoke. "It was a bad situation that grew worse after Peter was born. That was when Bruce started drinking heavily and drifted from one job to another. Each month he seemed to be more depressed and more angry. He claimed I'd trapped him and he was going to make sure I paid for what I did." She closed her eyes and he heard her sigh. "I did pay, and so did Peter. My life became a nightmare."

Alex had suspected things were bad for her, but he'd no idea how ugly. "Did he beat you, Carol?"

Her eyes remained closed, and she nodded. "When Bruce drank, the demon inside him would give rise to fits of jealousy, fear, depression and hatred. The more he drank, the more the anger came out in violent episodes. There were times I thought that if I didn't escape, he'd kill me."

"Didn't your family know? Surely they guessed?"

"I hardly ever got to see them. Bruce didn't approve of me visiting my family. In retrospect, I realize he was afraid of my father. Had Dad or Tony known what was happening, they would've taken matters into their own hands. I must have realized it, too, because I never told them, never said a word for fear of involving them. It was more than that.... I was too humiliated. I didn't want anyone to know about the terrible problems we were having, so I didn't say anything—not even to my mother."

"But surely there was someone?"

"Once...once Bruce punched me so hard he dislocated my jaw, and I had to see a doctor. She refused to believe all my bruises were due to a fall. She tried to help me, tried to get me to press charges against him, but I didn't dare. I was terrified of what Bruce would do to Peter."

"Oh, Carol." The anger Alex was experiencing was so profound that he clenched his fists. The idea of someone beating this warm, vibrant woman filled him with impotent rage.

"I'd lost any respect I ever had for Bruce shortly after we were married. Over the next three years I lost respect for myself. What kind of woman allows a man to abuse her mentally and physically, day after day, week after week, year after year? There must've been something terribly wrong with me. In ways I can't even begin to understand, all the hurtful, hateful things Bruce accused me of began to seem valid."

"Oh, Carol…" Alex's chest heaved with the weight of her pain.

"Then Bruce didn't come home one night. It wasn't unusual. I knew he'd come back when he was ready, probably in a foul mood. That was what I'd braced myself for when the police officer came to tell me Bruce had been killed in an accident. I remember I stared up at the man and didn't say anything. I didn't feel anything.

"I was hanging clothes on the line, and I thanked him for letting me know and returned to the backyard. I didn't phone anyone, I didn't even cry."

"You were in shock."

"I suppose, but later when I was able to cry and grieve, mingled with all the pain was an overwhelming sense of relief."

"No one could blame you for that, my love," Alex said, wanting with everything in him to wipe away the memories of those years with her husband.

"Now…now do you understand why I couldn't tell you about Bruce?" she asked. "Your marriage to Gloria was so wonderful—it's what a marriage was meant to be. When she died, your love and James's love surrounded her. When Bruce died—" she hesitated, and her lips were trembling "—he was with another woman. It was the final rejection, the final humiliation." She drew in a ragged breath and turned, her eyes burning into his. "I don't know what kind of wife I'll be to you, Alex. Over the years I've thought about those three nightmarish years and I've wondered what would've happened had I done things differently. Maybe the fault *was* my own…maybe Bruce was right all along, and if I'd only been a better woman, he wouldn't have needed to drink. If I'd done things differently, he might've been happy."

"Carol, you don't truly believe that, do you?"

"I… I don't know anymore."

"Oh, love, my sweet, sweet love. You've got to realize that any problems Bruce had were of his own making. The reasons for his misery lay within himself. Nothing you could ever have done would've been enough." He cupped her face in his hands. "Do you understand what I'm saying?"

"I… I can't make myself fully believe that, and yet I know it's true. But Alex…this time I want everything to be right." Her eyes were clouded and uncertain, as if she suspected he'd be angry with her.

"It will be," he promised her, and there wasn't a single doubt in his heart.

Carol awoke when dawn silently slipped through the lush drapes of the honeymoon suite. She closed her eyes and sighed, replete, sated, unbelievably happy. Deliriously happy.

From the moment Carol had agreed to become Alex's wife to this very morning, exactly one month had passed. One month. It hardly seemed possible.

In one month, they'd planned, arranged and staged a large wedding, complete with reception, dinner and dance.

True to her word, Carol's mother had prepared a reception dinner that couldn't have been surpassed. Angelina had started dragging out her biggest pots and pans the Sunday afternoon she brought Alex back to the house to introduce him to the family.

Last week, Carol's sisters and their families had all arrived. The wedding became a celebration of love, a family reunion, a blending of families, all at once.

At the reception, Alex had surprised her with the honeymoon trip to Hawaii. The boys were mildly put out that they hadn't been included. Hawaii would have been the perfect place to "check out chicks," as Peter put it. To appease them, Alex promised a family vacation over the Thanksgiving holiday. Peter and James had promptly started talking about a Mexican cruise.

Carol smiled as she savored memories of her wedding day. Peter and James had circulated proudly among the guests, accepting full credit for getting their parents together.

Alex stirred and rolled onto his side, slipping his hand around her waist and tucking his body against hers as naturally as if they'd been married three years instead of three marvelous days.

Carol had been crazy in love with Alex before she married him, but the depth of emotion that filled her after the wedding ceremony made what she'd experienced earlier seem weak by comparison.

Never had she been more in love. Never had she felt so desirable. Just as she'd known it would be, Alex's lovemaking was gentle and unselfish while at the same time fierce and demanding. Thinking of how often and well he'd loved her in the last few days was enough to increase the tempo of her heart.

"Good morning," she whispered, as Alex turned to face her.

"Good morning."

Their eyes met and spoke in silent messages.

He was telling her he loved her. She was saying she

loved him back. He was saying he needed her. She echoed that need.

Alex kissed her again, lightly, his lips as weightless as the creeping sunlight.

"Oh, love," he whispered reverently, spreading moist kisses over her face. "I don't think I'll ever get tired of making love with you."

"I certainly hope not." She smiled at him, brushing a stray curl from his brow. She fought back the ready tears that his love brought so easily to the surface. But it would've been impossible to restrain them. Alex didn't understand her tears, and Carol could find no way to explain.

He tenderly wiped the moisture from her face and kissed her eyes. "I can't bear to see you cry. Please tell me if there's anything I can do...."

"Oh, no..." After all the times they'd made love, learned and explored each other's bodies in the past three days, he still couldn't completely accept her tears, fearing he was the cause. Once again, Carol tried to make him understand. "I... I didn't realize making love could be so wonderful...so good."

Alex momentarily closed his eyes, his look full of chagrin and something else she couldn't name. "We didn't take any precautions last night."

His words triggered a slow easy smile. "I know, and I'm glad."

"Why? I thought we decided to wait a few months before we even considered starting a family.

"What do you think your chances of getting pregnant are?" he asked after several minutes of kissing and touching.

She smiled again. "About a hundred percent."

The room went quiet. When Alex spoke, his voice was strangled. "How would you feel about that?"

"Unbelievably happy. I want your child, Alex."

His mouth found hers again for a kiss that grew wilder and wilder. Nestling her head against his strong shoulder, Carol sighed. She felt happier than she'd ever imagined possible. Happy with her husband, her family, herself.

Epilogue

After all the years Carol had worked as an obstetrical nurse, after all the birthing classes she'd taught, she should be able to recognize a contraction. Still, she wasn't a hundred percent sure and had delayed contacting Alex until she was several hours into labor.

Resting her hands on her distended abdomen, she rubbed it gently, taking in several relaxing breaths. Twins! She and Alex were having *twins*. He felt as excited, as ecstatic, as she did. Maybe even more so… Everything was ready for their babies. The nursery was furnished with two cradles, each with a different mobile hanging above it, and Alex had painted a mural, a forest scene, on the wall for his daughters. All their little sweaters and sleepers were stacked in twin dressers he'd lovingly refinished.

Carol took another deep breath as the next pain struck. Then, knowing she shouldn't delay much longer, she reached for the phone and called Alex at the office.

"Yes," he cried impatiently. This last week he'd been as nervous as...a father-to-be.

"It's Carol."

She heard his soft intake of breath. "Are you all right?"

"I'm fine."

"You wouldn't be calling me at the office if you were fine," he countered sharply. "Is something going on that I should know about?"

"Not really. At least not yet, but I think it might be a good idea if you took the rest of the afternoon off and came home."

"Now?"

"If you're in the middle of a project, I can wait," she assured him, but she hoped he'd be home soon, otherwise she was going to end up driving herself to the hospital.

"I'm not worried about *me*," he said. "Are the babies coming now? Oh, Carol, I don't know if I'm prepared for this."

"Don't worry. I am."

Alex expelled his breath forcefully. "I'll be there in ten minutes."

"Alex," she cried. "Don't speed."

She used the time before his arrival to make some phone calls, then collected her purse and her small suitcase—packed several weeks ago. Finally, she sank into her favorite chair, counting the minutes between contractions.

From a block away, Carol could hear the roar of his truck as he sped toward the house. The squealing of brakes was followed by the truck door slamming. Seconds afterward, Alex vaulted into the house, breathless and pale.

She didn't get up from her chair; instead, Carol held out both hands to him. "Settle down, big daddy."

He flew to her side and knelt in front of her, clasping her hands in his. It took him a moment to compose himself.

"This is it, isn't it? We're in labor?" he asked when he'd found his voice.

"We're in labor," Carol told him and stroked his hair.

"How can you be so calm about this?"

She smiled and bent forward to brush her lips over his. "One of us has to be."

"I know... I know...you need me to be strong for you now, but look at me," he said, holding out his hands for her inspection. "I'm shaking." Gently he laid those same shaking hands on Carol's abdomen, and when he glanced up at her, his eyes were bright with unshed tears. "I love these babies—our daughters—so much. I can't believe how lucky I am. And now that they're about to be born, I feel so humble, so unworthy."

"Oh, Alex..."

"I guess we'd better go. Is there anything we need to do first?"

"No. I've phoned my mother and the doctor, and my suitcase is by the door." She made an effort to disguise the intensity of her next contraction by closing her eyes and breathing slowly and deeply until it passed. When she opened her eyes, she discovered Alex watching her intently. If possible, he looked paler than he had before.

"Are you going to be all right?" she asked.

"I... I don't know. I love our babies, but I love you more than anything. I can't stand to see you in pain. I—"

His words were interrupted by the sound of another car pulling into the driveway and two doors slamming. James burst into the house first, followed by Peter, both looking as excited as if it were Christmas morning.

"What are you two doing home from school?" Carol demanded.

"We heard you were in labor. You don't think we'd miss this, do you?"

"You heard?" Carol echoed. "How? From whom?"

The two boys eyed each other. "We've got our sources," James said.

This wasn't the time or place to question them. "All right, we won't discuss it now. James, take care of your father. Peter, load up the car. I think it might be best if you drove me yourself. James, bring your father—he's in no condition to drive."

Their sons leaped into action. "Come on, Dad, we're going to have a couple of babies," James said, urging his father toward the late-model sedan the two boys shared.

By the time they got to Ford Memorial, Carol's pains had increased dramatically. She was wheeled to the labor room while James and Peter were left to fend for themselves in the waiting room.

Alex was more composed by now, more in control. He smiled shyly and took her hand, clutching it between both of his. "How are you doing?"

"Alex, I'm going to be fine and so are our daughters."

Janice Mandle came bustling in, looking pleased. "Okay, we all ready for this special delivery?" she asked.

"Ready," Carol said, nodding firmly.

"Ready," Alex echoed.

With Janice's help and Alex's love, Carol made it through her next contractions. As she was being taken into the delivery room, Alex walked beside her. The pains were coming faster, but she managed to smile up at him.

"Don't worry," she whispered.

"I love you," he whispered back. He reached for her hand again and they met, palm to palm, heart to heart.

"Grandma, can I have seconds on the zabaglione?" James called from the large family kitchen.

Angelina Pasquale's smile widened and her eyes met those of her daughter. "I told you my cooking would put some meat on his bones."

"That you did, Mama," Carol said, exchanging a private smile with her husband. She and the babies had been home for a week. Royalty couldn't have been treated better. James and Peter were crazy about their sisters, and so far the only tasks allotted Carol had been diaper-changing and breastfeeding. She was well aware that the novelty would wear off, but she didn't expect it to be too soon. Angie and Alison had stolen two teenage hearts without even trying.

"I brought you some tea," Alex said, sliding onto the sofa beside her. His eyes were filled with love. From the moment Carol was brought to the delivery room, the light in Alex's eyes hadn't changed. It was filled with an indescribable tenderness. As she gave birth, his hand had gripped hers and when their two perfect identical daughters were born, there'd been tears in both parents' eyes. Tears of joy. Tears of gratitude. They'd each been granted so much more than they'd ever dreamed. New life. New love. A new appreciation for all the good things in store for them and their combined families.

The soft lilting words of an Italian lullaby drifted toward Carol and Alex. Eyes closed, Carol's mother rocked in her chair, a sleeping infant cradled in each arm. The words were familiar to Carol; she'd heard her mother sing them to her as a child.

When she'd finished, Angelina Pasquale murmured a soft, emotional prayer.

"What did she say?" Alex asked, leaning close to Carol.

A smile tugged at the edges of Carol's mouth. Her fingers were twined with Alex's and she raised his knuckles to her lips and kissed them gently. "She was thanking St. Rita for a job well done."

* * * * *

Also by Lee Tobin McClain

Love Inspired

Rescue Haven

The Secret Christmas Child
Child on His Doorstep

Redemption Ranch

The Soldier's Redemption
The Twins' Family Christmas
The Nanny's Secret Baby

Rescue River

Engaged to the Single Mom
His Secret Child
Small-Town Nanny
The Soldier and the Single Mom
The Soldier's Secret Child
A Family for Easter

HQN

The Off Season

Cottage at the Beach
Reunion at the Shore
Christmas on the Coast
Home to the Harbor

Safe Haven

Low Country Hero
Low Country Dreams
Low Country Christmas

Visit her Author Profile page at Harlequin.com,
or leetobinmcclain.com, for more titles!

THE NANNY'S SECRET BABY

Lee Tobin McClain

This book is dedicated to all parents of children
with autism, especially my friend Laura,
who read parts of this manuscript to help me
portray the condition accurately.
All remaining mistakes are my own.

Therefore if any man be in Christ,
he is a new creature: old things are
passed away; behold, all things are become new.
—*2 Corinthians* 5:17

Chapter 1

Jack DeMoise watched his eighteen-month-old son bang a block against the doctor's desk drawer.

"He's going to need as much attention and support as you can give him," Dr. Rutherford said. "We're learning more and more about this condition. His best odds would be to get a TSS—therapeutic support staff—team on board right away. Hope your wife is organized!"

Jack drew in a breath and let it out slowly before meeting the other man's eyes. "There's no reason you should remember this from the intake papers, but I'm a widower."

The doctor's face fell, just a little. Most people wouldn't even have noticed, but Jack was accustomed to reading emotions carefully, from small tells. It had been a crucial skill with his wife. "Do you work full-time yourself?" the doctor asked.

Jack nodded. "My job can be flexible, though." *Except when it isn't.* "I'm a small-town veterinarian. I've had several good babysitters, but I'm not sure any of them are up to…" He reached down and squeezed his son's shoulder. "To helping me manage Sammy's care the right way."

The doctor frowned. "You need someone experienced with kids, someone who connects well with him. Ideally, a person with special-needs experience, though that's not a requirement. A full-time nanny would be ideal."

And where was he supposed to find such a person in his small Colorado town?

The doctor stood and smiled down at Sammy. "Cute little guy. You can see the people in the front office to schedule his next appointment."

As the doctor left the exam room, Sammy lifted his arms, and Jack knelt to pick him up and held him close.

Autism.

The diagnosis didn't shock him—he'd had suspicions—but the reality of figuring out a coping strategy was hitting him hard.

Two hours later, back at their new home at Redemption Ranch, Jack had just gotten Sammy down for a nap when the sound of a loud, mufflerless car broke the mountain silence. He hurried to close Sammy's window, glanced back at the crib to make sure his son was still sleeping and then looked outside.

From this angle, all he could see was a tangle of red curls emerging from a rusty subcompact.

Arianna. He'd heard she was in town.

He took another deep breath before double-timing it down the steps to anticipate his former sister-in-law's loud knock on the door. Once Sammy was asleep, you didn't want to repeat the complicated process that had made it happen.

He opened the door just as Arianna was lifting her hand

to knock. Under her other arm, she held a giant painting, done in her trademark primitive style.

"When I heard you'd moved, I wanted to bring a house-warming gift," she said. "And a treat for Sammy. Sorry I didn't call first. Is this a bad time?"

"I just got him down," Jack said. He half felt like closing the door in Arianna's face, but he couldn't. She was his son's aunt after all, even if her chronic disorganization and flamboyance had driven his wife crazy, causing some disturbing family fights. Arianna was way out of his comfort zone. "Come on in," he said. "What are you doing in Colorado?"

She waved a hand. "I'm in town visiting family. Thinking about moving back to the area. Penny had mentioned she might do some art therapy with the vets, so I came up to try to sell myself."

"Out of a job again?" he asked as he carried the canvas she'd brought to the middle of the living room. "Pretty," he added, gesturing at the wild yellow painting.

"Jack!" She blew out a sigh he could hear from behind him and then flopped down onto the couch. "Yeah. I'm out of a job. How'd you know?"

He shrugged and sat on the big chair catty-corner to the couch. "Just a guess." He let his head rest against the back of the chair.

"You look awful," she said with her usual blunt honesty. "What's going on?"

He looked at her sideways without lifting his head. "Sammy and I visited the doctor today," he said.

She sat up straighter. "Bad news?"

"Yeah. No. I don't know." He kicked off his shoes and put his feet up on the ottoman. "We got a diagnosis I was hoping we wouldn't get."

"Oh no!" The panic in her voice was real. "Is he going to be okay? What's wrong?"

Her concern brought him upright, and he leaned forward, waving a hand to calm her. "He's fine, he's going to be just fine. It's not some horrible disease."

"Tell me!"

"It's autism."

She sucked in a breath, looked up at the ceiling. He thought she was looking in the direction of Sammy's room. Maybe even praying—she was a fairly new Christian, from what his wife had said only weeks before she'd died.

But when Arianna looked back at him, he realized her eyes were glittering with tears she was trying not to let fall.

"Hey," he said, moved by her concern. Everyone in town liked him and Sammy just fine, but there was nobody who felt the intensity of this diagnosis like he did. Or so he'd thought. "He'll be okay. It's just… I have to figure out how to cope, make some new plans."

"I'm sure." She drew in a couple of deep breaths and looked out the window. He wondered if the view of the Sangre de Cristo Mountains would calm her, like it did him.

"He'll be okay," he repeated. "There's so much help available these days."

"You don't sound that surprised." She studied him, head cocked to one side, eyes confused.

"I… No." He looked at her. "I kind of knew."

She frowned. "I *should* have guessed. I've done art therapy with kids who had the condition a fair amount, and now that you mention it…he does seem kinda like those kids. Although he's his own sweet, wonderful self," she added fiercely. "If he's going to grow up a little different from neurotypical kids, that's okay. I'll still love him just as much."

"I will, too," Jack said mildly, surprised at her vehemence. But on the few occasions she'd spent time with him and Sammy, she'd been an enthusiastic aunt. More enthusiastic about Sammy, when it came to it, than her sister, Chloe, his wife, had been. "The problem is that I have to hire a nanny, and there aren't many candidates in Esperanza Springs."

"I could do it," she said.

Jack stared at her. "You?" He couldn't keep the surprise and doubt out of his voice.

"Just until you find somebody permanent," she amended quickly. "I mean, no way could I do that long term, of course, but I'd like to help if you're in a spot."

"Wow, thanks, Arianna, but..." He trailed off.

How to tell Arianna that she looked too much like her sister? That she was too disorganized? That her liveliness and fun were a direct contrast to his own staid, boring life... and that they disturbed him?

She leaned forward, one eyebrow raised, a long leg crossed over the other. "What, Jack? Go ahead, say it."

"It's just... I guess I was thinking of a Mary Poppins type," he said, trying to make a joke of it. "You know, laced up and experienced and efficient."

"Sure. You're right, of course." She sighed and stood up. "I'm nobody's idea of a good employee apparently. But I'm here to help if you need me."

He felt like a heel as he followed her to the door, unable to keep his eyes off her chaotic, shining curls. "I appreciate your coming by and bringing the gift," he said, although truthfully, he had no idea where he'd put the giant sunflower. It didn't exactly match the couch. "Stop back and see Sammy anytime."

That comment made her whole form brighten, and she

turned to him. "Thanks, I will. I miss seeing the little guy. I need a Sammy hug."

It occurred to him to wonder why she needed a hug, but that wasn't his business. He opened the door for her and held it while she walked out, the scent of musky roses tickling his nose.

Sometimes he wondered what it would be like to get involved with a woman like Arianna, colorful and warm and relaxed. But he always stifled the notion. He realized, almost instantly, that it shouldn't and wouldn't happen.

Love and marriage weren't about fun; they were about sacrifice and responsibility and hard work.

And getting drawn to Arianna made his face heat and his stomach churn with guilt, because of Chloe and all her suspicions. She'd died fourteen months ago, but her angry accusations still rang in his ears.

Anyway, and fortunately, no woman like Arianna would be attracted to a methodical, scientific nerd like him.

One minute later, his business phone buzzed, and five minutes after that, he was trying to figure out how to get someone to come watch Sammy while he drove to one of the neighboring ranches to help with a cow that was suffering from a dangerous case of bloat.

He'd moved from town up to Redemption Ranch because he'd seen how happy the wide-open spaces made Sammy. Made him, too, really. The fact that he believed in the ranch's mission as a haven for struggling veterans and senior dogs was a factor, too. Living here, he could serve as the ranch's on-site veterinarian, which was a needed role and one he relished.

On the downside, moving up here meant he was thirty minutes away from his normal babysitters, and they had both just refused to come at this short notice. He hated to impose by asking Penny, the ranch owner, or Willie, a Vietnam veteran and permanent resident of the ranch.

You could just ask Arianna.

The thought came to him, and before he could second-guess himself, he was out the door. Arianna was walking back toward her car from Penny's house. "She's not home," she called in explanation.

"Could you stay a couple of hours with Sammy now?" he asked, holding up his phone. "Vet emergency."

Her face lit up like he'd offered her the world. "Of course! I'd love to!"

He beckoned her in and showed her the laminated instruction sheets he'd made for Sammy's care. A little ridiculous, but Sammy was particular.

Now Jack knew at least a part of the reason why.

A smile tugged at the corner of Arianna's mouth. "It'll all be okay, Jack, really," she said. "I know Sammy, and I've worked with autistic kids before. Go help your…steer or whatever. We'll be fine."

Three hours later, Arianna patted Sammy's back as he bounced a bedraggled blue-and-white-checked bear. Whew. She'd finally found the toy he needed, and for the moment, he was content.

She, on the other hand, was anything but. Getting to take care of Sammy was sweet torture. She loved him with all her being, and Chloe had never let her be alone with him. She leaned forward and kissed the sweaty top of his head as he pushed his stuffed bear back and forth, humming tunelessly.

He glanced back at her as if slightly surprised but didn't reject the contact. Good. She knew that some kids on the spectrum resisted physical touch, but Sammy didn't seem to be in that category.

She looked around the living room, noting the bare walls, the end tables devoid of decoration, the shortage of pillows on the couch. Of course, Jack had just moved in. He hadn't had time to add the small touches that made a house a home.

Would he ever? Was he the kind of man who could do that, could be both mom and dad?

Oh, how she'd like to stay nearby and care for Sammy. But the job situation in the small ranching town of Esperanza Springs was bleak. At most, she might be able to cobble together some part-time gigs, but to support herself...not likely.

She'd find work aplenty in a bigger city, where her education would be valued and her references—which were actually stellar—could help her to get a job.

But she liked Esperanza Springs, had spent a lot of time here as a kid and young adult. Now, with her parents living in Europe and her sister gone, Sammy, plus the aunt and uncle she was staying with, were the only family she had.

And she was the only one who knew the truth about him.

The sound of a vehicle pulling in outside, the slam of a car door, made her jerk to attention. Was Jack back already?

Sammy held his bear to his chest and stared impassively at the door.

It opened.

It was Jack. And his handsome face went from gladness to amazed frustration as he looked around the living room.

Arianna looked around, too, wondering what his expression meant. As she took in the overturned basket of toys, the three sippy cups she'd tried until she'd found the one Sammy would accept, the box of diapers she'd brought down from Sammy's room and not found time to take back up, she realized what was bothering him.

"I meant to clean up," she said. Why was she so messy? When was she ever going to get organized? Chloe, thin and disciplined and neat, would never have let her house get into such disarray.

Of course, Chloe would never have let her care for Sammy at all.

"It's okay." He walked over to Sammy. He knelt beside the boy, picked him up and swung him high.

Sammy struggled to get down, and Jack let him. Then he sat and rubbed circles on his back.

Sammy went back to his bear, gently bouncing it.

"Up, down. Up, down." Arianna said the words in rhythm with the bear's bounces and watched Sammy for any recognition of the words.

"He doesn't talk," Jack said, his voice bleak. "I've done some reading, listened to some podcasts on autism. I guess that's part of it."

"It's probably a delay, right? Not a life sentence."

"I hope."

"When he heard your car, he sat there looking at the door until you came in. And when he wanted water instead of juice, he, um, *persisted* until I understood. That's all communication." If Jack got discouraged, gave up on Sammy, she couldn't handle it.

"Thanks, Arianna." He gave her a brief, haggard smile. "And thanks for staying with him on no notice. It was kind of you." He gave the messy room another glance.

Oh brother. "Let me go clean up the kitchen," she said. "You stay here with Sammy."

"No, it's fine." Jack stood and followed her. "He plays well by himself."

She hurried in and knelt by the overturned trash can, stuffing garbage back into the container. When she looked up, Jack had stopped at the doorway, looking stunned.

"I'll clean it up!" She grabbed paper towels to wipe up the floor where the garbage had spilled, then rinsed her hands and started putting away beverage containers.

"Arianna." His hand on her shoulder felt big and warm and gentle. She sucked in a breath and went still.

He pulled his hand away. "It's okay. I can do this."

"No." She spun back toward the cracker-scattered counter to hide her discomfort, started brushing crackers and crumbs into the sink. "I made the mess. It's only fair I clean it up. See, especially for kids with disabilities, low blood sugar is the enemy. But you have all these special requirements—" she gestured toward the laminated sheets "—so it took a little longer."

"There's leftover chicken and rice in the fridge. You could have served him that."

"I didn't see it." But another, more practical person—like Chloe—would have looked harder.

"Look," he said, "I appreciate what you've done, more than you know. But right now, I'll be fine."

You didn't have to be a genius to read the subtext. *I want to be alone with my son.*

"Of course." She sidled past him out to the living room and found her purse. She knelt down by Sammy, swallowing hard. "Good to hang with you, little man," she whispered.

Then she went to the door, where Jack stood, no doubt impatient for her to go. "See ya," she said, aiming for breezy.

He tilted his head to one side. "You okay?"

She nodded quickly, forced a smile.

"Thanks again. Stay in touch."

Stay in touch. The same thing you'd say to a friend you encountered after some time away, a friend you really didn't much want to see again.

Her throat tightened, and she coughed harshly as she hurried to her car. She didn't deserve to cry.

Didn't deserve a job. Didn't deserve to spend time with Sammy. Didn't deserve any kind of warmth from her former brother-in-law, Jack.

She drove carefully down to the ranch's entrance, glanced back to make sure she was out of sight of Jack's new house, and then pulled off the road.

She drew deep breaths, trying to get calm, but it was impossible.

She'd just spent time—botched her time, really—with precious Sammy.

Her adopted nephew.

And, unknown to anyone on this earth but her and Sammy's adoption agency, her own biological son.

Chapter 2

The next Thursday, Jack walked out onto his porch with nanny candidate number four, Sammy in his arms. His son's wails died to a hiccup.

"Aw, he's such a cute peanut," the nineteen-year-old said, flicking a long lime-green fingernail under Sammy's chin, which made him cry again. "Just give me a call about when to start, okay?"

"Um, Mandy," Jack said to her retreating back. "I don't think this is going to work out."

She turned back in the process of extracting a cigarette from her purse. "What do you mean?"

"Sammy didn't seem to connect with you," he said. In the course of four nanny interviews, he'd learned to be blunt.

The teenager gave him a disbelieving stare. "He's *autistic*," she said, enunciating the word as if Jack were hard of hearing. "He's not *gonna* connect with people."

"Thanks for your time," he said, "but I won't be hiring you."

She lit her cigarette, inhaled deeply and blew out a lungful of smoke. "What a waste coming up here. I *told* my mom I didn't like babysitting."

Jack blew out a breath as he watched her drive off and then sank down into one of the rockers on the porch, Sammy in his lap. "We dodged a bullet," he informed his son.

Sammy looked at him solemnly but made no answering sounds, and worry bloomed anew in Jack's chest. They needed to get started with treatment, but how could he find the time to interview nannies *and* therapeutic support staffers? He'd already maxed out Mrs. Jennings, his main caregiver in Esperanza Springs; although she'd assured him before that she'd be glad to continue babysitting Sammy after he moved, she'd quickly discovered she didn't like driving ten miles on mountain roads to get here. And Penny had been sweet, taking care of Sammy twice, but he couldn't continue asking that of the owner of Redemption Ranch.

From the newly renovated activities center, the sound of laughter made him turn his head. Four men emerged, one of them Carson Blair, his pastor, and another a veteran Jack knew a little. The other two were new to the ranch.

At their center was Arianna.

Before he knew it, he was on his feet, walking over.

"Everything okay here?" he asked. When the conversation abruptly died, he realized he must have sounded harsh.

Carson lifted an eyebrow. "We're fine over here, Jack. Something up with you?"

I don't like seeing Arianna surrounded by men, and I don't know why. "No, everything's fine," he said.

Arianna seemed oblivious to any undercurrents. "Oh, hey," she said to Jack. "What's up with the little man?" She held out her arms for Sammy, and Jack was about to tell her not to bother, Sammy was upset. But his son considered her offer and then lifted his arms for her to pluck him from his father's hold.

Immediately, Sammy quieted down. Arianna nuzzled her cheek against his, looking blissful.

Gabe Smith, the veteran Jack had met a few times, greeted him with a friendly handshake. "Hey, Doc, I hate to ask it of you, but could you take a look at Rufus?" He gestured to the porch of the activities center, where a large gray-muzzled dog sprawled. "He's got a raw spot on his leg."

"Sure. I'll get my bag." *And pull myself together.*

He had no right to care what his sister-in-law—former sister-in-law—was up to. He had to focus on getting help for Sammy. Another nanny candidate was arriving soon, hopefully better than the last.

He brought out his bag, glanced over to make sure Sammy was still content with Arianna, and then joined Gabe on the porch. Examining Rufus would ground him. Dogs were so straightforward compared to people, and Rufus was a steady, respectable senior dog.

"Where's Bruiser?" he asked, and as if in answer, an elderly Chihuahua rushed out onto the porch, yipping. He postured stiff-legged in front of Rufus, teeth bared, growling at Jack.

"Hey, whoa, little buddy. I'm not gonna hurt your friend." He moved closer, sideways, not making eye contact, so as not to threaten the pint-size protector.

"Bruiser!" Gabe scolded. "Quit that." He picked up the little dog and sat down on the porch step, holding him.

Jack examined the hot spot Gabe was worried about and bandaged it. "We don't want it to get infected. If he can just go a couple of days without licking it, it'll heal."

"Does he *have* to wear a collar of shame?" Gabe asked. "He hates it."

"I might have one of the new soft kind in the truck. It'll be more comfortable for him." He rubbed Rufus's big head and ears, and the dog lolled onto his back, panting.

Jack massaged the dog, enjoying the cool mountain breeze on his face. Despite his problems, he had a good life. New friends like Gabe, old friends like Penny, a healthy son, work he loved. And an environment where God's grandeur was continually on display.

When Arianna approached, Sammy in her arms, he was surprised to see the warm expression on her face.

He gave her a smile in return, and their eyes linked and stayed for a second longer than was polite. Heat washed over him.

A black PT Cruiser chugged up the road then, breaking the mood. It stopped in front of his place, and a woman stepped out. She looked to be a few years older than Jack and was dressed in black slacks and an old-fashioned white blouse. Her hair was caught back in a tight bun. She marched up to his front door and knocked.

"Uh-oh," he said. "Looks like Sammy and I have an appointment. Gabe, I'll dig out one of those collars for Rufus and bring it over later. You going to be home?" He waved a hand toward Gabe's cabin a short distance down the ranch's main road.

"Sure thing, we'll be around all day."

The nanny pounded on his door again and then returned to her car with visible exasperation. She got in and leaned on the horn.

A drop of rain fell, then another. The clouds that had been coming in clustered over them.

The prospective nanny got out of her car, snapped open a black umbrella and marched toward the cabin's porch again.

"You said you wanted Mary Poppins," Arianna murmured, a smile tugging at her mouth.

"So I did," he said with a sigh.

None of this was going to be as easy as he'd hoped.

"Thanks for letting me stay with you, Aunt Justine," Arianna said the next morning as she dodged stacks of magazines and newspapers to get their breakfast dishes to the kitchen sink.

"You're as welcome as can be," her aunt said. "I just wish the place were in better shape for visitors." She looked toward the hallway that led back to the bedrooms. "He won't let me throw anything away, and his stuff is filling up the whole house."

"I know how hard you try." Arianna submerged the dishes in soapy water and started to scrub. "I'm either going to find a job and a place to stay within the week, or I'll have to move back to Chicago."

"Don't do that!" Aunt Justine sounded horrified. "You should have settled down here like your sister did, not in that soulless city, when your parents moved overseas. I never could figure out why you chose to live there. I thought you loved it here, especially when you spent that one whole summer here during college."

Arianna rinsed the dishes and dunked a couple of dirty pans from the counter into the soapy water. It was good that Aunt Justine had never figured out the reason for Arianna's abrupt departure. Almost no one had known about the mistakes that had led to a surprise pregnancy. That was what had allowed Chloe to adopt Arianna's baby with no one the wiser.

Including Jack. Arianna sighed. She'd been adamantly opposed to Chloe keeping the truth from her husband. But Chloe had been as embarrassed about her infertility as Arianna was about her out-of-wedlock pregnancy. Somehow, adopting her sister's baby, and having people know it, made everything worse for Chloe.

And given how sensitive Chloe was, Arianna had given in. It was what she'd been raised to do. *Take care of your sister. She's not strong like you. Don't upset her.*

She pushed thoughts of her younger days out of her mind and asked Aunt Justine about her vegetable garden and the cat that had shown up on the doorstep yesterday. They had a nice chat while Arianna finished the washing up.

"There. That's better, at least." Arianna surveyed the empty sink and two feet of clear counter space with satisfaction. "Now, I'm going to go out and sell myself as an art therapist."

"Thank you for cleaning up, hon. I'll keep praying for a wonderful job for you."

Arianna strolled through the town of Esperanza Springs, inhaling the fresh scents of pine and sage that blew down from the Sangre de Cristo Mountains, watching a black-and-white magpie land on someone's fence post to scold the pedestrians walking by. From the Mountain High Bakery, the cinnamon scent was so powerful that Arianna was sorely tempted to pop in for a scone, even though she'd just had breakfast. But she didn't need to outgrow her summer clothes, so she walked resolutely past the bakery. She waved at the woman washing the windows of La Boca Feliz Mexican restaurant, and peeked in the hardware store window, then focused on her destination: the children's summer program housed in a local church. She was hoping they'd jump at the chance to have a real art therapist visit with the kids each week for the rest of the summer.

It had been a long shot, and she'd known it, but she was still disappointed at the firm no she got. Disappointed enough that she stopped in the town park to look out at the mountains, breathe in the fresh air and regroup.

She hadn't expected to land in a bed of roses when she'd come back to Esperanza Springs. She'd known the market for art therapists would be tiny; this town was about the basics, not the luxuries, and art therapy was considered a luxury by most of the folks around here.

The exception was up at Redemption Ranch. Penny and her staff were forward thinking; they knew that it took various types of therapy to reach veterans, to help them work through PTSD and other mental health issues related to their wartime service.

Maybe she could talk Penny into giving her more work than just the single class per week that she'd offered. And maybe one of the cabins was empty. If she could live rent-free…

It was another long shot, but at least it was worth trying. For the chance to live near her son, it was definitely worth a try. None of her attempts to put the past behind her and get on with her life had worked, so she hoped being near Sammy would help to settle her soul. That was the real reason she'd come back to Colorado.

Although, if Jack found out the truth, he'd be furious. Understandably so. She and Chloe should never have kept something so important from him.

What if he got angry enough to keep her away from Sammy? Could he do that? Would he?

And what about Sammy, when he got old enough to wonder about his adoption and his birth parents?

She shook her head to try to shake off the circling thoughts and tuned back in to the world around her.

"That poor little thing," a woman was saying. She was on a bench behind Arianna, facing the playground. "They have no idea where he came from."

Idly, Arianna turned to see who the ladies were talking about.

And then she sucked in a breath. There was Sammy on the playground, just a few feet away from the women, toddling from the slide to the climbing structure, where a set of chimes was available for the kids to bang on.

"Turns out he has autism," the same woman said to a younger mom seated beside her, who was nursing a baby. "And now that I think about it, look how he just stands there banging on one thing over and over. I should have guessed."

"What's Dr. Jack gonna do? He's a widower, right?"

"I don't know, but I'm not as young as I used to be. And I didn't bargain for babysitting an autistic kid."

Arianna didn't know how she got to Sammy, but she found herself beside him, facing the two women on the bench. "Look," she said to the white-haired one, who'd been talking, "he's a child first. And he might not like to have his condition broadcast to everyone in the park."

"Who are *you*?" the white-haired woman asked.

That made Arianna pause, because she couldn't tell the whole truth, obviously. "I'm his aunt."

The woman pursed her lips. "I wasn't expecting to be eavesdropped on and criticized when I took this job," she said. "I've been planning to tell Dr. Jack I'm through. Maybe I'll just do it today. I don't need this."

Arianna studied her and saw tears behind the angry expression. "Look, maybe I spoke too harshly. I just feel like a child's medical condition is private."

"No, you're right, I'm a terrible babysitter." She sighed and held out a hand toward Sammy, who looked at her and then turned back to the chimes. "I talk too much, don't I, sugar? And you don't talk at all."

The other woman finished nursing her baby, packed up and hurried away with her little one.

"I shouldn't have said anything, maybe," Arianna said to Sammy's babysitter. "I just… Well, I was thinking, it's not other people's business what condition little Sammy has. Strangers, I mean. Like her." She gestured toward the rapidly departing young mother.

"I suppose," the woman said. "But honestly, I have to talk to someone. I can't deal with all the things this child is going to need. Dr. Jack is lovely, but he brought up supervising therapists and having people come to the home to work with him each day… I didn't sign up for that. I'm retired. We didn't even *have* autism when I was growing up."

Well, they'd had it, they just hadn't diagnosed it, but whatever. "I'm sure it can all be worked out. Jack and Sammy really need the help."

"I'm overwhelmed," the woman admitted. "I'm also a grandma, and I'm not sure whether my grandkids should be around him. Oh, not that he'll hurt them or anything, but they might be too rough or tease him. It's just all so complicated."

"I'm sure Jack will help," she said soothingly, watching Sammy. Did he really act autistic? Was he banging for an unusually long time on those chimes?

Maybe he was exhibiting musical talent. How could you even tell the difference?

Just then Sammy saw them watching and toddled over, arms extended toward Arianna.

"See, and he never comes to me. And he doesn't speak. He's a difficult child to work with."

Arianna picked Sammy up and held him loosely against her. "Do you have one of his toys?"

The woman fumbled through her bag, but she was obviously more intent on venting her feelings as she absent-mindedly handed Arianna a cloth block that jingled when shaken. "I don't think he likes me," she said.

"He might just not be very expressive," Arianna said, feeling defensive for Sammy. "Kids with autism don't always smile a lot." How had this turned into a coaching session for a woman more than twice her age?

And what if the coaching didn't work and the woman decided to quit?

"To think, I'm sitting here in the park and getting in trouble for a chat I have with an acquaintance." The woman waved off in the direction of the woman who'd left with her baby. "You know what? I've had enough. You're his aunt, you say?"

Arianna nodded. She was getting a very bad feeling.

"He obviously knows and likes you. Better than he likes me." The woman stood and plunked the diaper bag into Arianna's lap. "Here," she said. "You take care of him. His father will be here in half an hour. Tell him he can mail me my last paycheck."

"But…but…"

It was no use. The woman left, and there was Arianna, literally left holding the bag.

The bag, and her secret son.

Chapter 3

Jack's last Saturday appointment was with a longtime patient: Mr. McCrady's Irish setter, Cider. He ran his fingers over the dog's hunched haunches and manipulated her legs, noticing when the stoic creature gave a little flinch. "Her arthritis is bothering her more?"

"Hers and mine, both." Mr. McCrady's forehead wrinkled as he stroked his dog's ears. "She has trouble getting out of her bed some mornings. Can we get her on pain meds?"

"Absolutely." Jack finished the exam and then scratched Cider's chest, glad to note that her plume of a tail wagged. "There are risks to her kidneys that come with that type of medication, so we'll want to keep up with her bloodwork. But I think she's earned some pain relief."

"That she has," Mr. McCrady said. "She's been my best friend since my wife died. I don't know what I'd do without her."

The dog panted, seeming to smile up at her owner. Her white face and warm brown eyes communicated pure, uncomplicated love. Jack had really come to appreciate senior dogs since he'd been working at Redemption Ranch.

He got Mr. McCrady and Cider set with a prescription and an appointment for a follow-up visit and then stepped into his office to check messages.

He skimmed past seven he could handle later, and then his fingers froze.

Why was Arianna messaging him?

Problem with your sitter. I have Sammy and he's fine. Come to my aunt's house, 30 Maple Ave. ASAP

A problem with his sitter? He scrolled on through but didn't see a message from Mrs. Jennings.

"Gotta run," he said to his receptionist, who was gathering up her things. "There's an issue with Sammy. Can you and Thomas close up?"

"Sure thing, Doc. Hope everything's okay."

Jack drove the four blocks to Maple Avenue without his usual pauses to enjoy the town's Saturday bustle and then hurried up the front sidewalk to Arianna's aunt's house. He'd been here a couple of times in the early days of his marriage, but Chloe hadn't gotten along with her aunt and uncle—hadn't gotten along with a lot of people, including Arianna—so he didn't know them well.

When he rang the doorbell, Arianna's aunt Justine answered. "Hey, Dr. Jack, you sure you want to come into the craziness?"

"I got a message that my son's here," he said.

"In the kitchen." She gestured behind her. "Come on in."

Jack's eyes widened at the stacks of magazines and

newspapers that allowed only a narrow path through the hallway.

"I don't want any more people in here!" came a bellow from the other end of the house.

"It's just Dr. Jack," Aunt Justine yelled back. "He's here to get his baby."

"Well, send him on his way."

She gave Jack an apologetic shrug. "Go on in and see Arianna and Sammy. He—" she gestured in the direction from which her husband's shout had come "—he's embarrassed about how the house looks. I just have to calm him down." Justine turned and hurried toward the back of the house.

Jack picked his way through the mess, his uneasiness growing.

When he got to the kitchen, his focus immediately went to Sammy. His son sat straight-legged on a clean blanket next to Arianna, who was talking at a computer screen.

Sammy held a wooden spoon and was tapping it against a plastic bowl with intense concentration.

"I have experience with teenagers, yes," Arianna was saying to the screen. Her wild curls were pulled back into a neat bun, and her peach-colored shirt was more tailored and buttoned-up than what she usually wore.

She also had a streak of what looked like blueberry jam across her cheek that matched the streaks on Sammy's shirt. Oops.

"I'm staying with relatives in Esperanza Springs right now," she said, apparently in answer to an interview question. "But I'm able to relocate for the right job."

She was doing a Skype interview and, for whatever reason, she was also taking care of his son.

And she was thinking about relocating? Jack's chest tightened.

But he didn't have time to wonder what *that* was about. "Come here, buddy," he said quietly, holding out his hands to pick up Sammy. The steady banging noise his son was making couldn't help Arianna's cause.

Sammy noticed him for the first time and pumped his little arms. Jack's heart lifted, and he swung Sammy up.

But not before Sammy's flailing feet made a stack of plastic containers clatter to the ground. The noise startled Sammy, and he began to cry.

Jack glanced at Arianna in time to see her slight cringe. The person doing the interview, blurry on the screen, frowned.

"I can send you reference letters or give you phone numbers," Arianna said over the din.

She turned up the sound and Jack heard the fatal words: "We'll be in touch."

He carried Sammy out of the room, waved to Justine, who stood at the end of a hallway arguing with her husband, and went out the front door. He started toward his truck, then paused. He needed to get Sammy home, but first, he'd better wait and find out from Arianna what was going on. And apologize for disrupting her job interview.

Putting Sammy down on his blanket, he showed him a smooth stick. True to form, Sammy found it fascinating and began to bang it on the ground.

It wasn't three minutes before Arianna came out. "Hey," she said when she saw him.

"How'd your job interview go?" he asked. "I'm sorry for all the noise."

She shrugged. "What will be will be," she said. "I was just hoping… It's my only semilocal opportunity." Her words were casual, but her eyes were upset. She was fingering her necklace, and Jack saw that it was a cross.

Yeah, he'd heard she'd come to the faith in a big way.

"So what happened with Sammy?"

She sighed. "It's my fault."

"What's your fault?" Arianna meant well, but chaos followed her wherever she went. Chloe had always said as much.

"The sitter was talking about his autism in the park, where everyone could hear," she said. "I sort of got upset and told her she shouldn't share his diagnosis—which wasn't my business, and I'm sorry—and she ended up dumping him and all his stuff on me."

"She was talking about his diagnosis? At the park?"

"She didn't mean any harm. I think she was just trying to figure out how to cope."

That sounded like Mrs. Jennings.

Sammy looked up, and Jack sat down to be closer, rubbing his son's back. How was he going to do right by Sammy? The child needed careful, consistent care, and he'd known for a while that Mrs. Jennings couldn't fit the bill, even before they'd gotten the diagnosis. But now, his interviews with so-called serious sitters weren't going any better. He'd even tried Skyping with a couple of women from out of state, but he'd not gotten a warm feeling from any of them.

"I don't know what I'm going to do," he said. Right now, he felt like just a struggling dad and was glad to have a relative to vent to, someone who seemed to care about Sammy almost as much as he did.

She tilted her head to one side. "This could be a God thing."

"What do you mean?"

"I need a job," she said slowly. "And you need a nanny."

He saw where she was going and let his eyes close. "Look, Arianna, I don't want to hurt your feelings. But I just don't think—"

"*Don't* think, then," she said.

"But I'm responsible for—"

"Don't think—pray." She stood smoothly, leaned down and ran a finger across Sammy's shoulders—which he normally hated, but accepted from Arianna with just an upward glance—and then walked toward her car.

"Arianna…"

"Don't answer now. Pray about it," she called over her shoulder. "See you at church tomorrow."

The next morning, Arianna thought about how much she loved art. One reason was the way it distracted you from your problems. It had distracted little Suzy Li from missing her mom, right here in the second-grade Sunday school class, and it had distracted Arianna from thinking about her own ridiculous offer to Jack DeMoise the day before.

"I'm sorry Suzy got a little paint on her shirt," she said to Mrs. Li as Suzy tugged her mom's hand, pulling her over to look at the picture she'd painted, now drying on a clothesline with the rest of the primary kids' paintings.

"I'm just thrilled she made it through the whole class," Mrs. Li said in between hugging Suzy and admiring her picture. "It's been a long time since I've gotten to stay for a whole church service. What a big girl you were, Suzy!"

"I missed you, Mommy." Suzy wrapped her arms around her mother. "But Miss Arianna said I was brave."

Mrs. Li smiled at Arianna. *Thank you*, she mouthed.

Arianna was glad she'd helped, but she felt a pang; she couldn't deny it. It was fun and rewarding to get her kid fix through helping with Sunday school, but in the end, those precious little ones wanted their own mommies. In the end, Arianna went home alone.

Fortunately, there was no time to dwell on what she didn't have. Sunny and Skye, the pastor's twins, needed their hands washed before heading out with their mom, who introduced herself as Lily. "Don't worry about it," Lily said as Arianna tried to scrub off the paint that had inexplicably splattered both twins' arms. "As long as they're happy, it's fine."

"That's what I said." Kayla, the main teacher of the primary-age kids and the mother of one of them, Leo, came over, and she and Lily hugged. "Kids are supposed to get messy and have fun."

Yeah, they were right about kids, Arianna thought, but what about her? When was she going to grow up and stop getting messy? She wet a paper towel and used it to wipe the biggest smudge from her cheek. The green streak in her hair was probably there to stay, at least until she could get back to her temporary home and shower.

"Hey, Dr. D," Kayla said and went to the door to greet Jack, who was leaning in with Sammy parked on his hip. Arianna sucked in a breath. He was good-looking to begin with, but when he smiled, he was breathtaking.

Finn Gallagher, Kayla's husband, showed up and sidled past Jack into the classroom. He reached out to Kayla and gently rubbed her shoulders, his eyes crinkling. She smiled up at him, love and happiness written all over her face.

Arianna's chest tugged. What would it be like to have someone touch you as if you were infinitely precious? Someone with whom to share your deepest thoughts, your hopes and dreams, your secrets?

But she couldn't tell anyone her deepest secrets, not

and have them look at her the way Finn looked at Kayla. An out-of-wedlock pregnancy wasn't that uncommon, and there were plenty of people who took it in stride, raised the child and got on with their lives. Arianna wished she was that person, but she wasn't. Not given her family and the way she was raised.

As a result, she'd given away her child…and lied about it.

Jack was still standing at the half door. "Are you coming to the church lunch?" he asked her abruptly.

She hesitated. The church had a lunch after services every Sunday, for members and anyone in the community who needed a free meal or fellowship. She should go, since she was trying to make some kind of a life here. "Um, I guess."

"Good. I'll see you there." And he was off.

What did *that* mean? That he wanted to see her, have lunch with her, hang out, accept her offer of helping with Sammy? Or that he wanted to let her down easy?

She blew out a sigh as she wiped down the tables where the kids had been painting. Thanks to an abundance of newspapers, cleanup wasn't that difficult, but she found herself lingering, carefully putting things away in a most uncharacteristic way.

She knew why she was stalling: she didn't want to go to the lunch and face Jack. Not after she'd made such a ridiculous offer.

Why had she suggested—again—that she could serve as Sammy's nanny when Jack clearly didn't want her to? Had she turned into one of those desperate women who couldn't take no for an answer?

Jack was kind and he would be nice about it, but rejection was rejection. She wasn't looking forward to it.

But, oh, for the chance to take care of her son, even briefly! To get to know him, to help him, to watch him grow.

No, said the stern voice in her head. She didn't deserve it, and it wasn't for her.

She was tempted to just skip the lunch and go home, avoiding Jack altogether, except she didn't have a home, not really. Aunt Justine and Uncle Steve had been kind to take her in, and hospitable, but trying to make space for another person in their crowded home was putting a strain on their relationship. She could see it. The more hours she could stay away the better.

Which pointed to her other problem: she needed to make new living arrangements. It was just that she didn't know whether to make them here or somewhere else.

Meanwhile, she'd get her aunt and uncle take-out meals from the church lunch, she decided. It was so hard to cook anything in their kitchen, piled high with appliance boxes and recycling and newspapers. It wasn't much, but a good meal from the church would be a small token of her gratitude to them.

Penny caught up with her and walked alongside. "You doing okay? You look a little blue."

She couldn't tell Penny the big reason, of course. "Just thinking about my living situation," she said as they walked into the fellowship hall, where the meal was already being served. "I'm wearing out my welcome at my aunt and uncle's place, but I'm on a tight budget until I find more work."

"Hmm, that's tough." And then Penny snapped her fingers and stared at her. "You know what? The pastor was right. With God all things are possible."

"Oh, I know that's true—"

Penny interrupted her. "No, seriously. I just got a brainstorm."

"What's that?"

"I've got a mother-in-law apartment upstairs at my house on the ranch, and I've been meaning to clean it out and fix it up forever. You're energetic and artsy. How would you like to stay there for the next few weeks? Rent-free, if you'll clean it and fix it up nice, so I can rent it out at the end of the summer."

Arianna's jaw dropped. "That would be so perfect!"

And then the other ramifications of Penny's offer rushed into her mind.

She could live so close to Sammy. Across the lawn, basically.

But how would Jack feel about that? Would she appear to be stalking him?

Penny was studying her face and no doubt saw her mixed feelings. "You think about it," she said. "There's no need to decide today."

"Thank you." Arianna gripped Penny's hand, her eyes filling with tears. "That's such a kind, kind offer. I just... have to figure a few things out, but I'm incredibly grateful to you for suggesting it."

"I'd be getting as much out of it as you are," Penny said. "Now, you'd better go grab a bite to eat while they're still serving."

Arianna did just that, accepting a generous portion of enchiladas, rice and beans. She sat down next to an older woman who introduced herself as Florence, and they chatted a little while Arianna ate.

The fellowship hall was just a big tile-floored room with a stage at one end and a kitchen at the other. Long tables covered with cheerful red-checked tablecloths and lined by metal folding chairs filled one half of the room. Only about half the seats were full now; Arianna had lingered in the kids' room long enough that people were finishing up and heading home.

All of a sudden, Florence's eyes sharpened. "Would you look at that," she said, nodding toward a woman who was settling her two children at the other end of the table. "Pregnant with kid number three and not a husband in sight."

Arianna registered the disapproval and was aware that she would have faced the same if she'd kept Sammy. But she couldn't tear her eyes away from the woman, smiling and tickling her toddler while a slightly older child clung to her leg.

It would have been so wonderful to keep Sammy. And while she knew there had been many blessings in his adoption placement—not least his responsible, loving father, who was seated with Sammy at the far end of the room, where it was quieter—she couldn't help but wish she'd found a way to keep her baby, to raise him herself.

Then she wouldn't be caught in this web of lies, trying to decide whether it would be possible to live next door to her son without revealing her true relationship to him.

She barely realized she was staring dreamily into space until Florence waved a hand in front of her face. "I think Dr. Jack is trying to get your attention," she said, her eyes alight with curiosity. "You'd better go talk to him."

Arianna snapped to awareness, looked in Jack's direction and saw that he was indeed beckoning to her.

Quickly, she finished her last bites of rice and beans. "It was nice talking to you," she said to her extremely observant neighbor. She took both their dishes to the washing area and then headed over to Jack, mixed gladness and dread in her heart.

Any day she could see Sammy was a good day. But she was pretty sure Jack was about to turn down her nanny offer. And then she'd have to tell Penny she couldn't take the apartment, and leave.

The thought of being away from her son after spending precious time with him made her chest ache, and she blinked away unexpected tears as she approached Jack and Sammy.

Sammy didn't look up at her. He was holding up one finger near his own face, moving it back and forth.

Jack caught his hand. "Say hi, Sammy! Here's Aunt Arianna."

Sammy tugged his hands away and continued to move his finger in front of his face.

"Sammy, come on."

Sammy turned slightly away from his father and refocused on his fingers.

"It's okay," Arianna said, because she could see the beginnings of a meltdown. "He doesn't need to greet me. What's up?"

"Look," he said, "I've been thinking about what you said." He rubbed a hand over the back of his neck, clearly uncomfortable.

Sammy's hands moved faster, and he started humming a wordless tune. It was almost as if he could sense the tension between Arianna and Jack.

"It's okay, Jack," she said. "I get it. My being your nanny was a crazy idea." Crazy, but oh, so appealing. She ached to pick Sammy up and hold him, to know that she could spend more time with him, help him learn, get him support for his special needs.

But it wasn't her right.

"Actually," he said, "that's what I wanted to talk about. It does seem sort of crazy, but…I think I'd like to offer you the job."

She stared at him, her eyes filling. "Oh, Jack," she said, her voice coming out in a whisper. Had he really just said she could have the job?

Behind her, the rumble and snap of tables being folded and chairs being stacked, the cheerful conversation of parishioners and community people, faded to an indistinguishable murmur.

She was going to be able to be with her son. Every day. She reached out and stroked Sammy's soft hair, and even though he ignored her touch, her heart nearly melted with the joy of being close to him.

Jack's brow wrinkled. "On a trial basis," he said. "Just for the rest of the summer, say."

Of course. She pulled her hand away from Sammy and drew in a deep breath. She needed to calm down and take things one step at a time. Yes, leaving him at the end of the summer would break her heart ten times more. But even a few weeks with her son was more time than she deserved.

"Would you like to go get a cup of coffee?" he asked. "Nail down the details? I think Penny would be willing to take Sammy for an hour or two."

Arianna found her voice. "That's okay," she said, trying not to sound as breathless as she felt. "We can just talk it over at your house. Or here. Wherever."

He frowned and cleared his throat. "I'd like to be a little more formal and organized about it," he said as he started to collect Sammy's things into his utilitarian gray diaper bag. "Draw up a contract, that sort of thing. We need to hammer out the terms."

Hammer out the terms. What were the right terms for an aunt to become nanny to her secret son? "Okay, sure, I guess."

"Meet you at the coffee shop in half an hour?"

"Sure." Dazed, she turned and headed out to her car.

With God all things are possible. The pastor had said it, and she'd just witnessed its truth. She was being given a job, taking care of her son and had a place to live.

It was a blessing, a huge one. But it came at a cost: she was going to need to conceal the truth from Jack on a daily basis. And given the way her heart was jumping around in her chest, she wondered if she was going to be able to survive this much of God's blessing.

Chapter 4

Jack walked into the coffee shop half an hour later, still in his business-casual church clothes, briefcase in hand. He had a sample contract on a clipboard, a tablet to take notes, his calendar on his phone.

Having all his supplies made him feel slightly more in charge of a situation that seemed to be spiraling out of control.

He felt uneasy and uncomfortable and wrong every time he thought about hiring Arianna as a nanny, even temporarily. Partly, it was what he knew about her being disorganized and messy. More than that was the fact that Chloe had had real issues with her sister and would never have approved of her taking care of Sammy.

And even more than all that, he just felt strangely uncomfortable with his former sister-in-law.

When he thought about Sammy, though, he knew what he had to do, what was right. Sammy liked Arianna, and she was good with him. And they needed to start his treatment now, not when the perfect nanny showed up in six months or a year.

Inside the shop, the deep, rich fragrance of good coffee soothed him. He waved to a few patrons and headed for the counter. He'd order before Arianna got here, get her some coffee, too.

"Jack!" came a sunny voice from the other side of the shop.

He looked up and saw a mass of coppery curls, then Arianna's wide smile. His muscles tightened, and he felt a strong urge to back out the door. Stronger was the urge to go toward her, even though it felt like he just might be headed for disaster.

She gestured him over, holding up a drink. "I already got you something!" she called over the buzz of the small crowd.

As Jack turned and walked toward her, he was aware of several people watching. Arianna wasn't quiet.

And she'd gotten him one of those expensive whipped-cream-topped iced coffee drinks he didn't even like.

"Thanks," he said as he reached the table and sat down. "You didn't have to do that. How much was it?" He got out his wallet.

"It's on me," she said. "You've got to try this. I had one the other day and it's so good! It's a mocha java supreme. Of course, I shouldn't have it, it's full of calories, but you certainly don't need to worry about calories."

"Thanks." He sat down, feeling concerned, and studied her. She was talking fast, even for Arianna. She was stressed out, too, he realized, as much as or more than he was.

Compassion washed over him then. Arianna was living

in that hoarder house with her aunt and uncle and probably very low on cash. She needed this job, and his own worries paled.

He got out his clipboard and notes. "Before we start going through this," he said, "are you sure you're interested in the job? It'll be more responsibility than most nanny jobs, because you'd be supervising some of his therapists and doing the exercises they suggest. You'd have days off, of course, but you wouldn't be able to pursue a full-time art therapy position."

"I'm sure," she said, her eyes shining.

He got tangled up in that gaze for a few seconds, then looked away and cleared his throat. "Okay, then. Most of the sample contracts I looked at—" he pulled out the one he'd printed to show her "—have clauses about what will happen if either party decides to back out early. And we need to nail down an equitable schedule so you don't get burned-out." He drew a breath to continue.

She put a hand over his. "Jack. I trust you. Whatever you think is best."

Her hand on his felt soft and delicate and warm.

He straightened and pulled his hand away. "I can draft a schedule if that would work for you. Then we can go over it and finalize the details. Now, let's talk about pay."

"I'd do it for free," she said promptly.

"Arianna!" Jack shook his head, frowning at her. "You should never say that to a potential employer."

"You're not just that, you're my former brother-in-law. And Sammy is my nephew. Jack, we don't have to hash out every single detail, nor get everything down in writing. We can make it happen with a handshake."

He pointed his mechanical pencil at her. "You're way too trusting. People will take advantage of you."

To his surprise, she nodded. "It's happened before," she said. "But should I let that change me into a suspicious person?"

He really wanted to know who'd taken advantage of her, because he wanted to strangle that person. Some guy, most likely. "Not a suspicious person," he said, "but maybe a cautious one."

"You're probably right," she said with a shrug. "But for now...I'm super excited to be working with Sammy. I know I can help him."

Jack had to admit that her attitude was enormously appealing. If a stranger he was interviewing had acted so enthusiastically, he'd have hired her immediately. Well, after checking her résumé and background, of course. Unlike Arianna, he wasn't impulsive.

And there were a lot of details to straighten out. "Now, as far as where you'll stay," he said. "I have plenty of room in the house, but I'm afraid that would raise a few eyebrows. I wouldn't want your reputation to suffer."

"Or yours," she said, sipping her drink. "But actually, I've got it covered. Penny offered me the use of her upstairs apartment if I'll clean it out and decorate it so she can rent it in the fall."

"That's perfect." Another thing that was working out better than he expected. Not what he was used to. He often expected the worst.

He plowed on through his list of things to discuss. "How do you feel about organizing the TSS schedule? Is that something you can handle?"

A smile quirked the corner of her mouth. "I *can* be organized, Jack," she said with exaggerated patience. "I'm just not when it doesn't matter."

It's important to sweat the small stuff, he heard in his

mind. Chloe's voice. The same as his mother's and father's. Chloe had gotten along so well with them, partly because she'd tried so hard to do everything right.

Guilt suffused him. Chloe hadn't trusted Arianna and wouldn't think that hiring her was doing things right. She'd never sanction this arrangement.

Arianna fumbled in her oversize bag and brought out a tablet computer. "I can print this out for you later, if you want," she said. "It's my résumé." She enlarged it so he could see. "I've taken two classes focused on kids with special needs. They were a little older than Sammy, but the principles are the same." She scrolled to another section. "And I did an internship in an early-childhood program. I love babies." For just a moment, her eyes went wistful.

Jack studied those eyes as questions he'd never thought to ask before pressed into his awareness. Had Arianna wanted to have kids? Did she ever think about it? Was there a boy-friend in the picture?

Around them, the buzz of conversation indicated that the coffee shop was getting crowded. But Jack couldn't seem to look away from Arianna.

She didn't seem nearly so affected. "This section is my coursework," she continued on, scrolling down the tablet's screen and highlighting a section to show him. "We did a lot of psychology, life-span development, counseling work. Here, take a look." She handed him the tablet.

He scanned it quickly, then read more closely, impressed. "You have so much coursework in special education."

She laughed, a sunny, lilting sound. "Don't look so shocked, Jack. It's part of most art and music therapy programs."

He met her eyes over the tablet and couldn't avoid smil-ing, almost as big as she did. "There's a lot more to you than meets the eye, isn't there?"

"You haven't scratched the surface." Was there a tiny bit of flirtation in her tone, in her expression as she looked at him over the rim of her cup?

He took a long pull on his own drink, sucking up frothy sweetness. "You know," he said, "these are actually good."

Again, their gazes tangled.

"Son!" The deep voice penetrated his awareness at the same time a familiar, beefy hand gripped his shoulder.

He glanced up as the usual tension squeezed his chest. He knew *exactly* what his father was thinking. "Hi, Dad. Do you remember—"

"Arianna Shrader. How could I forget." His father didn't extend his hand for shaking and neither did she, instead inclining her head slightly, as if she were a queen and he, a lowly peasant.

The attitude wasn't lost on Dad, Jack could see. But looking at Arianna, he could tell his father's attitude wasn't lost on her, either.

"What brings about this meeting?" Disapproval dripped from his father's voice.

"I'm going to be working for Jack," Arianna said. "Taking care of Sammy for a while."

"You're *what*?" Dad's voice squeaked, and his face reddened. He looked at Jack as if he'd just committed a federal crime. "Was this *your* idea?"

"It was my idea," Arianna interjected before Jack could open his mouth. "It made sense, given my background and Jack's needs. Is there a problem?"

"Sure seems like a problem to me, you moving in with your sister's husband."

Arianna gasped.

At the same moment, Jack stood and stepped forward so that he was in between his father and Arianna. "Arianna is

Sammy's aunt," he said, "and there's nothing inappropriate about her caring for him."

"Perceptions mean a lot," Dad said, but his voice was quieter. He stepped sideways to look at Arianna. "It's your reputation that would suffer the most. This is a small town."

"I won't be living in." Arianna's normally expressive eyes were cool and flat. "Your son's virtue is safe with me."

His father's face went almost purple, his mouth opening and closing like a dying fish.

"It's under control, Dad." Jack put a hand on his father's arm. "Nothing to worry about."

Dad looked at their half-empty cups, pursed his lips and shook his head. "I hope so," he said abruptly and walked away, weaving through the coffee shop's small tables.

"I'm sorry for that," Jack said. "Dad can be a little…"

"Judgmental? I'm familiar," Arianna said, and suddenly, Jack wondered what kinds of things his father had said to her on the few occasions they'd all gotten together.

Certainly, the buoyancy had gone out of her face and voice, and he continued to think about that as they agreed on a few last details and a start date—tomorrow.

But as he walked her to her car, Jack couldn't forget what his father had said. Perceptions were important. At least a few people in their small town might start to link their names together.

Chloe would have felt that as the ultimate disrespect. If that wretched blood clot hadn't already killed her, this would have.

Was he making a huge mistake hiring Arianna?

"The place is kind of a mess," Penny warned Arianna that evening as they climbed the outside steps to Arianna's new apartment. "It's been a rough year."

Arianna had heard bits and pieces of Penny's story: how she and her husband had bought the ranch with high hopes. How they'd worked together—she with enthusiasm for the mission, he with enthusiasm for their pretty young office assistant. How he'd left Penny high and dry, and absconded with the funds *and* the assistant.

Penny was so kind and so beautiful, Arianna couldn't imagine how anyone could do that to her.

But then again, men could quickly tire of a woman when there were responsibilities involved, or when they found a new obsession. She'd learned that the hard way from Sammy's father.

Penny threw open the door at the top of the steps, then put a hand on Arianna's arm, stopping her. "You'd be doing me a favor if you'd move in and fix it up, but it'll be a lot of work. You be honest, now. If it's too much for you, say no. I'll understand."

Little did Penny realize how few options Arianna actually had. "I'm sure it'll be fine," she assured the older woman. "I love a good project." Not least because it would keep her busy and push her worries away.

"Just take a look before you say anything," Penny said and held the door for Arianna to walk through.

Inside, hard-back chairs stood at odd angles amid boxes, a big cooler and a bike that had to date from the 1980s. The place smelled musty, and through the giant dirty window, sunbeams illuminated the dust motes that danced in the air.

Arianna looked past the surface, something she'd always loved to do. The place had great bones and amazing potential. She clasped her hands together. "This is perfect!"

"You're kidding, right?"

"No! That slanted wood ceiling is gorgeous. I love a non-boxy space. And the view from the windows… It'll look out on mountains, right?"

"The Sangre de Cristos, once it's clean. You can barely see them through that coating of dirt and dust." Penny picked up a photo album covered in white lace. She grimaced at the happy couple on the cover and then dropped the album into the trash.

Arianna lifted an eyebrow but didn't comment. Not her business.

She looked around, scoping out the space. "I'd put the bed there," she said, gesturing to a space directly across from the big window. "Wall hangings should be big, with these tall ceilings. A sitting area over here." As she spoke, the place came to life in her imagination. "It's so much more than I expected in a place to live."

Penny put her hands on her hips and stared at her. "Now, why would you say that? Where were you living before, that this place seems so fabulous?"

Arianna flushed. "Oh, just here and there." No need to tell Penny about how unsettled the past couple of years had been, and how she hadn't been able to commit to anything since giving up her son. "Two days ago I was out of a job and practically out of a home, and now I have both." She bit her lip and shot up a prayer of thanks. "God's so good."

Even as she spoke, worry crept in. Penny was wise and saw a lot. Would she guess the truth about Sammy? Would Jack?

They worked together hauling boxes down the stairs and throwing them into the ranch foreman's truck. "Finn said once it's full, he'll drive it over to the dump," Penny said.

"Just look at the floor," Arianna commented once a big

square of it was cleared. "With a bright rug and a polish, these plank floors will come to life."

"You're so positive," Penny said. "You're going to be good for Jack." She hesitated, then added, "In a way your sister wasn't."

"Oh!" Color rose in Arianna's face. "It's not the same at all. I'm just the temporary nanny." Jack had made that very clear. He'd sent her a text after their conversation just to confirm that she understood that.

Penny didn't seem to have heard her. "His parents were so rigid. His mom's passed, rest her soul, but his dad seems to have gotten even more… What? Judgmental? Tense? Your sister had some of those same qualities." Penny smiled at her. "It strikes me that you don't."

Yes, true, to her detriment. She'd been the one to get pregnant without being married and disgrace the family. While poor Chloe, always such a perfectionist—and so perfect—hadn't been able to have the one thing that meant everything to her: a baby.

"Anyone home?" came a call from downstairs.

"We're up here, Willie." Penny brushed the back of her hand over her sweaty forehead and gestured toward a door Arianna hadn't seen before. "This is where the downstairs connects. You can lock the door for privacy or come down to use the laundry machines whenever you want."

A short, rotund but muscular man with a long gray pony-tail huffed up the steps. "There you are," he said, sweeping off his Vietnam veterans hat. He gave Arianna a quick nod, but his eyes were fixed on Penny. "Can I offer you lovely ladies some help? Before I offer to take you to lunch?" he added to Penny.

Color rose in Penny's cheeks. "Willie, have you met

Arianna? She's going to be living here and working as a nanny for Jack."

Willie smiled at her, his face breaking into a million creases. "I'm pleased to meet you," he said. "That Jack works hard. He could use some help." He turned back toward Penny. "Now, what about that lunch?"

Penny gestured at her dusty work clothes. "Look at me. I can't possibly go out. And we wouldn't ask you to do our grunt work."

"I was a grunt in the service," Willie said with a wink at Arianna. "The company's a lot better here."

"No, thanks, Willie," Penny said. "Another time."

"Maybe tomorrow night?" he asked. "I've got a gift card for the Cold Creek Inn. You could wear that red dress you have."

Penny's cheeks went pink. "I… We'll see," she said and turned back to the box she'd been sorting through.

"Talk her into it, will you?" he asked Arianna. "You know where to find me," he added to Penny and then descended the stairs.

"Looks like you have an admirer," Arianna said, waggling her eyebrows at Penny.

"Oh, he's just lonely because his friend Long John is off on his honeymoon," Penny said. "Those two have been best friends forever and lived next door in the ranch cabins until just recently. Long John married a woman from town, Beatrice Patton, just as soon as her chemo treatments ended. I think they kind of bonded over their health issues, since Long John has Parkinson's."

"Wow." The older woman's matter-of-fact words put Arianna's own problems into perspective.

"Anyway," Penny continued, "Long John getting married and moving down to town is an adjustment for Willie."

"I don't know if the invitation is all about missing his friend," Arianna teased. "I doubt he'd want Long John to wear a red dress to lunch."

"Oh, stop it!" Penny said, laughing a little. "Willie's a nice man, but…"

"He's older than you are. By kind of a lot."

"It's not that. It's that I'm not ready." Penny sighed. "Truth is, when my husband left me, he took that part of me that used to trust people. Or trust men anyway."

"I can understand that." Arianna hadn't dated anyone since Sammy's father for that very reason. But while her own loneliness felt well deserved, Penny's made her sad. "Sounds like he just wants to take you to dinner. Maybe you should go."

"I don't want him to spend his gift card on me. He'd think it means more than it does, and I don't want to hurt anyone, but especially someone who lives on the ranch. We have to be able to coexist."

Coexist. That was what she and Jack had to learn to do, too. But it was hard to look at it so impersonally when there was a child involved.

His child. Her child.

The sound of footsteps trotting up the steps interrupted their conversation. There was a tap on the door, and Jack's face appeared in the glass. "Need any help?" he asked.

Yes, Arianna wanted to say. *Can you help me make my heart stop pounding?*

"Absolutely," Penny said. "We have a bunch of boxes that need to be moved down to Finn's truck. You look like just the man for the job."

"It's good to be needed," Jack said. "Sammy's TSS kicked me out. She said I was hovering."

"Is Sammy okay being alone with her?" Arianna stood and looked out the window toward Jack's house.

"For now, yes," he said. "She has me on speed dial, and I'm to stay within shouting distance. She and Sammy were doing work with his vocalizing and I was distracting him, apparently."

"Do they know what caused his autism?" The question seemed to burst out of her. She hadn't even known she was wondering that. But she must've spoken intensely, because the other two stared at her.

"No one knows for sure," Jack said. "There's definitely a genetic component, and there's a lot about Sammy's background we don't know, given that it was a closed adoption. There's supposed to be a work-around if he develops any health problems, so maybe…" He trailed off.

Arianna's stomach roiled. She couldn't talk about Sammy's genetics with Jack. She couldn't hold it together, couldn't keep him from guessing the truth. At the same time, she wanted to do anything she could to help her son. "Would it make a difference if his genetics were known?" She tried hard to keep the question casual.

"I don't think so. We're still diving into the same type of intervention, and as early as possible. As you'll find out, the more you're around him and his therapists."

"I'm looking forward to working with him." And she should change the subject. She pointed toward the corner of the room. "Those boxes over there need carrying down."

Had she pulled it off? Or did both Penny and Jack think she was acting weird?

Fortunately, her worries were interrupted by another knock, this one on the downstairs door.

Penny rolled her eyes. "I can go weeks without anyone ever coming to visit, but today, when I'm trying to get something done, it's Grand Central Station." She headed down the stairs.

That left Arianna alone when Jack trotted back up the steps. "Ready for another load," he said.

Arianna indicated a stack of three boxes. "You take two. I'll take one," she said, trying for a businesslike tone.

But as she watched him pick up both boxes with ease, noticed his muscles straining the sleeves of his T-shirt, Arianna felt anything but detached.

Moving here, living here, spending time with Sammy... Was it a huge mistake? She'd promised Chloe never to reveal the truth, had reiterated that promise when Chloe was dying. How could she go back on it?

Besides, revealing the truth might very well erase her new, tentative relationship with her son. If Jack knew about the huge secret she'd kept from him, he'd be furious. He might consider her character fatally flawed and refuse to let her see Sammy anymore. Which was his right; he was Sammy's father by adoption and by law.

But now that she'd gotten a taste of spending time with her son, she couldn't imagine giving up the privilege. More important than her own feelings, Sammy needed the help she could offer.

She just had to make sure to keep her distance from Jack. She liked him too much, but she didn't dare start to confide in him, to get close. No sense torturing herself.

They carried several more boxes and then paused at the same time, surveying the attic apartment. What to do next wasn't clear.

"Are you going to be okay living here? Looks like there's

a lot of work to be done." Jack frowned at the remaining mess. "It would drive me crazy."

"Think where I've been staying," she said. "At least this mess is clean-up-able."

"You have a good attitude," he said, nodding approval.

It was the same thing Penny had said, and it shouldn't have warmed her as much as it did.

They carried one more load down. Penny stood beside an expensive sedan, talking to a man in a suit. They seemed to be arguing, and within a few seconds, the man threw up his hands, climbed into the car and drove away. Penny watched him go, then turned back toward the house. When she saw them, she shook her head and rolled her eyes. "I think I'm going to have to get out of here for a little bit," she said. "These men are driving me crazy."

"Is Branson Howe bugging you for a date?" Jack asked.

"Now, why would you say that?" Penny looked irritated.

"Because I think he's been trying to get up the courage to do that for a long time. You didn't shut him down, did you?"

"Yes, I did. I shut everyone down."

"You're breaking their hearts," Jack said.

"Don't you start." Penny bustled inside and came back with her purse and keys. "I'm serious. I'm leaving. I'm going to go see a woman friend, got that? A woman. Because women are a lot more sensible than men." She climbed into her truck and drove off in a flurry of gravel.

Jack winced as he looked at Arianna. "I shouldn't have said anything. It's just that all the men in town talk about Penny. They're all thinking that it's been over a year since her divorce, and they can approach her now."

Arianna felt a stab of pain. Penny could start over, but she couldn't. Instead, she was living in a shabby, dirty place, as shabby and empty as her own life. Because she might have a good attitude in front of others, but in her heart, she knew an educated woman in her late twenties should have been doing a lot better.

There was a sound on the porch, a low whine. Arianna looked at Jack. "Did you hear that?"

"What's over there?"

They both hurried over and discovered a box, lined with a towel and holding one sad-looking, crying, cream-colored puppy. Arianna sank to her knees. "Oh, little guy, who left you here?"

Jack frowned in the direction that Branson's, and then Penny's, car had gone. "Could Branson have brought it?"

"I don't know him. Could he have?"

"He doesn't seem the type," Jack said. "More like the type who would arrange everything carefully."

"I wonder how long it's been here?" Gently, Arianna pulled the puppy out of the box and cuddled it close. Its little pink tongue licked her arm, and her heart melted. She looked up at Jack. "You know, this might be just what I need to make my house a home."

"No." He shook his head, hands on hips. "Animals aren't accessories."

"Well, I know that, silly," Arianna said. "But dogs are companions, and I'd take good care of it."

Jack sighed. "Let me run and check on Sammy, and then I'll take a look at him," he said. "He looks kind of young to be away from his mama."

"That's not good, right?" Arianna had heard that dogs needed to be with their mothers for the first eight weeks to learn good dog manners and be socialized properly.

"Right," Jack said. "There *is* a new mama out in the barn. In fact, she only has one pup, and he's about this one's age. Want to help me?" He smiled at her, and his whole face lit up, and Arianna's heart melted.

Which it shouldn't be doing. She needed to focus her affection on Sammy, and maybe a puppy. Not on Jack. Definitely not on Jack.

Chapter 5

After making sure the puppy was in no immediate distress, Jack hurried over to his house, caught the tail end of Sammy's session with his TSS and got instructions for following up. Then he grabbed Sammy and two bags of supplies—one for his son and one for the puppy.

As he carried Sammy over toward Penny's front porch, magpies scolded and mountain bluebirds twittered and swooped. The late-afternoon sun warmed his shoulders, and the weight of his son in his arms felt good and right.

Finally, he was starting to manage Sammy's condition, get him help and get their lives back on track.

Arianna sat on the top porch step, her auburn curls glowing like fire. She cradled the small, cream-colored puppy in her arms, talking softly to it.

The sight of Arianna's nurturing side tugged at his heart, and when she heard them coming and looked up, the warm glow in her eyes melted something inside him.

"I really want to keep him," she said.

"He's a cute little guy. Let me take a look." He set down his bags and took the puppy from her, carefully, and she held out her arms for Sammy.

They worked well together. An automatic trade without words.

The puppy whined a little as Jack examined it, and Sammy turned his head to stare at the dog.

"He really noticed that." She patted Sammy's back. "See the puppy?"

"He notices animals more than he notices people," Jack said, and then he wished he hadn't.

Arianna looked up quickly. "That must be hard to deal with."

He nodded. "I'm used to it, but it makes me sad." He held up the puppy so Sammy could see it. "Dog," he said.

"See the dog?" Arianna added.

Sammy looked thoughtful but didn't speak.

"Does he know the word?"

"He used to," Jack said, and pain twisted his heart.

He met Arianna's eyes and saw a matching sorrow in hers.

The intimacy of their shared emotion felt too raw, and he looked away, focusing on the puppy. He examined eyes, ears, tail and paws. "He's healthy," he told her, "just too young to be left alone. That's why he's crying."

"Poor thing. I wonder what his story is."

Jack shook his head. "There are all kinds of reasons why a mother can't raise her pup," he said.

Arianna drew in a sharp breath, and when he looked up, her eyes glittered with unshed tears. Funny, he hadn't realized she was so sensitive. He put a hand on hers. "We'll find him a new mama," he reassured her.

She swallowed hard and nodded, and then Sammy started to fuss and the moment was over.

Half an hour later, at the barn, Jack inhaled the clean, lemony smell and smiled. "The volunteers keep this place really clean."

"It's staffed by volunteers? I thought the veterans cared for the dogs."

"It takes a village," Jack said. "Sometimes we don't have as many veterans, or they're working off-ranch, and then the community steps in to help."

The dogs started their usual uproar, and Sammy clapped his hands over his ears and started to cry.

"They'll quiet down in a minute," Jack told Arianna over the din. "Just bounce him, kind of hard." When she fumbled, he held out the puppy and they traded again.

Soon enough, the dogs quieted down and Sammy did, too. They walked down the aisle, and he could have predicted Arianna's reaction.

Puppy in hand, she knelt beside first one pen, then the next. She talked softly to the senior dogs, rubbed grizzled snouts, read the little cards on the front of each enclosure that told the dog's age, gender and something about them.

"Oh, look, Jack. This one's been here for over a year!" She studied the pit bull–rottweiler mix. "Why hasn't anyone adopted him?"

"We're not really so much about adoption, although we're thrilled when it happens," Jack said. "The veterans who stay here each pick out a dog to care for. Max is big, and he needs medication every morning and evening. He's a lot for anyone to handle, let alone a struggling veteran." Even as he said it, he knelt and reached into the pen to scratch behind the big black dog's ears. Normally he didn't let himself think too much about how long the dogs spent here or what their lives were like. As a veterinarian, he had to maintain some detachment.

Around Arianna, detachment was harder and harder to come by.

In Arianna's arms, the puppy started whining louder, causing Sammy to stare. Jack stood. "Come on, Buster," he said, spontaneously naming the pup. "Let's find you a mama, or at least, a mama for now."

The dog he'd been thinking of was at the end of the left-hand row of crates, and he hurried Arianna past the rest of the dogs on the line and knelt in front of the last pen. "Hey, Millie," he said gently.

The large beagle mix looked out at him with soulful eyes, her tail thumping.

"How's your pup doing, huh?" He opened the pen's door with one hand, still holding Sammy in the other. Millie was gentle beyond words and wouldn't dream of escaping or hurting anyone.

"Why does she only have one pup?" Arianna asked, kneeling beside the dog.

"Lots of possible reasons. She's old to be breeding, and she's had a lot of litters. That's why she was dropped off here. No use as a breeder anymore, and the owners were disgusted that she just had one pup."

"Well, I'm disgusted with them," Arianna said, rubbing the long, soft ears.

"It could be a blessing in disguise. She'll have plenty of extra milk, and her baby..." He nudged at the adorable pup sleeping beside her. "He's not had to compete for resources, so he's gentle as a lamb, too. What do you think, Millie? Can you take on another baby?"

Arianna held the whining puppy out, and the beagle let out a low woof, then sniffed him all over.

"You can put him down," Jack said. "I think she'll be nice."

Millie's pup lifted his head sleepily and then dropped it back down again. Millie licked the new, tiny pup all over, from head to toe, then nudged it toward her stomach. Soon the new baby latched on and began suckling with all its might.

Jack swallowed a lump in his throat. If only people could be as simple as animals, the world would be a better place. He glanced over at Arianna.

Her eyes were shiny again. "So sweet," she said, and then he noticed the tear running down her cheek. It was only natural for him to hold out an arm, bringing her into a hug. He wasn't sure why she let out a couple of sobs against his shirt, but hey...women, hormones, puppies... He rubbed his hand up and down her back.

After a moment she looked up at him, and he suddenly realized how close they were standing, how good her hair smelled and how wrong and forbidden it was to notice such things. He took a big step backward, forced out a laugh. "Well, that's our good deed for the day. Sammy and I have things to do. We'll see you tomorrow to get started figuring out nanny duties."

She didn't speak, and he didn't dare stay. He swung around and, God forgive him, he practically ran away, leaving her to find her way out of the barn and back to her apartment by herself.

Helping her just might prove too much, and too dangerous, for Jack.

The next morning, Arianna showed up at Jack and Sammy's house five minutes early—something of a record for her—only to find Jack with his jacket and shoes on, brief-case in hand. She blinked. "Am I late?"

"No, no. It's fine," he said. "I just need to give you some instructions before heading out."

Duly noted: on time for Jack meant at least ten minutes early.

She wasn't about to complain. She was still marveling over the blessing God had given her, allowing her to care for her son. She looked around and spotted Sammy, contentedly pushing blocks through holes on the top of a bin. Then she shed her own jacket and purse and pulled out her phone. "I'm going to record what you say, if that's okay," she said. "I don't want to make any mistakes."

He glanced over at her coat and purse. "Okay, first off, let's make sure that your purse is hung up out of Sammy's reach. I don't want him choking on small items or getting into medications. Even a little bit of aspirin or the like can make a baby sick."

She was already messing up. "Of course, I should have thought of that." She followed him to a closet where she could hang her things.

He brought her into the kitchen. "I know this is going to seem like overkill, but I have even more instructions than the last time, since you'll be with Sammy all day."

"It's fine. It's good." Her throat tightened unexpectedly. Jack was so careful, so thorough, at caring for Sammy. God had made sure Sammy was in a good home, that was for sure.

After walking her through the instructions and showing her where everything was kept—all in that flat, business-like tone—Jack finally left. It felt like a relief.

Until she sat down with Sammy. "Hey, pumpkin," she said quietly.

He ignored her.

"Sammy?"

He continued pushing blocks into his bin. Or did he pause? She wasn't sure.

"Are you hungry?"

He looked up at her, a fleeting glance, and then back at his blocks.

"Daddy will come back," she said. "He always comes back."

No reaction there.

She blew out a sigh. These were going to be long days if she couldn't do even basic communication with Sammy. She was incredibly grateful for the opportunity, but it came accompanied by worry.

Problem solve. She'd claimed to know about autism when she'd asked Jack for the job, and she hadn't been lying. She needed to use that knowledge to help Sammy communicate. She couldn't freeze up just because he was her secret son.

She shook off her emotions and cast her mind back to the kids she'd worked with before, kids she'd cared for, a lot, but not with the depth of emotion she felt for Sammy.

A few of them had been nonverbal, although they'd managed to communicate through art.

She studied Sammy, thinking. Now that she was paying closer attention, she realized that he wasn't poking the blocks into the correct holes as she'd thought. Instead, he was putting all of them into the larger side hole, and struggling plenty to do that much.

Fine motor skills delay. It was typical, and no doubt his TSS workers would help him with it. In fact, maybe that was why he was playing with the blocks at all.

But it meant that having him express himself through art probably wasn't a good option.

Okay, she needed to try something else. She thought back to the kids she'd worked with and had a lightbulb moment: sign language.

That was something even young babies could learn. It didn't take a lot of coordination, nor verbalization skills.

She got on her phone and looked up "sign language" and "babies."

When Sammy stopped playing with the blocks and instead started banging one against his head, hard, she figured something was wrong. A check of the detailed schedule Jack had left confirmed that it was time for Sammy's midmorning snack.

She got out the whole-grain crackers Jack had told her to serve and handed Sammy one. He stuffed it into his mouth and then looked at her expectantly.

"Do you want more?" She put her thumbs against her fingertips, making her hands into ovals, and tapped them together. "More?"

Sammy stared.

Gently, she reached out and formed his hands into the same shape, then tapped them together. "More!" she said and handed him another cracker.

They went through the entire snack that way, and while she was still assisting him after his designated ten crackers, she thought she saw a glimmer of understanding in his eyes.

Later in the day, she noticed he was looking at the door frequently. She found the sign for *daddy* on her phone. Then she found a photo of Jack and Sammy and brought it over to him. "Daddy," she said, pointing to Jack. Then she flattened her hand, splayed her fingers and tapped her forehead with her thumb. "Daddy. He'll be home soon."

She reached to help him, but he took the picture and grasped it in both hands, pulled it close to his face and stared at it.

Then he flattened his hand and tapped his forehead with his thumb. And looked at her.

Her heart expanded almost to bursting. He was smart! He *could* communicate. "That's right, Sammy!" she said and reached out to hug him, making it short and loose in deference to his likely preference for nonintense cuddling.

Indeed, he twisted away, but gently. Then he looked pointedly at the kitchen and made the "more" sign.

Arianna couldn't keep the smile off her face. He'd just asked for more food! And though it wasn't strictly his mealtime, she went and got him a bowl of fruit and more crackers. For him to communicate deserved a celebration.

They finished the snack together, and then she had Sammy sit with her in the kitchen while she made a modest dinner for him and his father. Pasta and cheese sauce with broccoli on the side. Cooking wasn't one of her duties, not officially, but she saw no reason not to help Jack out that way, since she was here all day.

A little later, Sammy looked at her with peculiar intent. He pointed at the picture of Jack and made the "daddy" sign. Then he pointed at Arianna and waited.

"He'll be home soon, buddy," she said.

He pointed at her again, and she stared at him. Could it be that he wanted to know the sign to use for her?

Before she could stop herself, she looked up the sign for "mother." Five spread fingers, thumb tapped on the chin.

Should she teach her son to call her "mother"?

The temptation tugged hard at her. Who on Redemption Ranch, or in Esperanza Springs, would know what the sign meant? It could be her private little communication with her son.

But that would be wrong. She'd be using Sammy for her own selfish satisfaction. Throat tight, she punched the keys to look up the sign for "aunt." Make a close-fisted *A*, circle it beside the cheek a couple of times. It was a sweet sign.

She taught it to him, and he caught on quickly, his face lighting into something like a smile.

It was enough.

It would have to be enough.

"You're sure these colors are okay?" Arianna asked Penny several days later. She was unloading discount paint from her car and doubting herself. "I know you gave me free rein, but sometimes that's better in theory than in practice."

"Believe me, that's the least of my problems." Penny was carrying cans of paint from Arianna's car to the outdoor stairway that led to Arianna's apartment. "With Willie and Branson both bugging me for dates I don't want to go on, as well as running the ranch, I've got my hands full. Besides, your taste is better than most people I know."

"If you're sure." Arianna had a vision for the upstairs apartment, and she'd gotten a little carried away with it at the paint store.

Daniela Jiminez, one of the women who worked as a therapist at the ranch, pulled up in her Jeep. "Did I hear there was a painting party out this way?"

"You sure did," Penny said and flashed a grin at Arianna. "I figured you might need some help. You don't mind, do you? I asked a couple of the other gals, too."

As if in response to her words, a truck pulled up. Kayla,

who worked with Arianna in the church nursery, and Lily, who'd picked up those adorable twins, climbed out.

"Ready to work," Kayla said.

"I love painting," Lily added.

Their kindness warmed Arianna's heart. "You guys didn't have to do this. I'm sure you've got plenty to do at your own houses. And husbands and kids to take care of." In fact, all three of the other women—Daniela, Kayla and Lily—were relatively newly married. Both Kayla and Lily had kids, and Daniela had a suspiciously round belly.

"Oh, believe me, we welcome the chance to be away from our mom responsibilities for a little while," Lily said. "A girls' night is fun, even if it has to take place in the middle of the afternoon."

"And I brought chocolate." Daniela opened the passenger door of her Jeep and pulled out a tray of very fancy brownies. "To make up for the fact that I can't paint while I'm pregnant. I'm a whiz with masking tape in well-ventilated rooms, though."

Arianna inhaled the rich fragrance of them and regretfully patted her hips. "These jeans are already too tight. Don't tempt me."

"Jeans are made to be unsnapped," Lily said. "Besides, you have a beautiful figure. You have actual curves." She gestured at her own rail-thin self. "I dream of a figure like yours."

"Curves are beautiful," Daniela said, "or at least, that's what Gabe tells me." She blushed, and one hand rose to the scar on the side of her face.

Another vehicle, this one a giant SUV, sped up the long driveway and stopped in a flurry of gravel. A woman closer to Penny's age than Arianna's, wearing a Mountain Malamutes T-shirt, jumped out. "Am I late?"

"Yes, but it's okay." Penny hugged her and then introduced her to Arianna. "Thanks for coming, Marge. I know between the dogs and six kids, it's tough to get away."

"Tough, but welcome." Marge walked around, hugging the other women, then gripped Arianna's hand. "I'm real glad to meet you. Thanks for letting me in on your girls' night."

"Thank *you*," Arianna said, slightly overwhelmed by these women's willingness to help a near stranger.

They hauled the paint up the stairs and started spreading drop cloths and taping off the trim. "This is going to be so cute," Lily said. "I love the primary colors you chose. With a nice braided rug and the pine floors, it'll look great."

"You think so? I was afraid the bright blue and yellow would be too much."

"Bold but perfect," Lily declared, and the others nodded agreement.

They painted together for a couple of hours, making small talk. Arianna was impressed that they all worked hard. It wasn't their place, and they barely knew her, and yet they dug in and helped as if she were family.

"So how's it going with Jack?" Kayla asked as the afternoon light went golden. Then she slapped a hand over her mouth. "Sorry. I didn't mean to be nosy."

"But we're all curious, because he's seemed a little happier." Lily was pouring more paint into a roller tray.

"He was so unhappy before," Marge added. "With his wife."

"That's her sister!" Penny slapped Marge's arm gently. "Be nice."

"I'm sorry," Marge said. "Nobody ever knows what someone else is going through."

Jack had been unhappy with Chloe? That was the first

Arianna had heard about it, and she doubted it was true. "It's okay, don't worry about it," she said. "Chloe was… Well, she was the perfect one out of the two of us. We didn't have a whole lot in common."

"Perfect, huh?" Penny raised an eyebrow.

"She wasn't perfect enough to forgive a rude remark like I just made to you," Marge said. "I was forever offending that woman. You seem a lot more relaxed."

"Um…thanks?" Arianna ran her brush carefully along the trim beside a window. "I just figure I don't have room to judge other people, that's all. But it's not Chloe's fault she was that way. Our parents were really, really rigid."

"Like Jack's," Marge said. "That must be why they got along so well."

Arianna thought back to Jack's father, sputtering in the coffee shop. He'd always seemed difficult to Arianna, making awkward comments and assumptions about young single women, and artists, and pretty much everything Arianna was. Jack's mother hadn't been as vocal, but she, too, had tended to judge first and ask questions later. And she'd seemed to particularly target Arianna.

"Chloe ran that True Love Waits club at our church with an iron fist," Marge continued on. "Those teen girls were terrified of her."

Marge had her mouth open to continue talking, but at a glance from Penny, a subtle head shake, she shut it again.

Daniela leaned forward. "Did I hear right that you're teaching little Sammy some sign language?"

Arianna nodded, relieved at the change of subject. "It's really cute. He already understands the signs for *more* and *Daddy*."

"Oh, *more* was Leo's first word!" Kayla chuckled. "Kids. They're actually a little bit predictable."

"I think you're going to be really good for Sammy," Daniela said.

"And good for Dr. Jack," Marge added with a sly smile.

"Speaking of," Lily said, looking out the window. "He's coming this way with his adorable baby."

Arianna checked the time on her phone and clapped a hand to her forehead. "Guys, I have to take a break. I'm supposed to watch Sammy while Jack does some work with the rescue dogs out in the barn." She went out to the back porch-like area, a square with room for a chair and small table, surrounded by a railing.

Jack was trotting up the steps, the sun behind him adding gold to his light brown hair. He reached the top, not even winded, and smiled at her. "Ready for Sammy?"

"Yes, I'm sorry you had to bring him over." She had to keep better track of time if she was going to make a good impression as a nanny, good enough that Jack might let her stay awhile.

"No problem. I'll get my work in the barn done and then come back and get him so you can finish painting," he said. "I saw you made a meat loaf. You've been cooking for us all week, and I appreciate it. You should at least stay for dinner with us so you could benefit from your hard work."

An electric prickle raced up and down her spine. She didn't want to impose on Jack and Sammy's family time, nor establish a habit of being too close and personal. But if Jack were asking her to stay because he wanted her to...

"The therapists say it's good for him to witness interaction," Jack said. "If he's having dinner with us, and hears us talking and laughing, it might stimulate his own communication centers."

Arianna's face heated. How stupid of her to think Jack was interested in hanging out with her. "Oh, sure, if it's for Sammy." She glanced back into the kitchen, where the other ladies were working and, most likely, listening in. "I can have a quick dinner, but then I'm going to finish painting while it's still light. You guys go on home," she called back through the screen door. "You've been an amazing help, but I'm going to need to be gone a couple of hours."

"Go, go," Daniela said. "We'll just finish up what we're doing and let ourselves out."

She took Sammy from Jack's arms. "I've got you covered," she said. "We'll be hanging out at home." Then she felt stupid to have said that. Jack's house wasn't home, not to her.

He just gave her his usual sunny smile and trotted back down the steps.

She went back into the kitchen, where Sammy permitted some pats and cooing from the ladies before starting to fuss. Arianna gave each woman a quick hug. "Thanks so much, you guys. With all of you helping, it's almost done. I owe you big-time."

They all assured her they'd enjoyed it, and Daniela wrapped up a giant brownie for her to take along.

As she carried Sammy back to Jack's place, melancholy washed over her. She had loved the taste of community that she'd gotten with those women. She would love to build on those friendships.

Except how real were the friendships when nobody knew the truth about her?

If they knew that Sammy was actually her son, she was fairly certain they'd all despise her. As would Jack. And unfortunately, she couldn't avoid spending more and more time with him, it seemed. Time when she needed to be on her guard, to make sure the truth didn't slip out. Starting with their cozy family dinner tonight.

Chapter 6

When Jack walked into his house after working in the barn with the dogs, the first thing he saw was Arianna, stirring something in a pot on the stove. Her wild curls were back in a ponytail, at least mostly, and her cheeks were flushed. She was humming.

In the doorway between the kitchen and the hall, Sammy bounced contentedly in his jumper. The smell of meat loaf and onions and potatoes made Jack's mouth water.

He stopped for a moment just to take it in, this unfamiliar, deep feeling: *I'm home. This is home.*

He must have made some noise, because she turned, and her wide smile made her even prettier. "Oh, hey, glad you're home," she said.

Did she hear how domestic that sounded? Could she be feeling anything similar to what he was feeling?

Probably not. It was probably just wishful thinking on his part.

After all, what did he know about having a loving family? His own mom had usually looked angry at this time of day, because someone was late or unappreciative or inappropriately dressed for dinner.

"I should go shower," he said. Chloe would have already waved him upstairs, grimacing. Working with animals meant he picked up a little bit of their fur and smell even if he'd just been doing quick exams, as he had this afternoon.

Arianna lifted her hands, palms up. "Don't worry about it. Just wash up in the kitchen sink—it's your house." She stepped closer. "And you don't smell too terribly doggy," she said with a grin.

She smelled good, like flowers.

Jack swallowed and took a step back and looked around the kitchen. Arianna had laid out plates and cutlery on the plank table in the kitchen. Sammy's high chair was there, in between the two set places. Ketchup and salad dressing were set out in their original bottles, and the napkins were paper, although neatly folded.

He thought about his parents, their formal style of dining. Chloe had loved it, had loved going to their house and eating well-prepared food on their fine china.

Obviously, Arianna wasn't much for formal dining. Or she wasn't going to try to make it happen at the end of a workday with a hungry baby.

He liked that.

Confused by his feelings, he strode over to the doorway and knelt in front of Sammy. He was delighted when his son held out a hand to him, and he picked Sammy up and swung him high. Sammy didn't chortle like a lot of babies would, but his expression changed, his mouth quirking up a little and then opening.

"He's loving it!" Arianna stood, watching and smiling. "Look at that happy face."

More emotions nudged at Jack's heart, emotions that made him uncomfortable. Undeniably, he and Arianna were on the same wavelength. He drew in a breath and, after one more swing, took Sammy to his high chair.

"Thanks for staying for dinner," he said. "I should have thought about the fact that you're still commuting to your aunt and uncle's place. I hope this won't make your drive down the mountain too difficult."

"It's fine," she said as she carried a big bowl of salad to the table. "Truthfully, I'm glad to have a nice meal in a clean place."

Jack thought of her aunt and uncle's home, how messy and disorganized it had been. "It must have been hard for you, living there."

"Oh no, don't get me wrong," she said quickly. "My uncle and aunt have been fabulous to me. I'm so grateful that they let me stay with them this long. Could you grab the potatoes?" she added, nodding toward the steaming bowl. She tipped the meat loaf, draining the grease into an empty can, and then carefully put slices onto a plate. "There," she said as she carried it to the table. "All of this can cool while you say a blessing."

"Sure," Jack said, even though he hadn't prayed publicly in a long time. They each took one of Sammy's hands, and then there was an awkward hesitation before he reached out and trapped her fingers in his. Long and slender, with calluses. Just as he'd imagined. He cleared his throat. "Father God, we thank You for this food and the chance to enjoy it together." He was about to summon up more to say when Sammy let out a series of bleating sounds, his usual signal for hunger.

"In Christ's name, amen," Jack said quickly, and when he opened his eyes, Arianna was smiling.

"Short prayers are the best kind sometimes," she said, and he laughed and nodded.

She insisted on serving, which gave him a few minutes to look around the kitchen. Of course, it was messy. This was Arianna, and she'd been taking care of Sammy as she cooked.

But he also noticed that she had put up the curtains he'd had sitting in their package for weeks and hung a small painting he didn't remember seeing before on the wall above the table. "You did some decorating."

"I hope you don't mind," she said as she handed him a steaming plate. "It just seemed like you needed little bit of... I don't know..."

"A woman's touch? Yes. We do."

She was looking at him while he said that, and something flashed in her eyes. He would have given a lot to know what it meant.

But it wasn't his business to go digging into her psyche. He needed to keep his distance. He busied himself with cutting Sammy some small pieces of meat and potatoes, and Sammy ate with a surprising amount of enthusiasm. "Wow, he seems to like it."

"I was hoping he would. I noticed he's a little picky about texture."

"Soft, but not too soft," he said. "This is perfect."

"For him. Sorry I made you baby food."

"No, this is really good," Jack said, meaning it. He scooped in several more bites before continuing, "I love comfort food, and your sister never made it."

Silence.

Jack replayed what he'd said in his mind and then felt

like a complete jerk. He shouldn't be making comparisons. He shouldn't speak ill of the dead.

After a moment Arianna spoke, her voice more thoughtful than condemning. "Chloe was more like our mom, who really wanted to be sophisticated about food," she said. "She was a wannabe foodie."

"So that's where Chloe got it," he said, relieved that she had ended the awkwardness. "What about you?"

"Oh, I was a disappointment. I was always so ordinary." She laughed dismissively.

Oh no, Arianna. You're anything but ordinary.

Even the thought made guilt overwhelm him. Arianna might not know it, but Chloe had been pathologically jealous about Jack and other women—for no reason Jack could understand—and her jealousy had focused on her sister. Chloe had suspected that Jack was drawn to Arianna. That was one big reason she had pushed her sister away. And it was one reason Jack had always tried to keep his distance from Arianna. He didn't want to stir Chloe's anger or give her any cause at all to feel more jealous.

Now Chloe's frequent disapproval echoed in his mind.

What was he doing, having Arianna in his house, in the mother's role, having a family dinner?

Unfortunately, Chloe had shared her belief that Jack was attracted to Arianna with his parents, with whom she was quite close. And considering how negatively Jack's father had reacted to them having coffee together, if he heard that they'd shared a home-cooked dinner, say, it would create a big uproar.

Jack could deal with his father, but Arianna shouldn't have to. Dad was blunt, sometimes rude. He could hurt Arianna. That was the last thing Jack wanted.

Oblivious to Jack's inner turmoil, Arianna was spooning bites of meat loaf into Sammy's mouth. She glanced over at Jack. "Look, he's starting to eat with a spoon a little bit," she said. "The next step will be to have him hold it himself. I've been reading about breaking everything down into small steps, and the TSS who was here yesterday helped me figure it out."

Mixed feelings coursed through Jack. Arianna was warm. She was wonderful with Sammy. He'd done the right thing hiring her.

Except that he liked her way too much. Admired her. Could fall for her.

He stood and started clearing off the table, aware that it seemed abrupt but unable to sit still a moment longer. He brought a cloth over to the table and wiped Sammy's face. Then he nodded at Arianna's still half-full plate.

"I'll take Sammy up to his bath and bed," he said. "That will give you a chance to finish your dinner in peace."

But as he picked Sammy up, Arianna pushed her plate away. "Do you mind if I come with you?"

As she tagged along to the bathroom, as she watched Jack kneel to gently wash Sammy, ignoring the fact that he was getting soaked himself, Arianna swallowed the tight knot in her throat.

She was absolutely blessed among women to be able to participate in her son's care. To watch his loving father bathe him, to help put him to bed.

She didn't deserve it. How well she knew that. God had given her grace.

Jack had gone quiet, but that was okay. Sammy liked quiet and peace. So did Arianna, for that matter. She handed Jack the hooded towel that hung on the back of the door, and he pulled Sammy out and wrapped him in it.

Sammy almost smiled, and Arianna's heart melted at the sight of Jack holding his son in such a loving way.

If there were ever any question about whether adoptive parents could care for their children as much as biological parents did, it was answered in this tender moment. Jack clearly adored his son. And although Sammy wasn't expressive, the way he stared up at his father, his focus and intensity, made Arianna believe that he adored Jack just as much.

God works all things for good.

Tears pushed at the backs of her eyes as she followed the father and son into Sammy's room. She was tired, that was all. Like every day, she'd gotten up early to take a stab at cleaning her aunt's kitchen, and then she'd driven up the mountain. She'd been working with Sammy most of the day and then painting in what little time off she had.

That had to be the reason she was emotional. She wasn't getting enough sleep. She was tired.

"Pick him out a pair of pajamas," Jack said as he sat on the edge of the rocking chair, Sammy bundled in the towel in his arms.

So Arianna knelt and opened the drawer of Sammy's cute, pale blue dresser. She stared in amazement at the folded pajamas lined up perfectly in the drawer. Wow, Jack was neat. "Is there a particular pair he really likes?"

"The blue ones with teddy bears. They're the softest."

So she pulled them out and helped Jack diaper Sammy and then put him into the one-piece pajamas. Sammy rubbed the backs of his little hands over his eyes.

"Somebody's tired," Jack said. Tenderly, he set Sammy down in the crib and rubbed his arms and legs with gentle pressure. "It helps relax him," Jack explained. "Helps him drift off to sleep."

Hesitantly, Arianna reached in and did the same, rubbing her fingers gently along Sammy's pajama-clad arms and legs.

What would it be like if this were real? If Jack was the father and she was the mother and Sammy was their child?

She already knew: it would be all she'd ever wanted in the world.

But no way, no way could she have it, and she was going to break her own heart if she kept having these crazy fantasies. She coughed, trying to clear her throat of the golf ball–size lump that had lodged there. "I think I'm going to go downstairs, give you two some privacy," she said in a rush. She backed out of the room, and then, at the doorway, she spun and hurried down the stairs, her feet clattering. She'd probably woken Sammy up again, just when Jack was getting him to sleep, but it was better than falling apart in front of Jack and then trying to explain it.

She went into the bathroom, locked the door, sank down on the edge of the bathtub and turned on the fan and the water. Then she let the sobs come.

How had she ever given her precious baby away? Why, oh, why had she done it?

Intellectually, of course, she knew that it had been the right thing to do. She believed in adoption, and she'd read all the research showing that parental love in an adoptive family was just as strong as parental love in a biological family. Sometimes better if a biological parent wasn't ready.

But what the literature hadn't said was how much it could hurt the birth mother. How the thought, let alone the sight and sound and smell, of the child she'd grown in her own body could tug her heart straight out of her chest.

Arianna had been drifting through life ever since she'd given birth, and this was why. Because there was a hole in her. Because she felt incomplete and didn't know if that would ever change. Because she was grieving the fact that she couldn't see her son, spend the days with him, get to know him, watch his every move.

She heard Jack's heavy tread on the stairs, and it brought her back to reality. She was in a better position than a lot of birth mothers, because she'd placed her child with family. And now she *did* get to help with Sammy. She did get to know him, at least some, and she could see for herself that he was fine, doing well. It was more than she had ever expected, because it was more than Chloe would ever have permitted. It was more than many birth mothers had, and it would have to be enough.

She splashed water on her face and ran her fingers through her hair. Maybe, in the dimming light of evening, Jack wouldn't notice that she'd been crying.

But when she came out of the bathroom, he was standing in the middle of the living room waiting for her. He studied her face, tilting his head to one side. "You okay?"

She nodded quickly. "Fine," she said, afraid to say any more. She hurried into the kitchen, started gathering up her things. "I hate to leave you with this mess," she said to him when he followed her. "Just let it go and I'll clean it up tomorrow."

"You're already doing enough for us," he said. "Besides, you know I like to clean."

Even in the midst of her distress, that made her smile. "You're strange," she said.

"In a bad way?" His tone was light, but his gaze lingered on hers.

She licked her lips. "I better get going," she said nervously.

"I feel terrible about having you drive down the mountain," he said. "Why don't you just stay up here tonight?"

His offer seemed to hang in the air between them. What was he actually suggesting? Why was he looking at her that way? And why was her own heart beating so fast?

She reached for her newfound faith and values. "Jack, I would never... That's not what I do." She was about to say more, to describe the change she'd gone through.

But he held up a hand as color climbed from his neck into his face. "I didn't mean that the way it sounded," he said, his words tumbling over each other. "I just meant, I hate to have you drive so late at night. I'm sure you could stay with Penny."

"No, no," she said. "I have to go. I need to go home. I'll be fine." She headed toward the door. When she went to open it, he was there, opening it and holding it for her.

He was so close that she could smell his spicy, masculine scent.

He stared down at her and lifted his hand. One finger brushed her cheek.

She drew in her breath with a gasp. He was going to kiss her. And God forgive her, but she was going to let him.

But something came into his eyes and he pulled back, his expression disconcerted. "Go get in your car," he said, his voice rough. "I'll watch you."

"Jack..."

"Go on. Now." It was an order.

And there was something in his eyes, some wildness that she had never seen in her gentle brother-in-law. She spun and scurried to her car, her heart pounding so hard that it made her breathless.

Chapter 7

Two days later, Jack still felt like an idiot.

He had gotten carried away when Arianna had stayed for dinner, acted ridiculous. He'd behaved like a boyfriend, not a former brother-in-law and an employer, and it was inappropriate and wrong.

It wasn't possible that he was attracted to Arianna. It had just been the emotions caused by having her there for a homey dinner. Her love of Sammy, the home-cooked meal, the sunset…all of it had contributed to a romantic feeling, and he had let himself go there when he shouldn't have.

Ever since, his emotions had been in such turmoil that avoiding Arianna had felt like a necessity. Yesterday he'd managed to keep his distance aside from a few instructions in the morning and a quick handoff of Sammy in the evening.

But today, Willie had driven his truck down to town to help Arianna bring her few things up to move into the new apartment.

Now she, Penny and Willie were carrying boxes up the outdoor stairway that led to her apartment.

Jack was young and able-bodied, more so than Willie, and what kind of gentleman would let ladies and an old man do a bunch of lifting and hauling?

He had to help. Even though he sensed that her moving in was going to be a disaster.

He'd help because it was the right thing to do, and then he'd stay away. She didn't work for him on Saturdays and Sundays, and there was no reason for him to be around her, not at all. After a half hour of carrying boxes, he'd leave Arianna alone for the rest of the weekend.

He picked Sammy up and parked him on his hip. Sammy was still sleepy and leaned his shampoo-smelling head against Jack's shoulder.

This is for him.

Arianna was great with Sammy, and for his son's sake, Jack could handle her presence. Even though he was attracted, he didn't have to act on it.

As soon he'd crossed the yard, Penny came over and held out her arms, Willie right behind her. "Let me hold that sweet baby while you help carry boxes," she said.

Sammy went to her willingly, and she tickled his chin. "You see what I did there," she said to Willie, laughing. "Now I get to chill out with this beautiful boy."

Willie gave her a tender smile. "If it were up to me, you'd sit in the shade and relax all the time."

Penny blushed.

Leaving them to what looked an awful lot like flirting, Jack strode over to the truck, picked up a couple of boxes—one coming open, the other ripped on one side—and carried them upstairs, shaking his head. Ariana had probably packed at the last minute, like she seemed to do most things.

When he walked into the apartment, the sight that greeted him made him stop still.

Arianna was shoving a chair to one corner of the main room. Sunlight glinted on her hair, turning it into a fiery mane as she tilted her head to one side, studying the effect. Then she spun around, found an empty box and set it beside the chair as if it were an end table. She rummaged through another box, found a large scarf and draped it over the box. Suddenly, the little corner looked cozy, a nice place to curl up with a book.

Something tightened inside him. Arianna had a passion for beauty and color, and she was so creative. So different from him—opposite, really. Maybe that was why he found her fascinating.

To cover his reaction, he cleared his throat as he set down the boxes he was carrying, then crossed his arms as she turned to him. "You went pretty outrageous with the wall color," he said, looking around.

"Outrageous?" She lifted an eyebrow as she turned a slow 360, studying the walls, three blue and one yellow. "I wondered if it was too much, but Penny seems to like it and so did the ladies. They finished all my painting the other night while I was with you." The color in her cheeks heightened, and she looked away. "Wasn't that nice of them?"

"It *was* nice. They're good people." *And it gave you the chance to hang around with me and Sammy, like you were part of the family.* Remembering the domestic evening they'd spent together made Jack feel a little warm, too.

And those were thoughts he didn't need to be thinking, feelings he didn't need to be having. "I'll, um, run up the rest of the boxes if you'd like to keep setting up."

After that, he'd take Sammy back to his house, where he felt a little more in control.

As he was bringing up the last load of boxes—surprising that Arianna had so few possessions—Penny and Willie followed, Penny carrying Sammy.

"There's my little man," Arianna cooed.

He glanced back from where he was setting down the boxes in time to see Arianna leaning toward Sammy, smiling and gently rubbing his arm. Sammy rocked a little and vocalized, an *ah-ah-ah* sound Jack hadn't heard him make in a long time.

"Such a cutie," Penny said, and Willie reached out a finger to tickle Sammy's neck, making him half flinch, half giggle.

That warm feeling in Jack's heart as he watched was unfamiliar, but he knew what it was: family.

Penny and Willie and Arianna felt like family. And they were a lot more affectionate than his own family had ever been.

But he had to be careful. Penny and Willie were fine, they'd most likely stay around. But Arianna was here temporarily. She obviously wasn't the "put down roots" type, if the few boxes that constituted her possessions were any indication.

Best not to let that family feeling penetrate too deeply in regards to Arianna. Yes, she was Sammy's aunt, but she was a free spirit and would probably just be in and out of his life.

"I can help you unpack your kitchen stuff," Penny said to Arianna.

Arianna did a mock cringe. "I, um, actually don't have any."

"How have you managed to cook for yourself?" Jack blurted out.

She shrugged. "I've mostly been renting rooms in friends' houses or furnished places," she said. "There never was a need. It's okay. I can pick up some stuff in the next few weeks."

"Or this one could take you to town to get some stuff, and pick up your car, too," Willie suggested, nodding at Jack.

"Oh, that's not really necessary." Arianna looked uneasy.

Of course she did. He'd come on pretty strong when they were last alone together.

"Penny and I will watch the baby," Willie went on. "And Jack would probably even advance you the money from your first paycheck." Willie nudged him.

Arianna glanced quickly at Jack, as if to see whether that was true.

She was broke and she needed some basics to survive. He couldn't leave her to make do without a pan or cup or plate to her name, could he?

Willie leaned closer to Jack. "Gives me a little more time with Penny," he whispered. "And I figured it might be a good thing for you young people, too."

Great, Willie was matchmaking. "Penny," Jack said with a feeling of desperation, "you probably have a ton of other stuff to do, right?"

She shrugged. "More important than taking care of this little peanut? Not hardly. Go on, go."

"I could use a few things from the general store," Arianna said hesitantly, "and I need a ride down to my car. But I don't want to put you out."

"It won't put me out," he said, giving in to the forces pushing him into a shopping date with Arianna. A shopping date brimming full of forbidden fruit.

Oh no. Not Donegal's Hardware.

Arianna didn't move to exit Jack's truck as he pulled

into one of the diagonal parking spots in front of the hardware store that had supplied the town with wrenches and mousetraps and road salt as long as she could remember.

"I might do better at one of the big-box stores out on the highway," she said to Jack. "I need a little bit of everything, and I don't think the hardware store has it all."

"You'll be surprised at what they've done to the place," Jack said. "It's not Donegal's Hardware anymore, even though most townspeople still call it that. It's Donegal's General Store, and they have a little bit of everything."

She sat still in the truck, trying to figure out how to escape and whether she needed to. But Jack had come around and was opening her door, and that distracted her. When did a guy do that, except on a date? She flushed, ignored the hand he extended and climbed out.

"Who's running the store now?" she asked. "Surely not Mr. and Mrs. Donegal?"

He shook his head. "Old Mr. Donegal passed away, but Mrs. Donegal is still there sometimes. Her daughter-in-law, Courtney, is the one who really runs the place."

Arianna's heart started thumping, slow and heavy, even as she tried to calm herself. The Donegals didn't know anything, she reminded herself. As long as she could stay calm, everything would be okay.

They walked inside, and it was like the old Donegal's Hardware, but different. There were the same bins of nails and extension cords and the faintly chemical smell of fertilizer and weed killer. From the back of the store came the grinding sound of someone making a key. Sweet, soft memories of simpler times assailed her.

But it wasn't the same. Nothing stayed the same. The store was bigger now, with a candy counter, displays of home goods and even some clothing.

"They knocked out a wall and took over the soda fountain next door," Jack said, gesturing toward the far side
of the store, where a row of turquoise-covered stools sat
along a counter lined with napkin holders and salt and pep-
per shakers.

Jack led the way toward an aisle with a sign proclaiming
it held kitchen supplies. "Courtney's husband, Malachi, is
still a professor at the community college," he explained.
"And did you know their son, Nathan? Real smart guy. I
heard he's teaching at the University of Colorado. Chemistry, I think."

Hearing Nathan's name on Jack's lips caused a flutter in
Arianna's stomach, but she was relieved to learn that Nathan was living up north and doing well. *Breathe*, she told
herself. *Everything's going to be fine.*

At least, as fine as it could be with the secrets she
guarded in her heart.

There was Hannah Johnson from the bakery, buying
mousetraps. "You didn't see me with these," she said with
mock sternness. "Preventative measures. That's all."

"Just keep making your cinnamon muffins, and my lips
are sealed," Jack said.

One of the store's workers called out a greeting, and Jack
waved back. "How's school, Marla?" he asked.

"I'm loving it," she said. "Photography is my life." She
glanced around quickly and added, "After Donegal's General, of course."

Arianna looked at the pots and pans and selected an in-
expensive skillet and pot. The initial expense was going
to be tough to cover, but she'd be able to eat much more
cheaply if she cooked, and healthily, too.

"Chloe used to love these," Jack said, holding up a
heavier pan.

"Yeah, well, Chloe could afford it," she said and then bit her lip.

Jack was looking at her quizzically. "Does it bother you when I mention her?"

"No. No, it's good. And I didn't mean to sound bitter, not at all. I'm glad she had all the nice things, since they meant a lot to her."

"They did," Jack said, and their eyes met for the briefest moment. But it was enough to read a meaning: Jack wasn't the type to care much about material things.

Neither was Arianna. But the last thing she needed was to focus on what she and Jack had in common.

"I wish I hadn't gotten rid of so much," Jack said. "The church was helping a family whose home burned down, and I just boxed up a lot of Chloe's cookware that I'd never use myself and drove it over." A shadow passed across his face, and Arianna could imagine why.

A lot of people coped with loss by clinging to the loved one's stuff, but Jack wasn't that type. He'd want to clean up and move on.

"I can't afford a set of heavy-duty cookware," she said quietly. "Anyway, I like to travel light."

Jack studied her. "If it's a question of how much I'm willing to advance your salary, it's whatever you need. Don't let money keep you from getting what you need to be comfortable."

"Thanks," she said, wondering why he was being so generous. Was it just his nature, would he do the same for any employee or was he treating her differently because she was Chloe's sister? "I appreciate it. I'll get what I need, but these—" she held up the lightweight skillet and pot "—these are fine."

He hesitated, then asked, "How come you've lived like that, traveling light? It seems like the opposite of what Chloe wanted."

No need to tell Jack that the reason she'd stopped thinking about the future, that she'd never wanted to settle anywhere, was that she'd given up her precious baby for adoption. When she'd done that, she'd given up her dreams of a home, as well. "We're—we were—pretty different." *Leave it at that.*

"Chloe was so keen on making a home, trying to have it warm the way you guys didn't have growing up." He picked up a couple of serving utensils and dropped them into the basket. "I hope you don't mind my saying that. I know your parents could be sort of..." He trailed off.

"Cold and judgmental?"

"Yeah. That's pretty much how Chloe felt, and even though I didn't see them often, I got that vibe from them. Do you like these?" He thrust a purple pot holder set into her hands. "I guess that's why Chloe and I understood each other. We grew up a similar way."

She nodded as she took the pot holder set out of his hands and set it back on the shelf. There wasn't much else to say about her family of origin, and truth to tell, she was surprised Chloe had revealed so much to Jack, even surprised Chloe had experienced their parents that way. She'd always come so much closer to meeting their exacting standards than Arianna had.

Of course, Chloe had tried a lot harder. And the stress of that had taken its toll in all kinds of ways.

After they'd gathered a few more things Arianna needed, and Jack had insisted on paying for them—which, however embarrassing, definitely helped, but she made sure to reiterate that he should take the balance out of her first pay-check—Jack stopped in the middle of carrying things out to the car. "You know what I'm hungry for?"

"What?" She lifted her eyes to his strong jaw and hand-some face and then looked as quickly away. Not things she should focus on.

"A hot-fudge sundae," he said. "And they make really good ones here at Donegal's. They'll even give you extra fudge if you ask. Want one?"

Yum. Stress eating was her downfall, always had been. "Don't tempt me," she said.

"They're really good. They have small ones, if you're not super hungry, but I'm getting a large. Come on." He took her hand and tugged her toward the soda fountain side of the place.

She followed, the feel of his work-calloused hand steal-ing her breath. She didn't normally think of a veterinarian as doing physical work, but Jack trimmed horses' hooves and birthed calves. A country veterinarian relied on his own strength, and Jack had plenty.

They sat next to each other on stools that seemed to be placed just a little too close together. She could feel the warmth of his jeans-clad thigh next to hers, and suddenly, she was finding it hard to breathe.

"The usual, Dr. Jack?" The woman behind the counter sounded amused.

"Two of them," he said and then turned to Arianna. "That is, if double hot fudge on coffee ice cream sounds at all good to you."

"Don't forget the whipped cream and extra nuts," the server said.

Arianna's restraint lasted at least three seconds. "Okay. I'll have one, too."

"Arianna Shrader!" The high, raspy voice behind her went right down Arianna's spine and back up again. She turned and half stood to face a hunched, white-haired woman leaning on a cane.

She'd aged more than Ariana would have expected in just a couple of years, and it squeezed Arianna's heart. She'd always liked Nathan's grandmother. She leaned in and kissed the woman's dry, powdery cheek. "Hey, Mrs. Donegal."

Mrs. Donegal gave her a surprisingly fierce hug, then released her and waved a hand at Jack, who'd stood when she'd approached. "I see you all the time, but this girl's like the prodigal daughter. How have you been, honey?"

"Good. Doing art therapy," she said, blinking a little.

"That boy made a big mistake when he let you go," Mrs. Donegal declared. "You know, he's never found another." She looked sharply at Jack. "Are you two dating?"

"No!" Arianna said, her face heating.

"Not at all," Jack said at the same time.

"Well, good. Because I don't mind saying I'd like to see Nathan settle down with someone like you. Maybe you could pull him back here where he belongs."

Jack cleared his throat. "I heard he was doing something important at the University of Colorado," he said.

"That's right," old Mrs. Donegal said, her face visibly lifting. "Working on a fertilizer that'll double crop production, and they want to use it somewhere in Africa. Help people get more out of their land." She sighed. "Oh, I know he's a different one, and he says he's perfectly happy being single, but I just don't know. I'm afraid he gets lonely."

"Here you go." Two hot-fudge sundaes appeared in front of them, brought not by their original server, but by Courtney Donegal, Nathan's mother. "Hey, Arianna, good to see you. Mom, stop trying to find Nathan a woman. He's doing fine. Doing the work he loves. He and Arianna were never serious."

She ought to speak up, agree, laugh, congratulate them on Nathan's success. And she *was* happy for Nathan, and not surprised he'd done so well.

It was just the enormity of discussing him with Jack here.

Fortunately, Jack carried the conversation, asking about Nathan, encouraging them to brag, which gave Arianna a chance to regain her composure.

Wasn't his success evidence that she'd done the right thing, not telling Nathan about her pregnancy? He was following his calling, making a difference, using that mighty, impressive mind of his.

"Come on, Mother. Let them eat their sundaes before they melt," Courtney said firmly, taking her mother-in-law's arm and leading her away. "It was good to see you both. Enjoy."

Arianna stared at the giant sundae in front of her so she wouldn't have to look at Jack. Some women's appetites would have been demolished by a stressful encounter with an ex's family.

Not Arianna. The sundae looked fantastic.

"Dig in," Jack said. He stuck his spoon into the ice cream, took a bite and smiled, the pleasure going all the way up to his eyes.

Arianna swallowed. Wow. Hastily, she looked down at the sundae and took a bite of creamy richness.

"Good, isn't it?" he asked, and they focused on their food for several blissful moments.

"You know, Chloe would never slow down enough to

enjoy a sundae with me," he said, and then, when she looked up at him, he covered her hand with his, giving it a quick squeeze. "I'm sorry I keep talking about her. It's just that you look like her, I guess, and make me think of her."

"I understand." She put down her spoon with her sundae half-finished. "Chloe had a lot of self discipline, unlike me. That's why she was able to stay so thin."

Jack frowned. "Even when she wanted to gain some weight to try to get pregnant, she couldn't make herself relax and eat more." He shook his head. "I've always wondered whether stress was a factor in her getting that blood clot. They say it wasn't, but…still, I wonder if there was something I could have done differently to help her, maybe avoid that fate."

"I've wondered the same thing," Arianna admitted. "I wish I spent more time with her, with you guys." It would have been painful, but if only they'd been able to work through that, maybe she could have lightened Chloe's load, helped her cope.

Jack nodded, his face grave.

She'd always wondered what Chloe had told him about Arianna, if she'd ever shared reasons for the obvious fact that they didn't get along.

"I know God has a plan," he said finally, "but sometimes, it's hard to fathom."

"We'll understand someday. Chloe does now, I'm sure." Because despite all her issues, Chloe had been a believer, strong in her faith.

"It's good we can talk about it together." Jack gave her a warm smile. "I'm glad you're here, Arianna."

Their gazes met. She couldn't look away.

Until a tall man approached them from behind. "Arianna? Listen, I just got into town. Haven't even checked in with the family yet, but I'd heard you were living here now. I was hoping to see you."

A prickle of doom crackled through Arianna's body. "Hi, Nathan," she said.

Chapter 8

"You sure you're okay?" Jack asked Arianna two hours later, as they walked slowly toward the barn. Jack was carrying Sammy on his shoulders. He probably should have left Sammy with Penny for another hour while he did the required vet checks on the dogs, but he wanted to maximize his time with his son on the weekend. He'd figured that Arianna would see his need for assistance and offer to help, because that was the type of person she was. He'd been right, and he was glad. Because he also wanted to spend a little more time with Arianna on this warm summer Saturday.

He wanted to find out more about her relationship with Nathan.

As they opened the barn door, the dogs registered their presence with barks and howls and yelps, high and low and everything in between.

"Jack, he's not putting his hands on his ears!" Arianna

said, her voice excited. "Oh, well, wait, there he goes. But he listened to the noise for a few seconds first."

He smiled at her enthusiasm. "We take what progress we can get."

He moved ahead into the barn, checking on a couple of dogs, an ear infection and a dog recovering from being spayed. Arianna wandered around with Sammy, kneeling to show him various dogs, talking in a gentle, upbeat voice.

What had been her relationship with the brilliant Nathan? What was it now?

Had the talented, nerdy professor broken her heart?

He didn't like the idea of it. And he was her brother-in-law, the closest thing she had to a male relative. Who better to offer her support and protection?

He came out of the second pen and knelt beside her and Sammy. True to form, Sammy had discovered a stick and was beating it on the front of a pen. The old dog inside didn't seem to mind.

"Did Nathan want to see you again?" he asked quietly.

She glanced at him and then focused on Sammy, tugging up his little jeans and straightening his sweatshirt.

Jack tried again. "I don't think I even knew you were dating him. Was that during the summer you spent here?"

She nodded, still not looking at him.

"Was it a serious relationship?"

Rather than answering, she rose to her feet and grasped Sammy's hand. "Let's go look at the mama and pups," she said, tugging Sammy along. She held him by his hands, encouraging him to walk.

Briefly, Jack was distracted by his son's heels-up, halting gait. Sometimes he noticed things that made him think Sammy didn't have autism. That gait, though, was a sign that he did.

Arianna was distinctly ignoring him. "Look," he said, "if you don't want to talk about Nathan…"

"Isn't that pretty obvious?" She continued to back away, holding Sammy's hands, all smiles for his son.

The idea of Arianna having a boyfriend, back then or now, did strange things to Jack. He had no right at all to feel possessive, but he most certainly did feel that way.

It was just that a guy like Nathan wasn't right for Arianna. She was creative, fun, a little wild. Nathan was dead serious, the type to spend every free moment at work.

He tried one more time. "If Nathan bothers you, let me know."

She met his eyes then, and to his surprise, hers were brimming with tears. Automatically, he stepped forward, reached to touch her shoulder. "You're upset. I'm sorry."

"No, it's fine. I'm fine." She stopped in front of the pen that held the mother and pups and reached up to open it. The new puppy stumbled out in cute, awkward puppy style.

"Look, Sammy, a puppy!" Arianna's voice was uncharacteristically shrill.

Sammy waved a hand toward the animal, batting at it. The puppy latched onto his tiny hand and gnawed with sharp puppy teeth.

Sammy wailed.

"You have to be careful with him around a puppy!" Jack whisked Sammy away.

"I'm sorry," she said as Jack checked Sammy's hand and then bounced him in the vigorous way that he liked.

Slowly, Sammy's cries subsided.

Jack's thoughts were in turmoil. Arianna was in tears because of Nathan. If the man came up here to see her, could he handle that? Would it be good or bad for Sammy?

And what was this powerful jealousy he was feeling?

He gave Sammy to Arianna. Quickly, he checked the two puppies and the mama dog, then gathered the few things they'd brought up and led the way back down to the house.

Given his weird feelings, the last thing he should do was to invite Arianna to come in. He felt as if an inner judge was setting a boundary. The judge's face morphed from Chloe's to his mother's to his father's and back again.

He couldn't start anything up with Arianna, not without playing into every one of their suspicions.

But Arianna looked sad, a little lost, standing with him on his front porch.

He shouldn't pay attention to the way her expression, her slightly slumped shoulders, tugged at his heart.

But Jack was tired of doing exactly what he should. "Do you want to come in?" he asked. "Sammy would like it."

"I should go unpack boxes and get settled," she said, but then Sammy reached out a hand toward her hair, glowing like fire in the late-afternoon light.

Jack couldn't blame him. He'd like to know what that hair felt like, too.

"Aw, sweetie," she said, her face softening.

He opened the door, and she followed him inside.

Feeding Sammy, sharing a frozen pizza while he played on the floor, giving him a bath… All of it went as smoothly as if they'd been a long-established couple. "You read to him, right?" Arianna asked when Sammy started to rub his eyes with the backs of his hands.

"Every night." Sometimes Jack felt sheepish about that; Sammy was too young for stories, really, and had enough delays that it wasn't clear how much he followed. "It's just a nice way to spend time together. I try to keep the TV off until after he's in bed."

"Good." She knelt beside Jack's bookshelf, where board

books mingled helter-skelter with Jack's own preferred reading—military and legal thrillers. "How about a little *Hungry Caterpillar*, Sammy?"

Sammy watched her impassively.

"Brown Bear?" she asked, holding up another book.

Sammy patted his own head, rhythmically.

"He wants *From Head to Toe*," Jack said.

"Oh, with the gorilla!" She grabbed the book from the shelf and brought it over. She sat down on the other side of Sammy and handed the book to Jack.

"No, you read," he said.

"Because you like to act out the pictures?" she teased.

"You bet." He usually did, hoping the concepts would get through to Sammy. But today, he was just glad that the melancholy look was gone from Arianna's face, the tears from her eyes.

She opened to the first page and held up the book so both Sammy and Jack could see. "Look at the penguin, how it's bending its neck. Can you do like the penguin?"

Jack turned his neck.

Sammy watched.

"Good job!" she said to Jack, grinning at him.

She went on, reading slowly and expressively, through the animals and their various abilities: giraffe, buffalo, monkey, seal, with Jack doing the actions in response. He felt silly at first, but Arianna's smiles and occasional giggles made him comfortable.

"Look at the gorilla, guys. Can you thump your chest like a gorilla?"

"I can," Jack boasted and did it.

Sammy thumped his chest, too.

Arianna sucked in a breath. "He did it," she whispered. "He imitated you and he did what the book said."

Jack was hardly breathing, his heart too full of joy. At the same time, he was willing Arianna not to make a big fuss; Sammy hated that. "Good job, buddy," he said quietly when he could speak.

Arianna leaned over and planted a kiss on Sammy's head, and then read on.

It was the only response Sammy gave, but it was a first, and it was enough.

His heart was full as he picked Sammy up. "Time for bed, my man."

"I should go," Arianna said.

"You don't want to help me put him to bed?"

"I...I'd better not."

Sammy gave a great yawn.

"Don't leave," Jack ordered. He carried Sammy upstairs before she could answer, not even looking at her. Because what right did he have to ask her to stay?

He put Sammy down and patted his back for a few minutes, prayed over him as he did every night and added an extra prayer for guidance and wisdom for himself. He didn't have to specify what situation he needed guidance in. The Lord knew.

When he walked downstairs, he didn't know whether to hope she'd listened to him and stayed or ignored him and left. But she was there, looking out the window to the moonlit yard.

He walked up behind her. Seemingly of its own volition, his hand came up to rest on her shoulder. "Pretty night."

She nodded. And didn't shrug him away.

"Thanks for helping with Sammy tonight. He's never responded to that book before."

She turned her head a little, her dimple showing. "That was amazing."

"It made me very happy."

"Me, too."

In a circle of moonlit intimacy, sharing joy about his son, there didn't seem to be a lot of decisions to make. What to do seemed obvious.

He tugged at her shoulder until she turned around, then touched her chin.

She looked up, her eyes wide. "Jack—"

When she didn't finish what she was saying, he let his finger trace her full lips, light as you'd touch a newborn kitten. "I want to kiss you."

She drew in her breath, and he expected her to pull away. Instead, she lifted her hand to cup his cheek.

"I need to shave," he said.

"It's okay."

He took that as a yes and kissed her.

Jack's lips moved gently on hers, but the kiss swept through Arianna like an electrical current. She sighed and pulled him closer.

He responded immediately, deepening the kiss, his fingers rising up to fork through her hair, then settling on the back of her head. And instantly, as if the mountain breeze had blown them away, her doubts and worries disappeared.

Being this close to Jack was all the warmth and love and caring she hadn't even known she was missing. It penetrated, too, that warmth: all the way through her, settling into her heart. It was as if something deep inside her sighed and said, *You're safe*.

His hand circled over her back in a gentle massage.

She breathed and let herself feel the emotions and kissed him back.

Until a jarring inner voice scolded through her romantic haze. *Chloe would really, really not like it if she knew what you were doing.*

And that thought stole away the safe, happy feeling. Because what *was* she doing, kissing the man who'd been Chloe's husband? The man from whom she was keeping a terrible secret?

It took every ounce of willpower to turn her head away, then her body, then to step outside the circle of his arms.

"Um, I..." She trailed off. There just weren't words, and if there were, she wasn't sure she could get them out past the thickness in her throat.

Jack looked a little dazed, as well.

She needed to leave. She couldn't look at his vulnerable face anymore, that warmth in his eyes. She needed to focus on her duty, what was best for Sammy.

But what *was* best for Sammy? Couldn't it be this?

No, it can't be this. The voice in her head sounded like her mother, but it could be Chloe's or the counselor at the church she'd attended—once—in the city where she'd gone as a single, pregnant mother-to-be. Maybe it was even Jack's voice. He'd admired how pure Chloe was.

Arianna, unlike her sister, had made bad decisions, and she had to pay. Had to pay for lying by omission, too; Jack would be furious if he knew the secret she was keeping.

With his special needs, Sammy didn't need the additional confusion of having his nanny turn out to be his mother. "I should go," she said. Her voice sounded odd, breathless. "That was... Look, Jack, I don't want to do that again."

It wasn't true. She *did* want to do it again. She wanted to feel his arms around her and his warm lips on hers, to see that intense, caring look—already fading now—in his eyes.

"I'm sorry," he said. "I didn't mean to overstep." He

was looking at her a little puzzled now, as if to say, *but you seemed to like it.*

"I'll see you later."

"We should talk about it."

She looked away. "Not now."

"Okay, then. I'll watch you get home safely."

"No need for that." Because if he did, she might turn around and run right back into his arms.

Sammy, bless him, let out a cry before Arianna could fall apart. "Go, take care of him," she urged Jack. "I'll just run across the yard and be home."

"Then we'll talk tomorrow," he said firmly. He tucked a stray strand of her hair behind her ear, his hand lingering on her cheek.

His touch burned. "Okay, sure." She spun away and headed toward the door. She had to escape. She wanted so desperately to melt into Jack's arms, to savor his embrace. Her whole chest ached with the longing for it.

Tough. You can't have it.

After letting herself out, she marched across the lawn. She reached the driveway that led to Penny's house.

Keep going.

She walked across the yard toward the outdoor stairs that led to her apartment.

Keep going.

She could do it. She could make it inside before she broke down.

"Arianna." The jarring sound of a male voice—*not* Jack's—startled her, and then the shadowy figure of a man came into view. She yelped out a scream and spun away from the intruder, her heart pounding fast.

"Arianna! Arianna, it's me, Nathan."

Oh. Her knees went weak, and she sank down onto the bottom step. "You scared me half to death."

"I'm sorry," he said, kneeling beside her. Wrinkles formed between his heavy eyebrows. "I just… You rushed away so fast, back at the store. Can we talk for a few minutes?"

No. She wanted to forget about Nathan and what had happened between them. Especially now, when her emotions were raw. "I'm very tired and I have to work tomorrow. Can't it wait?"

He bit his lip and shook his head back and forth. "I'm only in town for a few days, and this has been eating me alive."

She opened her mouth to refuse. But his face was tortured, and she'd once cared about him. "Okay," she said. "A quick talk. I guess I can do that."

"Thank you." He knelt on the pavement, shivering. He wore a short-sleeved polo shirt and khakis, not nearly warm enough for a mountain night.

"Come on in," she said with a sigh. "We can have a cup of tea and talk about whatever you want to talk about."

"Half an hour maximum," he promised. "And…despite the past, you can trust me."

"I know I can," she said, patting his arm as she walked past him, leading him up the steps.

From Sammy's bedroom, Jack watched Arianna lead Nathan Donegal up the steps to her place and slammed his fist against the wall beside the window.

He felt like a complete fool.

Here he had laid his heart out for her, exposed his feelings, and now she had a date with her ex-boyfriend?

Not that Jack's time with her had been a date, of course.

She was his employee, his former sister-in-law. She didn't have any obligation to him. She had probably set something up with Nathan when she'd seen him in town today and had been eager to get over to her place to meet him. It was Jack who had mucked everything up by kissing her.

But she responded. She seemed to like it.

Well, he thought she had. He'd thought he had heard a little sigh. Had thought she'd kind of melted into him. And when they'd broken apart, he'd thought he had seen some kind of warm emotion in her eyes.

But he wasn't the best at understanding women, as Chloe had let him know often enough. The other thing Chloe had pinned on him was that he had always had a crush on Arianna. Jack didn't think that was true. He had loved his wife and had never allowed his thoughts to venture toward her sister. He knew right from wrong.

But maybe Chloe had seen something he hadn't even been aware of himself. Maybe he had more feelings than he realized, and now they had led him astray, led him into thinking Arianna liked him when she didn't.

Sammy stirred in his crib, and Jack turned away from the window and went over to tuck his blue-and-white-checked bear back into his arms. Sammy's face smoothed, and his breathing became regular again.

This was what was important. That Sammy had a good life, that he get the treatment he needed, that he have loving caregivers.

Arianna's nanny gig had never been intended to be permanent. It was just until the end of the summer.

And now that Jack knew the boundaries he needed to set, he'd do it.

He would stay strictly professional with Arianna. He wouldn't comment if she went out with Nathan. He wouldn't set up any more of these late evenings that created feelings he shouldn't be having, feelings that could only lead to unhappiness. At the end of the workday, he would wave goodbye and send her away without a personal element in it. His father would be proud. Chloe would be proud.

He drew in a couple of deep breaths and tried to congratulate himself on the rightness of his decision.

The fact that he himself felt empty, gutted even, shouldn't signify.

Arianna watched Nathan drain the last of his tea, his Adam's apple bulging.

"I can't believe Chloe told you about my pregnancy," she said. Although she kind of could. Chloe wasn't one to leave any loose ends if she could help it.

"She said you were going to place the baby for adoption, and she didn't want me to show up later and cause problems. I guess she didn't realize you hadn't told me at all."

"I should have." Arianna's heart twisted with regret and misery. She'd made so many mistakes. "It's no justification, but I was immature. Naive and so confused. And when I came to you to ask if you wanted to continue the relationship, you said—"

"I said I didn't. I know." He leaned forward, elbows propped on knees. "You suspected you were pregnant then, didn't you?"

"I knew it," she admitted.

"I wish you'd told me."

She shook her head. "I should have. I meant to, but you were so excited about your new research fellowship in Boulder. And you said you'd be working day and night."

"Yes, but it was my responsibility," he said. "If we made

a baby together, I should have taken care of it." He splayed his hands in front of him and studied them.

Arianna's throat tightened. It was a gesture she'd seen Sammy make.

Nathan glanced up at her and then back down at his hands. "I only realized how wrong I was when my pastor spoke about how important fathers are, and how many don't take responsibility for their children. It hit me like a brick to the head that I was in that group, too."

"I suppose, though it wasn't on purpose. You can't be blamed for it."

"There's no way to find out more about the family who adopted our baby?"

Heat rose from her chest to her neck and spread to her cheeks. She prayed that the light was too dim for him to see how red her face was. "Like I said, it's a closed adoption," she said and hoped his steel-trap brain wouldn't close in on the fact that she hadn't answered his question. "You can put a letter on file, and when he comes of age, if he wants to, he can contact you. But, Nathan…think about it, okay? You'll probably have a wife and kids by that time. You might not want to be in touch."

"So it's a boy." He rested his cheek on his interlocked hands, looking away from her.

"It's a boy."

He blew out a sigh and stood. "I'm sorry, Arianna. Sorry for pushing you into what we did together, and sorry for not standing by you."

She shook her head. "Don't apologize. We were equally at fault. I'm sorry I didn't insist on your hearing the whole truth."

They hugged, and she stood at the door and watched him go downstairs and out of her life. For now.

She sagged back against the door after she'd closed it behind him, too distraught even to think. "Lord, forgive me," she whispered.

It was the millionth time she'd prayed that, of course. But now there were new prayers to add. "Forgive Nathan and help him to find peace. And turn all of this messy situation to good. Amen."

She slid down the door to a sitting position, forehead on upraised knees. And there she sat for a long time in wordless prayer and meditation, desperately needing the peace that only God could give.

Chapter 9

One awkward week later, Jack found himself at the office after everyone on his staff had gone home. He was catching up on paperwork, sure, but more than that, he was avoiding Arianna.

Every time he saw her, he thought about kissing her. Relived it, really—her warmth and tenderness and the way being close with her had filled a hole in his heart he hadn't even realized was there. His hands practically ached to pull her close to him again.

But there had always been reasons not to be with Arianna—Chloe's criticism and his parents' warnings—and those reasons hadn't gone away, not really. Yes, Chloe was gone. But for him to pick up with Arianna as much as proved that her suspicions had been right, that Jack hadn't really loved her, that he had been that neglectful, uncaring husband she had so often accused him of being.

And Chloe's critical glare, so vivid in his memory, would

be mirrored on his father's face were he to get together with Arianna.

Even those things might have been surmountable, but now he'd found out she had feelings for somebody else. Her relationship with Nathan must have been more serious than he'd thought, and from the looks of things, it was ongoing. Otherwise, why would she have taken Nathan up to her apartment?

It was true that he hadn't seen Nathan around in the week since the man had arrived in town. If Arianna were spending time with him, she was keeping it very quiet. So maybe Jack had overreacted. After all, Nathan lived up in Boulder and was a busy, well-known scientist. It would be tough for him to start, or restart, a relationship with a nanny-artist who lived in the southern part of the state.

Whenever he got to this part in his ruminations, a little spark of hope would come to life inside him. Guilt, though, due to Chloe and his father, quickly put out the flame.

So he was stressed. And he noticed that Sammy was fussier than usual, which could very well be because he was picking up on the tension between Jack and Arianna. That and the fact that Jack was working longer hours, so he wasn't spending as much time with his son as he should.

And if his state of mind was affecting Sammy, then Jack needed to do something about it. He didn't like asking for help, but he knew he had to overcome that, to swallow his pride, when Sammy was involved. So he closed up his office and walked two blocks down the street to his church, where his good friend Carson Blair was the pastor.

He walked through the cool, dark hallways. The light was still on in the church office, so he knocked.

"Come on in," came a deep but nasal voice.

Jack pushed the door open.

Hawk, honk. Carson was blowing his nose, and then he tossed the tissue into an overflowing wastebasket and looked up apologetically. "Hey, Jack," he said and coughed. "Glad to see you, but you might want to keep your distance. This cold is getting the best of me."

"I have a strong immune system," Jack said. "But I'm not stupid. I won't shake your hand." He studied his friend more closely. "Are you sure you should even be at work?"

"I canceled my appointments," Carson said. "But sermons don't write themselves. And Lily and the girls are visiting one of her old army friends, so I'm a bachelor this week. I may as well sneeze and cough here at the office as at home." He held up a hand. "And don't worry. Mrs. Greer will scrub everything down when she comes in in the morning."

"Oh, true." Jack had seen their church secretary disinfecting doorknobs and microphones, and once, she'd rushed up to the front of the church right in the middle of Carson's communion prayers to give him the hand sanitizer she'd forgotten to place with the bread and grape juice.

"What brings you here at this time of day?" Carson asked.

"I need to talk to you about something, and it seems like you could use a good meal. Can I buy you dinner? We'll go somewhere in town, close by."

"Sounds good to me," Carson said. "But don't you need to get home to Sammy?"

"Let me see if my nanny can stay a bit late."

"Your nanny, huh?" Carson cocked his head to the side and glanced questioningly at Jack. Then he turned back to his computer. "I'll just make a couple notes while you call her."

But Jack had no intention of calling Arianna; instead, he sent her a text.

Almost instantly, she texted back. No problem. No plans tonight.

Hmm, interesting. She didn't have plans. And she was making sure he knew it.

There was that tiny spark of hope again.

Half an hour later, they were at La Boca Feliz, and Senora Ramos, known to everyone as Delfina, was fussing over Carson. "*Sopa de tortilla* for you," she said. "Why are you not home in bed?"

"Lily and the kids are away," Carson croaked.

Delfina put her hands on her hips. "And you are not capable of opening a can of soup?" She turned to Jack. "And you could not help your friend?"

"I *am* helping him," Jack said. "I've brought him here for your healthy food."

Delfina smiled, her brown eyes twinkling. "This is the good answer," she said and clapped her hands as she turned toward the kitchen. "Emilio, *dos sopas de tortillas, por favor. El pastor está enfermo.*"

They both watched as she disappeared into the kitchen. Around them, silverware clinked and customers talked and laughed.

"So, what's going on with you?" Carson asked.

In the course of helping Carson, Jack had forgotten about his own problems for a few minutes, and he didn't really want to reengage with them. He lifted his hands, palms up. "No big deal. Nothing you need to worry about."

"I always worry about my flock," Carson said. "It's in the job description."

Delfina bustled back toward them, carrying a tray with

two brimming bowls of soup. She set one before each of them. "Eat, both of you. More food is coming."

Jack lifted an eyebrow. "Did we order more?"

"You didn't have to," Delfina retorted. "I placed the order myself, because I know what's good for a cold. And—" she pointed at Jack "—don't tell me you don't have a cold, because spending time with him, you will."

"I hope not," Carson said after she'd left them for another table. "I'd hate to be the reason you and Sammy get sick."

Jack waved a hand to dismiss Carson's worry. "We have so many TSS folks in and out of the house, plus Arianna's got him in some baby lap-sit program at the library. I'm sure he's been exposed to whatever germs you're carrying." He started spooning up soup, hot and spicy and delicious.

"Good." Carson ate for a few minutes and then put down his spoon. "I'd like to hear about whatever's worrying you."

Jack could tell from the determined look in Carson's eyes that the man wasn't going to give up. They were the same age, but Carson was wise, far wiser than Jack, especially in matters of the spirit and the heart. "I'm just struggling some," he admitted. When Carson nodded encouragingly, he went on. "There's something Chloe thought about me that I'm having a hard time shaking."

Carson frowned. "Was it true, what she thought?"

"No. At least, I don't think so."

"It's no fun to be harshly judged," Carson said. "Believe me, I've been there. And that judgmental voice doesn't have to be true to nag at you."

"Makes me question myself," Jack admitted. Because if Chloe, and his mom, and his dad all believed that Jack had a crush on Arianna, was it possible that he did and didn't know it?

As if he were reading Jack's mind, Carson pointed his

soupspoon at Jack and spoke again. "How does it all connect with what you were told as a child? How you were raised?"

Jack laughed, even though he didn't find the question funny. "'Harshly judged' could have been in my parents' marriage vows, they made such a practice of it. Toward me, toward each other and toward themselves."

"So Chloe came along and fitted right in with your concept of love," Carson said.

His words echoed in Jack's ears as Delfina brought them plates of steaming enchiladas and rice and beans, explained that they were extra spicy and that was good for a cold, and admonished them to eat every bite.

As Jack dug in, he thought about what Carson had said. Was that his concept of love: Harsh judgment? Was that why he and Chloe had hit it off?

They ate until they had to pause to wipe the sweat from their foreheads. "She wasn't kidding about spicy," Jack said, gulping water.

"I think I'm sweating out my germs. I sure don't feel congested anymore." He studied Carson. "Why are these questions about Chloe and your past coming up now? Because of Arianna?"

Jack blew out a breath. "There's no keeping anything from you, is there? Is it obvious?"

Carson shook his head. "Not obvious. The two of you are very circumspect and professional around each other. But I know you pretty well. I'm seeing something different in the way you confront the world, something that seems like it might come from... I don't know. Interest? Love?"

Jack nearly choked on a mouthful of beans. He waved his hand. "Nothing close to love. Interest, maybe. But that's where the past is bogging me down." He didn't want to disrespect Chloe's memory by telling Jack about her jealousy issues. "I'm just not sure whether it's right to let Chloe go and get back in the game again. Or when that might be okay."

"It's tough." Carson looked unseeingly across the crowded restaurant, and Jack remembered the trouble Carson had had accepting the loss of his first wife and moving on, until Lily had come along and rocked the pastor's world.

But Carson *had* accepted his loss and moved on, and no one had judged him for it.

"I'm going to email you a list of Scripture verses about guilt, and how to get free of it," Carson said. "Once you've grieved and healed from your past hurts and losses, you have to make your own decisions, independent of what others might think. I don't know about your wife, but my first wife had mental health issues that colored the way she looked at everything. It took some work for me to realize that wasn't my fault. Work and prayer." He pushed his plate away. "I'll also be praying for you to discern the right next step," he said.

"Thanks." Jack was grateful that Carson wasn't the type to hold his hand and pray publicly.

There wasn't an opportunity anyway, because old Tecumseh Smith stopped by the table to tell Jack about the digestive difficulties his mule was having, in colorful detail. Jack kept eating and nodding and offering advice, until he noticed that Carson was looking a little green and brought the conversation to an end.

"Sorry," he said to Carson after Tecumseh walked away. "Forgot that not everyone likes to discuss mule intestines while they eat."

"You did not eat enough!" Delfina approached the table and frowned at Carson's half-full plate.

"Can you wrap it up for me, senora?" Carson asked. "I'll have it for lunch tomorrow. I'm feeling better already."

"I will box it up with another carton of soup," she said and whisked away their plates. Jack insisted on paying—it was the least he could do—and they walked the short distance back to their vehicles in the cool evening twilight. "Just remember," Carson said as they were about to part ways. "You're not doomed to repeat the past. God can make all things new, and that includes you. You're a new creation, and anything is possible with Him."

"I hope you're right."

"I *am* right. It's all in the Bible." Carson held up an arm as a barrier, avoiding Jack's handshake. "I don't want to get you sick. Thanks for the dinner, man."

"Thank *you*," Jack said and walked back to his truck with more of a spring in his step than he'd had in days.

He wasn't going to delude himself that one conversation with Carson had resolved all his issues, but it had helped. He no longer dreaded seeing Arianna back at the ranch. Truth to tell, he was looking forward to it.

"So, did you have a good time with Branson?" Arianna asked Penny. The older woman had come over shortly after Jack had texted her to ask her to stay late. Now she was trying to avoid Penny's perceptive questions about what was going on between her and Jack.

They were sitting in Jack's kitchen, watching the sun set over the Sangre de Cristos. Sammy had been exhausted from a trip to the Esperanza Springs library's baby lap sit followed by a TSS appointment, so Arianna had put him to bed half an hour early.

"Branson's a very nice man," Penny said. "He brought

flowers and a side dish—this couscous salad," she added, pointing to the dish she'd brought, "that he'd made himself."

"Which is really good," Arianna said, taking another bite of it. "I mean, how many guys would use fresh dill and oregano?"

"How many men even know what couscous is?" Penny asked, chuckling. "I had to sneak off to the bathroom and look it up on my phone so I didn't seem like too much of a country bumpkin."

Arianna laughed. "That's not the image I have of you, believe me. And that's also not what I asked. I asked if you had a good time." This was good. Looked like she'd be able to grill Penny for a little while here, help her figure out what was obvious to Arianna—that she preferred Willie to the banker—and, in the process, keep her own romantic issues off the table.

"I don't know. It's just not…comfortable, you know? I feel like he's trying to prove himself to me."

"As he should. You undersell yourself. You're a very attractive, smart, successful woman."

Penny snorted. "Who's barely gotten the ranch out of the red, and whose husband left her for the secretary. Not even his secretary, *my* secretary. But I don't want to talk about me."

"Let's talk about these kebabs, then. They're so tender. And not even fattening."

"Why you worry so much about your figure, I'll never understand." Penny sipped her iced tea. "Believe me, there will come a day when you'll look back on that smooth, perfect skin and those hourglass curves and wish you had them back."

"Doubtful," Arianna said. And then their conversation moved to the art therapy group Arianna was doing at the ranch, and how well the veterans were responding, and whether it was time to start a second group.

"Jack's keeping pretty late hours," Penny said finally, glancing up at the clock.

Arianna clapped a hand to her mouth. "Oh no, he'll be home any minute, and the place is a mess." She stood and started clearing plates. "Please stay, Penny, if you don't mind my doing a little cleaning while we talk." She hurried a load of dishes to the sink and then turned back for more.

Penny was looking at her, head cocked to one side. "Are you always this paranoid about the state of the house?"

"Oh, well, my mom was really a clean freak. So is Jack. And I'm more the slob type."

Penny stood and carried the serving dishes to the counter. "I look around this place—and your place—and I don't see a slob. I see someone who's creative and who's been taking care of a baby all day."

"Yes, but Sammy went to bed an hour ago." She should have cleaned up the living room right away rather than collapsing on the couch and reading a novel.

"And shortly after he went down, you got unexpected company," Penny said, pointing at her own chest. "Whom you greeted very hospitably, I might add."

Arianna loaded plates and silverware into Jack's state-of-the-art dishwasher. "You're sure of a good welcome when you come bearing food."

"I was glad for someone to share it with. Glad for some girl time." Penny found a sponge and started wiping down Sammy's high chair, and Arianna didn't have the heart to tell her that she was using the counter sponge, not the Sammy sponge. Or did she have that wrong? Maybe the blue one was for Sammy.

"Anyway," she said, "Jack's pretty orderly, and he's paying me well, so I'm trying to be neater than I would be on my own."

"This room looks fine," Penny said, returning the possibly incorrect sponge to the dish by the sink. "Come on, let's tackle the living room, and you can tell me about your mom."

They'd gotten the place into a semblance of order, and Penny was laughing about Arianna's stories of competing with her sister for neatness awards their mother had set up, when Arianna heard the rumble of Jack's truck.

Her stomach tightened.

Things had been so uncomfortable between them since that wonderful, terrible kiss. Jack had backed way off, obviously avoiding her. What was up with that? Was he one of the many men who preferred the chase to the conquest?

But it was you who told him you didn't want to do it anymore, she reminded herself.

And for very good reason. How could she justify keeping secret the fact that she was Sammy's mother if her relationship with Jack deepened?

And yet how could she justify telling Jack something she'd promised never to tell, and something that would undoubtedly sully his view not only of her, but of Chloe?

The door opened and Jack came in, and all of a sudden the house seemed the way it should again.

Well, except for the baby toys that still littered one end of the living room.

"Hey, Penny," he said as he stowed his briefcase and picked up the mail. "How's it going?"

"*I'm* going," the older woman answered. "Arianna and I were having a nice visit, but I've got an early morning tomorrow." She opened the door, then tossed over her shoulder, "Don't give her too hard of a time about the state of the house. It's tough to keep it looking like a showpiece when you're taking care of a baby."

As the door closed behind her, Jack stared at Arianna. "You've been keeping the place extra neat for me," he said.

"I've been trying," she admitted. "Fallen down on the job today a little."

He put down the mail and grabbed a can of soda from the kitchen while she finished straightening the living room. She was just about to gather her things when he came back into the front room, sat down and patted the couch beside him. "Penny's right," he said. "It's hard with a baby. And everything looks just fine. Can we talk?"

Arianna's heart stuttered. He was going to fire her.

She was going to lose the chance to care for her son. Lose the chance to be near Jack. And suddenly, her on-the-road life as an art therapist, a perfectly good and adequate life, didn't even seem palatable.

Tears pushed at the backs of her eyes and she drew in deep breaths, trying to keep them from falling. Miserably, she approached the couch and sat down beside him.

"Look, Arianna," he said, his expression gentle and kind, which meant disaster, of course. "It's been…awkward between us."

She nodded, both because it was true and because she couldn't speak.

"That kiss was…premature." He kept his eyes on hers. "I'm sorry for that. I've been happy—very happy—with your work with Sammy. And…" He hesitated, his face coloring a little. "And I like being around you," he added finally. "Do you think we could try to go back to that, to the way we were before?"

Her insides were dancing so fast that she could barely find the wherewithal to nod.

He'd said "premature." Not a mistake, not wrong, just premature.

Did that mean he was good with it happening? Even that he wanted it to happen again?

At any rate, he hadn't fired her, and that meant she could continue working with Jack and with her son. "I'd like that," she managed to choke out through a throat tight with gratitude.

But as she gathered her things, an uneasy feeling penetrated her happiness. She hadn't told Jack about Sammy's heritage, and that fact stood in the way of them ever getting closer.

Tell him.

It wasn't an audible voice, there in the moonlight as she walked across the lawn to her place, Jack watching from the porch. It was just a feeling in her heart, but she knew the author of that feeling, because it was the same message she'd gotten in prayer before.

It was true, probably; she should tell him. But she was afraid. Afraid of hurting this wonderful, tentative, fragile accord between them.

Afraid of being barred from caring for her son.

Chapter 10

"Are you ready, Sammy? Ready to take the dog to Miss Arianna?" Jack didn't have to strain to put excitement in his voice, something the TSS had recommended.

Sammy's face remained impassive, but he toddled over to the door, which, as Arianna always pointed out, was a clear form of communication.

Jack scooped up the eight-week-old puppy he'd just examined and wrapped it in a towel, and they headed over to Arianna's place.

It was a beautiful Sunday afternoon. From the mountains, a warm breeze blew the scent of pine, rich and resinous. A Steller's jay squawked from a nearby aspen tree, scolding them, maybe scolding Jack for the eager anticipation he was feeling.

He and Arianna had a new, fragile accord, and he treasured it. After the awkwardness of that week after they kissed, Jack was being cautious not to reveal the attraction he felt for his redheaded nanny.

That attraction had caused them problems before. He didn't want to risk their friendship by acting on it again.

Then what are you going to do with the attraction?

Because he wasn't going to stop feeling it, that much was clear. So was he just going to shove it aside and continue treating Arianna as a friend? That seemed like it might be really hard to do. But on the other hand, if he made another move to get closer to Arianna, he might scare her away entirely.

When he'd hired her, it had been for a temporary position, just for the summer. She'd planned to seek work elsewhere if she couldn't find a permanent art therapy job here. But now the thought of her leaving stabbed at his heart.

He looked up at the clear blue sky. *Father, You're going to have to take over, because I don't know what to do, and I keep messing this up.*

He helped Sammy climb the first couple of stairs and then knelt and scooped him up to carry him the rest of the way to Arianna's second-floor apartment. Sammy's walking was improving, but stairs were a challenge still, of course.

At the top, arms full of puppy and boy, he tapped on the door. "Dog delivery," he called through the screen.

From inside Arianna's apartment, a loud squeal erupted and then Arianna ran through her small kitchen to the door, talking a mile a minute. "Did you bring me my puppy? I'm so excited! I can't believe I get to have him!" She opened the door and held out her hands, and Jack carefully shifted the puppy into her arms before putting Sammy down.

"He is so precious! I can't believe how tiny he is. And how wiggly!" She knelt so she could be at the same level as Sammy. Of course. She was always conscious of that, always trying to include him, to teach him new things.

"Look how cute he is, Sammy," she said. "Oh, Jack, I love him already."

Jack could have stood there and watched her for an hour as she cuddled the puppy and showed it to Sammy and put it down on the floor to let it walk and laughed at its clumsiness.

Her feet were bare, her toenails painted bright pink. He swallowed, then cleared his throat. "Do you have everything you need? You got bowls and food and a bed?"

Great, he sounded like a scold.

But rather than being annoyed, Arianna bobbed her head up and down and rose to her feet, graceful, the puppy in her arms. "Come see. You can tell me if I got the right stuff."

So Jack took Sammy's hand, and they followed her through the little apartment. She showed him the food and water bowls, simple and basic, just what Jack would have purchased himself. "And I got the puppy chow you recommended. And a few treats." She smiled a bit guiltily and showed him four different kinds of dog biscuits. "Are these okay for him to eat?"

Jack had to laugh at her. "They're fine. It's okay to indulge a puppy. Everyone does."

In the living room, more of that indulgence was on display. In addition to a small crate, she had gotten the little dog a warm fleece bed and at least eight different toys.

"I know, I know, I went overboard," she said. "They had a sale. That's my excuse." She put the dog down, and they all knelt around it. The puppy pounced on a banana-shaped toy, then jumped back when the toy squeaked.

Jack and Arianna laughed, and then Sammy let out a sound that could or could not have been a laugh, and Jack's eyes met Arianna's. Her smile was brilliant. And Jack could tell his own face held a similar expression.

"You know," she said, "if it turns out that Buster would be a good dog for Sammy to have, I'll give him to you."

"No, he's yours," Jack protested.

"Sammy is the priority," she said firmly. "If I'm just the puppy raiser for his service dog, I'm okay with that."

Her words sent a wave of happiness through Jack. One, because of the idea of Sammy having a service dog. That just might make a big difference for him. And two, he was impressed by Arianna's generosity and willingness to sacrifice.

Strange, on paper Chloe had been the upright, perfectly behaved, rule-following sister. Women's committee at church, Sunday school teacher, always tastefully dressed, a great cook and housekeeper.

According to Chloe, Arianna was the one who had gotten in all kinds of trouble as a kid. She'd struggled in school and wrecked her car and gotten into fights with her parents.

But as adults, and maybe this was because of Arianna's childhood difficulties, Arianna was the more generous and compassionate one. It seemed like Chloe had gotten more and more rigid. And living with her, Jack knew better than anyone the anxiety and tension that had hovered just beneath her perfect facade. It had gotten to the point that it made her miserable, and Jack had begged her to seek counseling. But she had refused, because that would have destroyed her carefully crafted self-image.

After a few more minutes, Sammy turned away, his signal that he had had enough. Arianna read it as quickly as Jack did, and she found a board book and helped Sammy sit down in a quiet corner on his blanket. There, he turned the pages methodically, tapping his foot on the floor in a complicated rhythm.

The puppy seemed to be overwhelmed at the same moment. He walked and climbed and tumbled his way into the fleece bed, flopped down on his side and fell instantly asleep.

So now it was just Jack and Arianna, her on the couch and him in the armchair catty-corner, because he wasn't going to push himself on her by sitting too close on the couch. But that good resolution was negated by the question he couldn't help asking. "Have you seen Nathan lately?"

She looked at him, surprise evident in her expression. "No, I haven't. I think he's gone back to the university."

"Are you upset about that?"

Now she really looked puzzled. "No, I'm not. Why would I be?" Color climbed into her cheeks.

Jack observed her narrowly even as he shrugged and lifted his hands, palms up. "No particular reason."

She didn't *seem* upset about Nathan being gone, and that made his heart beat a little faster. Did that mean she would be open to exploring a deeper connection with Jack?

But on the other hand, he was pretty sure there was something about Nathan that she wasn't telling him.

Restless now, he stood and paced around the little living room. "You have it set up so nice." With the colorful pillows and throws, the rattan shades at the windows and the hanging plants, the place already looked artsy and fun, just like Arianna herself.

He glanced at the photos on the mantel and paused at a picture of Chloe and Arianna, probably taken when they were teenagers. They both had their heads thrown back, laughing. Jack swallowed. "This is a good shot," he said, nodding sideways at the picture.

Arianna came to stand beside him. "I love it," she said. "There weren't that many times when we laughed together, but I treasure the few happy moments we had."

"What was it that put you two so much at odds?" Jack really wanted to know. He felt like it would solve some of the mystery of Chloe, help him resolve the past.

She picked up the photo and then put it down again, sighing. "Mostly, it was our mom. I guess she was trying to help us both excel by pitting us against each other. But I don't think it really worked. Sisterhood shouldn't be a competition."

"Chloe was jealous of you, you know." As soon as the words were out of his mouth, Jack regretted them. He didn't want to betray Chloe by letting Arianna know her deeper feelings.

But to his surprise, Arianna just nodded. "We were jealous of each other," she said. "I always wanted to be perfectly groomed and well organized the way that she was. She was in every club and organization. She got straight As. She was the perfect one."

Jack knew what she meant, but he couldn't let that analysis go. "She didn't feel perfect. Not inside herself."

"I know." She sighed. "In some ways, it was easier to be me than it was to be her. She came close to meeting Mom's standards, and that motivated her to try harder and harder all the time. I was so far below them that I just did my own thing."

"She thought I was attracted to you."

Arianna sucked in a breath. "What?"

He nodded. *May as well go through with this now.* "She got kind of obsessed with the idea that I wanted to be with you. That's why she didn't want you to come to our house very often. When you did, it always left her in a terrible funk."

Color had risen in Arianna's cheeks. "Wow, I didn't

know that," she said. She glanced up at his face and then looked away just as quickly.

He'd better push it to the end now. "She was wrong," he said. "I never wanted to be with another woman while I was with Chloe. Our marriage wasn't perfect, but I loved her, and I was loyal to her. It's important to me that you know that."

"I never would have doubted it, Jack," she said quietly.

"It's a little confusing to me," he said, "because now I *do* feel attracted to you."

Again she flashed a glance at him and then looked away, biting her lip.

"But I guess you know that."

She nodded almost imperceptibly, not looking up at him.

"Look, Arianna, I don't know where it might lead, but I would like to know you better in a social way, not just this employer-employee way." He drew in a breath. Asking for a date didn't get any easier than it had been when he was a teenager. He cleared his throat. "Would you like to go to the Redemption Ranch fund-raising gala with me?"

Arianna stared at Jack, wondering if her ears had deceived her. "Did you just ask me out?"

"I did." Jack looked at her for a moment and then stepped away, pacing over to the window and back again. "But, Arianna, I hope you know you can say no without causing any kind of a problem in our employer-employee relationship."

Her thoughts raced faster than she could process. On one side of her mind, an excited girl jumped up and down and clasped her hands together and squealed, *He asked me out! He asked me out!*

Another side of her, the more rational side, tried to project out into the future. He'd asked her out. If she went, and if they had fun, maybe he would ask her out again. And again.

At what point would it be right for her to say, "Hey, Jack, you know your son Sammy? Well, he's my biological child"?

Never. It would never be right for her to say that. Especially when she had promised her sister she wouldn't. And her sister wasn't around for her to renegotiate their agreement.

But if she turned down his invitation, which was what all logic suggested, her heart would break.

"I don't have a formal dress" was what she ended up saying.

"That's no problem," he said promptly. "I still have some of Chloe's dresses in storage. I can pull them out for you, and you can try them on while Sammy is napping one day."

Did he have no concept of sizes? Did he not remember that Chloe had been a stick while Arianna was much more, um, full figured?

Did he not realize that wearing one of Chloe's dresses would feel just plain weird?

Maybe he did have a concept of size, because he said, "Chloe fluctuated in size quite a bit during our marriage, and I think there are formal dresses in every size she ever wore. So it would be like shopping. You could take your pick."

"Jack...I'm sure they wouldn't fit," she said. "But... maybe I could shop for a dress."

"Then you will go to the gala with me?" Jack's intense gaze left no doubt that he really wanted her to.

And it was that, that strong desire for her company, the sweet balm of it soothing her heart, that convinced her. "Yes, I'll go."

Go to her own doom, most likely.

* * *

The next day, Arianna ended up leaving the puppy with Jack and taking Sammy out shopping. "Best to get him out of here in the hopes he doesn't catch whatever I've got," Jack croaked. He was staying home from work because of the monster cold he'd contracted. "Me and Buster will catch up on our rest."

Willie's ancient pickup truck chugged up to the driveway area between Jack's house and Penny's, and Arianna took Sammy's hand. "We'll be a couple of hours, max," she said to Jack. "Penny's shopping for a dress, too, but I have a feeling she's not a shop-all-day kind of person."

"I'm not sure why Willie is taking you," Jack said. "One or both of you could have driven."

"True, but—" Arianna smiled "—if I had to guess why he made the offer, I'd say he wants to spend the time around Penny."

"You're probably right, but he must be *really* motivated to put up with clothes shopping."

"That's a bad attitude," she said with mock sternness. "I'll try to train Sammy differently. Now, you rest up and don't worry. Sammy's in good hands."

"I know that," he said, and his gaze on her was warm.

His obvious approval melted something that had long been frozen inside her. What would it be like to live in the warmth of that approval?

Flustered, she gathered Sammy and his bag and her purse and made her way out to Willie's truck. Penny helped her get the car seat from Jack's vehicle and they strapped Sammy in, and then the two women climbed into the front seat beside Willie.

"You're a better man than I am," Jack called out to Willie. "Guess you're *really* missing Long John."

"Long John ain't near as pretty as these two ladies," Willie said and gave Jack a wave as he pulled the truck out of the driveway.

Thirty minutes later, they were walking in the door of a funky little shop with a wild, psychedelic sign proclaiming they were entering Suzie's Gently Used Emporium.

The tiny shop was lined with clothing, with racks encircling the first floor and a narrow balcony above entirely lined with more clothes. Shoes and purses stood on display tables in the center of the store, along with colorful scarves and jewelry.

"If we can't find dresses here, they're not to be found. And Suzie's prices are very reasonable." Penny was already flipping through the nearest rack.

In Arianna's arms, Sammy stared, wide-eyed.

Having parked the truck, Willie came in and lifted Sammy out of her arms. "You shop. Sammy and I will walk around outside a little bit. It's a nice day."

As soon the door had closed behind them, Penny glanced over at Arianna. "In case you couldn't tell, he's mad at me," she said.

"Why?" Arianna had noticed the tension in the truck on the way down.

"Because just before we picked you and Sammy up, I told him I'm going to the fund-raiser with Branson Howe," she said. "He asked me first—what can I say?"

"Ouch." Arianna looked off in the direction Willie had gone, feeling sorry for him. "Which one do you like better?"

Penny lifted her hands, palms up. "I don't trust my feelings," she said. "They're what got me in trouble before." She pulled out a purple dress, frowned at it and put it back. "I've tried taking it to God, but so far, He's been quiet."

Arianna found a rack labeled with her size and started looking at dresses, too. "Do you sometimes hear from Him? God, I mean."

Penny looked at her quickly. "Yeah. I do. Do you?"

Arianna shook her head. "Not so far. I wish I would." And then she realized that wasn't quite true. She had heard from God. God had told her to tell Jack the truth.

She hadn't done it. Was that why God had gotten quiet on her?

A woman carrying a tablet and an armful of blouses came bustling out from the back. "Hi, Penny," she said. "Anything I can help you with?" She looked inquiringly at Arianna. "I don't think I know you. I'm Suzie, and I own this place. It's a bit of a jumble, but I can help you find what you need."

"Arianna Shrader. I'm helping out up at Redemption Ranch."

"We're both looking for dresses for a fund-raiser," Penny said. "Not exactly formal, but fancy."

"Cocktail length?"

Penny nodded. "Although there won't be any cocktails involved. It's a Redemption Ranch fund-raiser, and too many of our veterans struggle with alcohol."

"Right." Suzie climbed the steep stairs to the second level and made her way along that narrow walkway until she found what she was looking for. "Ready? Catch," she said from above and dropped a dress on Penny. Next, she walked a little farther along and pulled two dresses off hangers. "And these are for you, young lady," she said. "Beautiful with your red hair. Fitting room is in the corner, behind the cash register."

She and Penny took turns trying on the dresses. Penny came out in her elegant burnt-orange sheath just as Willie came back into the shop with Sammy. The older man stopped and stared. "You look so beautiful," he said with a catch in his voice.

The adoration in his eyes made Arianna decide right then: she was officially on Team Willie.

Judging from the way Penny colored up, Arianna thought she might be leaning in that direction, as well. How the older woman would work that out when she was slated to go to the fund-raiser with Branson, Arianna couldn't imagine.

After Penny had changed back into regular clothes, Arianna went in. She pulled on the turquoise dress and smoothed it down.

"Come out and show us," Penny called.

She did, and they oohed and aahed, but Suzie frowned. "Try the other one," she said.

"The other one is lime green," she protested. "I love the color, but I'm afraid it'll make me look fat. Don't you have anything in black?"

"I do," Suzie said, "and you'd look sophisticated in black, but try the green one first. Humor me."

Arianna put it on and smoothed it over her hips. It clung, maybe a little too much, but flared out into a wide ruffle at her knees. The bodice fitted perfectly, with a modest key-hole neckline and cap sleeves.

She loved it.

Hesitantly, she came out of the fitting room, and all three of the others exclaimed and nodded enthusiastically. Even Sammy offered the half smile that was becoming his trademark.

"It's so *you*," Penny said. "Creative and fun and lively. You have to get it."

"Not many of my customers could carry off that color," Suzie said. "So I'm going to give it to you at half price."

Arianna sucked in a breath. "You'd do that?"

"I would, as long as you promise to have a good time in it."

"I will," Arianna said. "God willing."

Only, if God willed her to have a good time, a wonderful time, on a fancy date with Jack…then what might He will for her to do next?

Jack was brooding, and he wasn't a brooder.

Oh, he was thrilled that Arianna had agreed to go out with him. But almost immediately, the worrier in him had kicked into action.

His father would undoubtedly hear about the fund-raiser, most likely be there. And he wouldn't approve of Jack taking Arianna.

He'd admitted the truth to Arianna, that Chloe had been jealous, and she hadn't found it upsetting. Maybe because she and Chloe already had their issues. So that was the biggest hurdle.

His father's disapproval was a constant in Jack's life, but his worry was that his father would say something rude to Arianna.

If this was going to be the reality going forward—that he and Arianna were exploring a relationship—and he fervently hoped it would be, then he needed to confront his father.

His opportunity came unexpectedly quickly, when his father dropped by the ranch to give Jack some of his old toys that Sammy might be able to use. They even had a good time pulling the old rocking horse and blocks from Dad's trunk and reminiscing about Jack's childhood, though Jack made sure his father kept a good distance, not wanting to infect him with his cold.

"Dad," he said, "there's something I'd like to discuss with you."

"What's that?" Dad put down the plastic push mower he'd been wiping off.

Jack cleared his throat. "I'm taking Arianna to the Redemption Ranch gala."

"What? Do you know how that will look? People will think you're dating!"

Here goes nothing. "I hope we *will* date. I care about her, and I'd like to see where things go between us."

His father went back to wiping off the push mower, his movements jerky. "Then it's true, what Chloe always said."

Jack shook his head. "No. I was loyal to Chloe. I never thought about Arianna as anything other than a sister when Chloe was alive."

"Humph." Dad looked over at him, a glare from beneath heavy eyebrows. "Your mother always thought there were problems in your marriage. I didn't."

"There were some problems." And Jack didn't want to go into them. "Doesn't every marriage have some problems?"

Dad lifted his chin. "Your mother and I had forty-five years of happiness."

"Really?" All too well Jack remembered the days of silence, the tight-lipped dinners, the icily polite interactions between his parents. But he certainly wasn't going to bring that up now. "I'm happy it was that way for you, Dad. Chloe and I had a lot of happy times, too." Before her anxieties had driven her to thoughts that had made her miserable. Again, like always, he wished he'd known better how to help his wife. He'd grieved double for her because he hadn't had time to do everything he'd meant to do to help her.

"I don't like it, son. You're making a mistake."

"I'm sorry you feel that way. I wanted you to know."

He was walking his father to the car when, unexpectedly, Willie's truck chugged up and parked beside Dad's Oldsmobile. The contrast was almost comical.

But Jack's tension rose. Would Dad say something awful to Arianna? Not everyone realized how sensitive she was beneath her fun-loving exterior.

Arianna jumped out, waved to his father and reached to extract Sammy from his car seat.

Penny climbed out. "You should see Arianna's dress," she said to Jack. "She's going to be the belle of the ball, and to think, she got the dress half-price from a thrift shop!"

Jack frowned. If Arianna were still so short on money that she couldn't afford a new dress, then why hadn't she taken him up on his offer of Chloe's dresses? They were all fashionable, some of them with designer labels.

His father was staring at Penny and Arianna. "Thrift shop? You're clothes shopping at a thrift shop?"

Penny smiled at him. "Hi, Mr. DeMoise. Suzie's Gently Used is one of Esperanza Springs' most successful businesses. Recycling at its best. I got my dress there, too."

Jack cleared his throat. "Actually, Dad, Mom sold a number of her dresses to Suzie's. As did Chloe."

"Selling clothes to those less fortunate is one thing. Buying them there is another," Dad said.

Arianna was standing against the car, a bag clutched in her hand. "Did Chloe, um, donate a lot of dresses to Suzie's?"

"She sold them on consignment, and yes." Jack could tell she felt uneasy from the look in her eyes. "Why?"

Slowly, Arianna opened her bag, pulled out a lime-green dress and held it up to herself. "There's no way this was one of Chloe's. Right?"

Jack stared at the dress he and Chloe had argued about.

He'd bought it for her as a surprise, early in their marriage, and she'd hated it. Too loud. Too unusual. And why did he even think she could wear a size twelve? She'd been size eight, mostly, for years!

What were the odds Arianna would have come home with Chloe's dress? He cleared his throat. "Actually, that *was* one of hers. She never wore it," he added hastily. "She decided it wasn't her style."

The words hung in the air as everyone processed the awkwardness of the situation.

"I should say not," Dad bluffed. "A little exotic for Chloe."

Maybe I wished she were a little more exotic. The very thought made Jack's face burn. But he forced himself to think back. He'd thought she would like the dress. She liked green, and he'd known the style would suit her figure.

Remembering Chloe's reaction to the dress made Jack tense up. Would Arianna be as emotional as her sister had been, although for different reasons? Would she freak out, get upset, cry? She had every right to do so.

"Well," she said, with cheer in her voice that was only partially forced, "we do have the same coloring. I'd be honored to wear a dress Chloe picked out. She had really great taste."

Dad opened his mouth, and for a horrible moment, Jack thought he was going to make a quip about taste in men.

Willie came to the rescue, slapping Dad on the back. "That young gal sure is pretty, but you ought to see our Miss Penny in her new dress. It's the color of a sunset and fits her to a T. Brings out those amber eyes of hers."

"Oh, now, Willie," Penny said, and then Dad said he had to leave, and Penny and Willie went off toward her place.

Arianna swept up Sammy in her arms. "You," she said,

pointing a finger at Jack, "need to get back to bed. You look terrible. And Sammy needs you to be healthy."

"I'm sorry about all that," he said, not moving toward the house, but pointing at the bag into which she'd stuffed the green dress. "I had no idea you were going to shop at Suzie's, and even if I'd known, I don't think I'd have imagined that you would light on a dress of Chloe's."

"I didn't light on it, exactly," she said, her voice thoughtful. "Miss Suzie went and picked it out especially for me. I didn't even think it would look good on me, but it was perfect. Was she friends with Chloe?"

"Let's just say they did business together. Chloe bought a lot of clothes and changed sizes a lot, so she tried to recoup some of her money there."

Arianna nodded. "It's just a little weird that the store owner would choose that particular dress for me to try on. I'm trying to remember whether Penny introduced me by name, whether she might have known my connection to Chloe."

"Arianna," he said, "anyone who looked at you would know you're connected to Chloe. You guys look so similar."

"Really?" Arianna cocked her head to one side. "I never thought so. And Mom always said…" She trailed off and looked away. "We should get you and Sammy both inside and into bed."

"What did your mom always say?"

Arianna frowned. "She said that Chloe was the beauty *and* the brains," she said slowly, "and that I was the ditz."

He blew out a breath and shook his head. Amazing what some people considered good parenting.

"If the shoe fits," Arianna said. "Believe me, Jack, 'ditz' is one of the nicer names she called me. I was always failing to live up to her expectations. I was a real loser in high school."

He wanted to put his arms around her so badly that his whole body ached with it, but he didn't. It would be inappropriate, and besides, he didn't want to pass along his germs. "You're not a loser in my book," he settled for saying.

Now wasn't the time to pull her closer. But maybe, just maybe, the fund-raiser would be.

Chapter 11

As they pulled into the parking lot of the upscale Mission Hotel for the fund-raiser, Arianna struggled with herself.

She couldn't deny it: she was completely thrilled to be on a date with Jack. He'd insisted on coming to her door, had brought her flowers, had moved quickly ahead to open the passenger door for her. He'd joked and chatted with her on the way down to Esperanza Springs, making her feel comfortable.

But it was more than that. He'd asked about her art therapy work with the veterans and talked about Sammy's TSS in a way that showed her he respected her work and her opinions. They shared a love for Sammy that made their relationship deeper.

She wanted this. Wanted to explore a relationship with Jack and see where it would go.

She wanted desperately to tell him the truth about Sammy. That secret was the only thing standing between them, but it was huge.

Tell him tonight.

But telling him tonight could, and probably would, ruin tonight.

And how could she tell him the truth, breaking Chloe's trust, when she was wearing Chloe's dress?

"Sit tight. I'll get your door." Jack jumped out and came around to open her door.

Oh, those gentlemanly manners, so rare in a guy her age. And Jack was so handsome in his dark suit and tie. He could have been a model in an ad for expensive cars or luxury vacations.

You sure couldn't be a model.

She shoved away the automatic negative thought as she took his hand and let him help her out of the car. She knew she looked fine in the dress, and her hair wasn't *too* crazy.

"Did I tell you how great you look?" he asked as they walked across the parking lot toward the stately old hotel.

"Thanks." She waved a hand at the dress. "Chloe had terrific fashion sense."

Now what had possessed her to say such an idiotic thing? She shot a sideways glance at him and saw an odd expression cross his face. "Actually," he said, "I picked out that dress as a gift for her."

"But it still had the tags on it."

"She didn't like it."

"Oh." She pondered what that meant. Why wouldn't Chloe have liked this dress?

But it wasn't hard to figure out. Chloe had liked more subdued colors and classic styles.

If Jack, conservative, orderly Jack, had picked out this dress…well, that was something else they had in common.

Flustered, she looked off toward the mountains where

the sun was sinking into a pink-and-orange streak of clouds. "It's a gorgeous night."

"It'll be cool later. And you didn't bring a wrap." Jack sounded chagrined. "You can wear my jacket."

Sweet Jack. She squeezed his arm tighter. "Is Sammy going to be okay with Mrs. Jennings tonight?"

"Yes, he's fine. She's been wanting to mend fences, and I figured tonight would be a good time, since we're close by." He greeted the doorman and ushered her inside with a hand on her back.

Arianna tried not to make too much of his touch, but her heart was pounding.

She greeted Penny, resplendent in her new dress, her hair in an updo that made her look incredibly sophisticated. As the owner and manager of the ranch, she was the public face of the fund-raiser, and she was obviously up to the task, greeting everyone, directing the staff, looking over the food and the silent auction.

Branson Howe watched her admiringly.

"I'm going to see if she needs any help," Arianna said and escaped from Jack before he could answer. She needed space to breathe, because being near him was sweeping her way too far away from anything like clear thinking.

"What can I do to help?" she asked as soon as she reached her friend's side.

Penny hugged her. "Don't even think about helping," she said. "You be a guest." She held Arianna at arm's length and studied her. "You look absolutely stunning."

"You clean up pretty well yourself. Hard to believe we were scrubbing kennels this morning." Arianna had started volunteering in the kennels a couple of hours a week. She took Buster and let him play with the other puppy who was still living there while she did whatever was needed with the senior dogs. The only problem was that she wanted to take all of them home. She was pretty sure she'd end up with at least one once Buster was a little older.

If she stayed around.

She turned to look for Jack and saw him talking intently with an older man in a suit.

Oh. It was Jack's father.

Her stomach sank. For whatever reason, the man really disliked her. She'd always felt judged by him, as if he could see right through her.

She turned away in search of someone else to talk to and was happy to see Daniela, looking lovely in a cream-colored dress, her pregnancy now more obvious. "You look gorgeous!" Arianna hugged her.

Daniela touched her scarred face in what looked like an automatic gesture, and Arianna's heart twisted. Daniela really *was* gorgeous, and her scars didn't detract from that.

Her husband, Gabe, wrapped his arms around her from behind, and Daniela's eyes and smile lit up her face, making her glow.

If only Jack could be so affectionate with Arianna. But even if their relationship were close enough to merit that, he couldn't show such physical demonstration in front of his father.

He was approaching now, and her heartbeat quickened, because he was looking at her almost the same way Gabe had looked at Daniela. He reached her side and greeted Gabe and Daniela, casually putting an arm around Arianna's shoulders.

She saw Gabe's eyebrow lift, just slightly. Daniela tilted her head and narrowed her eyes, looking at Arianna.

Arianna looked over at Jack. "Your dad's not going to like this."

He smiled down at her with all the confidence and certainty in the world. "His problems are his own, not mine."

She swallowed. "Oh."

His eyes held hers for a long moment, and then he smiled, a dimple showing in his cheek. "Come on, let's go look at the food. I'm starving."

Arianna had been hungry, too, until Jack had looked at her in that intense way. Now her stomach felt so fluttery that she didn't know if she could eat.

He still had his arm around her. He was being public about the fact that this was a date.

She had to tell him the truth, and soon. She'd promised Chloe she wouldn't, but everything had changed. Now that she'd forged a relationship with Jack and Sammy, keeping the secret had the potential to devastate both of them.

Her new friend Lily came up behind them. "You've got to try those little tarts," she said, indicating one of the many trays of food. "They're some kind of seafood and cheese, and they taste amazing."

"And high calorie," Arianna said. "You can afford it. I can't."

"You look fantastic. And don't you know that when you're at an event for a good cause, the calories don't count?"

"Second the motion that you look fantastic," Jack growled into her ear.

Her stomach fluttered again, but she gathered a small plate of appetizers and sat with Jack at one of the high tables that dotted the room. Along one wall, silent auction items were meeting with a lot of attention, mostly baskets of luxury goods, some pet items and a couple of handmade blankets.

After the crowd had mingled and eaten for a while, Penny took the podium and got everyone's attention.

"Thank you all so much for coming out to support Redemption Ranch," she said. "We're mostly going to let you enjoy the evening in a lighthearted way, but I've asked a couple of folks who have benefited from our services to tell you a little bit about what the ranch has meant to them."

There was polite applause, and then when Gabe, who'd grown up around here and earned a number of medals for his wartime bravery, approached the stage, the applause grew warmer.

"I was a wreck when I came to Redemption Ranch," he said, and the applause and murmurs died down. "Even my family was ready to give up on me. It was my last chance."

He pulled out a handkerchief and wiped his forehead. "It meant so much to me, it helped me so much, that I agreed to speak despite being terrified of public speaking." A sympathetic laugh went through the crowd.

He told about how he'd come to the ranch with severe PTSD and little desire to live, and how the ranch's counselors—here he looked at Daniela, who smiled back at him—had given him hope that life would get better.

"But in addition to the counselors," he said, "there was other help available at the ranch, help that really cemented my healing." He turned and spoke to someone just out of sight in the wings and whistled, and two dogs ran to him on the stage. One was a giant black dog, the other a tiny Chihuahua, and when they reached Gabe, he knelt to greet them with obvious affection.

He took the dogs through a few tricks and then sent them to the handler at the edge of the stage and explained how the animals helped the veterans, and vice versa.

Arianna was thoroughly charmed, and she could tell from the smiles around her that many other guests felt the same.

Penny was glowing, which made Arianna happy. Penny

deserved to have success at the ranch after everything she'd gone through. She didn't express rancor toward her ex-husband, who'd absconded with the ranch's funds and its executive assistant, but Arianna could tell the whole situation still tasted bitter to the older woman.

Tonight illustrated the admonition that living well was the best revenge, and Arianna was fiercely glad Penny was living well.

Penny came to the stage again as the applause for Gabe finally died down. "Now, even though they don't want us to, we want to thank our key donors," she said. "We'd like to ask each of them to come briefly to the stage. First, we have Branson Howe, president of our local branch of Western States Bank!" He ducked to the stage smiling awkwardly. "Next we have Marge Springer, owner of Mountain Malamutes!" The woman who'd helped with painting Arianna's apartment joined them. "And finally, our major donor, Esperanza Springs' favorite veterinarian, Jack DeMoise!"

Jack growled beside her. "I told her not to do this," he muttered, then made his way to the front of the room and trotted up the steps to the stage.

"Speech," someone called.

The three onstage looked at each other, and Branson and Marge gestured toward Jack.

Good-naturedly, he took the microphone. "I don't like public speaking any better than Gabe does," Jack said. "And I didn't get the chance to practice, so I'll just say…it's a good cause. And everyone should come up to the ranch and find a senior dog to adopt." To general applause and laughter, he added, "And that's as long as I'm going to keep you away from your food and drinks and dancing."

Arianna was proud of him as he came down from the stage and wove his way through the crowd toward her, ex-

changing friendly greetings with dozens of people along the
way. "I didn't know," she said when he returned.

"You're not supposed to." He held out his hands to her
as the music started up again. "Would you like to dance?"

She sighed. Would she?

She wanted nothing more than to dance with Jack. And
she'd resigned herself to the fact that this night wasn't the
time she was going to be able to tell him the truth about
Sammy. So she let him lead her to the dance floor and guide
her gently through a semislow dance.

Whatever else happened, she'd have this night to remember.

"Are you having fun?" he murmured in her ear.

"Yes."

"I am, too," he said. "Arianna, I—"

A hand on her arm that wasn't Jack's made her open
her eyes. She blinked at Mr. DeMoise. "For Chloe's sake,"
he said in a too-loud whisper, "could the two of you stop
making a spectacle of yourselves?"

When Jack saw the hurt expression on Arianna's face,
fury flashed through him, quick and hot. He gripped his
father by the shoulders, hard, and physically moved him
away from Arianna as he stepped in between them.

An expression something like fear came into his father's eyes.

Immediately, Jack dropped his hands from his father.
He turned and scanned the crowd, noticing in a distant
way that a number of people seemed to be watching. He
caught Daniela's eye and beckoned her over. "Could you
keep Arianna company for a few minutes?" he asked. "I
need to speak with my father outside."

"Of course." She put an arm around Arianna, who looked ready to cry.

Jack took his father's arm and steered him toward the exit. Dad had regained his composure and was blustering and resisting with every step.

"I'd like to speak to you privately." Jack continued urging his father forward. "What I have to say isn't pretty, and I would rather not say it in front of other people, for your sake. But I also am not going to physically force you outside. It's your choice." Again, he dropped his hand from his father. Dad looked at him, pressed his lips tight together, nodded once and led the way outside.

They managed to reach the parking lot before boiling over.

"I've put up with a lot from you over the years," Jack said. "But I will not accept you speaking disrespectfully to my friends."

"Friends? Is that what Arianna is to you? Somehow I doubt it."

Dad's snide, angry tone fanned the flames of Jack's anger. "What possible business is it of yours what my relationship with Arianna might be?"

"I don't like to see you making a fool of yourself in front of the whole community," Dad said. "And I don't like to see you disrespecting your late wife's memory."

"Dancing with a kind, good woman isn't making a fool of myself," Jack said. He drew in a couple of deep breaths and reminded himself that this was his father and he needed to show respect. "Look, I understand that it may feel uncomfortable because Arianna is Chloe's sister. Believe me, I wouldn't have chosen to be drawn to someone related to Chloe, but it happened. I have to believe God has a reason for it."

"Oh, don't bring God into this," Dad said. "Chloe knew what was going on between you two, and she hated it. There's nothing godly about adultery."

Jack stared. "You think I was committing *adultery*? You really think I'm the type of person who would do that?"

"I understand the temptations, son." His father looked away. "I'm trying to keep you from making the same mistakes I made."

"Whoa, whoa, whoa." Jack drew in a slow breath and let it out, staring at his father, who was still not meeting his eyes. "Really, Dad?"

His father didn't nod, but he didn't deny it. Jack's parents' strained relationship appeared in his mind's eye, a picture in a whole new frame. "That's something separate that you need to deal with," he said. "If there's something you need forgiven for, Carson can talk to you or recommend a counselor." Even as he was talking reasonably, Jack's heart ached for his mother. He'd known his parents hadn't had a good marriage, but he had never known why.

His father crossed his arms and looked out across the parking lot. Everything in his posture said he didn't want to talk about it, didn't want to be here with Jack.

Fine. "For now," Jack said, "I insist that you keep your negativity to yourself and don't spew it out over Arianna or me or anyone else I know. It sounds like you've got some thinking to do."

"You mean to tell me this thing between you and Arianna just started up?"

"There's not a *thing* between me and Arianna," Jack said. "She was my sister-in-law, and she's Sammy's aunt and nanny. I care about her a great deal, and I would like to pursue a relationship with her, but that hasn't happened yet. I don't know how she feels about it."

"I can tell you how she feels about it," Dad said. There was some kind of bitterness in his tone. "She looks at you like you're the king of the universe."

Really? That notion spread warmth through Jack's heart.

"Nobody ever looked at me like that," his father added.

Jack spread his hands. "I'm just a man, struggling to raise my son and do my work and follow God's laws," he said. "I'm not going to deny that I've made mistakes. I'm not going to claim that Chloe and I had the perfect marriage. We didn't." He looked upward at the stars. "If I'm fortunate enough to be in a relationship again, I hope I can do better. And I would appreciate it if you didn't interfere with that."

His father didn't answer, but he gave the tiniest of nods.

Jack's emotions spun from hope about Arianna to hurt about what he'd just learned about his father. "Thanks," he said, then turned on his heel and walked back inside.

Then, because his father was aging and upset, he approached Carson. "Calling in a favor, man," he said. "My dad is out in the parking lot, and he's…troubled. Any chance that you could talk to him a little and make sure he gets home okay?"

"You've got it. I'll take him home myself. Lily isn't here, and I don't like to stay out too late when she's home alone."

Jack met his friend's eyes. "I hope you know how good you've got it."

"I do." Carson clapped him on the back and then headed outside.

Jack found Arianna sitting with Daniela on a bench at the side of the room, partially hidden behind some potted palms. He gripped her hands and pulled her to her feet, and she ended up closer than he'd expected. He had the strongest urge to pull her in and kiss her.

From the way she sucked in her breath and stared at him, she might have let him.

But Daniela was here, and so were a lot of other people. He didn't want to embarrass her that way. "Can we talk?" he asked.

"And that would be my cue to leave the premises," Daniela said. "I've left poor Gabe alone too long. He doesn't like this kind of event."

After she walked away, he looked down at Arianna.

She was studying him. "Are you okay?"

"Exactly what I was going to ask you," he said. "Look, I'm really sorry about my dad. He's dealing with some things I wasn't aware of, but that's no excuse for him being rude to you."

She bit her lip. "Do *you* think we were making fools of ourselves?"

He lifted his hands, palms up. "No doubt there are some people who noticed us dancing together. Some of them know that you are Chloe's sister. Some of them will gossip about that." He took her hand. "But life is short, and I won't live it worried about what people will think. As long as I feel that I'm right with God, that I'm doing my best to be honest and kind and to do the right thing, then I want to move ahead."

She'd been looking at him when he had started talking, but now her eyes dropped. "I want to do the right thing, too," she said. She drew in a deep, shuddering breath. "And that's why there's something I need to tell you."

Chapter 12

Tell him now. You have to tell him now.

A sharp knife of dread lodged itself in Arianna's throat. She coughed past it, ruthlessly. "Jack, I—"

"Let's go somewhere more private," he interrupted. He put an arm around her shoulders and guided her toward a back doorway. "There's a little courtyard out here, and I don't think anyone from the gala has discovered it."

Relief washed over her at the brief reprieve, and then her anxiety thrummed back even louder. No matter how beautiful the spot, she was about to tell him something ugly.

Oh, Sammy's birth wasn't ugly. Any baby was a blessing, and Sammy felt like a special one. His adoption, too, was a beautiful thing.

But the cover-up, the fact that Jack had been raising Sammy for eighteen months, unaware of her and Chloe's conspiracy of silence... That was ugly and that was a mistake.

"Here we go." Jack led her out into a cool green oasis.

Small trees surrounded a tiled courtyard. In the center was a fountain with burbling water and two small benches. Some night-flowering plant scented the air.

Arianna was praying now. *Please, God, give me the right words. Help me explain in a way that does the least damage to Sammy, to Jack and to Chloe.*

The thought of her sister made guilt rise up in her. *I'm sorry, Chloe. I couldn't keep the secret.* She was picturing her sister's face, sad and anxious and judgmental.

Jack drew her to a bench and tugged gently at her hand. "Sit down," he said. "Now, what's this big secret you have to tell me?" His tone was indulgent.

She looked into his kind eyes and tried to memorize their tender expression, because she didn't think it was going to last much longer.

"If you keep looking at me like that," he began, brushing a stray strand of hair back from her face, letting his thumb trail along her cheek, "I'm not going to be responsible for what happens."

Her heartbeat accelerated. "Chloe—"

"Shh." He touched a fingertip to her lips. "I've made my peace with Chloe and how she'd feel about us being together. She's in such a better place now, I can't think she'd begrudge us happiness."

He leaned forward and gently brushed his lips across hers, releasing a tsunami of emotions inside her. Her heart cried out with longing to melt into his kiss.

It was the love and acceptance she'd always longed for. Jack knew her, had known her for years now, and he cared for her, wanted to kiss her. And not just to kiss her, but to be close in every way, a closeness of the heart and mind.

She tried to hold on to reason. The further she let this go forward, the worse the truth would be when it came out. Pulling back, she extracted herself from his arms and turned away. "I mean it, Jack. Remember when you and Chloe were trying so hard to adopt, and it wasn't happening because of her issues with anxiety and depression? Until finally, the agency let you know that they had a baby for you?"

His phone pinged, and he held up a hand. "Hold that thought. I have my phone on Do Not Disturb, except for Mrs. Jennings. Let me check what's going on."

Arianna grasped hard at the iron bench. She was launched now. She just had to keep the flow of words coming, and it almost felt like a relief to finally let Jack in on the truth. She waited as he paced a little away, head down, focusing on whatever Mrs. Jennings was saying. "Uh-huh. Did you take his temperature? Oh yes, I hear him." He glanced back at her, mouthed the word *sorry*.

"I'll be right over to pick him up," he said.

"What's wrong?" she asked as he clicked off the phone.

"I don't know. Mrs. Jennings says Sammy is really sick."

"Oh no!" Fresh anxiety cut through her preoccupation with herself. "What's wrong with him?" If something happened to Sammy, if he got sick…it didn't bear thinking about.

He held out a hand and took hers. "I'm really sorry, but I've got to go. I'm not too worried. Mrs. Jennings tends to overreact, but just on the chance that she's right and he's picked up something serious, I'm going to head over." They were walking rapidly back the way they'd come. They reached the door and he held it for her to walk inside. "Look, I'm sure you can get a ride home with Daniela or Penny. Stay and enjoy yourself."

As if. "No," she said. "I'm coming with you."

"You're sure?"

"Of course. I'm worried about him."

They made their way through the crowd and out to Jack's car, and Arianna's mind raced the whole time.

What if Sammy were sick enough to go to the hospital, and she couldn't even visit him because she wasn't thought to be related?

Keep him safe, Father, and I'll tell the truth, no matter what the outcome.

"We're almost there." Jack considered running the last red light before the hospital. He decided he could wait rather than potentially explaining himself to a police officer, resulting in more time wasted. "How's he look?"

Sammy wasn't bellowing out his usual wail; instead, he just let out a series of small, fussy bleats that almost broke Jack's heart.

"He's still pale and feverish," Arianna said from the back seat. "And… Oh no, he just threw up. It's okay, honey, it's okay. We'll get you cleaned up." Looking in the rearview, Jack could see her digging through the diaper bag, finding wipes, cooing at Sammy the whole time.

Jack checked the intersection carefully and then gunned through the red light. He swung into the parking lot of the hospital and looked around wildly. He'd never been here before, never had need. Sammy was normally as healthy as a horse, and so was Jack himself.

There, a red sign: Emergency Room. He turned toward it with a squeal of tires, and a moment later, they were at the door of the ER. He jammed the car into Park and jumped out.

Arianna unfastened Sammy from the car seat and handed him out to Jack. "I'll go park the car and then be right behind you."

"Thanks." He didn't know what he'd have done without her. Mrs. Jennings had gotten worried because, in addition to him having a fever, Sammy's diaper had been dry for hours. Initially, that hadn't seemed like such a big deal to him, but seeing Sammy's dull fussiness, feeling his high fever, he was getting a much more serious set of worries.

He carried Sammy inside—man, he was burning up—and rushed a lackadaisical clerk through infuriatingly slow intake procedures. Arianna hurried in just as the med techs came to get Sammy.

They wanted to put him on a gurney. But Sammy wailed and clung to Jack. "I'll carry him in," Jack said and headed toward the double doors.

"Sir, our procedure dictates that—"

Arianna sped up to interrupt, walking alongside the tech who seemed to be in charge. "He has autism. Change bothers him, and he has sensory issues. He can't be separated from his dad."

"Ma'am, what's your connection to this child?"

"She's his aunt and she takes care of him, and he needs her in here," Jack said over his shoulder. Then they were in a cubicle and everything moved in double time: an IV and blood tests—horrific trying to find Sammy's vein—and then waiting for the chest X-ray and renal ultrasound.

"Why are they testing his lungs and kidneys?" Arianna was holding Sammy now, rocking him gently back and forth, and Jack gave information to the doctors and then paced.

"The fact he hasn't been urinating. There might be something wrong with his kidneys. The chest X-ray…heart, lungs, bones, there's a lot they can see from it." He blew out a panicky breath, trying not to think about the radiation and its effect on a baby like Sammy. Right now, they had to find out what was wrong, and fast.

Somehow they got through the tests, and the IV started to help with his blood volume and electrolyte balance. Sammy was admitted to a private room in the pediatric unit—not the ICU, for now—and the sun had already risen over the hospital parking lot when the pediatric ER doctor finally came in with the test results. He checked Sammy over visually and looked at the monitors, but didn't wake him.

"He's stable for now," the doctor said then, pulling up a chair to sit knee to knee with Jack and Arianna in the room, crowded with machinery and supplies. "But this is serious."

"What's going on?" Jack's heart felt like it was going to fly out of his chest. It was only natural to take Arianna's hand and squeeze it tightly. He felt like he was holding on to a lifeline.

"He seems to have gone into renal failure."

Jack's stomach hollowed out, and emptiness filled him. His lungs felt empty, too, like he'd run a long race; it was hard to catch his breath.

The doctor looked from Jack to Arianna and then perched reading glasses on the end of his nose and looked down at the sheaf of test results in his hands. "Right now we don't know why, and figuring that out will help determine our course of treatment. He's going to be here a few days, I would think. But this could be the beginning of a long process."

As long as the doctor was talking about beginnings rather than endings. He slowed his breathing deliberately. He had to hold it together. What he wanted was to take Sammy in his arms and hold him tight, but the poor kid was sleeping, finally, and Jack wouldn't indulge himself by waking him up. He reached over and patted his son's blanket-covered foot instead. "Renal failure," he repeated, trying to take it in, to understand it.

"He's going to be okay?" Arianna sounded as desperate as Jack felt himself.

"I hope so," the doctor said, which wasn't exactly the re-assuring answer Jack wanted to hear. "Do you know if he's ingested anything new in the past twenty-four, forty-eight hours? Chewed on something, gotten into some medicine?"

"I don't think so," Jack said, and Arianna frowned and shook her head. "He's been with one of us constantly until tonight, and he was with a dependable babysitter tonight." Guilt suffused him at leaving Sammy with Mrs. Jennings. He didn't suspect her of leaving Sammy unsupervised, but if he'd been with his son himself, he might have noticed symptoms sooner.

"The other question is genetic," the doctor said. "For two reasons. One, is there any history of kidney disease in either of your families? And two..." He met their eyes again. "Is there a potential donor, if it should come to that? Which could include either of you."

Jack sucked in a breath.

"A *kidney* donor?" Arianna sounded as shocked as Jack felt. "Is that...likely? Is it that bad?"

"We just don't know yet. If it's needed, we'd want it to happen quickly, and that's why I'm bringing up the subject now." He reached over and patted Sammy's foot just as Jack had done. "I certainly hope not, and there's a good chance that he'll clear whatever infection or toxicity is causing the problem and be just fine."

Jack shook his head slowly. "He's adopted," he said. "Closed adoption. I can petition to have the records opened for medical reasons, but there's time and paperwork involved."

"Definitely get it started." The doctor frowned. "I'd like to see the family history ASAP."

Arianna let out a choked sound.

Jack and the doctor both turned to her, and Jack squeezed her hand.

Her breathing was rapid, her eyes huge, staring at Sammy.

"Are you okay?" Jack asked.

At the same time, the doctor patted her hand. "I know it's a lot to take in."

She cleared her throat and looked at the doctor. "I can actually answer those questions," she said. "About his genetics?" Her face was almost as white as the doctor's jacket.

"You're the aunt, correct?" The doctor consulted his records and then looked expectantly at Arianna.

"Ye-e-e-s," she said, drawing out the word. "I'm his adoptive aunt. But I have some information about his genetic background."

Jack had been holding her hand all this time, but now he dropped it, turned and studied her. What was she talking about?

Her gaze flickered over to him and then back to the doctor. "Sammy doesn't have any biological relatives with kidney disease," she said, speaking slowly and clearly, kind of like a person who'd had too much to drink and was trying to sound sober. "And he does have at least one direct relation who's willing to be tested as a donor if it becomes necessary."

Her words made no sense. "Arianna," Jack said, "how can you know that?"

The doctor looked up from his chart.

Arianna met Jack's eyes and took his hand again, swallowed convulsively. "I know it," she said, "because I'm his biological mother."

Jack stared at her. "What?"

She nodded. "I carried him and birthed him," she said. "He's my son."

Jack's world, as he knew it, seemed to spin faster and faster until it exploded.

Chapter 13

Arianna's heart raced, and her palms were sweating. At the same time, it was as if a giant boulder she'd been trying to hold in place had finally crashed down the mountainside. There might be massive destruction in its wake, but at least she could stop this ceaseless effort to keep it in place.

Jack's face was expressionless, his voice toneless. "That can't be true."

The doctor looked from her to Jack. "This is something you were unaware of?"

He shook his head, quick and hard. "Arianna, I'm sure you feel like his mother at times, especially since you've been taking care of him, but Sammy's adoption was closed."

"Yes, I know," she said and swallowed. "Chloe and I decided that was best."

"What?" Jack's word exploded from him like a gunshot.

Best to get it all out at once. "Chloe couldn't have a child, and I got pregnant and knew I couldn't raise one," she said, the words tumbling over each other. "It seemed to make sense at the time, if she raised my child."

Jack was staring at her. "This is no time for jokes."

She tried to breathe slowly, to calm herself down. But it was next to impossible, because this mattered so much, mattered almost more than anything had ever mattered in her life. *Jack* mattered, and every word from her mouth was hurting him, stabbing him, cutting him. Cutting apart their relationship, this sweet, precious thing that had just started to grow. "It's not a joke. I'm sorry."

"You're sorry. You're *sorry*?"

The doctor cleared his throat and closed the file folder. "Well. I have the preliminary answers I needed regarding the boy's genetics, if this…ah…*revelation* proves to be true. We'll keep a close eye on Sammy and keep running tests. I'll be back in the afternoon." He stood, his legs knocking his chair backward into some equipment, making a metallic clang.

Jack nodded distractedly. "Thank you."

"Thanks." Ariana glanced up at the man and then looked away from his curious frown.

They waited while the doctor left the room. At the doorway, a smiling nurse started to wheel in a cart. "Hey, everyone, another vitals check!" she called out.

The doctor stopped her, speaking in a low voice. She looked past him, curiosity in her eyes, and then backed the cart into the hallway. A little girl's voice rang out and was hushed.

The hospital room's door closed with a gentle swish.

And then Arianna and Jack were alone in the hospital room with Sammy. And the truth.

It wasn't the situation she'd imagined when she'd thought of telling Jack that she was Sammy's mother. She'd intended to prepare him mentally, sit down in a comfortable, private place. To start at the beginning and explain, carefully, what had happened, what had led to this horrible mess.

Instead, she'd piled a second shock on top of the jolt of Sammy's serious illness. No wonder Jack looked so stunned.

Even though she couldn't fix it, she had to try. "I know it doesn't help, but I'm sorry. So terribly, terribly sorry. Not for having Sammy, and not for placing him with you, but for keeping the secret. Chloe didn't want—"

"Stop." Jack held up a hand as if he could physically halt the flow of words. "I'm trying to take this in."

"Of course. Sorry." She was going about this all wrong. If she could only think of the right words, maybe she could soften the fact that they'd hidden such a vast secret, make it hurt him less.

Sammy stirred in his bed, and they both stood and hurried from the foot of his bed to the side of it. Arianna started to brush aside a wayward strand of Sammy's hair and then pulled back her hand. It wasn't her right. She waited, arms rigidly at her sides, while Jack straightened Sammy's covers.

He was so close that she could smell his aftershave, just a hint of it. Last night that smell had evoked another kind of strong emotion, but that seemed like a century ago.

He moved back to the chairs they'd been sitting in and she followed. She sat, and he moved his chair away from her.

Her heart was breaking, cracking in two.

He stared at the floor for a long time, and she watched him, forcing herself to stay quiet, to let him process the news in his own way. Finally, he looked up at her. "Chloe knew the whole time? And kept it from me?"

She nodded, and he looked away.

This was a third awful thing he had to deal with: the fact that his marriage hadn't been what he thought, that there had been a huge lie at the center of it. He didn't betray much with his expression, but a muscle twitched in his cheek.

"Why?" he asked in a low tone.

Here was her chance to explain. To find the words that would give him a little bit of peace, and that might allow her to still see Sammy, be there for him, at least a little. She chose them carefully.

"Do you remember when I went to Atlanta to live for a few months, and Chloe came to visit me? Did that seem a little odd to you?"

He nodded.

"Right, because we weren't that kind of close sisters. But she'd found out from our mother that I was expecting a baby."

He looked up quickly. "Whose baby?"

Oh, she didn't want to go there. She knew instinctively that finding out Sammy's paternity would be a blow to Jack. "Let me tell the story in my way?" she asked. "I'll get to all of it. I promise."

He nodded. He still wasn't meeting her eyes, and that was killing her. She wanted to sink down onto her knees and beg for forgiveness, to cry on his shoulder—anything to keep their connection alive. She reached for his hand.

He crossed his arms and turned, avoiding her touch. "Just tell it."

"Okay." She drew in a deep breath, let it out and started talking. "She came to ask me if she could adopt the baby. My plan had always been to place the baby for adoption. Well, almost always." She'd thought, at first, that maybe she and Nathan could marry and raise their child. But when she'd met Nathan for coffee, planning to tell him about her pregnancy and discuss what to do, he'd beaten her to the punch, telling her he didn't want to be involved with her anymore and that he'd gotten a wonderful postdoc up in Boulder, one that didn't pay well but would allow him to do his research.

She remembered looking at him, this man she liked but didn't love, this man whose bright future would be crushed by the requirement to support her and a child. She'd shot up a desperate prayer to a God she barely knew.

The next moment, a family had come into the restaurant, a Caucasian mother and father and a little girl with Asian features. "Can I have a milkshake, Mama?" the girl had asked.

The man had swung her up high, making her giggle, and then settled her into his arms. "Whatever you want, princess," he'd said.

Arianna didn't consider herself to be a true Christian back then. She'd only just started going to church again after several years away. But even she could recognize a divine moment. It was as if God had proffered a visual aid, just when she needed it: *adoption can be the perfect answer.*

"It's okay, Nathan," she'd said. "You've got to follow your dreams. I understand."

Now she looked at Jack, his shoulders hunched and tight, lines bracketing his downturned mouth. In trying to do the right thing by Nathan and Chloe and, most of all, Sammy, she'd done Jack a great wrong. "It seemed to make sense. We were both immature, not good at thinking about future consequences. And for different reasons, we both felt desperate."

He was quiet for a couple of minutes, and then he looked at her, his face bleak. "I get why you and Chloe would've made that arrangement. I guess. But why wouldn't you tell me?"

She lifted her hands, palms up. "Chloe insisted. For reasons she wouldn't explain to me, she didn't want you to know."

"But you knew what Chloe was like!" he burst out. "Why would you let her make a decision like that for you? A decision that was so wrong?"

Why *had* she? Yes, Chloe had been persuasive, and Arianna had been raised to take care of her. But she wouldn't normally have allowed Chloe to lead her into doing something she thought was wrong.

The part she'd barely admitted to herself, the part she'd shoved down and avoided, nudged into the hospital-bright light. "I wanted to know him," she admitted through a throat that had gone thick and achy. "I wanted to see him growing up and to know he was okay. I couldn't face just giving him to strangers, getting a photo once a year."

Jack's mouth tightened. He didn't say anything, but to Arianna, his expression was pure negative judgment.

"Do you know what it was like, going through pregnancy and childbirth, holding him in my arms, loving him more and more, and then letting him go?" Her voice was hoarse and tears were rolling down her face, but she couldn't stop now. "It was like tearing out part of my heart and throwing it aside. It almost killed me, Jack! But it was good for Sammy. And that was what mattered."

Jack was shaking his head. "No. Stop it. I'm not going to feel sorry for you."

"Of course not," she choked out. "That's not what I want, I was just trying to explain—"

"You came to me and offered to be his nanny," he said. "Knowing you were his mother. You've hung out with me and eaten meals with me and—" He broke off, looking at her with eyes that expressed pure pain, and she knew what he had been about to say.

She'd kissed him. Knowing this awful secret, she'd kissed him.

"Were you planning to try to get him back? Is that why you acted like you cared for me?"

"No, Jack, of course not. I wanted to tell you—"

"But you didn't, did you?" He swallowed and straightened. "Get out."

"What?" She met his eyes, saw the anger there and instinctively crossed her arms over her chest.

He waved a hand at the door. "Go on. I don't want you here."

"But Sammy needs—"

"I'm still his father," Jack interrupted, his voice hard and cold. "And I don't want you here."

She stood. "I understand, Jack, but I hope—"

"Now, please?" His voice cracked a little on the last word.

"Okay." She nodded rapidly, then looked over at Sammy. "Will you…" She wanted him to keep her updated, but that wasn't a favor she could ask, not now. "Can I bring you anything? Clothes, a cell phone charger? Coffee?"

"I'll get Penny or Willie to help." He turned away from her and went to Sammy's bedside. His shoulders were stiff and square, a wall against her.

"Right." She swallowed hard and headed out the door.

She had her hand on the door when he said, "Hey."

"Yeah?" She turned back, searching his face for any kind of softening, a hope of forgiveness.

There was none. "You didn't tell me who Sammy's dad is."

Right. And she'd promised to tell him everything. And

his attitude toward her was already about as low as it could go. "It was Nathan," she said.

His mouth twisted to the side, and he gave one nod. Looked away from her and waved her out with one hand, as if she were a pesky courtier and he were the king.

She couldn't fault him for it, though. He'd had shock upon shock. "He didn't know, Jack," she said. "Not until he figured it out himself, just a little while ago. Don't hate him."

His lips flattened and he planted his legs wide, his fists clenching. "Do I have to call hospital security to get you out of here?"

It wasn't fair, when he'd asked her a question that had held up her departure. But what she'd done was much, much more unfair. She opened her mouth to say goodbye, couldn't squeeze out the word and half stumbled into the bright corridor, feeling like her own heart had been surgically excised.

Jack got through the next few hours on the kind of autopilot he'd perfected doing long, complex surgeries on extremely fragile animals. He comforted Sammy when he woke up, tried to get him to eat the unfamiliar soft food diet and called Penny to bring in the blue-and-white-checked bear and a few other supplies. He didn't ask it, but she also brought a change of clothes for Jack.

"You should have called the moment this happened," she scolded him. "Honestly, we all thought you and Arianna had gone off for some quiet time together. You seemed like you were having a wonderful night. Where is she, by the way?"

Jack hadn't even thought about the fact that he'd have to explain things to people and figure out who should know the truth about Sammy. For now, he just shook his head. "We had a disagreement," he said.

She'd sat down on the side of Sammy's bed, and at his words, she looked quickly up at him. "That happens," she said, "but I'm sorry it happened now, when there's so much stress in your life. I'm sure you'll work it out."

"No." And he didn't want to talk about it. He sorted through the supplies she'd brought. "Look, Sammy, your cup!"

Sammy reached fretfully for it, then threw it down. He made a fist and rubbed his cheek, then looked expectantly at Jack.

"Does it hurt?" Jack put his hand on Sammy's cheek, then touched his forehead. His fever, thankfully, had gone down.

Sammy twisted away and curled around his bear.

"This has to be hard on him emotionally," Penny said quietly.

Jack nodded. "He doesn't even like it when he has a different food for dinner or gets a new shirt. Being in the hospital means everything is new."

"That's rough. Rough on you, too." Penny patted Jack's arm. "Look, why don't you get a shower and change clothes? I'll sit with Sammy. It looks like he's going to sleep anyway."

"You don't need to…" He trailed off. He wanted to do everything for Sammy himself, but he'd been going nonstop for more than twenty-four hours now. He was just so tired. "Thanks, I will."

After he showered in the little bathroom connected to Sammy's hospital room, and his energy returned, his anger grew. What had Arianna and Chloe been thinking, keeping the truth about Sammy from him? How disrespectful could you get? Had they never intended to tell Sammy, either? What was supposed to happen if Sammy got sick or, when he got older, wanted to know something about his heritage? Had they even considered those ramifications?

Moments from his years with Chloe pushed their way into his head. How brokenhearted she'd been about her infertility. How she'd closed down, turned away from him. How, when they'd adopted Sammy, it hadn't made her as happy as he'd expected it to.

How she'd avoided Arianna, felt competitive with her, been obsessed with the idea that Jack had feelings for her.

Looking at his face in the mirror as he shaved, he almost felt like she was a shadow behind him, hovering. Permanently unhappy.

She'd been beautiful, outwardly perfect. They'd wanted the same things when they'd married. But life hadn't worked out the way they'd planned.

Chloe had struggled with so many issues. He wanted to feel angry with her for her secrecy and lies, but he ran out of gas when he thought it through. She hadn't had full control of her thinking.

But Arianna did! Arianna, free-spirited, warmhearted Arianna, knew perfectly well what she was doing. She'd betrayed him without a second thought, had then come to be his nanny and acted like she was falling for him.

Had she done that because she wanted to get close to Sammy again, to be his mother?

He rammed his fist against the wall of the bathroom. It hurt, but not as much as his heart did.

He'd been falling for Arianna, hard. He'd *wanted* something to happen with her. He'd loved how warm and creative she was with Sammy. He'd even thought of marriage.

What a fool he'd been.

When he came back to Sammy's bedside, refreshed in body if not in spirit, Penny rose to meet him. "They came in and took his vitals, but he's sleeping again," she said. "And your phone's blowing up."

He checked on Sammy, pulled the covers up and stroked his sweaty head. His throat tightened. *It's just you and me, little guy. We'll make it alone.*

Then, to escape his emotions, he scrolled through his phone. For every message from a friend—because word had gotten out in Esperanza Springs, and everyone was worried about Sammy—there was a message from Arianna.

I'm sorry.

Do you need anything?

How is Sammy doing?

Her concern rang so false that he felt like throwing his phone across the room. Instead, he clicked into his phone settings and blocked her number.

Sammy stirred, and his eyes opened. He rubbed his cheek with his fist again.

"I don't know why he keeps doing that," Jack said to Penny. "What's wrong, buddy? Does your face hurt?"

"Oh! I think I know what it is," Penny said unexpectedly.

He looked at her, surprised. "What do you mean?"

"It's a sign. You know how Arianna taught him *more* and *milk* and *banana*?"

And *daddy*. She'd taught him to tap his forehead with the thumb of an open hand, asking for Daddy. He remembered when Arianna had pointed to Jack, and Sammy had half smiled and made the sign.

Arianna had swooped down on him with hugs, her eyes shiny with happy tears. When she'd calmed down a little, she'd explained the sign's significance to Jack.

It had made him feel hopeful. Sammy was learning to communicate. And he was communicating about people, being social. A double win.

In a way, it was Sammy's first time of saying, "Daddy." He remembered how he'd reached over and squeezed Arianna's hand, all full of emotion, and she'd smiled at him.

"So what does the cheek-rub sign mean? Do you know?" Because no way, no *way* was he calling Arianna to find out.

She nodded. "It's his sign for Arianna," she said. "He wants her."

Chapter 14

Sammy was crying. Again.

Arianna stared out the window of her second-floor apartment, looking at the house where Jack and Sammy lived. They'd come home from the hospital last night, but Arianna had no way of knowing how he was doing health-wise. It had been three days since she'd revealed the truth to Jack in the hospital, and she hadn't been able to contact him since.

She could tell Sammy wasn't doing well emotionally. The fussy, whiny sound of his wailing made her ache to comfort him.

She'd go over there. She picked up her purse, got the plate of cookies she'd baked in the hopes of seeing Sammy and started out the door. But two steps down the stairs, she lost her courage.

Jack didn't want her there. He wasn't answering her calls or texts. He had as much as threatened to call hospital security to keep her away. If she showed up on his doorstep, he wouldn't open the door. He might even call the state police.

She went back inside, put down her things and sat at her small kitchen table, staring out at the Sangre de Cristo Mountains, her gaze frequently turning toward Jack's house.

Sammy's cries stopped, and that was a comfort. Jack must have gotten him calmed down.

Thinking about Jack made her stomach twist into impossible knots. She would never forget the look on his face as the truth had sunk in. Shock. Betrayal. Anger. All understandable emotions, and she couldn't fault him for having them. But what had hurt the most was what hadn't been there: the love and caring that had been in his eyes every time he looked at her. Now that was gone. And it wasn't coming back.

She'd been happy about it, enjoyed it. But she hadn't realized how very blessed she was to have it, and how awful it would be when it was withdrawn. It was the acceptance she'd always wanted and never gotten before. Jack had liked her as she was, her messy, disorganized, slightly overweight self. He cared for her, even knowing her flaws.

Except he hadn't known the worst ones. He hadn't known what she was hiding, what she had concealed, and when he had discovered that, it had proven to be too much, even for his larger-than-normal heart.

She'd blown it. She blown the best thing she'd ever had.

The sound of a thin, high cry drifted across the space between the houses on a mountain breeze, quickly increasing in volume. Sammy was upset again.

It was killing her not to know what was going on with him, whether his prognosis was good, whether some kind of a transplant was going to be needed. Oh, she'd gladly give Sammy a kidney or any other organ that she could donate.

If Jack would allow it.

The crying didn't stop. It got louder. She shut the window so she wouldn't hear it anymore. Let him deal with it himself if he was determined to.

She stood with her hands on the window frame, trying to look away.

And then she grabbed her things again and clattered down the stairs. A moment later she was on Jack's front porch, knocking.

He didn't answer.

She knocked again, just a little louder. He had to hear her. She knew he was in there, could hear Sammy's cries distinctly now.

Behind her, she heard a car door slam. Finn, the ranch manager, emerged from the office and walked to meet the suited, cowboy-booted man, who'd apparently come on some sort of business. They walked into the barn.

"Jack! Please, let me come in, just for a minute!"

Sammy's cries escalated.

"Jack! Please!"

The door opened, and there was Jack, stubble thick on his cheeks and lines she'd never seen before bracketing his mouth and crossing his forehead. Dark circles beneath his eyes told the story of sleepless nights.

Sammy's face was red, but he looked far, far healthier than he had when Arianna had last seen him. Relief washed over her, even as his cries grew louder. He reached his little arms toward her.

"You need to leave us alone." Jack's words were clipped. "Seeing you just upsets him more."

"He wants me. If I could just spend a little time with him—"

"That just stretches out his pain." Jack's voice was cold, but his eyes were tortured.

"Look, I know how angry you must be, but we need to talk soon about some kind of an arrangement—"

He held up a hand, shaking his head, cutting her off. "We're not making an arrangement."

She sucked in a shaky breath. "You're not going to let me see him?"

"That's right. It's a closed adoption. You signed away your parental rights."

His words, each distinctly articulated, hammered her like steel.

"I need for you to leave. Now."

Arianna's heart seemed to stretch out toward her son, crying in Jack's arms. She could comfort him, she knew she could. "Please, Jack—"

"Don't make me be cruel."

Still, she stood there, staring, trying to memorize Sammy's little face, to remember what it felt like to hold him in her arms. Trying to memorize Jack's face, too, because she didn't know when she'd see it again.

"Arianna. Go."

She shook her head miserably. "I can't."

Jack closed the door, not with a slam but gently. The click of the lock, though, was decisive.

She stood staring at the closed door for a long moment and then set the cookies down on his porch. She walked back toward her apartment but found she couldn't bear to go back inside. Instead, she headed for a trail that led up into the foothills, walking faster and faster and then running, her throat thick and aching. Soon, tears were pouring down her face, making it hard to see, but she couldn't stop. Couldn't stop moving. Couldn't stop running away from the worst mistake of her life.

It was late afternoon when Arianna came down from the foothills and trudged back to the ranch. Her eyes were dry now. Her soul was dry, too.

She'd had the undeniable urge to just keep walking, walking into the mountain as the night grew colder, as storm clouds gathered. Her purpose in life, whatever purpose she'd had, was gone.

She couldn't see her son. Couldn't help Jack raise him.

She was so overwhelmed with shame and guilt that her forearms kept going across her stomach, as if she were going to fall apart if she didn't literally hold herself together.

Still, some survival instinct brought her back to the ranch. That same instinct told her not to go up to her apartment and spend the evening alone.

She needed help.

She'd poured her soul out to God on that mountain, but God had stayed silent. Maybe she wasn't praying right. She wasn't an experienced Christian.

She wanted to talk to Penny, or maybe to Daniela, but she didn't have Jack's permission to share the story of Sammy, and it wouldn't be right to start telling people something so private. She wouldn't add insult to the injury she'd already done Jack by spreading Sammy's story around town.

But there was one person that she could tell. She got in her car and drove carefully down the mountain road, staying well under the speed limit because she knew how close to the edge she was emotionally. Forty minutes later, she pulled into Pastor Carson Blair's driveway, parked her car and knocked on his front door.

Lily answered. "Arianna! Come in." She peered at Arianna's face. "You look awful. Is Sammy okay?"

Arianna licked dry lips. "Do you think Carson would be willing to talk to me in confidence?"

"Of course he can. Come in." Lily opened the door and ushered her in, then walked her through the house to Carson's study with an arm around her shoulders.

The unquestioning kindness made Arianna's throat thicken with unshed tears.

Lily tapped on the door and spoke to Carson in a low voice, and then he opened the door wider and reached out a hand to Arianna. "Come in. Make yourself comfortable."

Arianna looked at Lily. "This needs to be confidential," she choked out, "but I'd like it if you could stay and hear what I have to say, on those terms."

Lily bit her lip and looked at Carson. "Come help me make some tea and bring in something to eat, and we'll talk about it. Just relax, Arianna, and one or both of us will be right back."

Arianna sat in the comfortable chair in front of Carson's battered desk and let her forehead rest on her hand. She had no idea of what to do, how to handle any of this, but Carson was wise. Carson would help. Carson would pray with her.

There was a snuffling around her legs, and a heavyset, low-slung dog nosed at her hand. Almost immediately, another equally odd-looking dog rushed in, barking.

"Boomer! No, Boomer!" Sunny, one of Carson's twins, ran in and grabbed the barking dog.

Her sister, Skye, came in, too, and knelt by the quieter dog. She looked up at Arianna, and her head tilted to one side. "I'm sorry you're sad."

"She's sad?" Sunny looked up from her efforts to hold her squirming dog. "Aww. She *is* sad."

The twins looked at each other, seeming to communicate without words. Then Sunny pulled a large dog biscuit out of her pocket and broke it in half.

Instantly, the little dogs sat at attention, silent and alert.

"Now, be quiet. We have to talk to Miss Arianna." Sunny's tone was severe. She handed half of the biscuit to each dog, and they went to opposite corners of the room to eat them.

Still kneeling on the floor, Skye reached up and took Arianna's hand. "I'm sad sometimes, too," she confided.

Not to be outdone, Sunny leaned against Arianna's knees. "Do you need a hug?"

The identical, upturned faces were so full of sweet sympathy that Arianna couldn't help smiling through her tears. "Of course, a hug from you girls would really help," she said, sliding down onto the floor so they could all sit next to each other. The dogs, having finished their biscuits, trotted over and climbed into their three adjoining laps, sniffing pockets, looking for more treats. And then, as the girls told Arianna about their own problems, how they'd started a new school year and were in separate classrooms for the first time, Arianna listened and nodded her sympathy, and a tiny measure of peace rose in her heart.

There was still sweetness and caring in the world. And no, she wasn't going to get the kind she craved, from the person she craved it from, but it still existed, in good friends like Carson and Lily, and in sweet children like Sunny and Skye.

Lily and Carson came back in, Lily carrying a teapot and cups, and Carson a tray piled with cookies and chocolates and cupcakes.

"Girls," Lily said as she set down the teapot, "did you

ask if Miss Arianna wanted company? She might need some time alone."

"She doesn't, Mommy," Skye said.

Sunny shook her head. "She's sad, but we made her feel better."

"It's true." Arianna tightened an arm around each girl's shoulders. "They've been so sweet." She wanted to say more, but her voice was catching.

"Actually, girls," Lily said, "there's a new princess movie. For a special treat, would you like to watch it?"

"Yes!" Sunny jumped up.

"Can Miss Arianna watch it, too, with us?" Skye asked.

"No, she needs to talk with Daddy and me," Lily said. "You girls run along. It's all set up, you just have to push Play. And I put a bowl of popcorn up high, where the dogs can't reach it. Will you be very careful to keep the people food away from the dogs?"

Both girls nodded vigorously.

"Okay, then, off you go," Lily said, and the two girls rushed out of the room, the little dogs following after them.

"They are *so* adorable," Arianna said. "And so kind and sweet. And you're such a good mom, Lily."

Lily flushed with obvious pleasure, and Arianna thought about how fully Lily had become a mother to the twins. Indistinguishable from a biological mother, really.

She wondered whether Jack would meet someone soon, give some woman an opportunity to become a mother to Sammy. It was more than likely; he was a handsome, kind, good man. Any single woman in town would be happy to go out with him.

Her stomach burned at the thought. She didn't want anyone else to fill that role in Jack's life; she wanted to be the one. Had stood a chance of it until he'd found out the truth.

Pastor Carson smiled and took a seat across from her, and Lily sat down at his side, pouring cups of tea. "Why don't you tell us what's going on?" he suggested. "I can see that you're very upset."

So she told them, with a lot of pauses and a few tears. Told them about getting pregnant with Sammy, and about Chloe's proposition, and how she had decided to accept it.

"Why did Chloe want to keep it a secret from her husband?" Lily asked.

"It's complicated," Arianna said. "So complicated that I don't completely understand it. She struggled with some mental health issues, anxiety and depression. And…" She trailed off, thinking.

"Is there something else?" Carson asked gently.

Arianna drew in a breath. "We grew up with a lot of shame," she said slowly. "I've always felt shame about my body, my weight. Chloe didn't have that issue, but I wonder if she was ashamed that her body wouldn't do what she wanted. She couldn't make a baby."

"That could definitely be the case," Lily said. "She could have felt like an inadequate woman."

"There's biblical precedent for that," Carson said. "In ancient cultures, and in some cultures today, unfortunately, a woman's fertility is all tangled up in her sense of worth."

"I could have a baby and she couldn't." Arianna took a cookie and broke it in half. "I never really thought about how jealous that must have made her feel. I was so caught up in what I did wrong, getting pregnant without being married, that I didn't really consider how it must have made Chloe feel." Her heart ached for the sister she'd once been close to. There would be no more opportunity to mend the relationship, to talk about what it had all meant to them. Not on this earth anyway.

Carson and Lily looked at each other. Lily raised an eyebrow, as if asking her husband a question, and Carson gave a nod.

"You may have come to some of the only people who could really understand what you're talking about." Lily took a sip of tea and swallowed. "I kept a big, big secret from Carson when we first met. It had to do with his wife, who was my friend and who died. I thought keeping the manner of her death a secret was a kindness to Carson, but it actually caused us terrible problems."

"I didn't know that." And it made Arianna feel a little better, knowing she wasn't the only person who'd made the mistake of being too secretive.

Lily had even gotten through it and found love and a family.

"Secrets are almost always toxic," Carson said. "Even when they're kept as a mercy to someone else, it almost always backfires."

Arianna nodded. "I know that now. But at that time, I was so desperate, I wasn't thinking straight. Now I hurt Jack so badly. He—" her throat tightened, but she choked it out "—he doesn't want me to ever see Sammy again."

Lily put a hand on Arianna's arm. "Oh, honey, that has to hurt so bad," she said. The sympathy in her voice threatened to open the floodgates of Arianna's heart. She didn't dare speak; she only nodded.

"You know," Carson said, "we all make an awful lot of mistakes in this life. It's part of being human."

Arianna drew in a breath and let it out slowly. "I guess that's true. I hate that I hurt Jack so badly, though, and that…that Sammy will suffer." Again, she had to force the words out through a thick throat. "He keeps crying."

"And Jack won't let you see him?"

She shook her head. "I feel like it can't be fixed. Like it's an impossible situation."

Lily glanced over at her husband, a tiny smile pulling up one corner of her mouth. "Carson kind of specializes in those."

"Correction—Jesus specializes in those." Carson reached for a Bible that sat at the center of his desk. "I'd like to read some Scripture with you, if you don't mind."

Lily patted Arianna's arm. "I need to check on the girls and on dinner," she said. "Will you stay? In fact, why don't you stay the night with us?"

"Oh, I couldn't," she said. "I need to…" Her heart turned over in a low darkness. "Actually, since I'm out of a job, I guess I don't have to do anything."

"Then stay. I'll set an extra place at the table and make sure the guest room has clean sheets."

Arianna spent the next hour with Carson, reading passages he showed her from Scripture. They prayed together, sometimes aloud and sometimes silently. And they talked: about Arianna's childhood, her parents, the things that had led her to get too involved with Nathan.

Every time she felt discouraged, every time she cried, he was able to pull out a Bible passage that addressed what she was feeling. Not that he made her feel bad about crying, but he had real answers.

When Lily knocked and told them that dinner was about ready, Arianna went to the bathroom and splashed her face with water. She felt exhausted, but also clearer and cleaner. The tears she'd cried had been bottled up inside her since way before Jack had gotten angry at her, probably since Sammy's birth. A part of the heavy burden she'd been carrying since then had lifted. *Thank You, Jesus*, she thought. She checked herself in the mirror—impossibly red eyes, but that couldn't be helped—and went out to join the family for dinner.

The dogs begged and the twins were funny, and Carson and Lily were the warmest of hosts. Lily and the girls had made a cake earlier—"Just because," Lily said, "but maybe we sensed you were coming"—and Arianna accepted a big piece without her usual agonizing about her figure.

In the grand scheme of things, looking model perfect didn't matter. Carson and Lily accepted her. God accepted her.

It grieved her deeply that Jack didn't accept her, and that her easy access to Sammy had ended. But with Carson's help, she'd seen that there was a glimmer of a solution. Nothing had ever seemed so unsolvable by human standards, but according to Carson, that was usually where God stepped in.

Lily loaned her toiletries and a nightgown, and she went to bed early, prayed herself to sleep and slept all night without dreams.

Jack hadn't slept well.

Sammy had been up several times, crying. His temperature was normal, and he didn't seem physically sick, other than tired. But he kept making the "Aunt Arianna" sign.

Jack stood up from the breakfast table, where he was attempting to feed Sammy some eggs and toast, and looked out the window. He could tell himself he was looking for Mrs. Jennings, his reluctant substitute babysitter for the day. But the truth was, he was checking to see if Arianna had come home.

She hadn't.

Which probably meant she was spending the time with Nathan. Even as he had the thought, one side of himself realized it was irrational. Arianna's relationship with Nathan was in the past. He had believed her when she told him that, and nothing had changed really, not in Arianna and Nathan's relationship.

What had changed was Jack and Arianna's relationship, because she had lied to him.

Nathan was Sammy's father. Arianna was his mother.

He stared bleakly at his son, finally calm and tapping a spoon on the tray of his high chair. He didn't feel any less love for him, knowing his parentage. But the deception hurt.

Not only that, but Arianna and Nathan could so easily be the people raising Sammy, and maybe that would have been better for him. Nathan was incredibly successful on a scale that Jack, a small-town country vet, could never dream of. And Arianna... Well, Arianna was warm and loving and smart and creative, a mother anyone would like to have.

Except for the lying.

The sound of a car engine broke his concentration and he was ashamed of the way his heart rate picked up. Was it her?

But no, it was Mrs. Jennings, and Jack sighed as he looked around his messy home. Sammy's tantrums and meltdowns meant that Jack hadn't had a spare moment to clean up the place. The clutter, the spilled orange juice, the slight diaperish smell—all of it got to him, made him feel uncomfortable in his own home. In his own skin.

He still had feelings for Arianna. He couldn't deny it. But he wasn't going to act on them. Wasn't going to let Sammy start to get reattached to her when she was likely to flit off to another adventure at any moment. They'd only had an agreement for the rest of the summer, and summer was nearly over. He'd been a fool to stop his nanny search, somehow trusting that Arianna would stick around. She wouldn't, and even if she would, he wouldn't have her.

Mrs. Jennings bustled in, full of stories about her grand-kids. She set her purse on the floor and took off her jacket without even a slight break in her conversational flow. She'd always been like that, but her rate of speech seemed to have sped up now, and he realized she was nervous. He set out to reassure her, because he really couldn't do without her, not now. She wasn't the best with Sammy, but she was far, far from the worst. Sammy knew her, and that was important.

Mrs. Jennings looked around the room and raised an eyebrow. "I see why you wanted me to take care of him up here," she said. "Looking for a little light cleaning in addition to childcare, are you?"

Jack was too tired to tell if she was joking or seriously annoyed. "I'll pay you extra," he promised, "if you can get the house into its usual shape."

Sammy had gotten down from the table and was crawling directly toward Mrs. Jennings's purse.

"Oh, he loves that thing," she said, laughing. She didn't stop Sammy from reaching inside.

"I'd rather you didn't let him…" Jack trailed off and stared in horror as Sammy pulled out a colorful plastic container and banged it on the floor until it opened. He picked up a small white pill.

"Oh no, Sammy, no, no!" Mrs. Jennings reached down and took the pill and pill container from him. "Those are Mrs. Jennings's special candies."

Jack's insides froze. "Has he done that before?"

She seemed to hear something in his voice. "No, of course not."

"What did you mean, when you said he loves your purse?"

"Oh, well…" Her eyes shifted back and forth, not meeting Jack's. "He just always grabs for it. I'm sure he's never gotten in before."

"You keep your medications locked away at home, right?"

"Yes, I do." She looked indignant. "I take care of my own grandchildren. Do you think I wouldn't keep them safe?"

He hoped she would keep *all* the children in her care safe. "I'm just wondering," he said slowly, "whether Sammy could have gotten ahold of your purse and taken a pill or several."

"No! That's not possible."

"Like he was about to do just now," Jack continued as if she hadn't spoken. "Like he would have done in a second, if we hadn't both been looking at him. I'm just wondering whether his kidney episode could have been because he ingested some medication. That's one of the things the doctor asked about."

"Now you're blaming me for his kidney issues?" Mrs. Jennings grabbed her purse. "I knew I should never have started taking care of him again. You'll just have to find another caregiver, one who's up to your standards."

Yes, he would. "What kinds of medication do you carry with you?"

"Just one kind, and it's my personal business." Her face was pink.

He stepped in front of the door, blocking her way. "If I need to get the police to investigate, I will. This could help the doctors know how to finish treating Sammy."

"It was an antianxiety medication, all right? I don't even remember what it's called. I'll text you the name of it. Now, let me through!"

He did let her through and watched as she got into her car and floored it, gravel flying under her tires.

So the mystery of Sammy's kidney problem might very well be solved. Too bad there was only one person he wanted to share that knowledge with. And he'd barred her from ever again coming over or speaking to his son.

Her son.

Chapter 15

An hour later, Jack sat out on his front porch with Sammy, but *not* because he wanted to see Arianna. No, he was sitting there because he was at the end of his rope, with Sammy and with life generally, and sometimes being outside kept Sammy calmer.

Across the way, Penny's front door opened, and Jack felt an absurd hope that Arianna would come out, even though she didn't use that entrance and her car wasn't there.

Then the hope within him made him angry. It didn't matter if she showed her face; he wasn't going to invite her in for coffee. It wasn't like he was going to let her see Sammy.

And he had the feeling that if Sammy saw her, and wasn't allowed to go to her, the meltdown would be massive.

"Hey, Jack!" Penny's cheerful voice matched the cheerful barking of Buster, Arianna's puppy. "Okay if I bring him over?"

"If he's leashed. Sammy's still a little afraid."

"Sure." She held the pup at the bottom of the steps while Jack sat at the top, holding Sammy. Sammy reached toward the dog, so Jack scooted down another step, then another. Finally, he and the pup were only a couple of feet apart. "That's about where Arianna stopped," Penny said.

Even the mention of her name made Jack sweat. "What do you mean, she stopped there?"

"Desensitizing Sammy," Penny said. "She's been working to get him used to the puppy ever since she got Buster. Inch by inch, pretty much."

Why did he seem to know less than anyone about his own son?

"I thought you'd be at work," Penny said. "Wasn't Mrs. Jennings's car out here a little while ago?"

Jack explained about the pills. "I have a call in to Sammy's doctor, but I have the feeling we have an answer as to why Sammy got so sick. The information about what kind of drug it was is probably irrelevant by now, but it would've been good to know at the time."

Maybe Arianna wouldn't have been pushed to confess the truth, he thought darkly. Maybe he'd still be a happy idiot.

"Do you need someone to take care of Sammy today?" Penny glanced toward the barn. "I have some work to do, but I could bring him along."

"I canceled my appointments. I can't ask that of you."

She nodded, sitting down on the edge of the steps to rub the puppy's belly. "That's all well and good, but what are you going to do tomorrow?"

"I don't know," he said, sighing.

"Look, why don't you come up to the barn with me? You and Sammy don't need to sit here by yourselves feeling blue."

Jack had a "what does it matter" feeling that was pretty alien to him. "Okay," he said. He'd been fueled by anger since Arianna's big reveal, but it was starting to trickle away. Surging up now and then, yeah, but he just wasn't the angry type.

Instead, hopelessness pressed down on him like storm clouds pressing against the mountains, dark and ominous. Thing was, he'd started to hope for a future brighter than the past. A future where Sammy would thrive and they'd have a warm, happy home. A future where Sammy would have the love and warmth of a mother.

A future where he'd have the heart-filling, joyous, expansive experience of loving and being truly loved.

But that had evaporated with Arianna's stunning words, and now that anger wasn't filling the hole that remained behind, he just felt dry and empty.

Up at the barn, Penny let dogs out of their crates and Jack walked them outside to do their business, carrying Sammy on his shoulders. It was true, Sammy was much more comfortable with dogs now. He guessed he had Arianna to thank for that. Not that he felt the least bit thankful to her.

Willie came in and took charge of Sammy, and once again, Jack was surprised. His son went readily to the rough-voiced older man.

The ranch was good for Sammy.

It was good for Jack, too, because he had close friends, like Penny and Willie, who refused to let him sink into despair. And suddenly, he wanted to know what they thought of the whole wretched situation. "Did Arianna talk to you?" he asked Penny.

She frowned. "I spoke to her briefly last night, when she asked if I could take care of Buster."

Why'd she need that? Where was she staying?

He suppressed the questions he had no business asking, but Penny squinted at him. "She stayed down at Carson and Lily's," she said.

Had she read his mind?

And why was he so relieved that she hadn't slept over at Nathan's or traveled to see him?

"I tried to find out what was going on between the two of you," Penny said with a hint of a smile, "but she said it wasn't her story to tell. Said it was yours."

"Well, it's kind of hers," he said. And then before he could think himself out of it, he blurted out, "She's Sammy's mother."

Penny stared and sucked in a breath. "You're kidding me. And you didn't know?"

He shook his head.

"Chloe?"

"She knew. They kept it from me."

There was a cough behind them. "Sorry, didn't mean to eavesdrop," Willie said. "But no point pretending I didn't overhear. That has a whole lot of ramifications, doesn't it?"

Jack nodded once. "The main one being, I know now I can't trust her."

"That's... Well, I can see why you'd say that, for sure. But she's a good person. This just doesn't sound like her." Penny frowned.

In a strange way, Jack was relieved that Penny thought well of Arianna and was taken aback by what she'd done. Made him feel like less of a fool. "I guess none of us knew her as well as we thought we did."

They all took care of the dogs for a little bit, and finally, all three adults and Sammy ended up in the big field behind the barn, watching the puppy romp with the mother dog and her pup, the ones who'd taken him in.

"Dogs sure know how to be happy," Willie said, chewing on a blade of grass.

Penny gave Jack a meaningful look. "Even if someone kicks them or hits them, they jump right back up, ready to love again. Our rescue program is proof of that."

Was this some kind of heavy-handed lesson they were trying to teach? "I'm not a dog," he said. "My memory's a little longer."

"Believe me, I get it," Penny said, looking out across the horizon.

Jack realized with a jolt how much Penny had had to forgive, her husband having left her for another woman, an alleged friend.

"Did you ever hear how me and Long John got to be such good friends?" Willie asked.

Jack shook his head.

"He sought me out after 'Nam," Willie said. Now he was looking out toward the mountains, too. "He'd been in battle with my twin brother and he wanted to tell me about it."

Jack noticed that Penny put her hand on Willie's back, patting it a little. He was guessing this story wouldn't have a happy ending.

"They were in a firefight together, and Long John just… left him there," Willie said. "Saved himself. Ricky was down—and hurt pretty bad, sure. He probably wouldn't have made it. But…" The older man's eyes welled up, and he swallowed hard, got himself under control. "His remains were never recovered."

Jack blew out a breath. "I'm sorry."

"Me, too. But before I was sorry, I was mad. I knocked Long John plumb out when I heard."

Penny put a hand on Willie's arm. "What made you for-give him?"

He shrugged. "There were a lot of circumstances. He was sorry. He regretted it."

"Still," Penny said, "that must have been hard to do."

"It was," Willie said. "I wanted someone to blame. But when I let go of that, I ended up with the best friend of my life."

Both of the elders looked at Jack.

"You could end up with something good, too, Jack," Penny said softly. "Something that would be good for Sammy, too, because you know it's better for him to know his biological parents than not."

"*Parents*. Plural." Jack heaved a giant sigh. He couldn't imagine opening his heart to Arianna, let alone to Na-than, too.

"First things first," Penny said. "Why don't you talk to Arianna?"

"No, uh-uh. She lied to me."

"She was in an impossible situation, sounds like," Penny said. "She was pregnant and desperate, and she had the chance to have her baby raised within her own family with a stable mother and father, only there was a condition. That's what it sounds like anyway, right?"

Jack nodded. "Chloe apparently made her promise not to tell me or anyone."

"So Chloe is as much to blame as Arianna, right?"

"Was," Jack said. "Yeah. I guess."

They were all silent for a few minutes, watching the pup-pies frolic. Sammy was actually rolling around with them just like any other little kid, and Jack couldn't help but be warmed by that.

"Would you change anything that happened?" Willie asked finally.

The question stopped Jack short. Would he? If anything changed, he wouldn't have Sammy. "No," he said quietly, "I guess I wouldn't."

"Then it's just possible," Penny said, "that God had a plan."

Jack thought about that as he walked back down to his house, slowly, adjusting to Sammy's pace. He had to admit it was possible.

He just didn't understand what the plan was.

The next morning, Jack woke up with his heart in his shoes. He had to move forward, had to find care for Sammy, had to go to work and keep his appointments. People were depending on him. But he didn't feel like doing anything at all.

He'd spent the night looking out at the stars and thinking. He knew that Penny and Willie had his and Sammy's good at heart. He even knew they were probably right. But his heart was so raw.

Why had Arianna let him kiss her and acted like she was attached? Because she *was* attached, or because she was Sammy's mother?

He was ashamed to admit to himself that he could forgive her more easily if he knew she hadn't been faking her feelings for him.

But if he couldn't tell the difference between fake feelings and real ones, how could he ever succeed at a relationship?

He grabbed his phone and clicked off his "do not disturb" to start searching for sitters, and a text pinged in.

From Arianna. In a moment of weakness, he'd lifted the block on her number.

He didn't want to look at it, was mad when he couldn't resist.

These six sitters are willing to care for Sammy today and for the rest of the week. All experienced and highly recommended.

There was a list with phone numbers he could just click.

Her own name was last on the list.

Jack didn't want to accept help from her, but he did need care for Sammy. He only hesitated a minute before he clicked on the number of a woman who worked in the nursery at church.

He should have thought of her before; Sammy knew her. Soon, he'd arranged care for the rest of Sammy's week.

He should thank Arianna. But she was obviously just trying impress him. He turned off the phone and started packing Sammy's bag for the new sitter.

That night, when he and Sammy got home, there was a casserole on his doorstep with a note. "Pasta with Alfredo sauce and veggies. Microwave 2–3 minutes. Sammy loves it and you might, too. —A"

She needed to leave him alone. She wasn't getting back in his good graces just by providing a babysitter and a meal. In no way did that outweigh the horrible betrayal she'd committed.

He did take the casserole inside and serve it up, though, because both he and Sammy were starving. They ate almost all of it in one sitting.

She did it all week. A new interactive toy that Sammy

adored on sight. A six-pack of Jack's favorite soft drink and two bags of the kind of pretzels he loved but could rarely find around here. A new jacket for Sammy with a note clipped to it: "You should cut out the tags before putting this on him—they're too scratchy for him."

He hated it that she knew more about his child than he did. Hated that her gifts were so perfect.

None of it was going to open the door to his heart.

The next time, he caught her: she was delivering a big portrait of Sammy, laughing. It was in her trademark primitive style, but a perfect likeness for all that.

He flung open the door. "Why can't you just leave us alone?"

She paused in the act of setting down the portrait. "I can't. He's my son, and I'm not abandoning him again."

Sammy had fallen asleep on the floor and Jack didn't want to wake him, but he'd had enough. He was going to have to lay it out for her again. He came out onto the porch and shut the door behind him. "Do you realize how awful it is, what you did?"

She met his eyes steadily. "Yes, I do," she said. "I'm truly sorry, Jack. I made a horrible mistake of judgment."

He waited for the excuses, but they didn't come. She just stood there, watching him.

He *wasn't* going to forgive her.

"I'm hoping one day you'll forgive me," she said, seeming to read his mind, "and let me see Sammy."

"Not happening," he said. "Some things are unforgivable."

He went back inside, slammed the door and didn't feel nearly as gratified as he should have. Especially since the loud slam woke up Sammy.

Later that night, his father called. Of course, he'd heard that Jack had missed a couple days of work. More disturbing, he wanted to know if the rumors around town were true.

Someone at the hospital must have overheard Jack and Arianna talking, or read a notation in Sammy's chart. Or maybe Arianna had told one of her friends who'd spread the word. It didn't matter; there was no point hiding something that would soon come out anyway, so Jack confirmed the rumors. "It's true, Dad. Arianna is Sammy's biological mother."

They talked for a few minutes, Dad sputtering and angry. "Some things are unforgivable," he said as he hung up.

The words sent a sharp chill through Jack.

He'd said those exact same words to Arianna just a few hours ago.

Was he turning into his father?

"Am I, God?" he demanded, looking upward.

He seemed to sense God chuckling, telling him it was his choice. Jack had free will: he could turn into his father, or not.

He thought about what Willie and Penny had said: that Arianna had faced an awful and impossible decision.

It was hard for Jack to put himself in her shoes—he was a man after all, and would never bear a child—but he did know something about putting his own feelings aside for the good of his son.

If she had done it, he could do it, too. Before he could lose his nerve, before his usual nonspontaneous habits could kick in, he texted her. Can you come over?

He'd envisioned a quiet talk, a start toward forgiveness, but when Arianna came in, Sammy woke up again. Her look at him was stark, hungry, but she turned her eyes toward Jack and didn't go to Sammy.

Sammy saw her and his eyes widened. "Ah-ah. Aunt Ah-ah." He held out his arms toward her.

They were clear words, and the first he'd spoken since way before his diagnosis.

Arianna put a hand to her mouth, tears filling her eyes. "Oh, Jack." She glanced over at him and then back at Sammy. "Oh, sweetheart, come here. Is that okay?" she added, looking at Jack.

Jack nodded because he couldn't speak through the lump in his throat.

She held out her arms.

"Aunt Ah-ah!" Sammy toddled toward her.

She clasped Sammy in her arms.

Jack watched the two of them and wondered how he hadn't noticed that the glints in Sammy's hair were the same color as those in Arianna's. Even more, how could he have missed the loving, completely maternal way she held him?

He was in danger of breaking down and sobbing, especially as the significance of Sammy's speech dawned on him. If he could say two words, he could learn many more. If he could speak, he could communicate.

And he'd communicated out of caring for Arianna. Which was contrary to all the stereotypes about autism. Sammy had feelings, deep and loyal.

Arianna was unlocking them.

She'd unlocked Jack's heart, as well. He'd doubted his ability to have a relationship, doubted that anyone would care for him. But in word and action, Arianna had shown that she cared. For Sammy, yes, of course.

But she seemed to care for him, too, and he almost couldn't breathe with the joy of it.

Almost couldn't believe it, either. Maybe the texts and the babysitter list and the casserole were all for Sammy, all so that she could see her son. Maybe she cared nothing for Jack; maybe he was a means to an end.

Sammy struggled free of her arms and she let him go, making sure he was steady on his feet before releasing him. He toddled straight to Jack and made the sign for "father."

"Da!" he said. "Da!"

Jack did break down then. He scooped Sammy into his arms and buried his face in his son's sweaty hair and let himself cry a little.

All the emotions and hugging were too much for Sammy, of course. He wriggled free and crawled to his bear and flung himself down on it, rubbing the backs of his hands over his eyes.

Jack got control of himself and then passed the tissue box over to Arianna, and a few minutes later they put Sammy to bed.

"Thank you so much for letting me see him," Arianna said as they came back downstairs. "I know it's hard for you and I won't abuse the privilege."

Jack waited until she was down the steps and standing beside him. He smiled at her. "You can see him whenever you want."

Her eyes lit up. "Thank you!"

She was *so* beautiful.

They stood looking at each other, beaming, really, until a cloud flickered across Arianna's eyes. She shook her head a little and turned away. "Thank you again, Jack. I guess I should go."

"Arianna."

She paused in the act of picking up her purse.

"Do you want to go?"

"No." Her head was bowed. She didn't look at him.

"Why not?" Maybe it was cruel of him, but he wasn't content with guessing about her feelings. He knew his own—he'd realized them for sure when he'd seen her holding Sammy—but hers were still a mystery.

She drew in a breath, put down her purse and turned to face him, meeting his eyes. "I miss what we had, Jack, or what we were starting to have. Independent of Sammy."

Her warm words seemed to permeate his very core. She missed *him*.

"I've missed you, too," he admitted.

She reached out and put her arms around him in a hug that felt like nourishment after starvation. Neither of them let go for a long time.

Finally, he broke their embrace, took a step back and put his hands on her shoulders. "I'm sorry I've been so harsh and judgmental. I guess… I guess I was hurt, but that's no excuse."

She shook her head rapidly and reached out to put a finger on his lips. "There's no need to apologize. What you did was nothing compared to what I did, and I'll never stop being sorry for it."

"Ah." He cupped her face in his hands. "No, Arianna. Don't let guilt get in the way of something beautiful."

"What's that?" She was staring at him, eyes glittering with unshed tears.

"These feelings between us. I love you, Arianna," he said.

She bit her lip, a tear spilling out.

He wiped it away with his thumb. "I think it started when you came in here with that crazy sunflower picture." He nodded toward it, now proudly displayed over the couch that it most definitely didn't match.

She laughed a little. "Even though I made a mess of your house?"

"You brought in color and warmth and life. For both of us. I…" He drew in a breath, trying to phrase it right. "You've been helping both me and Sammy to heal, and I love you for it. And I love you for your creativity and your energy and your sense of fun. The way you care about other people and know just what to do to help them. The way you've helped your aunt and uncle clean up their house, and the way you've been training that puppy to be careful around Sammy."

A dimple quirked in her cheek, and she pulled away, her cheeks going pink. "You noticed."

"I think I notice everything about you," he admitted. "But I still wonder…how do you feel about me, Arianna? Can we…pursue this?"

She looked up at him through her lashes and brushed a stray curl back from her face. "I think…I love you, too."

"You think so?"

She nodded, smiling.

Jack's heart pounded like the hooves of a racehorse. He reached for her.

She held up a hand. "Wait," she said seriously. "There's something I want you to know."

He took her hand and tugged her to sit beside him on the couch, right underneath the sunflower painting. "You can tell me anything."

"I won't keep anything from you ever again." She clutched his hand tighter and looked into his eyes. "That's why… I know how it looks, the fact that I got pregnant out of wedlock. But that was a mistake I won't make again. I intend to wait for when, or if, I get married."

He looked at her, and love for the strong woman she was, for her values and her goodness, her ability to make a new start, seemed to fill his heart. "If I have anything to do with it," he said, his voice catching, "you won't be waiting long at all."

Epilogue

Eighteen months later

Balloons were flying at the entrance to the newly renovated Redemption Ranch lodge as Arianna, Jack and Sammy walked into the warm, welcoming great room. Arianna looked over at Sammy, worried he wouldn't like the colorful change to a familiar environment. And indeed, he studied the balloons impassively for a moment.

"Balloons, Sammy. How do you like the balloons?"

He studied them for a moment longer. "'Loons," he said and nodded once. The shadow of a smile crossed his three-year-old face. "Like 'loons."

She swept him up in a hug. "Good words!"

"You little pistol." Jack tickled Sammy's chin, making him giggle. "You knew you'd get a hug from Mommy for that."

Arianna still got a warm, happy feeling when she heard

her husband refer to her as Sammy's mommy, because there was no ambivalence or discomfort in his tone. With God's help, they'd worked through it and it wasn't a barrier to their happy marriage. Their *very* happy marriage. She leaned into him, and he put an arm around her.

All their friends were here: Gabe and Daniela with their baby, named Tommy for one of Gabe's fallen comrades, and Lily and Carson and the twins, Sunny and Skye, who had been so wonderful helping Arianna and Jack manage the hard time they'd gone through.

Finn and Kayla were here with Leo, now a big third grader. And of course, Penny, Long John and his wife, and Willie. And Branson Howe, the banker, which was a little bit surprising.

After everyone had eaten a kid-friendly meal of pizza and pasta, and the kids were playing with Sammy's toys— he had plenty, and no problem at all sharing his wealth— Penny gestured to bring the adults together. "I love you guys so much," she said. "And I want you to be the first to know that, thanks to our donors, including many of you, we're burning up the mortgage to Redemption Ranch, because it's all paid off."

The door opened, and everyone turned as Nathan came rushing in. "Sorry to be late," he said. "I didn't... Well, I appreciate the invitation." His eyes scanned the children, and his small smile told Arianna he'd found Sammy at the center of the kids.

"We're glad you came, too," Penny said to Nathan, "because your donation is the one that put us over the top in paying off the ranch."

Arianna lifted an eyebrow and looked over at Jack. His eyes had narrowed a little, and he looked surprised and interested, but not angry.

He was the best husband in the world.

"As long as we're making announcements," Willie said, "Penny and I have one, too."

Arianna sucked in a breath and looked at Penny.

She was smiling at Willie with eyes full of love.

Willie cleared his throat. "She and I, well, we're going to get married."

There was general cheering and hugging, and Arianna's heart was full. So much to celebrate, and these people were all so dear to her. She and Jack and Sammy were richly blessed.

Jack walked Branson Howe to the door. "You okay, man?" he asked.

"Yeah. I wish them well." He took one more glance back at the room, where people were toasting Penny and Willie, and shook his head. "Next time, if there is one, I'll try harder."

"There will be," Jack said. Sometime in the past year, he'd become an optimist about the future.

Jack looked across the room to where Nathan knelt in front of Sammy. They were both engrossed with a complicated and undoubtedly very expensive truck that Nathan had brought for Sammy's birthday.

They didn't look much alike, but the intensity they shared, their complete focus on what was in front of them rather than the din of the party around them, identified them, at least to Jack, as father and son.

It's good for Sammy.

Of course, Sammy was too young to understand about biological parents. They had started telling him a simplified version of his adoption story, but for now, he didn't have much interest.

As Jack watched, Arianna turned from refilling drinks and walked over toward Nathan and Sammy. She squatted down to admire the truck with them.

Emotion flashed through Jack, jealousy and longing, but it was clean now. He wasn't ashamed of how he felt, and that helped him be in control of it. He drew in a couple of deep, calming breaths and walked over to the trio.

"Daddy!" Sammy held up his arms, and Jack reached down to pick him up, his heart swelling with love. Nathan stood then, too. He met Jack's eyes and gave a little nod, and Jack understood.

It was a thank-you. Nathan was grateful to be involved in Sammy's life. And Jack knew that as time went on, that involvement might become greater. Nathan might be a huge resource to Sammy, and that would be a good thing. Jack felt big enough to let it happen now.

"Bus! Bus!" Sammy struggled to get down as Buster, now a full-grown retriever mix, let out one deep bark. Sammy wrapped his arms around the dog's neck for a none-too-gentle hug, which Buster endured patiently. Then the two of them headed off toward the other children.

Arianna slid an arm around Jack, and when he looked down at her, her eyes were warm with love. He tugged her closer, putting an arm around her slender waist and letting her his fingers stretch to touch her slightly convex abdomen. "You're sure we can't tell everyone tonight? Today?"

"It's only four months. I still feel like it's too early." She smiled at him and relented. "Pretty soon, I'll let you shout it from the rooftops."

And that, he reflected as gratitude flooded his heart, he would certainly do.

* * * * *

We hope you enjoyed reading

The Courtship of Carol Sommars

by *New York Times* bestselling author

DEBBIE MACOMBER

and

The Nanny's Secret Baby

by *USA TODAY* bestselling author

LEE TOBIN MCCLAIN.

Both were originally Harlequin® series stories!

From passionate, suspenseful and dramatic
love stories to inspirational or historical,
Harlequin offers different lines to
satisfy every romance reader.

New books in each line are available every month.

LOVE INSPIRED
INSPIRATIONAL ROMANCE
Uplifting stories of faith, forgiveness and hope.

Harlequin.com

BACHALO0821MAX

SPECIAL EXCERPT FROM

LOVE INSPIRED
INSPIRATIONAL ROMANCE

Newly guardian to her twin nieces, Hannah Antonicelli is determined to keep her last promise to her late sister—that she'll never reveal the identity of their father. But when Luke Hutchenson is hired as a handyman at her work and begins to bond with the little girls, hiding that he's their uncle isn't easy…

Read on for a sneak peek at
Finding a Christmas Home
by Lee Tobin McClain!

On Wednesday after work, Hannah drove toward home, the twins in the back seat, and tried not to be nervous that Luke was in the front seat beside her.

"I really appreciate this," he said. His car hadn't started this morning, and he'd walked the three miles to Rescue Haven.

Of course, Hannah had insisted on driving him home. What else could she do? It was cold outside, spitting snow, and he was her next-door neighbor.

"I hate to ask another favor," he said, "but could you stop by Pasquale's Pizza on the way?"

"No problem." She took a left and drove the two blocks to the only nonchain pizza place in Bethlehem Springs.

He jumped out, and she turned back to check on the twins, trying not to watch Luke as he headed into the shop. He was good-looking, of course. Kind, appreciative and strong. And he had the slightest swagger in his walk that was masculine and appealing.

But he was also about to go visit his brother, Bobby, if he kept his promise to his ailing father. And when she'd heard about that visit, it had been a wake-up call: she shouldn't get too close with him. The fewer chances she had to spill the beans about Bobby being the twins' father, the better.

He came out of the pizza shop quickly—he must have called ahead—carrying a big flat box and a white bag. What would it be like if this was a family scenario, if they were Mom and Dad and kids, stopping for takeout on the way home from work?

She couldn't help it. Her chest filled with longing.

He climbed into her small car, juggling the large flat box to make it fit without encroaching on the gearshift.

She had to laugh at the size of his meal. "Hungry?"

"Are you?" He opened the box a little, and the rich, garlicky fragrance of Pasquale's special sauce filled the car.

Her stomach growled, loudly.

"Pee-zah!" Addie shouted from the back seat.

"Peez!" Emmy added, almost as loud.

"That's just cruel," she said as she pulled the car back onto the road and steered toward Luke's place. "You're tempting us. I may have to order some when I get these girls home."

"No, you won't," he said. "This is for all of us. The least I can do is feed you, after you drove me around."

Her stomach gave a little leap, and not just about the prospect of pizza. Why was he inviting her to have dinner with him? Was there an ulterior motive? And if there was, would she mind?

Don't miss
Finding a Christmas Home *by Lee Tobin McClain,*
available October 2021 wherever
Love Inspired books and ebooks are sold.

LoveInspired.com

LOVE INSPIRED
INSPIRATIONAL ROMANCE

Save **$1.00**

on the purchase of ANY

Love Inspired book.

Available wherever books are sold,
including most bookstores, supermarkets,
drugstores and discount stores.

Save $1.00

on the purchase of ANY Love Inspired book.

Coupon valid until October 25, 2021. Redeemable at participating outlets in the U.S. and Canada only.
Not redeemable at Barnes & Noble stores. Limit one coupon per customer.

Canadian Retailers: Harlequin Enterprises ULC will pay the face value of this coupon plus 10.25¢ if submitted by customer for this product only. Any other use constitutes fraud. Coupon is nonassignable. Void if taxed, prohibited or restricted by law. Consumer must pay any government taxes. Void if copied. Inmar Promotional Services ("IPS") customers submit coupons and proof of sales to Harlequin Enterprises ULC, P.O. Box 31000, Scarborough, ON M1R 0E7, Canada. Non-IPS retailer—for reimbursement submit coupons and proof of sales directly to Harlequin Enterprises ULC, Retail Marketing Department, Bay Adelaide Centre, East Tower, 22 Adelaide Street West, 40th Floor, Toronto, Ontario M5H 4E3, Canada.

U.S. Retailers: Harlequin Enterprises ULC will pay the face value of this coupon plus 8¢ if submitted by customer for this product only. Any other use constitutes fraud. Coupon is nonassignable. Void if taxed, prohibited or restricted by law. Consumer must pay any government taxes. Void if copied. For reimbursement submit coupons and proof of sales directly to Harlequin Enterprises ULC 482, NCH Marketing Services, P.O. Box 880001, El Paso, TX 88588-0001, U.S.A. Cash value 1/100 cents.

® and ™ are trademarks owned by Harlequin Enterprises ULC.

© 2021 Harlequin Enterprises ULC

BACCOUP40620MAX

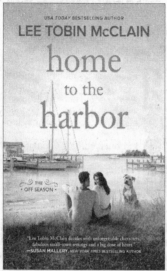

Love Harlequin romance?

DISCOVER.

Be the first to find out about promotions, news and exclusive content!

Facebook.com/HarlequinBooks

Twitter.com/HarlequinBooks

Instagram.com/HarlequinBooks

Pinterest.com/HarlequinBooks

YouTube.com/HarlequinBooks

ReaderService.com

EXPLORE.

Sign up for the Harlequin e-newsletter and download a free book from any series at **TryHarlequin.com**

CONNECT.

Join our Harlequin community to share your thoughts and connect with other romance readers!
Facebook.com/groups/HarlequinConnection